The Christmas Killer

JIM GALLOWS

PENGUIN BOOKS

PENGUIN BOOKS

UK | USA | Canada | Ireland | Australia
India | New Zealand | South Africa

Penguin Books is part of the Penguin Random House group of companies
whose addresses can be found at global.penguinrandomhouse.com.

First published 2014
001

Set in 12.5/14.75 pt Garamond MT Std
Typeset by Jouve (UK), Milton Keynes
Printed in Great Britain by Clays Ltd, St Ives plc

A CIP catalogue record for this book is available from the British Library

ISBN: 978–1–405–92025–4

www.greenpenguin.co.uk

Penguin Books is committed to a sustainable future for our business, our readers and our planet. This book is made from Forest Stewardship Council™ certified paper.

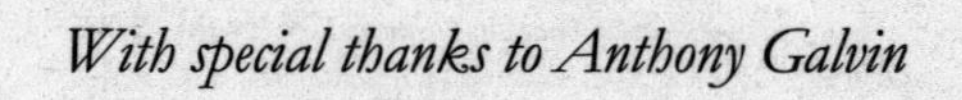

With special thanks to Anthony Galvin

I

Monday, 12 December, just after midnight

He walked down the street. His soft shoes barely made a sound on the sidewalk. His breath condensed on the cold air in front of him – for just a moment, and then it would fade away. Like he was never there. It had been a while since he had heard the chimes of the old bell tower strike midnight. It was close to freezing already, and snowflakes were falling lazily, which meant he would have to be cautious about where he stepped.

He bet it looked and felt 'Christmassy' to most people. But he could make his peace with it tonight. Because it was so Christmassy, no one would be outside. They would all be in their homes, beneath their garish decorations and the trashy lights he could see flickering behind some of the windows on the street. They were probably online shopping for toys and video games that would further soften the brains of their doubtless slow-witted children.

But tonight that was a very good thing, as far as he was concerned. It made his work easier . . .

Would you mind if it's too *easy?*

A line from Hamlet came back to him.

'Now could I drink hot blood and do such bitter business as the day would quake to look on' . . . *If I wasn't so damned tired and chilled to the bone.*

There she was, walking towards the end of the street. He would need to speed up, but only a little. He didn't want to run. Pounding footsteps and panting breath would only spook her. He wanted her to be scared . . . but not yet.

He could see her clearly now, wrapped firmly in her thin coat as she hurried towards the house. She was shouting into a mobile phone.

'You should have picked up Kelly ages ago,' he heard her say. 'Instead you're fucking around with your asshole friends. If I can't rely on you, then what's the fucking point?' There was more, but he tuned it out.

He was almost feeling sorry for her. What was the life of a single mother in this bleak neighbourhood? It must be tough, juggling work, a home and a young child with no support. Mostly he felt sorry for Kelly, a sweet little thing with a shy smile and big brown eyes, sleeping at the babysitter's place until someone picked her up.

How will she cope without a mother? Will every Christmas after this one be tinged with sadness, bitterness – heartache – at the memory of what happened the night her mother died?

He scanned the surrounding street. A narrow alley ran down the side of the house. That would be ideal. He would have to intercept her before she got there.

Timing would be everything. Already she was fumbling in her purse for a key, the phone clutched between her shoulder and her ear, still giving it good to the poor sap at the other end.

She had not even noticed him.

He smiled.

She'll notice me soon enough.

'Excuse me,' he said, tapping her on the shoulder.

She turned and squinted into the darkness. Her eyes were uncertain, alert. Then a faint frown crossed her dark features as she tried to place him.

Hissing into the phone she said, 'I'll call you back.' Then she turned to him.

He needed to get her off the street and into the alley.

'Please,' he whispered. 'My glasses . . . I dropped them in the snow. Could you help me . . . please?'

And then he was backing away slowly, into the alley that ran down the side of her small house. His nerves were tingling. If she followed now, the rest would flow with an easy inevitability. But if she hesitated . . .

'Oh, yeah. Sure.'

In his pocket, his grip tightened around the long black woollen sock filled with nearly a pound of nickels and dimes. Enough to knock over a horse.

They were always so cumbersome when they were unconscious, limp and heavy – uncooperative. But once he got her inside, things would get much easier.

He felt triumphant as she drew alongside him. She

was close enough for him to smell her perfume on a wave of body heat and end-of-day sweat.

He closed his eyes. 'You've asked for this.'

And then he swung.

2

Monday, 10 a.m.

Jake Austin plunged his hands deep into his trouser pockets. It was cold and the wind found its way easily through his coat and shirt. What should have been an easy morning policing a small protest was turning into a colossal pain in the ass.

He looked at the angry crowd in front of him. Half the reason he had left Chicago was for a quiet life, but now Littleton, Indiana was beginning to look like the LA riots. The group was only about sixty strong, but they were hot. And there was one man among them fanning the flames.

'You're pulling down our church,' the guy shouted. He was in his late thirties, with a scraggly dark beard and rumpled checked shirt open at the collar. Jake didn't need to see the notepad sticking out of his back pocket to make him for a hack – probably one of the local guys trying to raise his profile by turning this into a bigger story than it actually was. 'It's an insult to God – at Christmas, of all times!'

The crowd roared agreement, their roar falling to jeers and boos as Councilman Mitch Harper took to the makeshift wooden platform which had been erected just to the left of the church's nativity scene, which was a sad reflection of the building itself – old and bland, in serious disrepair. The Virgin's clothes were moth-eaten, and the cow that stooped over the manger was missing an ear. Jake watched Harper step as respectfully as he could over one of the two wise men, wondering if an APB had ever been put out on the third.

At over six foot, Harper looked impressive in his dark power suit, crisp white shirt and red tie, and did a good job of pretending he wasn't feeling the bitter cold – every inch the unflappable civil servant. But as he spoke into the microphone his pinched face and tight voice betrayed the fact that he was riled by the heckling. Jake could make out '. . . progress . . . and . . . infrastructure . . .' but that was about it.

Jake looked over at his partner, Detective Howard Mills, who just shrugged his thin shoulders and yawned. That was Mills all over; you'd need to put a match to his trousers just to get him to stand up. An OK guy, but he had about as much drive and ambition as a dung beetle.

Jake shrugged back. He hadn't been in Littleton long, but he knew that Harper would say whatever was needed to get the votes. Today, it wasn't working so well.

'We have to look to the future—'

'You're destroying the heart of this community for another interstate!' the journalist yelled.

Harper addressed his response to the crowd. 'We are

the only major route out of the capital not serviced by a proper road. The sea of progress is raging, and Littleton is being swept away.'

'Sweep this away!' a voice shouted, and a paper coffee cup exploded on the councilman's chest, the top popping off and hot coffee splattering his shirt and tie. He flinched, and first pain then anger flared in his eyes, but he quickly brought it under control, like steel shutters coming down.

The unflappable civil servant.

'I am as sorry as you are . . .'

Next came a Coke can, which Harper swatted, stumbling back a little as he did.

Jake rushed up the steps of the wooden platform, feeling his shin make contact with the Virgin Mary and hearing the dull thump of Baby Jesus landing in the snow. He threw a protective arm around Harper, who was still trying to talk into the mic. Mills came forward also. Between them they used their backs to shield Harper from the mob's missiles. They guided the councilman over to the side of the church, where silent earth movers stood behind wire fencing.

'Thank you, Officers,' Harper muttered, brushing furiously at the stain on his shirt. His hand was white and trembled slightly.

'Are you OK?' Jake asked, but then his mobile rang. Bad timing, but as a cop he couldn't ignore it. He took it out of his jacket pocket, glanced at the display – *Leigh* – and sighed.

He put the phone away. The protesters were beginning to press forward against the wire, shouting abuse at the construction workers. That was all Jake needed. More trouble.

Suddenly a voice rang out over the protesters: 'Friends, please!'

There was a momentary lull as the people turned back to see who was speaking. A man in black walked briskly to the platform. He stood behind the microphone and tried to take it from its stand but it wouldn't come loose so he stretched his neck upwards.

'Friends,' the man said again. 'I am as upset as you are.'

Jake looked quizzically at Mills.

'Father Ken Laurie,' Mills whispered. 'The parish priest.'

The priest, who looked to be in his late fifties or early sixties, struggled with the microphone, finally gripping the stand with his left hand and angling it down towards his face.

'We're all going to miss this church, and it's especially sad to have to say goodbye to it at this time of year. This is my twenty-second Christmas as your priest. I baptized many of your children. I presided over your daughters' weddings.' The crowd quietened to listen to him speak. 'But the church isn't a building. The church is in our hearts.'

There was a hum from the crowd.

'The diocese has agreed to Christ the Redeemer

being relocated, as a new road will breathe life back into this community.'

'What about the graves that will be buried under four lanes of concrete?'

The people jeered again and Father Ken held up his hand. 'Our loved ones' remains will be moved to the new cemetery with all the proper respect—'

'What about resting in peace, Father?' The hack addressed the priest, but his eyes were on the gathered protesters. 'Don't you give a shit about that?'

The crowd yelled angry agreement. This was getting out of hand. Jake stepped round the wire fence and pushed through the throng, opening his jacket and flashing his badge to make people move aside. Once he got to the middle where the journalist was standing he could see the man's accreditation: Chuck Ford.

'Why don't you cool it on the questions, Chuck?' he whispered. 'You're making a tricky situation into a volatile one.'

Ford just grinned back at him. He looked around at the protesters, even though his words were for Jake, the same trick he'd pulled to turn the crowd against Father Ken.

'Ever hear of freedom of the press? Why don't you want us to ask questions? Why the cover-up?'

Jake knew the type. He had seen it often. Big shows of anger delivered in a relaxed but challenging pose, the pose of someone who knew that he could say what he wanted without getting punched in the face. Probably bullied at school, now using his job to feel like a big man. Everyone with status was a substitute for those who had slapped him around.

'Cover-up!' One voice rose over the others. Jake quickly scanned the protesters and found the source near the front, shaking his fist up at the priest. He was a big man with wide shoulders, somewhere in his fifties. His eyes were dull but fixed. He was wearing blue jeans and a lumberjack shirt, open, with a black T-shirt underneath. The letters of the Metallica logo emblazoned on the chest were contorted by the man's broad but flabby chest. His red bobble hat barely made it around his cranium.

'Cover-up! Cover-up! Cover-up!' The crowd was taking up the chant. The lumberjack threw his cigarette at the platform, the butt hitting the priest on the leg.

Take out the bull-moose loony, the rest will fold.

Jake pushed through the crowd again towards the loudmouth. This time people weren't making way for him. Then his phone bleeped. Text message. He ignored it.

Twenty or so uniformed cops were coming in from the sides. They were trying to make a line between the inflamed protesters and the construction workers.

'Called for reinforcements, pig?' snarled the lumberjack. 'Big brave men when you have backup, right?'

'I need you to calm down, sir!' said Jake.

'Fuck you.'

'Calm down,' said Jake, 'or I *will* take you into custody.'

The man drew his fist way back – a haymaker. Jake stepped into the punch, bringing himself chest to chest with his attacker, and the wild swing sailed over his left shoulder. Jake gripped the lumberjack's shirt, then he spun sharply, bending his knees and throwing his hips back into the big man, who was bent at the waist and thus easier to flip. Jake pulled up sharply to make sure that the man didn't suffer any broken bones upon impact. Internal Affairs were still a little bit touchy about broken bones.

The two wise men were not so lucky.

As soon as the man landed Jake turned him on to his stomach and pinned his arm behind his back. He brought both arms together and cuffed them.

A few in the crowd backed away. One of the uniforms winked at him and muttered, 'Touchdown!'

Mills was grinning. Just as Jake was hauling the man to his feet, knocking aside the severed torso of Melchior, Caspar or Balthazar, Mills's phone began to ring.

'If it's my wife, tell her I'll call her back,' Jake said with a smile.

Mills answered his mobile, stiffened, listened for a few more moments, then put away the phone.

'You better hand this guy over to the uniforms, Jake,' said Mills, his expression more serious than Jake had ever seen. 'They've found a body.'

3

Monday, 11 a.m.

Mills drove because the roads were icy and he was local, which meant he not only knew the roads, but knew how to drive them at speed without getting them both killed. The blue light was on the roof and heat was blasting out of the dashboard as the sedan sped across town. It was about six miles to the site where the body had been found. Another point on the new interstate, where construction was cutting along the back of Glendale, a lower-class suburban sprawl.

'Female, African-American, late twenties or early thirties,' explained Mills as he drove. 'Whoever the sick fuck is who did it, she died a horrible death. Her eyeballs—'

Jake held up a hand. 'Don't tell me anything more. I want a clear mind when I look at the kill site.'

'Is that some big-city cop technique we hicks don't know about, Grasshopper?'

'No,' Jake said. 'It's, kind of, my own technique.'

More a curse than a technique.

They drove in silence for a few minutes, a silence eventually broken by Mills. 'Neat move on that protester. Karate?'

'Judo. We covered it in basic training.'

Mills sighed. '*My* training covered basic nose-picking and hamburger eating,' said Mills. 'I was good at the nose-picking.'

Jake laughed.

They lapsed into an uneasy silence for a few minutes, which Mills broke by flipping on the radio. Some local station DJ was rambling over a song intro, which was apparently number 14 on their 'Epic Yuletide Countdown'. Jake flicked the radio off.

'You not a fan?' Mills asked.

'Nope,' said Jake, resisting giving Mills the explanation he was clearly after. His new partner was the kind of man who had obviously—

'I've always loved Christmas.'

'One day of the year your dad showed an interest, right?' said Jake. Then he winced. 'Sorry.'

'It's OK.' Mills kept his eyes on the road as he said, 'Things between me and my dad are tough, that's all. Always have been. How'd you guess?'

Jake shrugged. How could he explain it to Mills?

'Go on then, what else you got?' Mills joked. 'When will I meet my Princess Charming, and how many kids will I have?'

'You have an aunt called Vonnie,' said Jake. 'Your wife has a phobia about cats. And you broke your leg in a skating accident when you were twelve.'

'Wrong, wrong and wrong,' said Mills.

'I know – it's a pile of shit.'

Both men laughed. 'First right thing you've said all day,' said Mills as they turned off the street.

They pulled in beside three black and whites, a medical examiner's van and an ambulance. Mills's eyes twinkled as he said, 'The ambulance is a bit optimistic.' He undid his seat belt but Jake didn't follow. 'Coming?'

'I need a minute to get orientated.'

'I can help there. North is to your left, south is to your right, and brutal death is straight ahead.'

Jake stepped from the car and stood, leaning his elbows on the roof. It was a highway construction site, simple as that. A broad swathe of land laid bare by the machines, a strip of brown mud dusted with snow frozen hard by the winter and dotted by diggers silent and still now because of the corpse. Construction workers stood around in small groups, talking. Most of them were congregated to the right of where the cop cars had pulled up.

When Jake looked left he could see the gleaming new interstate – six lanes of progress surrounded by suburbia. The construction site was fenced in, but it wouldn't have been difficult to get access, particularly at night. A cheap pair of wire cutters would have done the trick. Near where the new road petered out to levelled mud Jake could see a cluster of cops and paramedics, and a couple of technical guys in whites. The Indianapolis Crime Scene Squad, on loan for the forensics. Littleton didn't have its own body team.

The area was marked out with yellow tape. Jake

straightened up and walked over. He reached the tape and ducked under it. Immediately a uniform moved forward and put a hand on his arm. 'This is a crime scene, buddy. You can't come in.' Jake held up his badge and walked on.

He could make out the body, but the face was the first thing – the *only* thing – he saw, and the full horror struck him like a physical blow. The top half of her face was dominated by twin dark patches of dried and caked blood standing out against the flakes of snow that had settled on her skin. Something seemed to be hanging from both eyes. The murderer had inserted something into them.

'Whoa,' said Mills, covering his mouth with his hand.

Jake bent forward, then recoiled, the gorge rising in his throat. Experienced though he was, he hadn't prepared himself for this. Nothing had been inserted in her eyes. Instead both her eyeballs had been popped out and were hanging from their blood-blackened sockets by the optic nerves. Her jaw was strangely distorted. He could see that several teeth were missing, and one was dangling from her mangled lips. He was sure that when the medical examiner took the body, some would be found in her mouth and throat – maybe even her oesophagus, depending on how long she had lived.

'Christ,' said Mills. 'What did he do to her?'

Jake ignored the question and took in the secondary injuries. The woman was on her back, arms spread wide. Like an insect pinned to a display board. Jake took it all in at a glance. African-American, mid-to-late twenties or early thirties, just like Mills had said. Slightly overweight but probably attractive when she was alive.

There was a dark ring of bruising around both wrists and down her arms. She had been tied up. And there was a ligature mark around her throat. Jake hoped she had been strangled before the injuries had been inflicted. But he got the feeling she hadn't.

She was poor, that was obvious from the way she was dressed. Smart but cheap, probably Walmart. One shoe was half off her foot, and her mud-smeared clothes were crooked. There were two buttons missing from her blouse. Sign of a sexual motive? No . . .

She was dragged.

And the woman had fought, which probably prompted the blow that had mangled her jaw. The missing teeth looked like a quirk of the killer's rather than an attempt to frustrate police identification.

He looked around at the CSIs. 'Anyone find her purse?'

No one answered.

'Gloves.'

Scowling, a white-coated technician handed him a latex glove, which Jake pulled on. He bent down and reached a hand into the victim's coat. There it was. Her wallet.

'Don't most women keep their wallets in a purse?' asked Mills.

Mills was right. The wallet was probably put there on purpose.

You want us to know who she is.

Jake snapped it open. There was her driver's licence. Her name was Marcia Lamb.

A shadow hovered in front of him. He looked up. It was one of the lab people from Indianapolis. She was early thirties, with small glasses and brown hair tied back in a ponytail. She looked like a librarian.

'Detective, this is the scene of a murder,' she said. 'Please move behind the tape until we have examined it.'

He turned to her, wondering if he had been that arrogant when he had first moved from the city.

He shook his head gently. 'No, it's not.'

He looked slowly around. The whole area seemed to darken and sharpen. He could see that it was far too exposed. *You'd move furtively, like a small animal avoiding the predators. It would have been quiet here last night, but you'd still have to hurry in case someone saw you from the road. But you didn't hurry the killing. You wouldn't hurry something you get so much pleasure from. So why did you lay out the body here?*

The body – not the woman. She had to have been dead already. That's the only way it could have worked.

'This isn't the murder scene,' Jake went on. 'This is a dump scene.'

The CSI stiffened. Jake replaced the wallet, then turned to head back to the car, hearing the woman mutter, 'All that after two minutes?'

Jake didn't turn round.

Mills caught him up. 'How come you're so sure?'

'If I was going to kill someone this slowly, this deliberately, I wouldn't do it here.'

4
Monday, 4.43 p.m.

Crying was the one thing Jake couldn't deal with. And Bertha Sinclair was laying on the waterworks. A big woman in her forties, she described her missing friend between long drags on her Chesterfields, the smoke contributing to the stuffy air inside the cramped apartment, whose floor space was cut in half by the undecorated Christmas tree in the corner. Ms Sinclair had been dragging it into place when the detectives had arrived.

'Marcia is always so reliable – never left me waiting before.'

The address from the licence had proved a bum lead, being several years out of date. But they had got lucky: Ms Sinclair was Marcia Lamb's babysitter and she had been the one to report her missing.

'OK,' said Mills, who seemed less affected by emotions. 'First, we need to establish the facts. How long have you known Miss Lamb?'

'Since she was a kid. She grew up down the street from me.' Bertha sniffed through a large handkerchief.

'And you look after her child?'

'Yes, little Kelly. She's four. I take her in here while

Marcia's at work. She's got a job in a cocktail bar – Blue Dog, I think it's called.'

She sucked on her cigarette and blew out a shaky breath.

'But last night she never came.' She looked from one detective to the other. 'You will find her?'

Jake narrowed his eyes at Mills, who picked up on the sign. *Don't tell her yet.*

'You reported her missing?' Jake asked.

'Yes. Around two o'clock in the morning.' The woman's eyes suddenly blazed. 'But the cop who took the call tried to get rid of me. Told me I had to wait twenty-four hours . . . I told him straight, he should tell *that* to her little girl.'

Jake could hear Kelly – a cute little thing with her hair in neat cornrows – playing with some dolls in the back room. She was in a world of her own, oblivious to the darkness that was gathering around her life.

'Does she always pick up Kelly by midnight?' asked Mills.

Bertha nodded. 'Never once let me down. That night her boyfriend was supposed to get Kelly.'

Jake's head flicked up at this. Ninety-nine cases out of a hundred, the boyfriend was the killer. The statistics don't lie.

'When he didn't show, I called her and she said she'd come—'

'Tell me about the boyfriend,' Jake asked.

Bertha looked at him with wide eyes. 'Sonny's a

lowlife,' she said. 'Marcia could do a lot better. But who am I to judge? He picks up Kelly every so often, and . . . well . . . what do I know?'

'You didn't phone him last night, when he didn't show?' asked Jake.

'I don't have his mobile number,' said Bertha. 'I know where he lives, if that helps.'

'Where?'

'With Marcia. About two minutes from here. It's on Washington Street – 149, I think.'

There was a knock at the door. Bertha was about to haul herself up but Jake raised his hand and went to get it himself. Outside on the porch stood a sweet-looking woman in her early twenties wearing a colourful scarf over a plain beige coat. Jake knew she was from Social and Family Services even before she showed him her badge.

'I'm here for Kelly,' she said, her voice low.

Jake nodded and stood to one side to let the woman in. As soon as Bertha saw her she started crying again. 'The poor child. I'd keep her myself, but I just can't.'

From where he was he could see Kelly still playing in the back room. The woman from Social Services walked through the den, throwing a polite smile to Bertha as she passed, and knelt on the floor beside the little girl.

Kelly looked up at the woman and said, 'Are you bringing me to my mommy?'

Jake felt his fists clench.

5

Monday, 5.02 p.m.

When they left Bertha Sinclair's apartment, Jake let Mills walk ahead towards the car. He took out his phone and returned his earlier missed call.

Leigh, his wife, answered halfway through the third ring. 'So, you *do* have our number.'

'Sorry, honey. It's been a rough shift.'

'It's been a rough month back here,' said Leigh, any playful sarcasm thrown aside. 'The baby's been crying all day. He screams when I hold him, he screams when I put him down. The house is in a mess. And Faith is in another one of her moods.'

Faith, their eldest, was twelve and beginning to move awkwardly into her teenage years. His sweet princess had been replaced by a hormone-driven she-devil. Come to think of it, since the birth of Jakey six weeks ago, his wife had been replaced by a hormone-driven she-devil too.

'She needs to start pulling her weight around here,' Leigh continued. 'And so do you.'

'I know, honey. I'm sorry.'

'You OK?' she asked, sounding concerned. She

must have heard the catch in his voice. After fifteen years together, she knew him too well.

'We caught a bad one this morning,' he said. 'Young mother. Murdered. Her four-year-old has just been taken in by social services.'

'I'm sorry, babe.' She paused and then sighed. 'Wow, sometimes you just need things put into perspective.' There was a silence, then Leigh said in a smaller voice, 'But Jeanette isn't helping . . .'

Jake sighed. His mother had always got on with Leigh, but dementia had struck when she hit her seventies. She was no longer able to care for herself, so Jake had had her move in with his family when they came to Littleton. But it wasn't working out.

'I love you, babe. Don't hold dinner for me,' he said.

'Right back at you.' The line went dead. He put his phone back into his pocket and looked at Mills.

'Babysitter said it's a short walk. So we'll walk. Get a feel for the area.'

They went from the babysitter's down a side street, then took a left. The buildings were small single-storey houses, most with a porch and a tiny yard out the front. This was a poor neighbourhood but a family neighbourhood. It was quiet – kids at school, parents at work – but this wasn't a dangerous area. Jake would feel OK about Faith walking around here.

After another fifty yards they reached number 149. As they approached, Jake could feel the pressure building in his stomach, remembering the peptic ulcer he'd had the year before.

Don't make me kick your ass again, he told it.

It was a small wood-frame house with a postage stamp of grass in front and what looked like a junkyard at the rear: a blocky bundle covered with a tarpaulin – obviously a semi-retired barbecue – plastic chairs and piles of weathered children's toys filled the small space. An alley ran down one side. There was a low wire fence at the front, with a broken-down wooden gate leaning at a crazy angle. The gate threw a long shadow in the afternoon sunlight. Mills went straight up to it.

'Slow down,' said Jake.

Mills looked at him, but Jake just stood there. He looked up and down the road. *No cover, but late at night there'd be no one to observe. It might work.*

He looked into the yard, then up towards the door. Gently, using the sleeve of his coat, Jake pushed the gate open. He walked up to the front door and looked in through the pane of glass at the top. The hallway was dark, but nothing seemed disturbed.

He wasn't feeling it.

He looked around again and his eyes fell on something in the alleyway on the other side of the fence. There were some weeds trampled and tortured down in one corner. 'I think we've found our kill site,' he told Mills. 'He went in the back door.'

'How do you know?'

How *did* he know?

Mills shook his head in disbelief but stood back to let his partner lead.

Jake walked down the alley to the rear of the house. In his head it was almost as if he was watching a movie in silhouette. He couldn't see the details, but he could get the gist of what was happening.

You can feel the weight of the body. It's so heavy, inert. How long have you dragged her? Did she struggle? No, she was already dead. But that didn't gel either. More likely she was unconscious. *You wanted her awake when you killed her.*

The door was locked but seemed flimsy. This was where he had dragged her in.

'We have probable cause. I say we enter,' Jake said.

'No argument from me,' said Mills. 'I'll call it in.'

As Mills radioed the station Jake drew his knee up to his chest and thrust out his heel, hitting the door just below the lock. He kicked it three times in quick succession, then hit it with his shoulder. The door opened.

The two detectives entered the house.

Inside the kitchen there was a dirty coffee mug on the counter and a few plates in the sink. The bin was overflowing. There were three chairs around a small table – part of a set.

'Chair's missing,' said Jake, pointing to the table. 'She was tied to it.'

'Yeah, right. And the tooth fairy tickled her with a feather duster,' joked Mills. He was about to go into the next room when Jake placed a restraining hand on his elbow.

He closed his eyes and tried to see how it must have been. *You're under pressure because you've been dragging her for a while.* Jake could see it, he could feel an ache in his arms as if he had used them, could see the crumpled body at his feet, feel the panting from the exertion. But it was all vague, images replacing each other like photographs in a slide show. He needed those images to sharpen – he needed them to slow down. *It's late at night, she's coming home. Are you waiting for her or would anyone do? It's so cold the streets are empty, but you can't risk taking her in the open. You lure her into the alley and you chloroform her there. Or maybe you club her over the head? Then you drag her through the alley, across the backyard and into her house.*

'He's strong, and he knows the area,' said Jake. Mills was about to open his mouth, but Jake continued, 'And he knew where she lived. So he at least *knows* Littleton. Maybe he's visited, numerous times. He might have family here or something. But it's more likely he's a local.'

'The boyfriend?' asked Mills. 'He'd have a key to this place.'

'No sign of the door being kicked in,' Jake agreed.

'Until we came along,' Mills joked. When he saw that Jake was not smiling, he pursed his lips. 'Can we search the rest of the house now?' he asked.

Jake nodded.

Using his coat sleeve again, so as not to add his own prints to any left by the murderer, Jake depressed the handle and pushed the kitchen door open. He stood in the doorway and looked into the shadowy interior.

Mills stood behind him, taking in the scene over his shoulder. 'Jackpot,' he whispered.

6

Monday, 5.30 p.m.

The smell came first. The earthy, coppery odour of freshly spilt blood overlaid with other smells – faeces and urine – but the blood predominated. It was the smell of the slaughterhouse.

Jake reached for his belt and unhooked a small penlight. He swept the beam over the room. The living room – less disturbed than he expected: a knocked-over table, and the television had fallen from its stand. The floor was cluttered, but no more so than in his own home. Kids did that. In the centre of the floor, its back against the toppled coffee table, stood the fourth kitchen chair. There were dark stains on the wood.

'Ladies and gentlemen, we have ourselves a murder scene,' said Mills, and spoke into his radio, asking for the forensics to come.

Using the penlight to pick his route, Jake made his way slowly to the opposite wall and flipped the switch, throwing the room into harsh electric light. Now the stains on the wooden chair were visible as dark gouts of blood. There were also bloodstains on the threadbare carpet under the chair and some on the coffee table. Some snaked all the way to a limp, pathetic Christmas tree in the far corner, touching the edges of a present laid beneath it.

The red tag said, 'To Kelly, from Mommy xoxo'.

He stood in the centre of the room and saw how it must have happened. *It's late. The neighbours are in bed. You come to the door and leave the body down on the ground while you search her purse. You want to find her wallet so we can identify her quickly.*

Here Jake paused and scanned the room. He looked through the connecting door into the kitchen. Yes, in the corner, tossed casually away, was a woman's purse.

You shoved some junk aside, kicked the coffee table out of the way, overturning it. You laid her down in the centre of the room. Then you went into the kitchen for the chair. After putting the chair against the overturned table you tried to pull her up on to it. That must have been when she woke up. There was a brief struggle – the television was knocked over. But you got her under control again and tied her to the chair.

He scanned the floor again. No ropes.

'I'm not so sure I like the boyfriend for this,' said Jake. 'The killer brought rope with him and took it away again after. That's a murder kit. We might be looking for someone who has either done this before . . . or has been building up to it.'

Mills winced before he answered the question Jake was about to ask. 'I don't recall any recent reports of women attacked on the street, no attempted abductions. Nothing like that. You might be overthinking this one a little, city slicker,' said Mills with a dark laugh.

Was he? He had done so before – thrown himself into cases back in Chicago, ending up mired in the minds of the offenders. Sometimes the simple solution really was the right one. Sometimes the boyfriend really did do it. Grounding himself with that thought, Jake crouched. Near the leg of the chair was a white speck.

'Fuck,' said Mills, his eyes on Jake. 'I could have done without seeing that.'

It was a molar. Jake looked around quickly and found two more.

'She was conscious throughout the whole thing,' he said.

Mills exhaled a long breath.

Just then both detectives heard the clatter of the gate in the yard being roughly pushed aside.

The scrape of a key being inserted into the lock.

The whine of the front door as it opened.

Footsteps came down the short hall. Mills's breath caught in his throat just as the living room door swung open, revealing a large black man in his late twenties, wearing a puffy parka that had seen better days.

He paused in the doorway. 'The fuck are you assholes doing in my house?' he shouted.

Sonny. The boyfriend.

Mills reached for his badge.

'Ah, shit!' Sonny yelled, his sneakers scraping the floor as he turned and bolted.

Jake ran after him. *Sometimes*, he told himself again, *the boyfriend really did do it.*

7
Monday, 5.36 p.m.

Jake was out on to the street and running hard after Sonny – a big man in bad shape, and the sidewalk was slick and icy. Not the best conditions for an escape. In a few long strides Jake had closed the gap. He judged his lunge to perfection. He drew level, then placed a hand on Sonny's shoulder, gripping the jacket. At the same time he caught his right leg in between Sonny's legs, who went down hard. Jake went down too but was able to twist so that Sonny broke his fall. Almost as soon as he hit the ground Jake was spinning, muscle memory kicking in. Within a second he had flipped Sonny on to his stomach and pinned his hands securely behind his back.

By now Mills had jogged up. He came to a stop, both arms straight out and cradling a big Smith & Wesson.

'Get up, shit head, and assume the position,' he growled.

Jake looked up at Mills. 'I hope you're talking to him.'

Sonny got to his feet and stood with his arms raised. The movement pulled his parka up, revealing two handguns whose barrels disappeared beneath the belt line of his jeans. Jake stepped forward and took them, placing them on the ground. There was a beat-up old Chevy nearby. Jake marched Sonny over to it. Sonny knew the drill, placing both hands on the hood and spreading his legs.

'I'm not saying nothing,' he said.

As Mills stepped up to cuff him, Jake reached into his pocket and took out his mobile phone. Whatever niggling feeling he might have had about this case, there was no way to argue – Sonny was an armed man fleeing the scene of a murder. Time to call it in and hope it was one of those open-and-shut cases.

'Put me through to the colonel,' he said.

'Out at a meeting with the DA,' the desk sergeant replied, his voice robotic.

'If he gets back before us, tell him we're bringing in a suspect.' Jake ended the call.

When he turned back, Mills was standing there with a big grin on his face, the gun now held by his side. Sonny glowered, a sullen hulk radiating defiance.

Mills did the honours: 'I am arresting you on suspicion of the murder of Marcia Lamb.'

Sonny's eyes widened in shock. 'What the fuck?'

'You have the right to remain silent. Anything you say can and will be . . . Shit, you know the Miranda rights as well as I do.' Mills shook his head and pushed Sonny forward. 'Walk.'

They turned back towards their car. They weren't

within ten feet of it before Jake heard approaching steps.

'Is this where she was killed?' Chuck Ford asked as he appeared first at Jake's side, then hanging back to walk on their heels. He carried a pen and pad. His pupils were dilated like he was on something, but Jake had seen the buzz journalists got from a story before.

Jake glared at him. 'Who?'

'I was hoping you'd tell me,' he said, tapping his pen against his pad. 'We need official confirmation on the victim's name.'

Jake kept walking towards the car.

'I'm only doing my job,' said Ford.

Mills handed Sonny off to Jake before rounding on the reporter. 'You stepped over the line this morning. Almost caused a goddamned riot outside a church – at fucking Christmas time, no less. So don't talk to me about "doing my job". You are the pus inside the pimple on the ass of the department. Do you need me to spell that out for you? A-S-S.'

But Chuck wasn't listening any more. He was looking behind them. And he was smiling.

Both cops turned and Jake saw two black and whites and a big white forensics van pulling up on the street.

'I think I just got my confirmation,' said Chuck. 'But I can make you look good if you help me out.' He nodded towards the handcuffed Sonny. 'Can I tell my readers you have caught the killer – the deranged individual who slaughtered a young mom before she could celebrate Christmas with her kid?'

'You're a dick, Ford,' said Mills as they reached the car. 'One of these days you'll get what's coming to you.'

'Yeah, I will,' said Ford. 'A Pulitzer.'

Jake just stood there. *Keep calm*, he told himself. *Remember Chicago.*

Suddenly Sonny lunged towards the reporter, trying to break free from Jake and Mills. 'I didn't do it!' he shouted. 'They're trying to frame me, man!'

Jake pushed past Chuck and bundled Sonny into the car before he could give Chuck any more for his article. The big man cursed as his head bumped the roof, but Jake didn't care. He got in beside him while Mills got into the driver's seat. Within seconds, Mills was pulling away from the kerb.

Jake glared at the small, indistinct shape of Chuck Ford in the rear-view mirror.

'Fucking journalists.'

8

Monday, 7.15 p.m.

It was after six when they got back to the station, then it took an hour to get through the formalities of booking, taking prints and samples of Sonny's DNA. There was a numbness in the air – the station had been looking forward to the Christmas party that had been scheduled for the following day, but an unclosed case was likely going to put paid to that. Jake had heard the station administrator – a sardonic woman in her fifties named either Gina or Tina – sounding out others about rescheduling it to the new year. Assuming the murderer was locked up before the 31st.

Finally, with the district attorney called in, the detectives were ready to interview the boyfriend.

Ninety-nine cases out of a hundred . . .

'I'm telling you,' said Sonny, addressing every word to his attorney, 'Marcia was fine when I left her last night.'

The suspect's voice wavered, but that wasn't necessarily a sign of guilt. Maybe he was just cold. Jake had had the heat turned off in the interview room, and with his parka taken as evidence, Sonny's thin black T-shirt wasn't doing much for his core temperature in the small windowless interview room. Hard chairs, a black table and a tape recorder fixed to the wall made the place look about as luxurious as the average holding cell.

'Lots of things can happen in a night,' said Mills. 'She's dead now.'

Sonny fell silent. His big hands came up to his face and he clenched them. For a moment his hands struggled against the restraining cuffs. Then he dropped them again and scowled.

'Look, she was my woman,' he said. 'I wouldn't hurt her.'

'So what happened?' Jake asked.

'I don't know. She left for work at seven. Dropped Kelly over to that nosey bitch who watches her.'

'Why didn't *you* watch her?' snapped Jake.

'Busy, man. I was out of there by eight.' He looked again at his attorney, who nodded. 'Spent the night with my girl over on Cherry Orchard,' he admitted.

Jake looked at Mills. Cherry Orchard was a poor area very close to Glendale. That put Sonny near the dump site. He was looking better and better. On the other hand, his shock had seemed genuine. And he didn't strike Jake as the sadistic type. Was there a way to get Sonny to confess? Jake's plan was to bide his time with this one. Once the forensics were done and they could see if they'd found any DNA, they would have a better idea of whether he was their man. But for now he'd ask some questions and see what happened.

'And there's me thinking you had a girl here on Washington,' said Jake.

'No law says a man can't have two girls,' said Sonny, his voice so quiet Jake thought it might not register on the tape.

'OK,' said Jake. 'But it doesn't make you look like a decent guy.'

'My client has already told you where he was,' said the attorney, George Vincennes, with an exaggerated sigh, his puff of breath visible. 'He was dancing at the Boom Box, a nightclub in Indianapolis, with a Miss Penny Stokes.'

'We was clubbing all night,' added Sonny.

'You weren't clubbing all night,' said Jake.

'No, man. After we finished clubbing, we went back to her place.'

'And were you doing a bit of dealing at the club?' asked Jake. Sonny had a heavy rap sheet, lots of priors including possession and possession with intent. Speed, weed, blow – it didn't matter to him. He had served time for an aggravated burglary rap. He had been out a little over a year.

Jake nodded to himself. Sonny was certainly violent – but sadistic? He didn't see it.

And I've been wrong before.

'Are you arresting my client for murder or for

possession?' asked Vincennes, his tone telling them not to mess around.

'We need this Penny Stokes's address,' said Mills.

Sonny shrugged. 'Sure.'

It took them until after nine to locate Penny Stokes, but the story checked out. Stokes confirmed that Sonny had been with her all night, only leaving at six thirty in the morning, when he got up to go to his job at the city sanitation department.

By nine thirty Jake and Mills were back at their desks in a small cubicle at the end of the detective bureau, drinking coffee and eating drugstore sandwiches.

'You still like him for this?' Jake asked.

Mills paused over his sandwich and when he answered, he spoke slowly.

'I don't know. The alibi is holding, but we have nothing from the club. I'll go over myself in an hour with his picture.' He took a bite and carried on with his mouth full. 'Let's say he killed Marcia at midnight, dumped her, and got to this Penny girl by two. She loves him, or she's scared of him, so she alibis him for the night.' He swallowed his mouthful and shrugged. 'I think we got the right man.'

Jake couldn't dispute the logic. Forensics would throw light on it, he hoped – and with the low temperatures this time of year, Marcia's time of death might not be so easy to determine.

Ninety-nine cases out of a hundred . . .

He sighed and ran his hand through his hair. 'But we don't have enough to hold him tonight.'

Mills threw back a sigh at Jake like an echo. 'And the sonofabitch knows it,' he said. 'It's on us to build the case, I guess.'

Knowing they wouldn't get any more by tomorrow, they cut Sonny loose. His home was still a crime scene, sealed by forensics, so he had to nominate a friend to stay with and give the police the address. They were not surprised when he chose Penny Stokes and Cherry Orchard.

9

Tuesday, 13 December, 12.10 a.m.

When Jake got home, he was too frazzled from his shift to feel his usual irritation at the garish red reindeer on the roof of the house next to his. His own home was in darkness, which was no surprise. He crept into the kitchen like a burglar, flicking the light switch. He opened the fridge, feeling a pleasant sense of relief when he heard the clatter of beer bottles.

Just the one, he told himself.

He took out a Miller Lite and brought it over to the table. He popped the top as he sat down, taking a long swig. And as the cooling liquid flooded through his chest, he began to go over the day.

The case should have been an easy one. Sonny – a violent criminal on probation – had obviously killed his girlfriend, probably in anger but maybe with a more complex motive. Prison can change a man. Maybe a distressing episode or two in the showers. Rape, humiliation – a lunkhead like Sonny surely didn't have the psychological capacity to withstand such an experience. It might explain why he was cheating on his girlfriend, filling his time with an extra woman, looking to reassert his manhood now that he was back on the outside. Had he confided in Marcia, perhaps? Had she thrown it back at him, prompting a new kind of rage and violence in Sonny?

Would such a sequence of events be enough to push a man like him to the madness of the man who had murdered Marcia?

Jake rubbed his temples as if he could erase the tumbling thoughts from his brain.

He took another long swig from the bottle, almost emptying it. Motive and explanation were irrelevant. All they had to do was build the case and secure the conviction. The lab work should help there. A messy killing like that always left plenty of forensics. As long as the killer wasn't a pro. And Sonny, despite his record, was no pro. He would have made mistakes.

But Jake wasn't happy.

There was the purse. It had been flung casually across the kitchen, suggesting that the killer had let himself in with Marcia's key. Did the killer hold on to it? Sonny had his own key.

Jake cursed himself.

Why can't I just accept the obvious? Sonny is the killer. Mills is right: I overcomplicate.

A noise – someone coming down the stairs. The light came on in the hall. Leigh.

He looked up with a grin as the door opened, but it wasn't his wife who came into the kitchen. It was his mother. She was wearing a nightdress and fluffy pink slippers. But she had her woollen overcoat on over the top.

'Hi, Mom,' he said in a resigned but gentle voice.

'Hi, Bruce,' she replied with a bright smile. 'You're home early.'

Bruce? That's a new one. His mother's lucid moments were fewer and further between these days. She was beginning not to recognize family members. Her connection with the world was eroding.

'What are you doing up?' Jake asked.

'It's such a sunny day I thought I would take a walk.'

Jake's eyes flicked to the kitchen window – seeing his vivid reflection in the sheet of black cast by the night. 'I see.'

'The air will do me good. I might take the dog.'

They didn't have a dog.

'That's a great idea, Mom.' He stood up and went towards her. 'But have you taken your nap? I think you should take your nap first, and then go for the walk.'

Jeanette frowned deeply like he'd just asked her to solve a particularly complex puzzle. 'Yes, I think I will have a nap.'

Jake took her by the hand and led her back to the hall, where he took off her coat. He hung it on the rack beside his own and Faith's bright red coat. Then he led his mother up the stairs and into her bedroom. He stayed in the room until she had climbed back into bed, then he bent down and kissed her softly on the forehead.

‘Good night, Mom,’ he said.

‘Good night, Bruce,’ she replied.

Jake tiptoed out of the room, shutting the door behind him and wondering how he could keep her safe.

Time to call it a night. Outside his bedroom he shuffled off his shoes without undoing the laces. He crept into the bedroom and quickly stripped down to his boxers, dropping trousers, shirt, vest and coat on the floor at the end of the bed. Leigh would give him hell for it in the morning, but he was too tired to care.

He took a moment in the moonlight to look down at his sleeping wife. Her slim shoulders and golden hair still stole his breath. Then he took a quick glance at Baby Jakey, sleeping peacefully in his crib by the wall. They had converted the box room for him, but Leigh said he wasn’t ready to sleep on his own yet. Jake suspected it was she who wasn’t ready.

He pulled back the sheets and slipped into bed. Leigh stirred and rolled over.

‘Hi, babe. Good to see you,’ she murmured. She didn’t open her eyes.

‘You too,’ said Jake, stroking her hair.

‘Rough day?’ she asked, nestling into his chest.

‘The roughest. It’s too awful to think about.’ Jake changed the subject. ‘How’s my mother been?’

Now Leigh looked up at him. She considered her answer – maybe several possibilities – before settling on ‘The usual.’

'When I came home she was all dressed to go out for a walk in the sunshine. Has she been like that all day?'

'Pretty much.'

'Soon we'll have to put a lock on her door. We won't have to baby-proof the house; we'll have to grandma-proof it!'

Leigh giggled into his chest, which turned into a kiss. Jake allowed himself a smile. Over the past few months there hadn't been enough laughter in their house – or kissing, or anything else. Leigh's fingertips lightly brushed over his ribs, sending a pleasant shudder through his torso. Jake decided to push his luck. He playfully cupped her butt, prompting more giggles. And another kiss to his chest, this one just below his nipple.

'You're very hot,' she muttered.

'Not as hot as you are, honey,' he growled in his best Bogart accent.

'You're so cheesy,' she said. She lightly blew on the small trace of saliva she had left on his skin. She knew that drove him crazy. Maybe he wasn't pushing his luck at all.

He ran a finger down the path of her spine. His touch was light over her thin cotton nightie.

'That feels good,' she whispered.

Encouraged, he stroked her buttocks with his other hand, moving in big, slow circles, his fingers gliding over the cotton. Leigh drew in a sharp breath as she moved closer to him. Her body felt soft and warm. As his left hand continued to circle, his right reached the hem of the nightdress. Gently he pulled it up, but it wouldn't budge. Leigh's weight was pinning it firmly against the bed. He tugged a bit harder and was rewarded with the sound of tearing fabric.

'Jesus, Jake, have you torn my best—'

'Fuck it, it's ruined now,' he said, and he ripped up the front of the nightie.

Leigh laughed. 'You animal!'

Grinning, Jake turned Leigh on to her back and moved on top of her. His left hand pushed aside the torn nightie and slid down her body.

Suddenly, he heard a noise in the corridor. Jake reacted instinctively, sitting up and reaching for his gun. But a half-second later he realized it was his daughter, Faith. He took his gun from the bedside table and shoved it safely under the bed.

Faith stood in the open doorway, looking down the landing, not saying a word.

'Honey?' Leigh called out.

Faith didn't say anything for a moment, then in a soft voice she said, 'Mom?'

'Are you all right, honey?'

But Faith just stood there, looking ahead with a fixed gaze.

'I think she's sleepwalking,' said Jake, pulling up his boxers and reaching for his dressing gown. She hadn't sleepwalked in years. The move and the strain of a new baby and a live-in grandma were obviously taking their toll.

He went over and took her gently by the shoulders.

‘Faith, baby,’ he whispered, ‘you need to wake up now.’

Slowly the fixed look left her eyes. ‘Hi, Dad.’ She blinked slowly. ‘Can I sleep with you guys tonight?’

‘Sure, honey,’ Leigh said. They wouldn’t get to finish what they had started but suddenly Jake was too tired to care. He led Faith to the bed. She got in and curled up against her mother, her eyes closing instantly. Jake sat on the edge of the bed, wanting to make sure she was OK before heading downstairs to sleep on the couch.

‘It was a bad dream,’ she said to no one in particular. Her voice sounded dreamy, far away. ‘I was running, but I don’t know from what. And then I wasn’t running any more. I was hitting someone in the face.’

There was a long pause, and Jake thought it was all over. But then she carried on, her voice thick with sleep: ‘It hurt him, and I felt bad about that. But I kept hitting him anyway. And I was holding Jakey, and I was worried about dropping him.’ She sounded shaken. ‘That’s all I remember.’

Jake leaned forward and stroked her hair. ‘You shouldn’t worry about dropping the baby, little one. I dropped you on your head lots of times, and you turned out fine.’

Faith smiled, then snuggled into her mother and was lost to the world.

Jake took himself downstairs. And a few minutes later he was asleep, and smiling too.

10

Tuesday, 8 a.m.

The sun had barely risen when Jake drove up to the station. He could see a group of people gathered around the entrance. Some he recognized as reporters but some were complete strangers. Chuck Ford must have broken the story. Jake wasn't surprised, but he wasn't happy either.

He parked his car and walked up the path. As he pushed his way through the group some tried to get in front of him.

'Detective Austin, what can you tell us about yesterday's murder?'

'Will the police be issuing a statement today?'

'Why was your suspect released so quickly?'

He tried not to make eye contact with anyone.

Ford was leaning against the wall beside the station door. He uncurled himself as Jake came up.

'You going to be digging into Sonny's history?'

Jake just gave him a cold look. Ford shrugged and stepped aside.

As Jake turned into the detective bureau he could feel his shoulders hunch. The scant Christmas decorations of yesterday had been taken down – Gina (or Tina) had obviously made the call. Mills was already at his desk and a few of the other guys – what remained of the staff during the holiday season – were talking by the coffee machine. Outside the window the reporters had started up their questions again and flash bulbs strobed. Mills stood, then punched Jake on the shoulder.

'The eagle has landed.' He grinned.

Jake followed him to the window and looked out. Councilman Mitch Harper had arrived, and arrived with a bang. Dressed in a dark woollen coat, the councilman had planted himself on the top step of the station entrance. He stood tall, shoulders thrown back. His dark Lincoln was casually parked. Jake wondered if detectives could write parking tickets.

The reporters crowded around in a semicircle, looking up at him. Through the window Jake could hear everything.

'A single mother should not have had to die to show up the inadequacies of our city's social policies,' Harper thundered.

A reporter raised a biro as if to ask a question, but Harper held up a hand.

'Let me just say that there are two guilty parties here: the man who killed Marcia Lamb, and the system that sent her out to work when she should have been at home with her young child. We need proper affordable day care, so that women like Marcia can hold down proper jobs, and not be forced to waitress in the shadow economy.'

'Are you blaming—'

'If the school system had not failed Marcia, she might have had a shot at college, a different life. And she might still be with us.'

'What a prick,' Mills muttered. 'He's milking her corpse for votes, and she's not even cold yet.'

'Sick,' said Jake, remembering his thoughts about Marcia's body temperature, cooled by the weather. He made a note to check with the coroner on the time of death, on which any attack they were to launch on Sonny's alibi might hinge.

Just then Colonel Asher came in. 'Mills, Austin, I need a word,' he said. They followed him across the hall into his office. A stocky man whose muscles were beginning to turn to fat, he had a red face and a shaven skull that only emphasized his bullishness. 'Anything I need to know before –' he rolled his eyes '– *Harper* comes in here?'

'There's nothing yet,' Jake said, looking to Mills for confirmation.

'Nothing new,' said Mills, 'except nobody at the club remembers Sonny Malone being there, so maybe we can crack his alibi.'

'Good.'

Was it good? Jake strongly suspected that Sonny Malone was the one case out of a hundred.

Asher sat heavily behind his desk and pulled Sonny's file towards him. 'You two might as well sit in when I talk to Harper.'

Jake nodded. He could hear the councilman from a mile away. He was greeting every officer as he passed them in the hall and creating as much fuss as possible. When he got to Asher's open door he knocked twice before striding in. He walked straight to the colonel's desk, put out his hand and smiled. 'Colonel,' he said. 'Thanks for taking the time to see me.'

Asher shook his hand. 'Of course, Councilman.' He motioned to Jake and Mills. 'Councilman Harper, this is Detective Austin, the lead on the investigation, and Detective Mills.'

'I know Howard well.' Harper smiled, shaking Mills's hand. He turned to Jake. 'You were at the protest at the church the other day, weren't you?'

'Yes, sir,' Jake replied, taking his turn to shake the councilman's hand.

'And you're new?' he asked.

'Transferred from Chicago a couple months ago.'

'Glad to have you here.' He took the spare seat. 'Terrible business. Is it too early yet to say how the investigation is going?' He looked at all three men. Jake and Mills didn't react. Asher sighed.

Harper broke the silence.

'You'll appreciate this is a community that values law and order. Rumours are flying around about the vicious way this woman was murdered. People have got a lot of questions and we're not hearing any answers. What do I tell them?'

'We have things in hand,' said Asher with a smile.

'I just want to be able to assure people that you are on top of this situation, Colonel.'

Asher forced a smile. 'Of course.' Asher motioned to Jake and Mills. 'My detectives are making very good progress.'

Harper nodded. 'That's what I like to hear. We need to solve this one quickly – a murdered young mother is hardly going to do much for the Christmas spirit around here. I'll want regular updates on how the investigation is going.'

Asher rubbed his hands together with more of a nervous tic than eagerness. 'You'll be glad to hear that we already have a very strong suspect.'

'That fast?' Harper looked startled and impressed. 'That's great news! Who is he?'

'Sonny Malone,' Asher told him, looking down at the file on his desk. 'The victim's boyfriend.'

Harper nodded to show that he wasn't surprised. Figuring the political angles, Jake thought. Wondering how to play it with the public.

'He's done time for aggravated burglary,' Asher read from the file. 'Beat an old woman half to death.'

'And our great justice system let him out early?' sneered Harper.

'Yes, sir. Got six years, paroled after four.' Asher nodded.

Harper straightened in his chair. 'It's like I always say – if they sin, keep them in. If this fellow, Sonny what's his name, had been punished properly, maybe we wouldn't be sitting here talking about him. And Marcia Lamb would still be breathing today. Maybe if Sonny—'

'Sonny didn't do it.'

It was out before Jake could stop himself. But there was only so much electioneering he could stomach.

Harper was looking at him, startled.

Asher glared at Jake. 'Detective . . .'

'It doesn't fit,' Jake went on. 'The MO is wrong for a guy like Sonny.'

Asher's mouth fell open. Jake knew he was digging a hole for himself, that Asher would drill him for this later, but he wasn't going to let him say that Sonny did it when he knew he didn't.

'The killer was too controlled,' Jake went on. 'It's not the reaction of an angry boyfriend. I'm sorry to tell you, but this one is going to take time.'

Harper stood. 'I don't give a fuck what it takes,' he said, the veneer of politeness gone. 'Throw everything into it. We need to catch this killer before everything gets crazy.'

He turned and left the room. As the door swung closed behind him, they could hear his footsteps recede down the corridor.

'Hell, Austin,' said Asher in a low voice, 'you couldn't have saved that for later?'

Jake knew the colonel had a point. 'Sir, we need to be thorough with this,' he said. 'If it's not Sonny, and we spend too long running down that road, it's going to be a long way to turn back.'

Asher sighed again. 'All right,' he said at last. 'But let's do this properly. Get Sonny back in here for a follow-up. Chip away at him. By the end of the day, I want him ruled out if he's not to be ruled in. We're playing by the clock on this one, you understand?'

'Yes, sir.' And Jake knew his reputation was on the line.

11

Tuesday, 9.15 a.m.

'Ready?' asked Mills.

'Ready,' said Jake.

They walked into the same interview room as before. The table was bare except for a briefcase belonging to Vincennes. The heating was back on.

Jake and Mills sat.

'Morning, Vincennes. Morning, shit head,' Mills began.

'There's no need for that,' said Vincennes. 'My client has returned to the police station at your request, to cooperate fully in the investigation. Like you, my client wishes only to find the man responsible for the death of his girlfriend.'

'Your *client*,' Mills growled, 'beat in the skull of a young woman and left her daughter an orphan, Vincennes. I think "shit head" is just about right.'

Sonny flinched. Under the table, Jake tapped his foot against Mills's to shut him up. Mills sat back.

'Sorry about that, Sonny.' Jake smiled. 'My colleague needs to work on his anger management.' He angled the microphone towards Sonny and turned the recorder on. 'Let's start at the beginning. Where were you the night before last?'

'I've told you already.'

'We have to go over everything again,' said Jake. 'Procedure. To make sure we make no mistakes.'

'Keep the fat man under control, and I'll tell you,' muttered Sonny.

Mills slapped his hands on the table, making to stand. Jake pulled him back down.

Jake arranged his hands in a placating gesture. 'Let's all be polite for a while. Just tell us where you were,' he said.

Sonny leaned back, then looked at his lawyer. He leaned forward again.

'I told you. I was with my girl. Penny.'

'She'll confirm that my client was with her all night,' said Vincennes. 'She lives with her aunt, who will also confirm it.'

'I'm sure Miss Stokes will say anything Sonny has told her to say,' Mills interrupted.

'Her aunt—' began Vincennes.

'Her aunt was with them all night? She was in the bed with them? That's some kinky shit,' said Mills.

'Detective . . .' Vincennes's tone warned him to toe the line.

'Whatever,' said Mills. 'Just don't mention the fucking aunt to me.'

Jake gestured to Sonny. 'Please, go on.'

'Like I said, I was with my woman.'

Mills smiled. 'We know you were with your woman.' He was speaking slowly, calmly, but his eyes were blazing. 'We also know what you were doing with your woman. We know how you pummelled her head until it collapsed. We know how you knocked the teeth out of her mouth. You sick fuck, you pulled her eyeballs out.'

Sonny grimaced. 'No!' he shouted. 'I wasn't there.' He looked at each man in turn, his pupils dilated and his eyes wide. 'I loved that woman. Her kid too. Man, I bought her a computer for Christmas.'

' "Bought"?' Mills sneered. 'That might be your most ridiculous lie yet.'

Sonny shook his head and stared at the wall. 'I don't care what you think, fat man. Just know, I would never hurt Marcia.'

'And you don't think pulling her eyes out of her head hurt her?'

'Fuck you! I didn't do it.'

Sonny got to his feet and Mills jumped up too, but Jake grabbed his partner by the shoulders and pulled him down. Mills was laying on the bad cop act a little too thick. Vincennes dragged Sonny back to his chair.

'All of you, calm down!' Jake said. Sonny's chest rose and fell as he glared at Mills, seething. Jake continued: 'What time did you go out to meet Miss Stokes?'

'Look,' said Sonny. 'I didn't do it.'

'Say nothing,' snapped the lawyer.

'I didn't do it. I didn't kill Marcia. Sure, I was fooling around with Penny, but Marcia, me and the kid were tight, man. We were family. Kelly – thank Christ the sick bastard didn't get Kelly.'

Vincennes took Sonny's arm but Sonny brushed him away.

'Let me tell my story, man. This time I got nothing to hide.' He stretched forward and looked Jake in the eye. 'She called me that night. Said I was a fucking loser. Can you believe that? The last words we spoke, she was cursing me out.'

Jake hadn't heard this before. He made a note. 'What time was that call?' Jake asked.

'I was still in the Boom Box. I think it was before midnight. No, it was after. I don't know. The club was buzzing. I had to go outside to hear her.'

'What did she say?' asked Jake. For the first time in the investigation they were getting information that might help.

'She ripped me a new asshole, man,' said Sonny with a hurt look. 'I think she knew. About Penny, you know?'

'Was there anything unusual about the call?' Jake pressed.

'The same old same old. She was yelling, then – hang on – she ended the call quick. Said she had to go. Said she'd call me back. She never did.' Sonny seemed surprised at the memory.

Jake looked at Mills. This was good. Useful.

'Can we check your phone records?' Jake asked.

'Not without a warrant,' said Vincennes.

'Shut the fuck up, man,' Sonny told his defender. He

turned to Jake and Mills. 'You check whatever you want. Anything that will help you catch the sonofabitch that killed my girl.'

'For the record, suspect has given us permission to access his mobile phone records,' said Jake. Then he added, 'Thank you.'

Sonny looked shocked.

Vincennes scowled. He stood, and Sonny got up too. Jake let them go without saying a word.

Once they'd left, Jake looked at Mills and raised an eyebrow.

Mills shook his head. 'Sonny's not our guy,' he said. 'Who's going to tell the chief?'

Jake grinned. 'Sorry, pal, I'm the lead detective. I have other things to be doing.'

Asher was going to be mad. But worse, the killer was still at large. And because of the way Marcia was murdered, Jake had a feeling that he was going to do it again.

12

Tuesday, 11 a.m.

Jake didn't go back to his desk, which was in sight of the colonel's office across the hall. It was better to keep out of Asher's way. Instead he went out to the front desk. There was a computer there hooked into the system, and that would do.

Nothing new in his in-box apart from offers of cheap Viagra and an invitation to join an online casino. The department's spam filter was, like other things in Littleton, a bit behind the times.

Jake quickly fired off two emails asking for updates. One went to the medical examiner's office, the other to the forensics laboratory that shared the ME's morgue. He wasn't too hopeful; if there had been any news it would have been there waiting for him. But he wanted to keep the pressure on.

He stared at the shimmering screen. A shadow appeared behind him, and he was engulfed in a scent of jasmine: Sara Janesky, the desk secretary. He turned. She smiled and handed him a mug of coffee he hadn't asked for.

Every cop in the department had a thing for Sara.

Barely over five foot, the young divorcee was a little firecracker. She had long dirty-blonde hair, which hung over one ear but left the other bare, revealing a big silver Gypsy earring. She wore tight blouses that emphasized her cleavage, and her voice oozed smoke and honey, like a rich whiskey.

'You look like you need a pick-me-up, sugar,' she said.

'You're a mind-reader.' He smiled at her, knowing he offered a different sort of smile to the one she usually got at the station. Most of the guys talked about her like she was an easy score – based, seemingly, on the fact that she was good-looking – but he had not seen one of them even make it to first base. Jake thought she was smarter than she let on. He wondered if she had grown up with a father who was domineering, old-fashioned to the point of chauvinistic, the kind of man who preferred his ladies – her mom, especially – to keep their intelligence concealed. Not a violent man, just one set in his ways who Sara had learned how to handle at a very young age.

What she had learned, she could apply to the boys' club that was the local PD where she had ended up earning a living.

Sara sat down on her chair behind her desk. 'What you thinking about?'

He made a show of clearing his head. 'Nothing.'

'Working on a case or going through the personals?'

'I'm waiting on word from the lab.'

'You'll be waiting, honey. Didn't you hear?'

Jake looked up from the computer, puzzled.

'What they found over in Springfield.'

Springfield was two towns away, a more rural version of Littleton. Jake had driven through it once but nothing about the place stood out. He hadn't heard anything particular about Springfield today.

'Oh babe, you need to catch up. The interstate construction crew dug up a skeleton about two hours ago.'

Something jumped inside Jake. *Can it be a coincidence? Two bodies found at construction sites.* His eyes widened.

Sara was looking at him. 'Don't get excited, cowboy,' she said. 'It was an old skeleton. A child. From long ago. They were working in the grounds of an old asylum that used to house all the crazies and the stray kids.'

'A kid? How old do they make it?'

'Dunno. I mean, the place was probably full of skeletons. Who knows what went on in those places.' She gave an exaggerated shudder. 'Gives me the creeps.'

It gave Jake the creeps too. He could imagine the old stone building, the cold corridors, the small dusty windows, the attendants. He had a vision of blood in a basement. It was all in his head – too many movies when he was young.

'Hon, I need to go out for a few minutes.' She placed a hand on his forearm. 'I'm due a smoke break. Can you mind the desk while I'm gone?'

'So the coffee was just a bribe?'

'Such a sharp detective.' She gave him a wink as she swept out the front door.

Jake was doing nothing, killing time until the technical people got back to him. He might as well kill it here. He turned back to the screen and was googling 'Springfield Asylum' when he heard the main door opening. Putting on his friendly face, he looked up and smiled.

The man who came in resembled an extra from a zombie movie. He was tall and thin, with narrow shoulders and three-day stubble. His pale eyes had the bleary appearance of the habitual alcoholic; his clothes looked like they had been slept in, and his smell wafted ahead of him, as if trying to escape the body to which it was attached. As he reached the desk the man fumbled in the pocket of his torn coat and pulled out a pack of cigarettes.

'No smoking in the station,' said Jake.

'Sorry,' mumbled the man.

Jake stared at him.

'I want to talk to someone about the murder out by the new interstate. I have some information.'

Jake's heart quickened. 'I'm one of the investigators. You can tell me what you saw.'

The man's lips began to quiver. 'It's not what I saw,' he said. 'It's what I did.'

Jake waited, his heart now slamming against his sternum.

'I have a confession.' The man paused, took a deep breath and said, 'I killed Marcia Lamb.'

13

Tuesday, 11.15 a.m.

It was like a klaxon had sounded in Jake's head. *This is it!*

Every case broke at some point, but rarely this early. He stood up as deliberately as he could, putting on his blankest, most professional face. He had to handle this just right.

Don't spook the guy.

He came from behind the desk and gently took the man by the elbow. The man looked at him, pleading with his eyes. He came meekly as Jake led him around the desk and down a corridor to one of the interview rooms. The man kept glancing about, seeming like a little boy lost in a big world. Jake brought him into the bare room and sat him down on one of the chairs.

'I need you to just stay here for a few minutes while I get one of the other detectives to sit in on our conversation. Is that all right?' Jake asked.

'Yes, sir. I'll wait,' said the man. 'Thank you.'

Jake left the interview room and made sure to lock it behind him. He jogged down the corridor into the office.

'Mills! Someone's here with a confession.' All the staff nearby looked up at Jake. 'Says he's our guy.'

Whatever Mills was typing he dropped it fast. 'You think it's solid?'

'Too early to say,' said Jake. He could feel his heart thumping and he was trying to get himself under control. They started down the hall and everyone followed behind. 'We'll play it straight this time and just ask the questions. I think he wants to tell his story.'

Jake and Mills entered the interview room slowly and shut the door on the ten or so people standing outside. They approached the desk like the man was a dog who might freak with any sudden movement.

'Can I get you a coffee?' Jake asked him.

The man shook his head, not looking up from his lap.

'Fine.' Jake and Mills sat opposite him. 'I'm Detective Austin, and this is Detective Mills. We want to hear what you have to say, but before we begin, I have to ask you if you need a lawyer?'

He was a bit surprised when the man shook his head again. He seemed diminished in the chair, and Jake could see he was breathing deeply.

'OK,' said Jake. 'Let's begin with the basics. What's your name?'

'Johnny Cooper. I live on 42nd.'

Even Jake knew this was one of the roughest parts of town: skid row.

'What have you come here to tell us, Mr Cooper?' Jake asked.

'I killed her. I smashed her head in with a rock, God help me. I'm sorry. I didn't mean to.'

'Let's go back to the beginning,' said Jake gently. 'Did you know Marcia Lamb?'

'Never met her in my life. I just felt the urge. I was walking around the park . . . I got nowhere else to be most days.'

Jake nodded sympathetically.

'I saw her walking there,' said Cooper. 'I get so lonely. I didn't mean to – I just wanted to talk to someone. And she wouldn't stop. She just kept walking. And the red mist descended, and I killed her. Used a knife.'

'Because she didn't talk to you?' said Jake, wondering how he got her back to her house and how the knife was used. He hadn't seen knife wounds on the corpse, but maybe the medical examiner had found something. He took out a pad and made a note that this would need to be checked out.

'All I wanted was some company,' the guy continued. 'I didn't ask her for money or nothing. I just wanted someone to talk to me, to see me. And I wanted to fuck her.' He said this softly, his weak eyes watery. 'I'm sorry. I get urges, but I can normally fight them. If I could have just got her to stop . . .'

Jake looked at Mills, who had turned to face the wall. Jake frowned – was the confession getting to Mills? Jake knew that Littleton might not have seen much in the way of grisly murders – not in the same way a city tends to – but still, Mills had coped more than fine with everything so far. Jake turned back to Cooper.

'How'd you get into her place?'

'I'm good with locks. Always have been.'

Jake's hopes began to fade. He tested a theory: 'And her daughter?' he asked. 'Why didn't you kill the daughter?'

Cooper shrugged. 'I tried to. But she ran away too fast. Long legs on that girl.'

Jake looked back at Mills, who had now turned back from the wall. He had a hand over his mouth, holding in his laughter.

And Jake felt a sudden fury that he had walked into such a rookie mistake.

Mills cleared his throat as if about to say something but Jake stopped him. 'I'll ask the questions,' he said, an edge of steel to his voice.

Jake turned back to Cooper, who was now sobbing gently at the table. He couldn't believe it. The man looked sixty, but when Jake looked closely, he realized he was probably nearer forty. Jake knew the type. The type that wandered the streets. *People ignore you. You feel invisible. Parents died or gave you up at a young age. You were in the care of the state. Thrown out when you came of age. Since then you've drifted between cheap hotels, dingy one-room apartments, mission flophouses and the streets. You feel guilty because your parents abandoned you. You think it is your fault. You crave attention. You need to be noticed.*

'You don't need to do this, Mr Cooper,' Jake said gently.

'Confession is good for the soul,' Johnny replied.

Mills choked back a laugh, unsuccessfully trying to

disguise it as a cough. Jake calmly rose from his chair. 'Detective, can I see you outside?'

They walked out of the interview room and the people outside were laughing too. When they saw the look on Jake's face they quickly scattered.

'Office tradition,' said Mills. 'Everyone has to take a report from Johnny the Snitch. It's a rite of passage.'

'It's a fucking disgrace. That guy needs professional help.'

'Come on,' said Mills. 'He's confessed to more crimes than I've investigated. Son of Sam – that was him. The Milwaukee Cannibal – he did it. He'll confess to offing Santa one day, I'm telling you. He's just a harmless bum looking for some attention. We'll hold him until lunchtime, feed him and send him off with a twenty in his pocket. No harm, no foul.'

'You're a prick.' Jake walked away from Mills, too angry to look him in the eye.

Somewhere in Littleton a murderer roamed free. The murderer wasn't Johnny Cooper, but Johnny felt all the guilt. That was almost as sad as the murder itself.

14

Tuesday, 12.40 p.m.

Johnny Cooper needed help. The department had a database of psychiatrists they could call upon. Some were used to counsel cops who had discharged a weapon in the line of duty, or after fatal incidents. Some were called in if guys started drinking or their gambling got out of control. And a few were there for when the cops or the DA needed a quick take on whether a suspect was a nut job, or faking to slide out from under a charge. Jake didn't know any of the names, and he was too pissed off at Mills to ask him.

Jake went back to the front desk computer. He picked a name at random – Dr Greene – and called the number.

'Hello, Gail Greene speaking.'

'Hi, I'm Detective Jake Austin, calling from Littleton PD,' he began.

'Hi. How can I help you, Detective Austin?' Jake liked the music in her voice.

'We have a man in the station who has confessed to a crime he couldn't have committed, and I don't want to just send him back on the streets.'

There was a pause.

'It's not uncommon,' she said. 'I presume it's the interstate killing?'

'How did you know?' asked Jake.

'The big ones normally draw them out.'

'Is there anything we can do? I'd like someone to at least see him,' said Jake.

'I'll be there in . . .' Her voice tailed off. Jake could imagine her checking a tastefully expensive watch on a slender wrist. '. . . an hour.'

He went back to the interview room. Cooper sat on the chair where they had left him. He wasn't crying any more but was subdued.

Jake made a point of not looking at his partner. 'Can you go out and wait for the psychiatrist?'

Mills took his coffee and walked out without a word.

Jake sat down opposite Cooper again. 'We can get you help, Johnny. A doctor is coming in to talk to you.'

Cooper blinked and looked up.

'I need to be stopped. I'm not right in the head.'

'Don't worry about it. None of this is your fault; you didn't do any of those things.'

'I need to be punished. I fuck dogs.' He said this in a low voice, and he stared at the table as he spoke. He wouldn't meet Jake's eye. 'I—'

'It's all right.' Jake put a hand on Cooper's shoulder, who flinched under his touch. Jake wasn't sure why he felt so much pity for this man. But he did.

15

Tuesday, 2.10 p.m.

It was ten past two when Sara came into Jake's cubicle waving a fax. 'Just in,' she said.

Jake laid the paper on his desk. It was from the phone company, and confirmed that Sonny Malone had got a call at 12.34 a.m. from Marcia Lamb's mobile and that the call had lasted nine minutes.

Jake nodded at Sara. 'Thanks,' he said.

'There's a rather cute lady doctor here to see you too.' She smiled.

Just then Mills looked around the door. 'Shrink's here,' he announced.

'I heard,' said Jake.

He was relieved. He'd get Johnny off his hands and then he could get his mind back to the case. He joined Mills and walked towards the front desk. As they approached, a tall woman turned and smiled at them.

'Wow!' whispered Mills. 'Time to slip off the wedding ring.'

Mills had a point. Gail Greene was stunning. About five nine, with long red hair that fell over her shoulders. She could have passed for mid-twenties, though Jake knew she had to be a decade older at least, based on the length of time she would have spent on her degree, her postgraduate studies and later professional practice until she reached her current status. She walked towards him, although 'swayed' would have been more accurate. She moved with the grace of a ballerina – maybe she had studied as a child? Maybe her mom had had her heart set on her daughter going on stage, a wish that had eventually been torpedoed by a move into the medical profession. Her green eyes twinkled with every small movement she made. There was a tiny stud piercing the right side of her nose. He could also see the top of a tattoo peeping out from the neckline of her shirt. Sign of a disreputable past? Maybe part of the rebellion against the demanding mom?

'Detective Austin?' she said, extending a hand.

'Call me Jake.'

'Gail.'

'I'm Detective Mills,' said Mills, pushing himself forward and shaking her hand.

'Pleased to meet you.' She smiled sweetly. 'Where is he?'

Mills led the way back to the interview room. When they got to the door Gail laid a restraining arm on Mills. Instead of going in, she opened the grille and looked in at Cooper. Jake watched her watch him for a few seconds. He was reminded of the cowboys-and-Indians movies of his childhood, where patient Indian scouts waited in the hills, unmoving. Cooper didn't appear to notice that he was being observed. Finally Gail closed the grille.

'Well?' asked Jake.

'I'm a psychiatrist, not a psychic.' She smiled.

'But you've seen it before? This compulsion to confess, it seems to indicate a need to punish himself.'

'What college did you get your degree from?' she asked. Jake felt the rebuke and blushed slightly, but her smile softened it. She went on: 'You guys can go back to work. I'll look after him,' she said.

'Do you want me to come in with you?' Jake asked.

'I take my coffee with cream, two sugars. And a chocolate doughnut, if you have it,' she said.

Mills grinned as she entered the interview room and shut the door firmly behind her. 'She's a piece of work,' he said.

'Agreed,' said Jake.

'The most beautiful woman I have seen outside of a movie,' said Mills. He grinned again. 'And I think she likes you.'

'Then she needs a shrink more than Johnny does.'

He went back to his desk and checked his emails. He had a reply from the ME.

To: Detective J. Austin.

From: Dr V. Zatkin.

Re: Initial report on suspected homicide victim Marcia Lamb.

Detective Austin, got your messages. Initial examination suggests a time of death somewhere between 1 and 3 a.m.

Monday morning. Cause of death is trauma to the head. Initial examination suggests victim had not engaged in sexual activity in the day prior to her death. More in report to follow.

They knew most of this already. Sonny had got the call from Marcia half an hour after midnight, and the hang-up had come well before 1 a.m. Assuming Marcia had been disturbed by her killer, that meant he had killed her fairly quickly, but maybe not immediately. He could have had up to two hours.

The only real news from the ME was that Marcia had not been raped. Jake wasn't surprised. Sadistic killers were more often motivated by power than sexual lust.

He typed another email to the forensics lab:

From: Detective J. Austin
To: Greater Indianapolis Forensics Unit
Re: Marcia Lamb

Guys, I hate to ask but I need anything on this one quickly. Did she scratch his face? Did you find any DNA? Anything we can use, can you keep me in the loop as you find out, rather than keeping it for the final report?

Thanks
Detective Austin

He didn't hold out much hope. Forensics hated to be rushed, and Jake anticipated that the killer had been too organized, too careful, to leave any clues. He probably knew as much about forensics as most cops.

He became aware of a gentle floral scent that he vaguely remembered. Pure Turquoise by Ralph Lauren? He had bought that for Leigh on her last birthday. He turned to see Gail Greene standing behind him, a gentle smile on her face.

'You forgot my doughnut,' she said.

'Sorry. I can get you a coffee,' he replied.

'That stuff?' she said with a smile. 'No, thank you. You'll have to owe me one.' She propped herself against one of the desks. 'Let me tell you a little about your suspect. I don't think he killed anybody.'

'We guessed that.'

'He has Aquinas syndrome, a compulsion to claim crimes he had nothing to do with. It's named after—'

'Thomas Aquinas,' said Jake.

'You're Catholic?' she asked.

'My mother is.' He motioned towards the door of the interview room. 'Is he going to be OK?'

'I don't think he'll ever be OK.' She smiled sadly. 'He's a deeply damaged individual. Borderline retarded in terms of intelligence. His mother abandoned him, and he drifted in and out of care. I'm having trouble tracking down exact records. But now he's living in a project, among drug dealers and prostitutes. He's fallen through the cracks, and he could be very dangerous.'

'Dangerous enough to murder?' Johnny had got all

of the details wrong so far, but Jake would still have to look into it.

'Hmm.' Gail twisted a lock of her hair in her fingers when she spoke. 'Typically, people like Johnny are prone to violence and to abnormal expressions of sexuality,' she went on. 'For instance, during the interview he exposed himself to me.'

'You should have called me.'

'I'm a big girl.'

Jake put his hands up in surrender.

'He shows some signs of sexual deviance,' she went on.

'Paedophile?'

She shook her head and her red hair changed colour in the light from the window. 'Sufferers from Aquinas syndrome sometimes have predilections towards juveniles, but I don't think so in Johnny's case. Necrophilia seems more likely, given his obsession with death and dead people – he showed visible signs of arousal when discussing what he claims he saw.'

Jake groaned. Now they had another suspect, even if a blind man could see he didn't do it. Procedure was procedure.

'So, is he capable of having killed Marcia Lamb?'

'Capable, sure,' she said, clearly picking up on his tone. 'But it isn't exactly an easy pathology to anticipate.'

Jake nodded, unsuccessfully biting back a frustrated sigh. Johnny might not be a murderer, but he could still be a problem.

He would have to be watched.

16

Tuesday, 3 p.m.

Colonel Asher's face was redder than usual. And his shirtsleeves were rolled up – never a good sign. He nodded briefly at Dr Greene, then turned to Jake.

'Austin, when you have a moment can you come into my office, please? And bring your partner with you.'

'Duty calls,' Jake said to Gail. 'So, what do we do about Johnny?'

'Our resources are limited. I would love to get him into a residential programme and prescribe him the right meds. But it's not going to happen. And as you have nothing to hold him on, he falls between the cracks again.'

Jake stood. 'I'll get one of the uniforms to process and release him. We'll give him some money so he gets a good meal tonight.' He offered his hand. 'Thanks for coming in.'

She took it. 'See you around, Detective.' Her hand held his for a moment longer than he expected. Then she smiled. 'Remember, you still owe me that coffee.'

She turned and glided out.

Jake turned to Mills. 'Colonel wants to see us.'

'I heard,' said Mills. 'I'll follow you in a few minutes. I need a coffee.'

Mills walked a thin enough line without antagonizing the boss, but it wasn't Jake's place to say anything. He went into Asher's office, asking Sara to find someone to release Cooper as he passed.

'Sit down, Detective,' said Asher, making a show of speaking in a level voice. 'Where's Mills?'

'He'll be here in a minute.'

Asher rolled his eyes. 'Forget him for the moment; it's you I really need to talk to.'

'Sir?'

'I'm running a department here, Detective. We may think of it as a civic service, but we both know this is a business. City Hall budget us, and we produce results for them. We get the stats, the budget grows, and we can use the extra cash to do some real policing.'

It was sad but true.

'But it works the other way if we don't come up with the goods.'

Jake nodded.

'Austin, you're not giving me results. Why haven't we charged Sonny Malone?'

'Because he didn't kill Marcia Lamb.'

'Maybe,' said Asher. 'Or maybe you're thinking around corners when this is a straight-line case.'

'Sir, with all due respect –' Jake saw Asher bristle at the phony phrase '– no DA would ever pursue a case against Sonny Malone. Not without solid forensic evidence. The most clueless public defender would rip it to shreds. It would be a waste of time and departmental money.'

'So improve the case – find the evidence to make it stand up.'

Jake offered a single nod of his head: *I hear you, sir.* 'We'll keep him in the frame as we investigate, but we need to keep open minds. We can't exhaust the department's time and resources on just one lead.' Jake watched Asher's eyes, wondering how the punch of the 'open minds' insult and the we're-all-in-this-together nod to 'the department' would play.

Mills walked in and placed a coffee mug on the desk, sitting down beside Jake.

'You wanted to see me, Colonel?'

'Ten minutes ago.'

'I'm here now.'

Asher grunted. 'Do you agree with Detective Austin about Sonny Malone?' he asked.

''Fraid so. He didn't do it.'

'Let me get the facts straight,' said Asher, directing his words at Mills – the apathetic man in the room, more likely to agree with him simply to get out of there quicker. 'Sonny Malone is a violent criminal on early release. For an aggravated assault charge. He deals drugs. His girlfriend finds out he's screwing around, and she's furious. With me so far?'

Mills nodded. Jake didn't bother. Asher still wasn't looking at him.

'So he has motive.' He counted the points on his fingers. 'Did he have opportunity? Of course he did. He knew where she would be late last night. He could get there easily enough. I know he has an *alibi* –' Asher said the word with such disdain, Jake was surprised he didn't make air-quotes '– but the alibi of your girlfriend is hardly cast iron, right?' Now he turned to Jake. 'You interviewed this girlfriend?'

'It's on our list of priorities,' said Jake.

Asher gave a grim smile. 'How high?'

Jake didn't answer. He could tell Asher wasn't really looking for one. This little sit-down was more about asserting himself than getting the best out of his men. A trait he probably picked up from the mother who had had him at a very young age, and spent the rest of her life reminding any- and everyone that she had given up a lot for her kids.

Asher leaned forward over his desk. 'When you talk to the girlfriend, you make sure you hammer at this alibi. Make sure you've made the right call.'

Jake bit the inside of his cheek to keep from laughing. Asher didn't say '*we've* made the right call'; it was '*you've*'. This went wrong, Asher was going to protect himself before his men.

17
Tuesday, 9 p.m.

The room was dark except for the flickering screen. Marcia Lamb led the evening news. Interesting coverage – enjoyable, even.

The first images came from the interstate construction site. A tarpaulin covered the body lying on the ground. A reporter was talking about the police investigation. A suspect had been taken in but released without charge late last night: a large black man who protested his innocence to the camera. Then the clip changed to earlier in the morning, outside the police station.

A group of people was gathered around the door of the station, drinking coffee and smoking. The press were out in force. That mouthy reporter was there. Ford.

There will be more media as it goes on. I know that. It's a good thing. Necessary.

The screen showed Councilman Mitch Harper on the top step, addressing the press. He was dressed in a dark woollen coat, open to reveal his shirt and tie. The assembled reporters were in a semicircle looking up at him.

It won't be long now. I'm sure of it. The forces are building. I can't delay.

The report ended, and the broadcast moved on to the next segment. He was about to turn it off when something stopped him. A name from his past. The Chase Asylum. This was interesting too. *So the old asylum is being demolished? I haven't thought about that place in years. So many memories . . . secrets . . .*

The anchor's voice dripped concern as he said, 'A second skeleton has been unearthed. It is believed that both skeletons could be the remains of children who died in the very institution which was supposed to protect them.'

The report ended with an appeal for information by the FBI. *If the Feds are involved, they are taking this very seriously. More and more interesting.* The image of the missing man flashed on the screen. It was black and white, and clearly many years out of date. It showed a man in his mid-thirties with thinning hair and eyes that still radiated coldness.

The anchor concluded, 'Investigators are now looking for Fred Lumley, the warden of the Chase Asylum.'

Old Fred. Who'd have thought?

'Fred Lumley disappeared several decades ago, and has not been seen since.'

This is all meant to be . . .

He rubbed his hands together and smiled thoughtfully. 'This is what you wanted.'

18

Tuesday, 9 p.m.

Jake sat on the sofa, his shoes off, drinking a beer as he watched the news. The way they spun it both interested and repulsed him. They – whoever 'they' were – had wasted no time in attaching the most sensational nickname they could think of to the murderer, to match the snowy imagery and stark black and white shots of Christmas trees that seemed to accompany every report.

The Christmas Killer.

And he was fascinated by the news from Springfield.

Downstairs was empty. An air of peace filled the house. As the news went to commercials he heard footsteps on the stairs. Leigh walked in. She was dressed in a robe with stains on it, and looked tired.

'Babe, you look great,' he lied. 'I got us a Chinese.'

She smiled weakly. 'We ate two hours ago. You have it. Whatever's left I'll heat up for lunch tomorrow.'

The Chinese had been his peace offering – so much for that.

'I got a nice bottle of wine as well,' he said.

Her smile brightened a little. 'Now you're talking!'

'Tough day?'

'You could say.'

She walked into the kitchen and came back with two glasses of wine, taking Jake's beer bottle from him and putting it on the table.

'Scooch over.'

He straightened up in the sofa, making room for her, and flicked off the TV. She sat down, leaning into him.

'I could do with a head rub.'

Jake smiled. He enjoyed these moments when they made up, with the kids in bed, his mother in her room, and the den empty except for him and his wife. He unbuttoned his cuffs and rolled up his shirtsleeves. Gently he shifted his body into the corner of the sofa while Leigh slid down until her head was resting in his lap. He began to massage her temples, moving his fingers in small circles. After every six circles he softly swept his fingers over her brow. It was a routine he had perfected over the years. Generally Leigh would fall asleep, and he would cover her with a blanket.

But tonight he could feel her tension. Despite her tired appearance he knew her mind was churning.

'Where's my mom?' he asked.

There it was – he could feel her brow furrowing under his fingers.

'Gone to bed, I think,' she said. 'We were watching the news a few hours ago and she suddenly got up and left the room.'

Jake grimaced. It made his mother sound like a

troublesome child. He remained silent but continued with the massage.

After a few minutes Leigh spoke again. 'Faith is beginning to worry me.'

Jake had been married long enough to know that bland reassurance was not what Leigh wanted. Instead he made a non-committal grunt that could be interpreted as sympathy, encouragement or agreement . . . and waited.

'Her behaviour is becoming more of a problem. She's always moping. She doesn't talk to me any more.'

'She's a teenager, honey. Did you talk to your mother when you were a teen?'

He should have kept his mouth shut. Leigh shuffled under him, then sat up straight. The head rub was over.

'She's twelve, not sixteen! She needs to show some respect, and she needs to help more. She just comes home from school and goes up to her room. Have you been in there? It's a dump.'

'It's a phase.' Out came the bland reassurance. 'There's been a lot going on. She's just trying to cope.'

'It's more than that. Last night she was in our bed. That hasn't happened since she was five. She's clingy one minute, running away from me the next. And she's been having nightmares again.' She hesitated then dipped her head as she said, 'Do you think having your mother here is healthy for a young girl?'

Jake felt a pang of hurt, but she ploughed on.

'Jeanette's behaviour is becoming more erratic every

day. Most of the time she doesn't even recognize Faith. You've seen it too.'

He *had* seen it. He'd seen the rejection in his daughter's eyes when her grandmother didn't know who she was. But he wasn't going to let Leigh blame his mother and her illness for everything that was wrong in this house.

'There are other things going on that could have unsettled Faith.'

There was ice in her voice as she asked, 'Other things?'

'You know – the move and everything. New friends.' But his backtracking wasn't going to work.

'Do you think Jakey is the problem?' She looked incredulous, disgusted even. 'Are you seriously telling me that the arrival of a baby brother has upset her this much?'

Jake changed tack.

'I can't move my mother to a home.' He was pleading with her. 'We could get a nurse. We have some money saved up now, and it won't be for ever. I could get a good nurse, and that would help a lot.'

'And have another stranger living in the house?' snapped Leigh.

Jake felt his fists tighten. Now *he* was angry. 'My mother is not a stranger,' he said.

Leigh ducked her head. When she spoke again, her voice was softer. 'I'm sorry. That came out wrong.' She sighed and tried to place a hand on his leg, but Jake reached for his beer to move out of the way. 'What I meant was she's changing all the time. She sometimes knows me, and sometimes I'm her sister, sometimes a shop girl. She's *becoming* a stranger. And she needs more and more care every day. I already have a baby to look after.'

Jake downed the rest of his beer. He needed time to compose himself.

'If Jakey needed special care we would give it to him. My mother is family and we'll do what we have to. One thing we won't do is shove her in a home at *Christmas.*' He stood. 'I need to get some air.'

'Aw Jake, come on. Please . . .'

Jake could hear her but he couldn't talk to her right now. 'I'm going out for a walk.'

He went out to the hall and put on a heavy coat, pulling a woollen hat down over his ears. He almost slammed the door as he left but stopped himself.

His family was tense enough.

19

Wednesday, 14 December, 8.30 a.m.

They could hear the raised voices of the reporters outside the police station. Jake didn't have to go to the window to tell it was Councilman Harper again, walking up the steps with his usual bravado. He *arrived* rather than just entered, and the whole station saw him sweep through to the colonel's office.

The detectives got to their feet when he walked in. Harper looked a little pissed off. The team had spent the night trying to track down Penny Stokes, Sonny Malone's second girlfriend, to confirm the statement she had made over the phone. She wasn't home, she wasn't answering her mobile, and she hadn't shown up for work that night. A few more calls had revealed that Sonny had split after his release. No one knew where he was.

Harper clearly was not going to be stalled or played with, like yesterday. 'Gentlemen,' he said. 'Sit down.'

As the councilman sat down in the only comfortable chair in Asher's office, Jake was surprised to see he was wearing yesterday's shirt. Although he had shaved and showered, he looked a little less slick than the day before.

'So, what happened?' he began. 'You told me yesterday you had a strong suspect.'

Asher cleared his throat. 'We're building the case against him. That can take time.'

'Colonel, did this Sonny Malone kill Marcia Lamb, or didn't he?'

'He did,' said Asher. 'We're building the case against—'

'He didn't,' Jake interrupted. Asher scowled at him so Jake turned to Mills. 'Right?'

'A lot of the evidence could go either way,' said Mills with a wavering of his head. Jake could have knocked him off the fence he was sitting on.

Asher leaned forward. 'Councilman, we're looking—'

Just then the phone on Asher's desk buzzed. He picked it up and dropped it back, cutting it off. The phone buzzed again. This time he cut it off and left it off the hook.

The sound of running footsteps came down the hall. There was a knock on the door; Sara Janesky opened it and looked in.

'We're busy, Sara,' Asher snapped. 'Come back—'

'Sorry, sir, but you need to take line one. There's been another body.'

Jake had known it as soon as he'd seen the first victim. Littleton was now one murder away from dealing with a serial killer.

20

Wednesday, 8.50 a.m.

Asher spoke to a panicked construction foreman. It took him a few minutes to get the details, but by then everyone in the room knew the facial mutilations and the torn-out eyeballs made it the same killer. Jake could see the mixture of horror and anger and excitement in Harper as they listened: horror that someone else had died, anger – possibly affected – that the police had not yet caught the killer, excitement that fate had given him more to make political capital from.

Finally Asher dropped the phone. 'Let's go,' he said to Jake and Mills.

The two men were already on their feet. Harper stood too.

'Sorry, Councilman,' said Asher. 'No civilians.'

Jake thought he caught a smile on Asher's face as he said that, but it was fleeting.

As they rushed through the station to the car outside, Asher paused at Sara's desk.

'Put a call through to the forensics lab and the medical examiner,' he said. 'We need a team out there immediately.' He turned to one of the sergeants. 'We need three cars of uniforms – one to secure the scene and two for witness interviews.'

'Yes, sir,' said the sergeant, turning towards the rows of desks. 'Jones, O'Brien, you take the first cruiser. Get there quick. Olsen, organize four guys for the interviews.'

There was immediate movement. Jake, Mills and Asher took the back door to the car lot to avoid the reporters. Harper followed – despite being told not to – listening in as they walked.

'Dumped on the highway construction site,' Asher told them, 'just further down the road a ways. The foreman found her.'

There was no doubt about it. It was the same murderer. And with the sick way he was killing these people, Jake knew there would be more and more deaths until he was stopped. The question was, how many?

Asher turned towards Jake and Mills. 'If this turns out to be Sonny Malone, I swear to God . . .'

Jake wished it was Sonny, but knew better. They opened the doors of the patrol car and climbed in. *Fuck*, he thought. *I'm the one around here who's had the most experience in homicide, and I've never handled anything this bad.*

In the rush Jake didn't think about stopping Harper climbing into the back seat next to him. Mills was up front with Asher. They tossed random speculations back and forth among themselves, but Jake kept silent, tried to empty his mind. There was no point in thinking anything until they got to the scene.

Asher put the siren and lights on and drove quickly – more quickly than Jake would have expected. He took chances and rode red lights fearlessly. Seven minutes after leaving the station, and just nineteen minutes after taking the call, they pulled up at the construction site. Flat yellowy rubble stretched for miles, with just a few portable huts dotted around.

One minute to nine, and all the workers were already there. But none were out on the site. They clustered around the prefab office, holding their hard hats in their hands like funeral guests. A big man sat in the middle of the group on a chair that had been set out for him. He carried his head in his hands and he was pale. The guy looked like shit. Not surprising after seeing what Jake knew he'd just seen.

Jake, Mills and Asher walked up to the man. 'Wait here please, Councilman,' Asher told Harper over his shoulder.

'Are you Snipes?' Asher asked. Jake guessed he was trying to sound sympathetic, but he just sounded like he wanted to get this over with.

The foreman looked up. 'I . . . er . . . Yeah, that's me.'

'Are you OK, sir?' asked Jake.

'I'm . . . Yeah, I'm OK.'

'Can you show us where you found the body?' Asher asked.

Snipes nodded, stood up slowly and then looked at his colleagues. 'What about . . . ? Um . . .'

Jake nodded at him. 'We'll get our men to shut the site for you.'

'OK,' he said. 'Thanks.' Snipes led the three cops towards the ditch that marked the end of the previous day's construction. 'She's in there.'

'OK,' said Asher. 'We can take it from here.' He stopped them all and gestured around the area. 'Mills, take Mr Snipes back to the site office and take a preliminary statement. Austin, examine the scene. I'll stay here to secure the site until the uniforms arrive.'

Jake nodded. He knew that Asher had never dealt with anything like this before and was letting Jake do what he had been brought here to do. He took a deep breath to steady himself as Mills turned to walk the foreman away from the body.

But procedure was lost on Councilman Harper. He walked up to where the three cops were and began to walk around them, towards the ditch where the body was.

'Get Harper out of here,' Jake said. 'No civilians within a hundred feet.'

Jake saw Harper's face go white with rage but he moved back behind the cops.

Asher stepped towards Harper. 'I'm sorry, Councilman,' Asher said in his most conciliatory voice. 'It is vital we don't contaminate the crime scene. We can't run the risk of this sick bastard sliding out from under this because the crime scene is tainted.'

‘I understand, Colonel,’ said Harper, turning his back on Jake.

‘One of the cruisers will give you a ride to City Hall,’ the colonel went on. ‘I’ll update you as soon as we’ve taken it all in.’

‘Thank you, Colonel. I would appreciate that.’

Harper turned and strode off, his coat flowing behind him. Even in defeat he was able to make a hell of an exit.

Asher turned to Jake. He nodded slightly and smiled. Jake walked over to the ditch and prepared himself for the sight of another mutilated corpse.

21

Wednesday, 9.20 a.m.

Jake walked to the end of the construction zone. After a few yards he could see the leg that had drawn Snipes to the body. On the end of it was a shoe. He approached slowly, letting his eyes take in everything. It was a good shoe, a lot better than the shoes Marcia Lamb had died in.

Was that the best he could do? He needed more but his mind refused to play ball – no impressions of the killer or the events that had brought them here were coming to him. It was all blank.

He stopped and looked around, but that brought nothing. It was virtually the same view as Monday morning. No work had been done here since yesterday; construction had moved to a different part of the project. And despite what Jake had said to the foreman earlier, work would go ahead later today, after the body was removed. It would just happen further up the road. Nothing stopped progress when big business was involved. The interstate was too important to the politicians to be delayed by two bodies.

He walked a little closer, and now he could see the

way the woman was laid out. She was on her side, her lower arm stretched out and her head resting on it. She was curled, and her legs were drawn up, but not by much. Jake recognized it as the recovery position that paramedics and lifeguards put people into after CPR.

Was she still alive when you laid her out? I don't think so. There's no disturbance, no sign of a struggle. You killed her at home, just like the last one. Then you brought her out here. You laid her out gently, almost tenderly.

He looked again at her position.

You didn't hate her. You cared for her. After you killed her, you cared for her.

So why did you kill her?

Now Jake was close enough to be able to examine the body properly. It was not easy – his gaze was drawn to the mutilated face and the twin dark eye sockets that seemed to be the killer's signature. But Jake had to force down his humanity and allow the cop to surface. How he liked to work a scene was from the outside in, gradually moving from generalities towards details. She was a blonde woman – looked to be in her late forties. Death, and the pooling of blood post-mortem, tended to make people look older than they actually were, so more likely she was late thirties or very early forties. Slim. Her clothes looked expensive. She wore black trousers that clung to the contours of her well-toned calves, suggesting a relatively strict health regime, and her blouse had the sheen of good silk. This was a woman who cared about her appearance.

An ornate gilt belt circled her waist, and it was clasped.

Two women, both attractive, and you have no interest in their bodies beyond forcing the life out of them. It's not sexual with you – it's about power.

Ten feet from the body, and Jake moved slowly. He picked each step carefully so that he wouldn't disturb any clues. Brilliant detective work caught criminals, but it was forensics that put them away. He bent low and looked at her face. He could only see one side of it. It was dominated by a dark smudge where the eye should have been, the skull contorted out of shape. The eyeball itself lay six inches from her nose, slightly crushed.

He scanned around the corpse. Something white and glistening was lying on the ground. There was another, nearer her face. He took another step forward, reached into his pocket for tweezers, then squatted down. It was part of a tooth. Picking it up with the tweezers he looked at it carefully: it came from a good tooth, uncapped and without cavities. She had taken care of her teeth. The two roots of the fragment were intact, and showed no signs of decay. Interesting. What would cause a healthy tooth to shatter in this way? A blow with a blunt object? Maybe, but it wasn't like anything he'd seen before.

He stood up and took two steps towards the body. Now he was standing a foot from her face, and he squatted again.

He tried to focus on anywhere but her eyes. He

started with her hair: immaculately cut and styled, a fact obvious despite the gaping wounds in her face, and the blood and mud. Short, which Jake took as a confirmation that the victim was pushing forty, if she hadn't already passed it. He could see a little diamond stud earring. No zirconium for this woman; he would stake his salary on that. And a gold chain with a little pendant was still around her neck.

He tried to look underneath at the other side of the face. But it was resting on her outstretched arm and he couldn't see. He looked around. He was far enough away from the others, and half-concealed by the rubble. He gently put a hand on the woman's blonde hair, and turned her face.

Though he was expecting it, he still recoiled. Her second eye socket was also just a dark smudge of congealed blood, blackened by exposure to air. Her second eyeball dangled from the deformed socket, tethered by a tattered optic nerve. It hung down, staring at the ground.

If you cared for her, why did you do this *to her?*

He forced his eyes back to her clothing, and focused on her blouse and belt. The silk of the blouse was thick and the cut expensive. The belt was real leather not synthetic, and carried a Gucci label. Not a knock-off either.

What possible connection could there be between this rich socialite and Marcia Lamb, Jake wondered.

'What can you see, Detective?' asked the colonel from the top of the ditch.

Jake said nothing so Asher jumped down and took a look for himself.

Asher muttered, 'Shit,' under his breath. He took a quick look at the body, then busied himself searching the ground.

Jake could make out Mills interviewing the foreman, and he guessed forensics were about five minutes away. The assistant medical examiner would be another half an hour. But the site perimeter had been secured by a ring of cops. Just in time too; reporters were beginning to circle. Jake could make out at least four print guys over by the site office, and a big truck from the local television affiliate was unloading equipment. He couldn't see Chuck Ford yet, but where there was carrion the hyenas were never far behind.

'They are going to be on us non-stop,' said Asher, motioning to the press behind them. 'They'll say we let the suspect go and he killed again.'

'They can say what they like,' said Jake. 'Sonny didn't do this.'

Asher glanced nervously at the press, then lowered his voice. 'Then who did?'

Jake was stumped. He was picking up very little. Detective work was a grinding slog, collating interviews, clues, alibis and opportunities. But you needed luck. And Jake needed a feel for the killer. He looked at the body again.

'Serial killers – if that's what we're dealing with – are like serial daters. They target a certain type,' said Jake, 'and they almost never cross the colour line. Our guy has crossed social class *and* colour, like he doesn't give a damn who he kills. And, to be honest, Colonel, that kinda scares the shit out of me.'

He looked down at the body again and the undisturbed jewellery.

'Robbery doesn't account for any part of it,' he muttered. 'It's all about the power and violence with this one. For him the life he takes is enough of a trophy. No need to bother with possessions.'

'This one will have a swankier address than our previous victim,' Asher said. 'He's spreading himself around a bit.'

Jake gently touched the body: stiff but not completely. Rigor mortis was not fully established. That put the time of death less than twelve hours ago. With the cold night-time temperature, probably less than ten.

Mills whistled from the top of the ditch, then stepped down to join them. He looked at the body from top to bottom, as if checking out a lady in a bar. 'Whoa, she's a looker,' he said.

'Detective!' warned Asher, who glanced behind him at the reporters and construction workers and said no more.

'God, sorry,' muttered Mills. 'I was only trying to lighten the mood.'

Jake reached out his hand. 'Just give me the thermometer and keep your thoughts to yourself.'

Mills gave Jake a digital thermometer. Jake took a

flashlight out of his pocket and shone it into the victim's mouth. This was a delicate operation, and strictly speaking he should not have been doing it, but he needed an approximation on the time of death as soon as possible – any advantage he could get against a killer Jake was starting to fear may already have an eye on a third victim.

The mouth seemed empty – no clues to be disturbed – so he inserted the thermometer and waited a few seconds for the temperature to register. The thermometer had two displays: external temperature and body temperature. Jake looked at the numbers and noted the difference. The outside temperature was 38 Fahrenheit, the internal temperature just below 41. The body had almost reached the temperature of the surrounding area so the victim had been killed up to eight hours ago. Because of the coldness of the night it could be as recently as six hours ago. That was good enough for Jake now. The ME could further narrow it down later.

While he was kneeling down Jake shone the flashlight around, but he could see nothing new apart from a third tooth. He left it there for the lab guys and stood. There was an awkward silence. Mills was unusually quiet. Jake had nothing. No idea where to go from here.

'We need to know who she is,' said Mills.

'A woman like this will be reported missing before long,' said Jake.

Mills stepped forward.

'Taking another look?' asked Jake.

'You're not the only—' Suddenly Mills tensed. 'Oh shit!'

'What's up?' asked Asher.

Mills looked around. He nodded towards the press. Jake and Asher followed him as he walked away from the corpse. Once he was well out of earshot of everyone else, he turned and faced them.

'I know who she is.'

Just then Asher's phone cut in, its shrill tone jarring. Asher pulled it out of his pocket and was about to kill it when he recognized the number.

'Hang on – it's Harper. We'll let him hear this.'

'I don't think so,' said Mills, laying a restraining hand on the colonel's arm. 'It's the councilman's wife, Belinda.'

22

Wednesday, 10.20 a.m.

Jake, Mills and Asher stood in the small construction site office. It had been cleared out for them and turned into a temporary command post. There was a desk and chairs but they all stood. A cop was at the door, keeping the press at bay. A fresh pot of coffee was percolating, and the men were staring at each other gloomily. This was rapidly becoming bigger than they were able to handle.

'It's not a serial killer,' said Asher to no one in particular. Jake could have added 'yet' to his sentence. Of course he also could have pointed out that, technically, a killer only became a serial killer with three victims spread over a month or more. So what did that make his guy? A 'mass murderer'?

That didn't exactly sound any better.

'We could call in the Feds,' Asher went on, sounding like he was voicing all the thoughts his mind was running through. 'They have experience with this sort of thing. But since the deaths have not crossed state lines yet, it's our choice.' He looked right at Jake. 'Can we handle it?'

Jake considered the question. Instinctively, he agreed the smart play was to postpone any decision for another few hours. Who knew what the local investigation might throw up?

'I have a contact in Quantico,' said Jake. 'I can ask him to run through the bureau's databases, see if the MO rings any bells. That way we don't have to make it official for the moment.'

'Maybe they could do us a profile,' suggested Mills.

'That's overrated,' replied Jake. 'It can often lead investigations down the wrong path.' He took a second before saying, 'We can call in Gail Greene, the doctor who helped with Johnny Cooper. She might have a theory about what kind of man we're looking for.'

'I suppose we need to break this to Harper,' Asher sighed. 'I'll send a cruiser out to City Hall and get him to come to the station for a briefing.'

'Thanks, Colonel,' said Jake. Breaking news like this was the worst part of the job, in Jake's opinion. He was relieved he wouldn't have to do it. 'Mills and I will check out Harper's house.' *We have to. He's killing in a hurry, so hopefully he'll be careless and leave a clue somewhere.* And Jake had a feeling they'd find the kill site there.

Asher cleared his throat, the cue to end the meeting. He left the office to get a car to take him back to the station. So far only three of them knew the identity of the victim, and they were determined to keep it that way.

Jake and Mills followed him from the office and walked silently through the press. There were about six newspaper guys, two photographers and a TV news crew. Chuck Ford was near the front, a look of feral pleasure in his eyes.

'Did he pop the eyes again?' he shouted, pushing towards Jake. 'Is it the Christmas Killer?'

Jake and Mills pushed past the reporters and headed towards their car.

'Did you have a man tracking Sonny Malone last night? Do you know where he is?' Ford asked.

'No questions at this point,' said Mills.

'Who's the victim?' Ford persisted.

'She's the body over by the lab coats at the end of the blacktop,' said Mills.

'Are the police treating this whole matter as a bit of a joke?' Ford shot back.

Jake gripped Mills by the shoulder and propelled him towards the car. 'Enough,' Jake hissed. He was getting sick of Mills's jokes as much as everyone else was. 'Don't give the press an inch. You don't play with them. You don't say anything. Not even to be funny. They're scum.'

Jake got in the driver's seat and Mills sat down beside him. Jake prayed that Mills wouldn't utter a word. Jake was afraid he might lose it if he did.

'Bit of an overreaction there,' said Mills as they pulled out on to the road.

Jake didn't answer, carrying on driving while Mills made a noise like he was preparing to speak – which, if Jake was honest, he could have done without.

'Any chance Harper is our guy?'

Jake eased the car around a corner. He had been wondering the same thing. But did it fit?

'I don't see him as the serial killer type,' he answered, 'but you can never tell. This could be an elaborate set-up to kill his own wife. First he kills Marcia Lamb, then he goes after his real target while we're misdirected, chasing up a potential serial killer that doesn't exist.'

'I can't see Mitch having the balls for that.'

'You know him better than me,' said Jake. 'But we still have to regard him as a person of interest.'

After calling in for the address, Jake took a scenic route to Harper's house in case the press was following them. When he was sure they had no tail, he cut through the centre of Littleton and straight out to Oakland Downes. Mills, presumably distracting himself from the stress of the case, asked Jake what he was doing for Christmas and did his family have any traditions.

'Shit,' Jake mumbled. 'Just realized, I still have no idea what to get Leigh. And she's probably already figured mine out, which will be nice and thoughtful, and all that stuff. I tell you, this is why I hate Christmas.'

'I love it,' said Mills, cheer suddenly flooding his voice. Jake could feel the big man's relief at getting to think about something other than the case that had him rattled. 'Well, normally I do. Normally, you get to kick back, relax, hit the reset button. This year, though . . .'

Jake didn't answer. They were in Oakland Downes

now. The houses here were large, well spaced and each set in what Jake imagined were beautifully maintained, landscaped lawns. It was hard to tell with all the snow. Trees dotted the front yards, and the road wound indolently. Middle-America aspirations on steroids. There was less in the way of Christmas decorations in front of the homes, and Jake speculated that was because the residents of Oakland Downes were more likely to spend their holidays elsewhere.

They pulled up outside the Harper residence. It looked peaceful. Normal. A bright red SUV was in the driveway. Harper's black Lincoln was still parked outside police headquarters, where he had left it after his unscheduled visit led to him accompanying them to the site of his wife's body. The SUV belonged to Belinda, which meant she hadn't gone out last night. Jake felt more certain she was murdered here.

'Before we go in, tell me about Belinda,' said Jake. 'What sort of a woman was she?'

'Beautiful,' said Mills. 'At high school she was the cheerleader we all got woodies over. And she knew it. But she could be a bitch. She'd lure you in with her looks, then cut you in half with a few words. You didn't want her as an enemy.'

Jake drummed his fingers on the steering wheel, thinking. 'What were her interests?'

'Belinda was interested in Belinda. She was head of the cheerleading squad, home-coming queen, the all-round queen bee. We all knew she'd go to a good small college, get a Mickey Mouse degree, come home and marry well.'

'How did she get together with Harper?'

Mills shrugged. 'He was a couple of years older than her, and he was making money. No great mystery there.'

'Are they happy?' Jake asked, then caught himself. '*Were* they?'

'I'm no expert,' said Mills.

'That doesn't sound like a resounding yes.'

'Well, Mitch has his little flings on the side, the way you do.'

'Some of us don't,' said Jake.

Mills just shrugged. 'Good for you. And anyway Belinda played around too. I heard she had a thing going with their accountant for a while.'

It surprised Jake that Mills would know all this gossip. Sometimes he forgot how small small-town America was.

'And Mitch was OK with that?'

'Of course not. He fired the accountant.' Mills grinned. 'Hey, it might not even be true. It's just what I heard.'

'Do you think it could be the accountant killed her?' asked Jake. 'Jealous rage? Maybe Marcia Lamb was a dry run, a rehearsal?'

'Last I heard, the accountant moved out of state. We'll look into it.'

Jake opened the driver's-side door. 'You wait here.'

'Fine by me,' said Mills, leaning back in his seat and closing his eyes as if about to go to sleep.

Jake stood at the top of the drive and scanned the lawn. There were no fences separating the properties on this side of town. The lawns were probably maintained by a landscaping company employed by the residents. Jake couldn't see Mitch Harper pushing his own mower.

The snow on the lawn was undisturbed, the path was shovelled and gritted. No clue to the violence he suspected lay beyond the hall door. He didn't want to go in just yet. He circled around to the back of the house, looking for anything that seemed out of place. But it was the same: no sign of a disturbance. He took a cursory look into a wooden shed at the back, and saw two bicycles and some garden tools. Nothing for him there. He finished his circuit of the house and rejoined Mills, who was now out of the car and sitting propped on the hood.

Finally Jake walked up to the front door. A wreath had been pinned to it – the Harpers might not have had travel plans this holiday season. Pulling his jacket sleeve over his hand, he touched the door handle and pushed, but nothing happened. Somehow he expected it to just spring open.

'Locked?' asked Mills. He had joined Jake at the door.

'Flowerpot?' Jake suggested. But when he lifted the flowerpot beside the door, he saw nothing except spilled soil and woodlice.

'We can go to the station and pick up a key from Harper,' said Jake, 'but we're losing valuable time.'

Mills smiled. 'I think I hear a sound inside. We know the lady of the house is not home, so it might be burglars. That gives us PC.'

Jake shook his head. 'Nice idea, but probable cause or not, I don't want damage to the door. This is very likely our primary crime scene.'

'I'm way ahead of you,' said Mills, removing a pen from his jacket pocket. He unscrewed the pen and tipped it upside down. A straightened paper clip fell out. He slipped it into the lock and gently jigged it up and down. It didn't take long for him to twist the clip and pop the lock open. The door swung inwards.

'That was pretty neat,' said Jake.

'I have my uses,' Mills replied and held the door open for him. 'After you.'

'Thanks,' said Jake.

He stepped into the hall and prepared himself to see a bloodbath.

23
Wednesday, 10.50 a.m.

Everything in the hall was immaculate, top of the range. The floor was tiled in a black and white diamond pattern. Marble. A small off-white table stood over by one wall. The table held a telephone, with a notebook and pen beside it. A few unopened Christmas cards were stacked. Apart from that, and a coat rack, the hallway was empty. Jake waited for the impressions to come, for the sights of the room to sink into his subconscious, and for the inner voice to begin telling him what he needed to know.

A staircase led up from the hall. Running up the stairs was a series of small paintings. Four Gustav Klimt reproductions. Jake calmed his breathing and continued to look slowly around. He could feel it beginning: his thoughts were becoming cloudy, but a voice inside his head was waiting until he was quiet enough to listen to its whispered message.

The phone was an old model and, like the Klimts, repro. It lay on its side on the small table, with the handset on the floor. Jake's eyes followed a natural line, up past the table, the fallen phone and on to the stairs. One painting – the third one up – was disturbed. It was not just slightly crooked – that could happen by chance. No. It was leaning at about forty degrees. That was more than simple bad housekeeping. Belinda had struck the painting during her flight up the stairs.

'It will be on the second floor,' said Mills quietly. Jake tuned him out.

You didn't knock her out and drag her inside this time. You came to the door and she let you in. Why the change? Did you know her? What did you say to get her to let you in?

You're inside, and now she knows that she shouldn't have let you in. Ten, fifteen seconds between knocking and taking the first step into the hallway. What happened to tip her off so quickly? Did you show her the weapon? Did she see it herself?

Are you slipping up?

Jake looked back at the crooked painting on the wall. He turned his head to the angle it was set at.

Yes, you wanted to strike immediately, take her totally by surprise. But when you raised the weapon, she ran. You ran after her. You could see her ahead of you, her arms spread. She was frantic. Did she scream?

Jake walked slowly up the stairs, past the canvases on the wall, past the crooked one. The stairs turned then led to the landing, where a discarded shoe lay beside a broken mirror.

Her panic was increasing. You didn't catch her. Not immediately. But she had no place to run to. Did you deliberately let her stay ahead of you, or were you too slow? I think you were toying with her.

No, that doesn't feel right. You wouldn't toy with her – this is all too important to you. You set about it all too deliberately. You're not just acting on impulse . . . You see this as your work.

At the top of the stairs Jake had the choice of right or left. He chose left and walked down the landing, past more crooked pictures. Two doors led off on either side. Three bedrooms and the master bathroom, he guessed.

She was running towards her bedroom, her place of sanctuary. But it's a dead end. She wasn't thinking clearly. Who could, with you behind? Not a knife. Something blunt and heavy, something to crush and beat her skull.

The final door on the right. Jake didn't need his inner voice to tell him it was the one. The bedroom door handle was lying on the floor, broken, and the door was half off its hinges.

She was still ahead of you. She made it to the bedroom. She was inside, pushing the door closed against you. She got it closed. She was locking it, probably had a telephone in the room. You couldn't have that. You kicked in the door, using your relentless strength. The strength of a man on a mission. Whatever your purpose is, you needed her for it. Your purpose gives you a reason to remove their eyes and their teeth. That's your signature.

But why Belinda Harper?

She was screaming. Begging you not to do it. Asking why. She wouldn't stop. You'd make her stop.

Jake stopped at the mangled door. He composed himself, then put a toe on the lower edge of the door, and swung it open. The stench hit him like a punch in the face.

Mills stood behind him and drew in his breath.

The bedroom looked more like an abattoir.

24

Wednesday, 10.50 a.m.

A satisfying *plunk* sounded as the spoon dropped into the cup. He fished out the tea bag and put it on the saucer. Then he stirred in the milk and two spoons of sugar. He had considered a shot of Four Roses, but he found tea so calming. He needed calming. He was still high.

You planned this so well, he thought.

They would have found her by now. It was well past ten. They might even have identified her. When they did, they would be stunned. Struck dumb. Clueless as to how to proceed. Big, smart detectives trying to second-guess the motives of a man of far superior intelligence.

When he knocked, she had opened the door for him. Unbelievable. She had let him into the house. But then something spooked her. It might have been the look in his eyes as he tried to engage her in conversation. The determination in them – had she seen it? Perhaps she just knew on some level that she was finally going to get what she deserved.

She hadn't run right away. She had slowly backed away from him.

'You knocked over the phone, Mrs Harper,' he had said. Then she was running up the stairs. She had made it so easy. If she had gone into the kitchen and out to the backyard she might have made it to a neighbour's house.

And then how would I have continued with my work?

He smiled as he remembered, sipping the tea and slowly feeling a sense of peace suffusing him.

She was fast, I'll give her that. She made it up those stairs well ahead of me. She threw the mirror but she was clumsy and missed. Bad luck. She went down the landing, but that was a mistake. It was a dead end. She had nowhere to go.

She just stood there outside the door, looking at me. Terrified but still brazen. Even the way she was standing as she looked at me – she deserved it. I walked slowly towards her, and she stood there. Right up to the moment I reached out and touched her cheek. She jumped then. She got into the bedroom and nearly got the door locked.

'Please don't do this! Why are you doing this?' *She'd screamed the words. Pathetic!*

The door wasn't going to keep me out. She got the bolt home but she never got to turn the key. My second kick sent her flying back into the room. She had no place to run. But she didn't give up easily. She picked up the chair and swung. So brave, so determined to stay alive.

He grimaced as he remembered the big weal on his arm where the leg of the chair had made contact. He had only allowed her one swing. Then he had wrenched the chair from her grasp.

She looked stunned when I hit her with it and she finally shut up. I hit her hard. I drew blood. It sprayed and some of it hit me on the face. I never knew I would actually like the feel of it . . . the taste of it. The second blow put her on the ground. The chair broke when I hit her for the third time. But it didn't matter. I could see it in her eyes. She wasn't going to struggle any more. She was out.

So I went down to the car and brought up the crusher. I fixed myself a cup of tea and waited for her to wake up.

That was when the fun began.

25
Wednesday, noon

When they returned to the station the place was quiet. Jake understood why. He could see through the blinds into the colonel's office. Harper was there, his head in his hands as sobs racked his body. There was something unnerving about such naked, unselfconscious displays of grief, and Jake wished there was some other way to take the investigation.

Harper was still wearing his black overcoat, and there was an untouched coffee in front of him. No steam wafted from the surface. It had been there a while. The colonel was sitting silently behind his desk. When he spotted Jake and Mills he stood up and came out.

'She was killed in the house?' he asked.

Jake nodded once in the affirmative, then aimed a second nod at Harper. 'How's he holding up?'

How would I hold up if it was Leigh?

From somewhere in the room a tinny blast of Christmas music made everyone jump. Jake saw one of the admin staff fumbling for her mobile phone and switching it to silent; he knew she'd curse her choice of ringtone until well after New Year's.

Asher glared at the unlucky soul for a long second, then turned back to Jake. 'He's devastated. But he was capable of focusing when I asked him a few questions. I'll type up a report as soon as he's out of here.'

'I really need to talk to him myself,' said Jake.

The colonel looked at him. 'I suppose you do. At least don't march him down to the interview room. Keep it gentle.'

'Yes, sir.'

Jake and Mills walked into the office. Jake sat in the colonel's chair. He saw Mills's look of annoyance as he took one of the canteen chairs still there from the morning meeting. Harper seemed smaller, barely filling his expensive suit. His reddened eyes seemed to burn within his pale face.

This was difficult. Yesterday Jake had begun the interview with Sonny fairly certain that he was a viable suspect. So they had gone in hard. Today he didn't figure Harper for a double killer, and he trusted his instincts. So he was going to be a lot softer, more sympathetic.

He leaned forward on the desk. 'Councilman?' Harper looked up, his eyes watery. 'I'm sorry for your loss.'

'Call me Mitch.' His hand reached out instinctively – a politician to the core – but his grip was limp, weak. He was going through the motions, on autopilot.

'I'm sorry to do this, Mitch. I know it's a bad time, but I have to ask you some questions. Anything you can tell me and Detective Mills now could help catch your wife's killer. We need to catch him fast, before he does this again.'

'I understand.'

'We'll start at the beginning, and I'm sorry if we repeat questions you've already been asked. We just have to get everything clear. Did you know of anyone who might wish your wife harm? Enemies, people she fought with, anyone like that?'

Harper's face registered surprise. 'She was such a warm, giving person. Everyone loved her.'

Jake saw a flicker cross Mills's face, but he said nothing.

'When did you last see your wife?'

'I had dinner with her last night, then we watched some TV. That English thing about King Henry. She . . . loved that.' His shoulders shook, but he managed to get a grip on himself and looked at the two detectives.

'And after?'

Harper hesitated, but Jake already knew some of the answer. The two-day-old shirt told its own tale.

'You didn't spend last night with your wife?' he prodded gently.

Harper looked at his feet. When he answered his voice was small.

'No, I didn't.' He looked down for a moment, and when he looked up he didn't meet the investigators' eyes. He went on in a low voice: 'I had to go out around ten, to meet a campaign sponsor. I had a few beers with him, so I decided not to drive home. I slept in my office. The campaign headquarters office, not the City Hall one. I have a little pull-out bed there. I often sleep over when I'm working late. Election year and all.'

It was a lie. Harper had volunteered too much detail. But Jake still had to go through the motions. In any case, it was not a crime to lie about your whereabouts.

'We'll need the details of the man you met,' said Jake. He would be able to confirm what time Harper had been out, but that still left a full night with no supported alibi. Quite convenient.

'That's not a problem,' said Harper. 'But I'll have to call him first, to square it with him.' He fixed the detectives with a stern, patronizing stare as he explained: 'I know this is a murder investigation, but these guys donate big sums, and they expect a certain amount of discretion.'

Unbelievable. Your wife has been murdered, and you're playing politics. But Jake said nothing.

Harper was sniffling again, the tears never far from the surface. He took a linen hanky out of his suit pocket and dabbed his face. It was all very affecting. *A bit too affecting*, thought Jake. He had sympathy for the man, but somehow he felt the emotion was being displayed. Harper was genuinely grieving, but at the same time he was *aware* of his pain and playing it to the hilt. He and Belinda had been the perfect power couple, and now Mitch would be the perfect widower. Jake felt it was all a bit impersonal. Political grief. But he had to admit the guy was good.

The cameras would love it.

'At your earliest convenience,' said Jake. He was

beginning to tire of the bullshit, but what could he do? Some day Harper might be his boss.

The councilman was sobbing now. He held his head in his hands, and the tears flowed freely.

'If only I had gone home,' he railed, clenched fist raised like he was going to pound the desk. Then he stopped and let it slowly ease down on to the wood. Every gesture calculated, almost practised. That he was able to be so deliberate mid-sob was nothing short of impressive. Jake wondered if it could also be classed as sinister. 'I wasn't drunk. I could have driven. Then she might still be with me.'

Jake had no answer to that. He was saved by the sudden arrival of Sara. The bubbly receptionist was smiling as she looked into the office.

'There's a visitor for you, Detective Austin,' she said.

She looked at the sobbing Harper, and a look of maternal concern crossed her face.

'Excuse me, Councilman.' Jake got up and went out of the door. Mills followed.

Jake closed it behind him so that Harper could be alone.

Sara looked up at Jake, and a miniature smile was still hovering over her eyes. She whispered, trying to keep it for Jake alone. 'He says he's here to confess.' She giggled.

Jake could feel his blood pressure rising. And that ulcer, the one whose ass he thought he'd kicked, released its acidy sensation into his stomach.

26

Wednesday, 12.40 p.m.

Jake tightened his jaw and ground his teeth. He followed Sara down the corridor to where Johnny Cooper was waiting for him at the front desk, looking as dishevelled as on the previous day. He had a hangdog face, and he was fidgeting with a pack of cigarettes.

'Detective Austin,' he began, 'I need to speak to you in private.'

'I'm a bit tied up at the moment, Johnny,' said Jake.

'Belinda Harper, I know. That's what I need to talk to you about.'

'Sorry, buddy, I don't have the time.'

Jake had felt sorry for Johnny yesterday, but today the nut bag was adding to his stress levels, bringing up the acidic prickles in his belly. But Johnny wasn't smart enough to pick up on Jake's mood.

'I think you need to talk to me,' he said. 'You see, I did it. I killed her. The rage came on me again, because of the moon, so I went out and I killed her. She was walking round the construction site on her own. She was asking for it. I need help. I need to be locked away for the good of everyone.' Johnny dropped the pack of cigarettes on the desk and put his head in his hands. He began to weep. 'You could have stopped this,' he mumbled into his hands. 'Why didn't you arrest me yesterday?'

'I think you need to stop walking around construction sites at night,' replied Jake. He tried to keep his voice gentle, like how he spoke to Faith when she was in one of her moods. 'You don't need to keep coming in like this.'

'Are you going to arrest me now?'

Jake shared a look with Sara, who was pretending that her keyboard was the most interesting object in the world, then turned back to Johnny.

'If you just go down to the interview room, I'll have one of the guys come down in a while and take a statement from you. You know your way. Better still, why don't you get yourself a coffee and go home. I'll have one of the guys swing by later and you can tell him all about it.'

Jake reached into his pocket and took out a ten, which he tried to press into Johnny's hand. But Johnny pushed the bill away. He reached forward and grabbed Jake's jacket lapel.

'I need someone to talk to me!' he shouted. 'Don't put me back out there.'

Jake's frustration was growing, and this was all being played out in public. He took Johnny's hand and snapped it from his lapel, then looked the man straight in the eye.

'I've got it. You killed her. But we have procedures,'

he said in a low, firm voice. 'You go home, I'll send a guy out. It's the best I can do. I won't let you down.'

The two men stared at each other for a moment, then Johnny broke eye contact.

'Thank you,' said Johnny, seeming to relax. 'I needed to get it off my chest. Make sure someone comes by. I don't want to kill any more women.'

Jake took him by the shoulder and led him out the door and watched him shuffle down the steps and away. Sara, who had followed the exchange with growing amusement, giggled again.

Jake rounded on her. 'There's a man there who's just lost his wife,' he hissed. 'What the fuck were you thinking, disturbing me in the middle of an interview with this shit?'

'Aw, c'mon. It was a bit of fun,' she gulped.

'This isn't a barroom brawl we're investigating! If it's so fucking funny, why don't you go into the colonel's office and explain the joke to our new widower. What were you—'

When he saw the tears welling up in her eyes, he realized that he was towering over her in a very threatening manner. He was scaring her and he was out of control. Worse still, he didn't feel the least bit bad about it. With difficulty he took a step back and got himself under control.

'Sara, don't . . .' But he tailed off. There was no way to finish that sentence that would leave him satisfied so he turned from her and walked back inside. 'Just get back to work,' he said.

27

Wednesday, 12.50 p.m.

Jake was still boiling as he walked back to the detective bureau. As he reached the door his phone buzzed. He didn't want to talk to anyone now, but it was Leigh. They hadn't made up last night. Somewhere he had read that it was not good to go to bed angry, but life has a way of screwing up even the best of intentions. He forced some sunshine into his voice, hoping that she was just calling to ask if he could pick up a Christmas tree or something like that. Something mundane that they could not possibly argue over.

'Hi, Leigh. Everything all right?'

'No,' she sighed. 'Your mother has gone missing.'

Jake froze. She had gone walkabout before but Leigh had never needed to phone him in the middle of an investigation. 'What happened?'

'I don't know. She didn't come down for breakfast this morning. I thought nothing of it. It's happened before. But when I settled Jakey down for his nap I went into her room to check on her. Jake, I don't even know if she slept in the room last night. She's been gone for hours. I've phoned around the neighbours, and no one has seen her.'

Jake could feel the waves of tension banding his forehead. 'Maybe—'

'No "maybe", Jake,' Leigh interrupted. 'She's a danger to herself. You can't just look away from the fact that your mother is losing her mind.'

His stomach tightened and he felt that ulcer again. He squeezed his eyes shut for a moment, then said, 'I'll be right over.'

Mills was at his desk, phone in hand. He hadn't dialled yet. He cradled the phone when Jake walked in.

'Howard, I need to go out for a while.'

Mills nodded. He didn't ask where Jake was going. 'OK,' he said. 'Where do we take this case?'

Jake pinched the bridge of his nose, mentally shifting thoughts of his family to one side, allowing his professional mind to tick over unimpeded. 'Start with the victims. Both of them. See if there's something that links them. But something tells me Belinda Harper is the key. So find out everything you can about her – her friends, her enemies, who she calls, her personal trainer. We need to know everything.'

Mills nodded and Jake backed out of the room.

'I'll have a radio and my phone. Any breaks, let me know.'

As he turned to leave Asher was walking up the corridor towards him. Jake nodded at his superior and walked out.

He was not going to tell the chief where he was going.

28

Wednesday, 12.55 p.m.

Jake lost a bit of time finding a patrol car with keys in the ignition. But when he found one he pulled out of the precinct yard and into the street, keeping his head low. The car had a radio and flashing blues, so he could get back in a hurry if he had to.

For a moment he wondered where to begin the search, but then logic kicked in and he decided to start where she was last seen.

He drove home.

He didn't go in, though. This was just the starting point. Instead he drove slowly from there towards the convenience store that the family occasionally went to. His mother had been there once. As he drove he went through a mental checklist making sure Mills could find him if anything happened: mobile phone – on the dash; radio – tuned into dispatch. But mostly he just scanned the sidewalk on both sides, and peered into yards and down lanes. He saw no sign of her. He drove back towards his house, using a different route. Still nothing. So he began circling slowly, gradually expanding the radius of his search. He was forty minutes in and beginning to panic.

The radio crackled beside him, letting cops throughout the city know about traffic jams, muggings, all the minutiae of day-to-day policing. He had tuned it out – Mills would call his mobile if it was anything important – but suddenly his attention was drawn to the end of a bulletin. '. . . wandering on Berkshire . . .' *Shit!* He had missed it. He lifted the mouthpiece and pressed the button, putting him through to dispatch.

'Car 62, Detective Austin. Can you repeat that last announcement?'

'Sure, Detective,' said the dispatcher. 'It's an old woman wandering around, looking confused.'

'Where?' snapped Jake.

'On Berkshire. There's no cars in the vicinity so I put it out on the all-points bulletin.'

'Where is she now?'

'Five minutes ago she was passing the low fifties, heading east. She won't have got far.'

'Thanks, bud.'

Jake thought of putting on the lights, but then another thought hit him – what if another car responded? He didn't want the whole station knowing his personal business. Some things were best kept in the family.

Jake hit a button on the radio, addressing all cars on patrol and forcing the tension from his voice: 'This is car 62.' He didn't identify himself. 'I've got the woman on Berkshire. I'll see that she gets home.'

He slowed, found a spot for a U-turn and headed

across town. It was lunchtime and traffic was light, but three stop lights went against him. He was tempted to run one of them, but the junction was too busy. It took six minutes to hit Berkshire. That meant it was more than ten minutes since the call came into dispatch. Would his mother still be there? He turned on to Berkshire and drove briskly up the numbers, past the fifties, then he slowed. He scanned both sides. No sign of her. Then he was past the sixties, the seventies, up to the eighties. Where was she?

Finally he saw her. His heart rose and he breathed out a long sigh. She was coming down the street towards him, walking slowly, looking about her as if she was lost. He pulled up and got out of the car.

'Mom,' he called, feeling snow clutching at his feet, climbing above his ankles. His heart lurched with worry for her – these conditions were not good for a woman her age. 'Mom, it's me. Jake.'

She looked up at the sound of the voice, then smiled sweetly. She recognized him, a look of relief passing over her face.

He ran over to her and put his arm around her shoulders. 'Are you enjoying your walk?' he asked through gritted teeth.

'Jake! I can't find a street sign,' she explained. 'I was looking for a policeman to help me.'

'Don't worry, Mom. I know the street signs. I'll take you home.'

'Yes. That sounds good. Perhaps we'll do that.'

Jake helped his mother into the car and drove back in silence – what was the point of asking her what she was doing? She wouldn't answer, or she would talk nonsense. There was that band of tension around his forehead again, the stinging prickles of acid in his gut. This was just too much, on top of everything else. Something within him wanted to explode, but he was careful – it wasn't her fault.

This couldn't take long; he had just walked out on a homicide investigation that happened to be the biggest one the town had ever seen.

Jake pulled the car into his driveway and got out. His mother was just sitting in the passenger seat, waiting for the door to be opened for her. Sighing, he walked around and popped the handle. Then he put a hand on her arm and helped her out of the car.

'We're home now, Mom,' he told her.

'Home?' She looked up at the house as if she'd never seen it before.

He fished out his door key and took her into the house. She smiled gently, but when she thought Jake wasn't looking her lip trembled in terror.

29

Wednesday, 1.30 p.m.

Leigh was vacuuming. There was a time, when they had first got married and were living in a cramped apartment on Lake Shore Drive overlooking Lake Michigan, when they didn't even own a vacuum cleaner. Even when that changed, neither of them had been especially diligent about keeping their house tidy. That just wasn't their way.

Until they had come to Littleton. Now Leigh seemed to be cleaning everything two or three times a day.

Jake forced a smile to his face. It wasn't his mother's fault. It wasn't Leigh's fault. It was just life. It wore you down. Best not to say anything about the fight last night and see how the land lay.

'I found her,' he said brightly.

'So I see.' Leigh was smiling too, but he could see the tightness around her lips. 'Where was she?'

'Walking along Berkshire, not a care in the world.'

'That's a long way from here.'

'I know. Any idea how long she was gone?'

Leigh bit her lip. 'As I said, the bed doesn't even look slept in. We'll have to get a lock.'

Jake looked to see if his mother was taking any of this in, but she was pottering around the kitchen, oblivious. Jake knew it was wrong to be talking about her as if she wasn't there, but in a sense she wasn't. He frowned slightly, and Leigh caught the message.

'We'll talk later,' she said. 'Want a coffee?'

Jake did, but he was pressed for time.

'Sit down – I'll have it for you in a minute.'

Feeling guilty for each second he was away from the station, he sat on the sofa. The news was showing, sound muted, so he boosted the volume. The second killing was getting blanket coverage. Some reporter he didn't recognize was describing the scene to the anchor in the studio. She didn't have much information, but she was spinning it as best she could. Then it struck him that she was spinning the same vague information they had had a few hours ago – the press did not have the identity of the second victim yet. He was impressed. Asher was keeping a lid on this one. Out of respect for Councilman Harper? Unlikely. Much more likely Asher was simply trying to make sure he hogged the limelight himself when he finally broke the news to the press. Probably a late-morning press conference, feeding live to the lunchtime news shows. Police colonel was not an elected position, but the incumbent needed to be a good politician all the same.

Leigh came back into the room. She had a mug of coffee, which she set on the table before settling down next to him. He moved over on the sofa and killed the sound. He tried to keep any combative tone out of his voice. 'Can we talk about this later?' he said.

'We can't keep putting it off,' Leigh replied. 'We have to make a decision soon. Do we get a nurse, or do we find a place where they can take care of her? These aren't just bouts of forgetfulness. She has a medical condition, and it's getting worse.'

'Now's not a good time.'

'I know. But when will be? It's for her own safety as much as anything. She could get hurt on one of her wanders. And they're happening more and more often.'

'We can cope.'

'You're not here to help with the *coping*,' she said.

'I'm here now.'

'But in an hour you'll be back at work, and I'll be on my own – as I've been since we arrived. You do know it's Christmas, don't you?'

'Yes,' he said, aware that his voice was clipped. He softened it. 'I also know we have a potential serial killer at large, and that people are at risk until I've caught him. I have to focus on that.'

'Insurance would cover the costs,' was all she said, changing the topic to one where she had the higher ground.

'It's not about the cost,' he snapped.

'Fine,' she said. But he knew it wasn't. This would run and run.

He stood, gave her a quick kiss on the cheek and headed for the door. She hadn't turned towards the kiss.

As he walked briskly to the car, he was seething. Whatever Leigh said, he would not be putting his mother in a home. Never. Christ, they should be on the same side.

He saw Faith coming up the driveway towards him. 'Hi, Dad.' His daughter grinned. 'What are you doing home? Have you—'

'Sorry, Faith, I have to go back to work,' he said, opening the car door. 'We'll talk tonight.'

As he made to slide his body into the car, he caught the pained look that clouded Faith's face. But he did not have time to make it better. Not today. He closed the car door.

What sort of a man am I turning into? That's my daughter.

He opened the car door and stepped out, spreading his arms. He put a big goofy grin on his face.

Faith smiled back at him, running into his arms. He hugged her tight, feeling her small skinny body folding into his strong arms. She snuggled like she hadn't since she was seven or eight, and he felt the tension easing around his forehead.

'Are you coming in for lunch?' she whispered.

'I just came for the hug,' he replied.

30

Wednesday, 2.30 p.m.

When he got back to the station it was chaos. The whole place was buzzing, with three news trucks parked outside. He went in and saw Sara behind her desk, scowling at him. It seemed like she was still bothered by the Johnny Cooper incident.

'In the conference room,' she hissed.

This is it: Colonel Asher's moment of glory.

He walked down the corridor and slipped into the back of the room. Already the press were there en masse, microphones bearing all the major radio and television logos clustered around the simple podium near the door. There were a few chairs to the side, with one or two of the detectives in place. Mills was there. Asher was beside him in full-dress uniform, the gold eagle shining. He was whispering urgently, then he spotted Jake and beckoned him over.

'How did your lead pan out?' Asher asked him.

Jake looked at Mills, who shrugged as if to say, *I had to tell him something.*

'Anything new I can tell these guys?'

'Sorry, sir,' Jake replied.

Asher nodded, then stepped into the office beside the conference room.

'He's been like this the past hour,' said Mills.

'These cases take time. He has to know that,' Jake answered. 'The press have to know it too.'

'We did have a development while you were out. I'll fill you in as soon as we're done here. You handle your . . . *situation*?'

Mills was fishing. Jake gave him nothing. He just nodded.

Asher walked back into the room, leading Councilman Mitch Harper. The official looked paler than everyone was used to. His eyes were red.

'The onion effect,' Mills whispered.

There was something a little too staged about the councilman's appearance. Jake remembered when Leigh's father had died. She didn't shed a tear until ten days after the funeral. That was the way deep grief hit: it left you numbed and in shock. It wasn't a thing you turned on for the cameras.

The reporters were beginning to stir.

'Colonel, any lead on the two killings?'

'Is it true they are linked?'

'Councilman, will this double homicide help your law and order bid for the mayoral election?'

Jake winced. That reporter was going to regret that last question once the facts were revealed.

Harper sat on a chair set behind the podium. His head was bowed and he was looking at his shoes, which lacked their usual polish. Something about his attitude and bearing was beginning to sink in with the assembled press men. The room gradually quietened.

Colonel Asher stepped up to the podium, a few typed sheets in front of him. He frowned, looked up, scanned the crowd, looked down at his notes and then began to speak.

'I'll keep this brief. As you know, a second body has been found, out by the interstate construction site. We are satisfied this second killing contains several significant similarities to the murder of Marcia Lamb yesterday . . .'

A wave of sound grew in the room as reporters began to fire questions, but Asher held his hand up to stop them speaking.

The colonel went on: 'We believe that we are looking for one man for the two murders.'

'Are you certain the perpetrator is male?' one reporter shouted.

'Are you treating it as a potential serial killer case?' said another.

'No questions yet, please,' Asher said. 'I will read my statement, then we'll see about questions.' He looked down at his papers again. 'The murders are being treated as one case. At this point we are exploring several lines of inquiry. For operational reasons I will not be discussing those with you.'

Jake scanned the crowd. Chuck Ford was near the front, a Dictaphone lying on his knee and a spiral-bound notebook open in front of him. He was scribbling furiously. One of the old-fashioned guys. Other reporters were holding their recorders in the air to catch every one of the colonel's words.

Jake wasn't scanning the crowd out of idle curiosity; FBI profilers had determined that serial killers – if that's what they were dealing with – like to stay close to murder investigations. They often hung out in cop bars, even befriending the investigating officers. It was not a universal trait, but something to look out for. The killer could be here right now.

Asher droned on for a few minutes, doling out a carefully selected package of details. It was important to hold things back, things that could then be used to check the validity of statements the police took later. It was these kinds of details that would weed out the fake confessions, like the ones offered by Johnny Cooper.

The colonel paused, shuffled a new sheet of paper to the top, glanced down, then looked out at the packed room.

Here we go, Jake thought.

'Every killing strikes at the heart of a neighbourhood, but this one has struck home especially hard,' he said. 'Our detectives have identified the second victim . . . and she was a pillar of the community, someone who worked tirelessly for others.' He took a deep breath before saying, 'Belinda Harper.'

The room went silent. Then pandemonium broke

out. The voices and the questions seemed to come all at once.

The colonel shouted over the top of them, 'The councilman has agreed to make a brief statement, appealing for any information that might help apprehend this killer. He will not be accepting questions.'

Harper's shoulders were hunched as he walked towards the podium. Jake had to admire the way he was holding it together. His voice shook as he spoke briefly about the shock of the discovery, then he blinked away tears as he turned from the reporters. There was a moment's silence, then he turned back to them.

'We were together so long,' he said. 'She was my life. I don't know how I will carry on without her,' he said in a small voice. Then he stepped from the podium.

Immediately the questions began, but Asher was on his feet, hustling Harper from the room. Ten minutes, start to finish. Show over.

Except it's not, Jake thought, feeling the acidic tingle of the ulcer in his gut. *Not yet* . . .

31

Wednesday, 2.50 p.m.

Jake stirred sugar into another coffee as he watched the last of the reporters pull out from the parking lot. 'You said there were developments?' he said to Mills, who had appeared beside him.

'Nothing dramatic,' said Mills. 'But we have a new suspect in the frame. Someone you know.'

'Who?' asked Jake.

'Guy Makowski.'

Jake looked at him blankly, so Mills went on: 'The guy you ju-jitsued at the church protest on Monday morning.'

'How is he in the frame?' asked Jake. He was surprised.

'You asked me to do a background on Belinda Harper. She had no enemies. I mean, nobody liked her, but nobody hated her enough to kill her either. However, she did have a very public fight with Makowski a few weeks back. It was at that meeting about the interstate.'

Jake remembered it vaguely. He had not been working that night. The city council and the contractors had made a presentation at City Hall about the interstate and how it would affect Littleton. It was supposed to be a routine town hall debate, but the event had been hijacked by protesters and the cops had been called out to calm the situation down. Which is why they'd been better prepared for the church event.

Mills pulled out a notebook. 'I was talking to a friend of Belinda.'

Jake found it jarring hearing the deceased being called by her first name, but he hadn't known her like Mills had.

'It seems that Makowski is one of the ringleaders of the anti-interstate faction, and he was at the meeting with his cronies, kicking up a rumpus. They weren't allowed in, but they were on the steps of City Hall as people arrived, trying to intimidate everyone. Makowski blocked Belinda as she arrived.'

'Did he target her specifically?' asked Jake.

'I don't think so. She was just another rich bitch getting out of a nice car, and he picked on her.'

'Where was Harper while this was going on?'

'Inside, with the other councilmen.'

'Interesting.'

'According to Belinda's friend, Makowski accosted her as she walked up the steps of the building, and blocked her way in. He had a bunch of guys with him, all following his lead, but he was the loudmouth.'

'Did he touch her?'

'You'll love this. When he started giving her the spiel

about our heritage being bulldozed, she just looked at him for a moment, and asked him if he'd finished high school. She said, "Even a moron can understand that two hundred jobs in construction is a fair trade for some heritage." '

Mills laughed, but Jake was focusing on the humiliation Makowski must have felt at that moment. No one liked being put down, especially not in front of friends following *your* lead. But when you are put down by a beautiful woman who is smarter than you, and more successful, it can be a painful thing. Guys like Makowski thrive on their machismo. He didn't have the words or the wit for the cute girls, and he wouldn't have coped when she had cut him down to size in front of everyone.

'He must have been mad,' said Jake.

'Yeah. Boiling.' Mills consulted his notebook. 'And then – get this – after he calls her a fucking bitch she bent forward and whispered something in his ear. No one caught what she said, but it must have been good, because he made a lunge at her, but he was held off. So he ran over to her car and kicked in a panel.'

'Did she bring any charges?'

'Yes,' said Mills, glancing down at his notebook. 'Misdemeanour assault and criminal damage.'

'So he has motive. That makes him a person of interest, to say the least.'

'Moving towards a strong suspect,' Mills agreed. He leaned back in his chair, a satisfied smile on his face.

Jake nodded, agreeing that – procedurally – it was something to keep in mind. Except that it didn't fit. He had tackled Makowski on Monday and that gave him a feel for the man's character.

You're a boaster. You like to boost yourself up. You could kill someone in a bar fight, but it would be an accident.

But . . . There was always a but. As well as the voice in his head, Jake could hear the voice of reason. Makowski *did* want the interstate stopped. And two dead bodies had certainly slowed things down. Of course, two bodies wouldn't stop the work permanently, but Makowski was not a deep thinker. And then there was the choice of victim. Kill Belinda Harper, and he killed the charges against him. That was added motive.

'Howard, I need you to check for priors. You have a three-strikes rule in Indiana, don't you?' Three strikes – three felony convictions – and you could be facing twenty-five years without parole.

'Yup,' said Mills, and he nodded at Jake because they both knew what that meant. If Makowski was on his third strike, he had all the motive in the world to off Belinda Harper.

'Let's go then.'

32

Wednesday, 3.30 p.m.

Figuring the odds were good, they drove to Makowski's house. They had an address for him, and a few calls established that he worked night shifts at a steel mill. The shift was from midnight to 8 a.m., and he had been late the last two nights. He was becoming a person of more significant interest to Jake, especially where Belinda Harper's murder was concerned.

Jake just wondered where Marcia Lamb would fit in.

Assuming Makowski slept after his shift, he should have been just about waking up.

'How are we going to do this?' asked Mills.

Jake paused. He knew this would have to be handled delicately. They had no probable cause at this stage and didn't want to let Makowski know he was in the frame for the double homicide.

'Let's ask him about the scuffle on Monday,' said Jake. 'Shake the tree and see what falls out.'

Makowski lived on the outskirts of town, where the city merged into the agricultural hinterland. They arrived a little after three thirty. It was little more than a clearing in the trees, with a forty-foot caravan pulled back from the road. The yard was littered with broken bits of furniture and truck parts, and a flatbed pickup was parked outside. The caravan needed work, and the pickup wasn't new.

'Give me the projects,' muttered Jake.

'Don't knock it – it's good hunting country,' Mills replied.

They pulled off the road and into the yard, stopping beside the pickup. They stepped from their car and crossed to the door of the caravan. In addition to the regular lock – which was about as secure as a shoelace – there was a big padlock on the door. But the padlock was open. There were two signs on the door. The first read, WHATEVER YOU'RE SELLING, I'M NOT BUYING, the second, TRESPASSERS ARE IN SEASON.

'Nice guy,' muttered Mills.

Jake rapped on the door. There was no response and no sound from inside. He rapped again. Still nothing.

'If he's not at home, can we snoop?' asked Mills.

Jake turned at the sound of heavy footsteps behind them.

'That would be breaking and entering,' a gruff voice rumbled. 'I would expect cops to know that.'

Makowski was standing about twelve feet away from them. He was dressed in a different Metallica shirt from the last time Jake saw him, but it was as tortured as the first had been. He looked like he hadn't shaved since that day. His face was blank, neither threatening nor alarmed.

'I'm Detective Austin, this is my partner Detective Mills.' He reached towards his pocket for his badge, but the movement brought a smirk from Makowski.

'I don't need to see your badge. I can smell cop. Besides, I know you. You're the guy who sucker-punched me at the church.'

Jake took his hand away, letting it fall by his side. 'From where I was standing, you went for me.'

'Hey, it was a peaceful protest until you clowns came along. Now get off my property.'

Mills stepped in. 'We only want to ask you a few questions.'

'Without a warrant?' asked Makowski, as if he were explaining the nuances of police procedure to *them*.

'What law school did you go to?' asked Jake. 'We're standing in an unfenced yard. Now let's all stop dicking around and have a talk inside.'

'Not gonna happen.'

'Fine. We can talk out here.'

'And if I don't?'

'Then we'll be back,' said Jake. 'And I can tell you're the kind of man who doesn't want the attention of cops.'

Makowski scowled. 'Fine. But make it fast, then get the hell outta my yard.'

'Mr Makowski,' said Mills, doing his best to sound cheery and breezy, 'we just want to know why you seem so interested in this whole highway business.'

'Why?' said Makowski. 'You think a guy like me

shouldn't be interested in the issues that affect the people of this town? You think I'm too dumb to understand?'

'Of course not,' said Mills; at the same time Jake was thinking, *Now that you mention it . . .*

Jake finished Mills's response: 'We've just noticed you're clearly passionate about the issue. We were curious as to why.'

Makowski shrugged. 'I'm just a citizen who cares about the earth and shit. Littleton doesn't need an interstate ripping through our town and digging up the churches.'

'No argument from me,' said Mills. 'But I don't see you as the community leader type.'

'The call came and I answered. You don't have to wear a suit and tie to care about things.'

'And what's in it for you?' asked Jake, ignoring the urge to tell Makowski he doubted he could even knot a tie.

'My town staying just the way I like it.'

'So you bring along a mob and try to start a riot?'

Makowski shrugged. 'Just exercising my right to protest. First Amendment and all.'

This was going nowhere, but Jake didn't want to let him know the real reason they were there because Makowski would clam up. He was stupid, but not stupid enough not to call a lawyer when he was threatened with a murder charge.

'You struck a police officer during your protest,' Jake told him.

'And you're going to bring me in for that? I don't think so. If you were, you'd have done it already. And it wouldn't be just the two of you come to pick me up. And you'd have that warrant we talked about . . .'

Makowski was right. Jake felt the tension returning to his head, doing a duet with the burn in his gut. The case was full of dead leads. Jake needed to shake something loose before the killer struck again.

'It's an offence,' he said.

'I don't recall striking anyone. Near as I can recall, I was waving my banner, shouting my slogans, and the next thing I know some cop puts me flying through the air like we're in the Octagon. And, you know, I don't feel so good. Maybe I should sue.'

Mills smiled. 'You've been very helpful, Mr Makowski. Do you have a phone number in case we have any other questions?'

'Tell you what – if I have any other information, I'll give *you* a call. We done here?'

Mills looked at Jake and shrugged. He turned towards the car. 'Thanks for your time, Mr Makowski,' said Mills, making no attempt to seem genuine.

As he made to follow his partner, Jake's mind was racing. He needed to think of something fast, something to give them the leverage they needed. He stopped and turned, heading over to Makowski and standing a few feet in front of him. Not right in the guy's personal space, but close enough for the subtle challenge to be received, loud and clear.

'Nice place you got here,' said Jake. A guy like Makowski would respond to patronizing. He probably couldn't spell the word, but he would understand the concept. 'Good mortgage rate?'

He sensed Makowski stiffening. He had found the button. Now it was time to press on it – and the other buttons that Jake knew were clustered around it.

'But I suppose, between you and your sister, you're making ends meet pretty well, huh?'

Makowski moved fast for a big man pushing fifty. But he moved without thought, without technique. He lunged at Jake's shoulder and shoved him back violently. On any other occasion it would have been a dumb move to make. Makowski should have known that the man he was attacking was trained, adept. The worst thing he could have done was to shove him back, creating distance between them – distance that would allow Jake to set himself, get his balance and counter-attack.

On a normal day this altercation would have been over inside three seconds. But this was not a normal day. Instead, Jake let his body fall into the reverse momentum created by Makowski's shove; he let his right foot land in the big empty paint-bucket he had clocked when they arrived; he let his balance tip back, as if the bucket was upending him. He hit the ground and let himself roll.

By the time he had sat up, Mills had done an about turn and pulled his service weapon, which he now had aimed directly at Makowski's head.

'Oh dear, Makowski,' he said. 'That's the second time you've assaulted an officer in three days.'

Jake smiled. Now they had a real reason to bring in Makowski.

By the end of the day they would know just how seriously to take him as a suspect.

33

Wednesday, 5 p.m.

They were glad when they got back to the station. Makowski had bitched the whole way, and only calmed down when Mills threatened to mace him. They had to drag him to get him inside.

Mills grinned at Sara, who was just getting ready to leave for the evening. 'Any news while we were out? Any more bodies dug out of the asylum?'

'No – still at two, just like our body count,' she replied.

'Looks like everything is under control then. Feel like going out and getting shitfaced with a cute detective?'

Sara barely looked at Mills as she sauntered out of the station with a smirk. 'If a cute detective asks me, I'd consider it.'

Jake led Makowski to a cell. 'Need a lawyer?'

'I ain't done nothing. I don't need a lawyer. This is just a jackass complaint to harass me.'

No lawyer was fine by Jake. He gently pushed Makowski inside, then shut the door on him. He planned to leave him there for an hour. A cooling-off period often softened someone up for interrogation.

Jake used the hour to do paperwork. A second killing in two days had done wonders for the ME's focus, and they already had a preliminary report. It made horrific reading.

Belinda Harper had suffered terrible injuries before her death. There was evidence of considerable blunt-force trauma to her head, just like in the killing of Marcia Lamb. Several of the teeth were missing, the jaw left mangled and deformed.

Jake read the clinical details: 'Both eyeballs were extruded. On initial examination, neither eyeball showed extensive trauma or tearing. Conclusion: eyeballs not levered out with a sharp instrument. One tooth missing from the upper jaw. Four teeth missing from the lower mandible, which is fractured in six places. Considerable damage to the cranium, all ante-mortem. Severe bleeding within the cranium, and within the brain, which was the likely cause of death.'

He skimmed through to the preliminary conclusion: 'Initial findings indicate that blunt-force trauma to the head resulted in internal bleeding within the brain. The victim was probably conscious for the infliction of most of the injuries. Bruising indicates that the length of the assault was between thirty and forty minutes.'

Mills, reading over his shoulder, muttered, 'Jeez. I've seen my share of heads beaten in, but none like that. And the eyes . . .'

That was bothering Jake too. A blow to the head, however strong the assailant, would not pop the eyes out of a victim's skull, and yet the ME was clear that they hadn't been scooped out. Something deep in his memory was sending signals to him. It took a few minutes, but when Jake thought about the eyeballs it finally came to him.

'I've seen this before.'

'Yeah?'

'Not the whole thing, but the eyes. Back in Chicago. I need to speak to the ME.'

Mills reeled off the number, and Jake punched it in. A busy assistant fielded the call.

'Dr Zatkin is tied up at the moment. Can I take a message?'

Jake looked at the clock on the wall. It was nearly six. The doctor might have left already, but he thought not. He hoped not.

'This is Detective Jake Austin,' he said, 'the lead investigator on both homicides. If the doc can be pulled away, it would be a big help.'

The ME was on the line quickly. 'Detective, what can I do for you? You've got my initial report? It will be a few more days before I have the full version.'

'I've got the report, Doctor, thank you. You describe the head injuries, but there's not much speculation as to how they could have been caused.'

'That's not my place, Detective. And, to be honest, the injuries were like nothing I've ever come across in all my years in the profession.'

'I might be able to help with that,' said Jake. 'I'm

going to throw a scenario at you and see what you think.'

'Go ahead.' The ME sounded interested.

'Back in Chicago I came across a homicide with similar features. It was a drug dealer, one of my informants. When we found him his head was crushed and one of the eyeballs was missing.'

'And did you ever determine a cause of death?' she asked.

'We did. He was found in a car chop shop, and that's what gave us the clue. He was held down and a car was lowered on to his head until they had all the information they needed.'

'That's charming.'

'Could this be a crushing injury?' Jake asked.

'Difficult to see how – both primary crime scenes were indoors, weren't they? There was nothing heavy that could have done this.'

'But in principle?'

There was a long pause on the line, then the doctor came back. 'It's an interesting idea,' she said. 'I'll bear it in mind when we're doing the detailed examination of the skull.'

Jake thanked her and hung up the phone. He looked at Mills, who had been working the computer with one ear on the conversation.

Mills raised his eyebrows. 'I've got Makowski's file.'

Jake was beside him in an instant and scanning the screen. Makowski had priors. But as they looked at his rap sheet some of their enthusiasm waned. None of the priors was recent. The last was twenty-two years ago, for felony possession. It was his only felony.

'So much for three strikes,' said Jake.

'Not quite. If he gets charged with assault on Belinda and attacking her car as separate offences, that's three felonies. Twenty-five to life. A good lawyer could probably prevent that, of course, but if he ended up with an incompetent public defender, who knows?'

'So he's got motive,' said Jake. 'I like him for this a hell of a lot more than I like Sonny Malone.'

'Does he tick enough boxes for us to go to the judge?'

Jake looked up at the clock on the wall.

'Let's take our time. If we apply after six, he's too late to get a lawyer, and we can hold him overnight.'

He smiled to himself. Things were looking like they might be starting to go his way.

34

Wednesday, 8 p.m.

Makowski hadn't taken it well when he found out he was going to sleep over. But it left the way clear for Jake and Mills to execute the search warrant – after Mills had reminded Jake that they'd be having a Christmas party at the station that night.

'That's still happening?' Jake had asked as they left the station.

'It'll be low key,' Mills insisted, zipping up his jacket and stuffing his hands into the pockets. It wasn't snowing, but the air was sharp. 'Unofficial, almost. I guess everyone feels like they could use a break, you know? A distraction, just for a couple of hours or so.'

As he opened the car and they got in, Jake thought he could see the sense of that.

'I tell you,' said Mills as Jake started the car and pulled away, 'anything after last year's would be low key.'

Jake didn't ask what happened last year, but Mills told him anyway. As he drove, Jake barely listened, but he did hear, '. . . me . . . three uniforms . . . Jäger-bomb contest . . . vacuum cleaner . . .'

Whatever filled in the gaps, Mills seemed to think

was hilarious, but when they came within sight of Makowski's caravan, his laughter died away. Distractions were all well and good, but they had a job to do.

Jake parked, and they got out, stepping towards it with natural, instinctive caution, even though they knew exactly where the occupant was. From what they could see in the darkness the caravan was exactly as they had left it a few hours earlier. The padlock was still hanging from the door. They pushed, but the door was locked. Mills pulled out a penknife and opened a blade. He pushed the blade in the door jamb near the lock and levered slightly. The door gave a little. He put his hand on the handle and pulled sharply. The door popped open, no damage done.

They stepped into the caravan. It was not big. There was a main room – an indoor junkyard – with a bedroom leading off it, and a small kitchen. At the other end of the trailer Jake knew they would find a shower unit and a small toilet. He had thought it wouldn't take long to search the place, but there seemed to be stuff everywhere.

Which meant that he was going to be late home. Again.

'Where do we start?' asked Mills. 'What are we looking for?'

'Souvenirs,' Jake replied. 'A lot of serials keep them. Maybe an item from a lady's purse, a small bit of jewellery. Or we could strike lucky and he might have kept a tooth. The ME doesn't have a complete set for either body. Also look out for porn – these guys tend to use it.'

'I hate to think what you would make of my house.'

Jake laughed as he opened a drawer and started looking through it. Keys. Bills. Receipts. 'I mean unusual stuff. A copy of *Penthouse* doesn't count.'

'*Hustler*?'

'Now you're borderline.'

The two men began systematically searching the main living area. They worked quickly but thoroughly. Every cupboard was opened, every pile of junk moved to check behind it. They lifted the sofa and examined the floor beneath. They shifted chairs. They found plenty of beer cans, more than a few empty bottles of Jack Daniel's, but no body parts. Near the television they found a box of DVDs, and Jake's interest was piqued as he scanned the titles.

Top of the list was *Mad Max*, and then *Monster*, the story of the female serial killer Aileen Wuornos. There were a couple of Second World War documentaries about the Nazis too. In the bottom of the box Jake found a pamphlet: a history of Littleton from its founding in 1816 to the end of the Second World War.

What are you doing reading this? Maybe you do care about the town.

'Howard, the guy seems to have an interest in the dark and violent,' said Jake, showing Mills the DVDs and the pamphlet.

'And history,' said Mills. 'Keep looking.'

They found his porn stash a few minutes later. The guy had made no attempt to conceal it. There was a locker under the television, and when they opened it they found a stack of magazines and about a dozen films. Mills took out the magazines and began flicking rapidly through. Jake removed the DVDs and quickly checked the titles.

'Notice a theme?' asked Mills. All the material was about bondage and S & M.

They took the search next into the bedroom, but found nothing. The place was probably crawling with things it was best not to think about. No way Makowski brought dates back here. But it gave no more insight into the man's character. The toilet and shower were checked, then they moved into the kitchen.

It took about ten minutes to check the shelves and the cupboards. Then Jake turned to Mills. 'Come on. The warrant covers the yard.'

They headed straight to the small locked timber shed near the trees.

Mills got to work on the lock, and a minute later they had the door open. It was a small space with plenty of carpentry tools. There was a worktable with a light overhead. Jake found the switch. He threw it but it stayed dark.

'I guess it takes power from the trailer,' said Mills.

Jake looked around using his penlight, followed the wire from the bulb to the switch, from the switch to a small hole in the wall of the shed. He stepped out. Just as Mills said, there was a weatherproof socket and an extension lead going back to the trailer. He connected the socket, and the light came on.

It was the only place that was cleaned regularly. The floor was swept, and all the tools seemed to be where they should be. There was a gun rack on the wall, with two rifles and space for a third. Jake speculated as to how and where Makowski could have lost it. He hoped the weapon was not going to be turning up in any Littleton investigations any time soon. Misplaced weapons had a nasty habit of showing up again.

One corner seemed slightly less organized than the rest of the room. There were some unfinished bits of furniture and a Black & Decker Workmate, a portable bench with clamps that carpenters take on the job with them.

Mills pulled it out. Something caught Jake's eye.

'Steady – be gentle with that.'

He took out his penlight again, and shone it on the clamp at the top of the bench. He moved closer. The dark stain looked like blood. Both men stared at the smudge.

Mills pointed to a small whitish speck on the smudge.

'What's that?'

'I think it's skin,' said Jake.

'Does that mean we just closed the case?' asked Mills, a smile beginning to appear.

'I guess so,' Jake replied, waiting for that sudden rush of adrenaline he always got when he was certain, *convinced.* But there was something missing.

He wasn't seeing it.

Despite the evidence, Jake did not feel like he was standing in the lair of a killer.

35

Thursday, 15 December, 8 a.m.

Jake sensed the mood when he arrived at the station the following day. It wasn't a high-fives-all-round sort of morning, but there was an air of restrained jubilation among his colleagues. The colonel even smiled at him as he passed his office. At his desk, Mills was grinning through his hangover – the 'low-key' Christmas party had obviously been anything but.

Within an hour they had Makowski and his public defender in the interview room.

'You were late to work two nights in a row. Two nights in which women were brutally murdered. Where were you?' Jake asked.

Makowski addressed his answer to the table. 'Like I said, I was with a girl.'

'We need a name for your girl.'

'Good luck with that,' he said with a shrug.

Mills butted in. 'The way this works is, you tell us the girl's name, we bring her in, we question her, and if the alibi flies, so do you. But if the alibi sinks, you fry like a rasher of bacon.'

‘I’d love to give you her name,’ Makowski said in a low voice. ‘But I never asked her.’

‘C’mon! How long have you been seeing her?’ asked Jake.

Makowski shrugged, still looking at the table. A slight smirk crossed his lips. ‘Varies. Usually twenty minutes, but sometimes I can go the full half-hour. Sometimes I take her to a motel and we make a night of it. Monday, we did it in the cab of the pickup. Tuesday was in an alley.’

Spent the night with a prostitute. It was an easy way to get an alibi. Worse comes to the worst, a guy in need could usually pay a prostitute to say what he needed her to.

‘And you never asked her name?’

‘I was more concerned with her price.’

Jake bit back an angry growl. Makowski seemed confident, untroubled, and Jake felt like pointing out to him that as these were violent misogynistic murders with a potential sexual motive, his bragging about having sex with hookers was putting himself more sharply into the frame for the killings. ‘You’re going to have to give us a description at least,’ Jake said.

‘Juicy,’ said Makowski.

Jake leaned forward over the table, angling his head to find Makowski’s eyes. ‘Do you want to get charged with double homicide?’ he asked, keeping his voice even. In his experience blank dispassion was more likely to convince than the TV-cop outrage he'd seen other detectives go for. 'Because you're going down that road.'

'I didn't do no double homicide,' said Makowski, turning his face away from Jake's.

'You're not giving us any reason to—'

Just then the door burst open. Sara looked in. Her face was pale.

'We're busy,' Jake snapped. 'Tell Johnny to—'

'It's not Johnny this time,' she whispered. 'There's been another murder.'

Jake felt it like a slap to the face.

He could see that Mills was pale, and not just from his hangover.

'Time out,' Mills said to Makowski and his lawyer, and the two detectives left the interview room.

Colonel Asher was waiting for them outside the door. 'There's been another body dumped,' he said.

'The interstate again?' asked Mills.

'Not this time,' said Asher. 'Littleton Middle School.'

Mills's head dropped. 'Not a kid,' he said just as Jake asked the same question.

The colonel puffed out his cheeks, breathing a relieved sigh. 'Thankfully, no.'

'Might the body have been there a few days?' Jake asked, on autopilot. Little Middle was the school that Faith had just started.

'Don't know,' said Asher, '*yet*.'

Jake caught Asher's tone and emphasis. Makowski was in custody last night. So if the kill was fresh, they had the wrong guy – again.

'We better get out there quick,' said Mills.

In the car Jake said nothing. If Makowski wasn't the man, they'd wasted a day chasing smoke.

'Is it something to do with the time of year?' Mills asked.

'No one hates Christmas that much,' said Jake, staring out of the window at the passing houses. There was snow on the ground and over the roofs, and ornate displays in many yards, but with the pall of serial murder hanging over Littleton, all the joy had been drained from them.

'Tell me what you're thinking, psychic boy,' asked Mills.

'I'm thinking we might have blown this one.'

It might not be their fault, but it was their responsibility. They were dealing with a serial killer now. The nature of a serial killer was to keep killing until they were stopped. And the more they killed, the more violent they tended to become. Each murder had to top the previous one, resulting in victims made to suffer even more. And that was only the second-worst-case scenario.

Number one was that the killer got more proficient, less sloppy. Harder to catch.

Mills drove quickly, keeping the siren off. There was

enough panic in the community without that. Mills drummed on the wheel as he drove and the noise was echoing in Jake's ears, making him crazy. 'How much experience do you have with serials?'

'None,' Jake admitted. 'But I've done the basic fortnight in Quantico for detectives. I'm guessing you haven't.'

'Littleton doesn't do murder. So none of us have been sent on any of those courses. Are they any good? Could they put together a profile of who we're looking for?'

Jake wasn't sure about the usefulness of a psychological profile, but at this stage they needed any help they could get. 'It wouldn't do any harm, I guess.'

'What are you waiting for?' Mills growled.

Jake took out his mobile phone and dialled back to the station. He asked Sara to put him through to the FBI headquarters and training college in Virginia. The switch patched him through to the office of Agent Bob Ressler, second in command at Behavioral Science, the profiling unit.

'Agent Ressler's desk,' a woman answered.

'Is Bob in?' asked Jake after identifying himself. 'I need to consult on a case we have here.'

'Agent Ressler is on vacation for the next few days. If it's urgent, perhaps someone else can help.'

'We've had three bodies in three days.'

'Point taken,' said the voice. 'One unsub?' This was FBI-speak for 'unknown subject' – the perpetrator.

'We think so.'

'Look, Agent Ressler is in the Bahamas, but if you email through all the files – especially the crime scene photos and the ME's report – I can get them to him this evening.'

'Thanks,' said Jake. He hung up.

'Any luck?' asked Mills.

'We'll have a profile in the morning.'

'Can we wait that long?'

That was the question bothering Jake. Could they wait?

What's going through your head? Something is driving you, and it's more than anger. But I can't see it. Not yet.

They passed four warehouses and a lumber yard, and arrived at the school. Parents were already pulling up to take their children away. Word spread fast, and Jake knew Littleton was edging closer to panic. There would be no containing this one. The press and the cameras would be at the scene within minutes. The proximity to the school made this one sensational.

'Dad!'

As Jake got out of the car, he was almost bowled over by Faith jumping into his arms. Leigh was behind her, wheeling Baby Jakey's walker, her face pale and drawn.

'It's OK, sweetheart,' said Jake, talking into Faith's hair. 'Mom's taking you home.'

Faith drew back from him, looking up with eyes that glimmered with tears. 'Are you coming with us?'

'I'll be home later,' he told her. 'I have to work now.'

'But—'

'Faith,' said Leigh, her voice a weary rasp. 'You want your dad to catch the man who did this, don't you?'

Faith looked from one parent to the next, seeming genuinely uncertain of her answer for a moment. Then she nodded. Over her head, Jake mouthed, 'Thank you,' to his wife, who nodded back.

Jake saw that Mills was keeping a respectful distance from the family tableau. 'Honey, this is my partner, Howard Mills. Howard, this is my wife, Leigh.'

The two of them shook hands. Then Leigh reached to take Faith gently by the shoulder. 'We should get going,' she said. 'See you at home.'

'There's a quick way to the dump site,' said Mills after they had walked away. 'Through the school.'

Mills drove around the building and straight across the basketball court. He parked the car right under the net and got out.

'There's a gap in the fence over here. That's the best way to the crime scene,' he said.

'I'd like to come in the way the murderer did.'

'And how do you know he didn't come in this way? Everyone who ever went to this school knows about this gap.'

'If he was carrying a body he didn't crawl through a gap in a fence. He took the access road.'

'OK,' said Mills. 'Want to go around to the other side?'

Jake nodded. His pulse was quickening. He could feel him. The killer had been here.

36

Thursday, 9.15 a.m.

The access road led to a little path. To Jake's left it curved away, following the line of a small river. It was a narrow path, more a track beaten in the grass, with bushes to one side and trees lining the river. The river was almost blocked off by the thickness of the undergrowth. He looked in the other direction. The trail curved and he could see some buildings in the middle distance. These would be the backs of the warehouses. Near one there were two cops standing on the path with their backs to the river. That had to be where the body was. No sign of anyone else yet. The forensics must still be on the road. One of the cops was smoking.

Jake walked up to them.

'Hey, buddy,' the smoker said, 'this is a crime scene. Walk on and get out of here.'

Jake flashed his badge. 'I hope you plan on taking that butt away with you after you finish smoking it. I don't want the scene contaminated.'

The cop reddened.

'I want one of you to block the trail down there near the entrance, and the other to go up to the high-school fence and keep it secure. No one comes in without a badge. And no smoking, no chewing and no stepping on stuff.'

'Yes, sir,' said the cop, and both left for their new posts.

Jake stood where the cops had been. He too had his back to the river. He looked in both directions. The problem was walkers. There were snagged branches, broken-down plants and dropped litter all along the path.

'How popular is this spot?'

'In summer it would be full of kids every night, drinking beer, making out, smoking pot,' said Mills. 'Not so much in winter. But there's joggers and the occasional vagrant. It was a dog walker found the body.'

Jake knew dog people. They walked their animals daily. And dogs tended to have a nose for dead things. This meant the corpse could not have been lying there two or three days. It had been dumped last night. Which meant they had wasted a precious day on Makowski.

Jake swore under his breath.

It bothered him that he was not able to tell which direction the killer had come from; there was too much innocent contamination of the scene. It would be a forensics nightmare.

Now he was facing the river, and he could see her. He felt a tightening of his chest muscles, a burning in his belly. Violent death ages a body, but this one was young. She was probably only just out of her teens. She was slim, with a clear complexion and coffee-coloured skin, and she was showing lots of flesh. She wore a tight leather miniskirt and a vivid pink boob tube. Her shoes intrigued Jake. They were cheap stilettos with clear perspex heels and red synthetic uppers. That and the scanty clothes indicated that she was a sex worker.

She was lying on her back with her head towards the river; her legs, close together, pointed to the trail. Her arms were flung out like she was asking for a hug. She had been dumped rather than laid out carefully. Without moving, he took in the position of the body, the angle it lay at and the trampled grass. He slowed his breathing and tried to put himself into the scene.

You carried her in a fireman's lift.

With every second he could see it more clearly. From the angle that she fell, and the crushed grass where he stood, the killer had come from the left. So, the school.

You had her over your left shoulder, and you went up on your toes and you heaved her off. She fell like that, looking up at you.

Jake could feel the murderer's euphoria as the woman with no eyes looked at him. He felt the joy the murderer would have felt as he saw what he'd done.

You love removing their eyes. You pretend not to, but you get a kick out of it.

But hold it – there was a difference this time. Jake had missed it at first. Only one of the eyeballs was dangling from the socket. The other eye was just an empty hole. There was nothing there. An eyeball was missing.

'Mills?'

He heard the sounds of Mills leaving the path and coming towards him. Then the intake of breath. 'Aw no!'

'You know her?' Jake asked.

'I think so. I mean, the face is virtually gone. But the body, the clothes, the shoes. It looks like Candy.'

'Candy who?'

'Don't know. Probably, her name isn't even Candy. She works the streets. She's a bottom feeder, been hooked on crack since her early teens. I busted her once for soliciting.'

'Her eyeball is missing,' said Jake.

Mills bent and looked. He straightened. 'He's keeping souvenirs now?'

'It's a nice idea, but I don't think so. I think our killer came from the school side, and he carried her. So we'll probably find the eyeball somewhere along the trail.'

'Anything else?' asked Mills sarcastically.

'He's quite strong, slightly below average height, and he's right-handed.'

Jake saw the look on Mills's face, so he explained.

'He carried her over his shoulder from the school, which means he's strong. He stood here.' He indicated the crushed grass. 'And then he heaved her from his shoulder. Look at where she landed. A tall man would have got her further from the path.'

'Whoa,' said Mills. 'You know a lot about this fella.'

'Let's look for the eyeball,' said Jake, ignoring the wary tone in Mills's voice. Was Jake making him uncomfortable?

They walked back towards the broken fence into the high school, moving slowly, shining their torches into the bushes as they went. Before long they heard the rustle of movement, the pitter-patter of scurrying rodent feet. A rat burst out and raced towards the fence. They went to where the rat came from and found the eyeball on the ground. There wasn't much of it left. Several small animals had obviously taken a bite.

Jake didn't flinch as he put on a glove and picked up the eyeball, dropping it into an evidence bag.

'You know, in the Middle East they eat eyeballs,' Mills said. 'Doesn't look so appetizing to me.'

Jake ignored Mills's ham-fisted attempt at lightening the awful scene. A blanket of darkness was descending on him, plunging to the depths of his mind. It was like some of the colour was gone from the world around him. Almost like edges were becoming sharper, and tones muted to black and white.

He shook himself. He needed to get to work, and fast. The darkness, the depression, would simply have to wait. Jake needed help – an outside opinion.

37

Thursday, 1.10 p.m.

Gail smiled when she saw the doughnuts.

'I remembered,' said Jake.

She laughed. It was lunchtime, and Gail had told him she was squeezing this in between clients. Jake sat opposite her at his desk in the detective bureau and poured a coffee. 'Any word on Johnny?'

'It's too early to say. I got him into a programme. He'll have a few individual sessions with me then I'll move him to a group. It will help, but it's too soon to predict how much.'

'Sure,' said Jake with a slow nod.

'He missed his session this morning, but that's typical of patients with schizo-affective disorder.' She tilted her head to the side as she said, 'I'm delighted you care about his welfare.'

'I brought you in to discuss a different case.'

She looked up at the scraps of paper pinned to the wall around Jake's desk. 'The eye-popper. Will he kill again?'

'Almost certainly – unless we can catch him. But . . . I'm drawing a blank on how to go about this.'

She offered him a gentle smile. 'Is that difficult?'

He tried to smile back, but his face felt too tight with irritation and frustration. 'Asking for help? No. The health of my ego can suffer when it comes to the safety of the town.'

She smiled and nodded. For a fleeting moment she even looked impressed. 'You know I'm not an expert on criminal psychology. I'm on the panel because someone in the area has to be.'

'Don't worry,' said Jake. 'What I need is the depth of knowledge a psychologist like you would have. What would be great is if we could look through the files together, bounce ideas around and see if we can't build a profile of our killer. It'll help us eliminate suspects, and also tell us what levers to use when we have someone to interrogate.' Gail looked hesitant so Jake quickly added. 'No pressure. I'm not expecting miracles. The profiling is just one strand of the investigation.'

'OK, Detective. Go ahead.'

Jake had the files on his desk and he laid out the photos of the victims in front of her.

'Oh God,' she said and winced as she saw the mutilated faces. But she didn't turn away. She picked them up one by one and examined them. 'These are three very different women,' she said, 'which isn't typical of a serial killer, as I understand it. They usually stay to type with Caucasian men killing Caucasian women and African-Americans killing African-Americans.'

'That's what I thought. It's not making my life any easier.'

Jake pulled out some other photographs, general shots of the crime scenes and dump scenes. Gail looked at them all carefully, but shook her head. They told her nothing. In twenty minutes he laid out the whole case. He showed her the crime scene reports, the limited forensics, the ME's initial reports. She asked a few questions, but in general let him talk.

At the end they sat and faced each other. The coffees were cold, the doughnuts untouched. There was a silence. Finally Jake said, 'I'll get fresh coffee, then we can get working on trying to make sense of all this.'

When he returned a few minutes later with two steaming cups, Gail was sitting back on her chair, a puzzled look on her face. She had three photographs in front of her, one of each victim. He noticed she had chosen two nicer pictures, Marcia Lamb from a photograph her neighbour and babysitter had given them, and a picture of Belinda Harper taken at a recent charity event. The third photograph was truly horrifying. It was too soon after the discovery of Candy for them to have obtained a similar picture of her.

'What links women of three different ages and three different places in society?' she asked.

Ethnicity links Marcia and Candy,' said Jake. 'And they were both poor.'

'That's not a link,' she said. 'There's a huge difference between a single mother with two jobs, and a sex worker who's living one step above the street. There's more linking Candy and Johnny, than Candy and Marcia.'

He was surprised. 'Is the difference that big?'

She nodded. Then she hesitated and went silent.

'Go on,' he urged.

'It's a bad thought.'

'This is a murder investigation. They're all bad thoughts.'

She looked away from him for a moment, then looked back. 'Have you considered the possibility that Belinda Harper was a user?'

Jake was surprised. No, they hadn't. But he knew that drugs were not unknown among the legal and professional circles in which the Harpers moved. It wasn't crack cocaine they used, but the guys who sold crack sometimes sold the upper-end product too. It was worth checking out. If Belinda had traccs in her blood, they would look for the dealer who supplied both women. Jake doubted that this dealer, if he existed, was a suspect, but any step in any direction had to be worth taking at this point.

'That's an interesting thought. I'll have the ME do a tox screen.' Jake looked at her; she was still thinking. 'There's more,' he prodded.

She nodded. 'You should ask about her sexual history. Anything unusual that might have made her vulnerable.'

Jake didn't mention the accountant Belinda had had an affair with, but the thought stuck. It was another avenue to look into.

Just then the door opened. Sara stuck her head in and scowled. 'Visitor for you,' she said.

38

Thursday, 1.30 p.m.

Jake tried to sound affable when he said, 'I'm in the middle of something, Sara.'

Sara replied with an equally bad version of an apologetic tone: 'Father Ken wants to see you.'

'Can you send him down to Mills or one of the others?'

Gail laid a hand on Jake's arm. 'Give him five minutes. I could use some time to think.'

Jake shrugged. 'OK, Sara.' He quickly gathered up the photographs on the desk and put them back into a folder. 'Send him in.'

Moments later slow footsteps sounded in the hallway. Jake tried not to let his irritation show. Standing, he stretched out a hand. 'Father Ken, how can I help you?'

Broad-shouldered and with a craggy face, the priest looked like a man who had laboured among his flock rather than led them from the library. He couldn't have contrasted more with the priest at the church where Jake's mother had worshipped when he was in his teens.

'I hope you don't mind me imposing,' he began.

'Not at all,' Jake said, the lie making his head pound. 'Take a seat. This is Gail Greene, a psychologist. She's helping with the investigation.'

The priest smiled as he shook her hand. 'Irish or Scottish?' he asked.

'Is the red hair such a giveaway?' she said with a chuckle.

'You know, they say that red hair is dying out; that fifty years from now, it'll be gone,' said Father Ken.

'I'll be grey by then,' she replied.

'What can I do for you, Father?' Jake asked, wondering how affable he sounded now.

'We are organizing an ecumenical service for the victims of this killer. Rabbi Weiss has agreed to take part in the service. We will hold it on Saturday, outside the Church of Christ the Redeemer. That's the old church being knocked down for the interstate. We thought it would be fitting for its last service to be a significant one. Bill Harrington will also help out. He's the Episcopalian minister.'

Jake looked at him blankly. 'Er, that's great, Father. How . . . er . . .'

'We would love it if you and some of the other detectives could attend,' said the priest.

Jake felt his eyebrows knit – he couldn't keep the puzzled look off his face.

'This is for the survivors,' said Father Ken. 'We want to show them that the community is standing shoulder to shoulder with them in this difficult hour.'

'I see your point, Father. I will do my best to be there,' Jake said, taking a half-step towards the door, hoping the priest would get the hint and leave.

'Can you spread the word around the precinct?' Father Ken asked. 'Colonel Asher said—'

'Of course. That goes without saying.' Jake was now actually walking towards the door. The latent, lapsed Catholic in him was mortified that he was almost literally hustling a priest out of the room, but the latent, lapsed Catholic in him was not working a triple homicide.

The priest smiled as he stood up and walked in Jake's wake. 'Bless you. It saddens me that this is last service at the old church before the bulldozers reach her. We'll even have to host it outside, as they've already gutted the inside. Let's hope it's not *too* cold, eh?'

'Yes,' said Jake, not giving him any more than that. It was all he could do to not wrench the door open and let the gesture speak for him. But the priest was receiving the message, offering Jake a surprisingly strong handshake before shuffling from the room.

Jake blew out a deep breath as he let the door close behind Father Ken. When he turned back, he could see Gail's raised eyebrow.

'Will that throw your weekend plans?' she asked.

'I shouldn't think so,' he replied.

She grinned. 'Of course not. You wouldn't be caught dead going to that service. Am I right?'

He laughed and felt the rubber band of tension lift a little. 'You're good.'

'You don't need to be a profiler to see you aren't the sort of person to let anyone into your head. Least of all God.'

Jake didn't answer.

Gail winced. 'I've said too much.'

'Maybe.' She was right about Jake not wanting people in his head, especially a smart shrink.

'But can I offer a word of advice?' she asked. Jake motioned for her to go ahead. 'You might consider going along to this church thing. The killer could be there. It will be a chance to glory in the chaos he's created.'

Jake sat back in his chair. He knew she could be right, but somehow it didn't fit. 'This guy has a short cooling-off period. He glories in the chaos by committing new ones,' he said. 'It's . . . his *work*, and he wants to continue it.'

'True. But I'll bet my diploma he'll be there. Or that he'll insinuate himself into the investigation in some way. Serial killers are normally cop-lovers.'

Jake leaned forward and forced a smile. 'Case closed,' he said. 'We arrest Colonel Asher right now.'

The soft tinkle of her laughter prompted a hazy, indistinct memory of sharing a moment like this with Leigh. Remembering this made them feel even further back in his past than they were.

He went back to the files. 'Serials are normally meticulous and organized, or frenzied and disorganized . . .' he prompted.

'From what I have seen, you're dealing with an organized killer,' she replied.

Jake groaned inwardly. An organized killer was, by nature, difficult to track down. An organized killer accounted for the possibility of making mistakes – accordingly, he tended to make fewer of them.

'His choice of victims doesn't seem opportunistic,' Gail continued. 'The one thing his victims do have in common is that they are women. He's targeting them. He approached Marcia Lamb just as she was nearing home. He attacked Belinda Harper in her home. The last victim, Candy, was a prostitute. My guess is that he picked her up on the street, posing as a john. She would have gone with him without a protest.'

'Probably his easiest kill,' said Jake, his impotence reflected in the lazy burn from the ulcer he had almost managed to forget until Father Ken had come calling.

'On the surface,' said Gail, 'he will appear to be a normal man, leading a mundane life. He'll have a job, friends, a certain status in the community. It wouldn't surprise me if he's married.'

Jake was surprised. 'A family man?'

'He might have a wife, but there will be difficulties in the marriage. At the very least a coldness.'

'That's every married man in Littleton,' said Jake.

Gail shot Jake a look.

He reddened a little. He'd given away too much and he wanted to get the subject off himself. 'His MO is very distinctive.'

'Yes, but MO doesn't tell us much. When we consider the minds of evil men, the signature is far more important. The MO is only how he *carries out* the attacks. It's a system he has that works for him. It meets no needs but the practical one of securing his victim. He approaches her in a friendly and non-threatening way. That gets him to where he wants to be. But we have to ask, what makes these crimes unique?'

She opened the folder that Jake had closed before the priest's visit. She looked at the face of the first victim, Marcia Lamb. When Gail spoke, there was a sense of urgency to her voice.

'I think it's what he does to the head. The mouth is crushed. That's not his MO. That's his essence, his signature. Is he trying to *silence* the women? Does the talk of women offend him, or belittle him?'

'And the eyes . . .' said Jake.

'The eyes are just a by-product,' Gail replied. Answering Jake's quizzical look, she continued: 'They don't mean anything to him. In the last murder one of the eyeballs was lost, and he didn't spot that. He didn't really care. The *mouth* is the signature.'

Jake nodded, thinking. It was certainly interesting stuff, but would it get him any closer to his killer?

'So what are we looking for?' he asked.

She began ticking points off on her fingers. 'One, he's not a hobo or a street person. He holds down a job and contributes to society. Two, he may be married, but not happily. Three, he's not a young man.'

Jake looked surprised.

'Young men tend to be sexually immature and are afraid to handle an adult woman. So they normally attack either prepubescent girls or the elderly. A man in his early twenties, especially a virgin or a sexually inexperienced man, would not attack someone like Marcia Lamb or Belinda Harper. And he certainly wouldn't have approached a prostitute on a street corner. You're looking for a man in his late thirties at the youngest. A man who thinks he knows the world, and doesn't like it very much.'

'Anything else?'

'His choice of victims is a little unusual.'

'They have nothing in common,' said Jake.

'Not quite true,' said Gail. 'Not only were they all women, but in their own way they were all *strong* women. Even Candy had street smarts. Why might he be angry with strong women?'

Jake was interested in this new line of thought.

'You'll find his father was a distant figure, and his mother overbearing. His father may well have abandoned the family, and he blames his mother for that.'

'Impressive,' he said.

'Thanks.' She blushed and looked away for a second. 'You're not totally useless yourself. How do you know about profiling?'

'We watch the TV shows like everyone else.'

But Gail Greene was not buying it. 'Spill,' she said. 'There's more.'

Now it was Jake's turn to feel uncomfortable. 'It's just . . . something I have a bit of a . . .'

'What?' she said, stepping towards him. 'A talent for?'

'You could say that.' He was hoping that would be the end of the matter, but when he realized she was neither going to blink nor avert her questioning gaze, he elaborated: 'I see things. When I am at a crime scene, I can walk through the scene as if I'm there, as if I'm the killer. I see through his eyes – or what I imagine are his eyes.'

Gail looked at him like he was a subject in a particularly intriguing lecture. Jake didn't like that. 'That's interesting.'

'You think I'm a freak?'

'It's called dissociation. You can get out of your own mind and see things in a new way. It's not a problem, as long as you are in control of it. If you dissociate deliberately, at will, it's a useful tool. But if it happens automatically, then you could be heading for trouble.'

There was an edge in her voice. Jake didn't answer.

She reached into her wallet and took out a business card. She scribbled a number on the back.

'Here's my home number. Anything I can help on, just call.'

As Jake took the card their fingers touched. For a moment he felt a tingle. This was getting dangerous. He was flirting with a woman, and he had got her number.

I need to focus.

39

Friday, 16 December, 9 a.m.

It couldn't be put off any longer. Jake had to drive into Indianapolis to see the lab people and see if he could get them to speed up.

The reception area was small, sparse and functional. There was a big desk and double swing doors to the left. He walked up to the desk. A big man in his twenties looked up.

Jake flashed his badge. 'Detective Austin, Littleton PD. I'm here to talk about the forensics on our triple homicide.'

'The Christmas Killer? That's a bad one,' said the desk guy. 'Have you got an appointment?'

Jake couldn't believe it. This was a crime investigation, not a trip to a hair salon. He had spent ninety minutes behind the wheel in bumper-to-bumper holiday traffic. Shoppers every-fucking-where. He had driven in circles for the last ten minutes just to find a parking spot. It was a real pisser of a journey, a reminder of why he had left Chicago for small-town policing. He wasn't about to see the rest of the morning go that way.

'Of course I haven't made an appointment,' he said. 'I just need to speak to someone who's working the forensics for us. Through here, is it?'

Jake made to walk through the heavy swing doors, but the receptionist was on his feet fast. 'No one is allowed through there,' he said, blocking Jake's path. 'If you call ahead, you can make an appointment and come back later, or tomorrow.'

There was something about the guy's arrogance. Jake knew the type and what he was trying to prove. 'New here? Or are you just a temp?'

The man pursed his lips. Angry and not fond of being talked down to, but undecided on whether messing with a detective, even one from a small town, could cost him his goal of long-term fixed employment.

Jake pressed home the advantage: 'Three people are dead; we have a killer on the loose, and I am going to talk to the forensic investigators.'

The guy held up a hand but Jake glared at him, and he dropped it.

'I'll call my supervisor,' he mumbled.

'I'd appreciate that.' Jake kept an eye on the fellow as he made the call.

A few minutes later the big doors swung open. A slight woman in her fifties walked through and smiled at Jake.

'Detective?' She reached forward and shook his hand. He scanned her quickly: short brown hair to her shoulders, straight. Glasses. Neat blouse under the white lab coat, and a single strand of pearls. Probably farmed. He smiled back, glancing at her name tag.

'Ms Zatkin. Jake Austin, Littleton PD.'

'Dr Zatkin,' she corrected. 'But everyone calls me Ronnie. We spoke on the phone yesterday. You're here about the Christmas Killer?'

'I don't like to call him that, but yes.'

'What a sad business. You'd better come through. Peter, the door.'

Sulking, the man behind the desk pressed a buzzer that opened the swing doors, and Jake followed Ronnie through. She led him down a corridor and into a small office. He saw the door plaque: DR ZATKIN, DEPARTMENT HEAD.

'Sit down.' She immediately began fussing with a small machine. 'Can I get you a coffee?'

'I'm fine, thanks.'

'Nonsense. You've driven all the way over. How's everyone back in Littleton?'

'You know the place?'

'I was raised there.'

'Everyone's on edge,' Jake told her. 'We're trying to catch a killer.'

She caught his tone and became more businesslike. She sat down at her desk opposite him. 'It's not an easy case. Messy forensics. The site yesterday had plenty of contamination, most of it from before the body was dumped. But it all has to go through the sieve. It takes time.'

'I appreciate that. But Monday's—'

'We've had a few days with Marcia Lamb and Belinda Harper. But then we've had a drowning, two drug-related deaths, one homicide, and that asylum business over in Springfield. Frankly, we're swamped.'

'Springfield is a cold case. Cold. With skeletons. Our guy is still killing. It should take priority over—'

'You *do* have priority, I can assure you. But we have to devote some time to each case as it comes in. We can't just put Springfield on the back burner. There were two children killed, after all.'

Jake had sympathy but he also had limited time. 'Ronnie, I need *something*,' he said. 'I'm chasing a guy who's killed three people in five days. Technically, he's not even a serial killer – he's on a killing *spree*.'

The doctor sighed, then opened one of the folders on the desk. 'I can tell you a little about the murder weapon,' she offered. 'Someone suggested that the injuries might be crush injuries.'

'That was me,' Jake said.

'So it was. Very good.' She beamed. 'But it's not as simple as that. Very specific pressures were applied to two points on the head, resulting in radiating fracture wounds to the skull. The pressures eventually led to the structural collapse of the front of the skull, resulting in teeth falling out and the eyeballs protruding.'

'Like a vice?'

'Not exactly. But that's in the ballpark. The pressure was applied to the top of the skull and the chin, and it was steady and cumulative. My guess, and I admit this is a bit left field, is an archaic device, some kind of a turning screw, slowly pushing the skull down until it bulged out and cracked. It would have caused the victims excruciating pain. The way we see it, the pressure would have caused the jaw to distort first, loosening the teeth. Eventually, as the squeeze became more severe, the jaw would clamp and the teeth would have nowhere to go.'

Jake tried not to think about what these women went through.

Dr Zatkin drew in a deep breath as she continued. 'The pressure would have increased, crushing the front of the face together. But the main structure of the cranium would still have survived, so the victim would have probably been conscious right through this process.'

Jake rubbed his temples.

'Eventually the orbital sockets cracked, and the eyeballs were pushed out by the pressure. At that point the pain would have probably caused the victim to pass out.'

'Fuck,' said Jake. 'Sorry.'

Dr Zatkin waved away his apology. 'Blood loss would have been significant but not catastrophic. Preliminary conclusion is that death was caused by asphyxiation, due to severe damage to the airways.'

She paused for a moment to flick through the file. 'I can't tell you what it looks like, but logic tells me the device is portable, though it must be big. I can tell you that once you find it, you'll know you've found it. And you'll have your killer.'

Jake nodded, still massaging his head as he wondered where a man might purchase an archaic torture device.

40

Friday, 11 a.m.

Jake wanted to take the report away with him, but Dr Zatkin filed it in one of the grey drawers behind her deck instead.

'The team are still working on it – you'll get the full and final version,' she promised. 'We're throwing everything at this. But the rest of the forensics aren't giving us much. The guy isn't raping the victims, and that means we are left with almost no physical evidence to work from.'

'I'm getting nowhere,' he said. 'Every suspect has had to be discounted. We've no witnesses. I can't find any connection between the three victims. He's killed three times in five days, and we're on the starting square waiting to throw a six. I was banking on forensics to give me a direction. Give me a lead I can chase, anything . . .'

She shrugged. 'I can't give you what I haven't got.'

As she escorted him from the building, Jake decided to get one more thing off his chest.

'Ronnie, can I ask you something?' When she nodded, he made a slight show of looking left and right – her ears only. Conspiratorial. 'It'd harm the investigation if the press got hold of details we wanted to keep quiet.'

She looked at him. He could see the frown and knew that he was stepping close to a line now. No one likes their unit to come under criticism from outside.

'The press know about the teeth,' he said by way of explanation. Softening the accusation, he added, 'They also know that two of the victims were killed in their homes, which didn't come from here. But I'm seeing all these reports in the papers, and their dumb headlines about the Christmas Killer, like he's some boogeyman made of smoke. It's obstructive – it puts the public at greater risk.'

The doctor frowned. 'We have a big staff. Almost thirty, if you include janitors, night staff and admin. And they all have family and friends. I suppose there could be some loose talk. I'll look into it.'

'This is more than loose talk. Someone is selling information, and—'

'As I said, I'll look into it.' Her voice was hard. 'I will tell my staff to be extra-vigilant, and I will make it clear that this is a disciplinary matter.'

'Thanks.' He smiled.

'Have you considered that you might *want* the press on board?' she asked, her voice softer. 'You could use them.'

Jake hated to admit it, but she was right: maybe an appeal for information would throw up the lead he was looking for. But that meant dealing with reporters. And after Chicago . . . after Adam Banks . . .

Jake blinked away the thoughts that were clawing at his mind. He extended a hand for Dr Zatkin to shake, turning away and trying not to dwell on a name and a face he had not allowed back into his mind for quite some time.

41

Saturday, 17 December, 11.25 a.m.

Jake arrived at the Church of Christ the Redeemer late. He was freezing cold on the outside, but boiling hot inside, with Leigh's parting shot ringing in his ears.

'Not even a Saturday dad,' she had said before slamming the front door behind him.

She's right.

In part the fight had been caused because Leigh had wanted to attend the service, but Jake had wanted her to stay at home. If Gail was right about the killer showing up there, he couldn't allow his family to be on display.

Mills was already there, mingling with the crowd. He was trying to look inconspicuous but failing miserably. A cop was a cop and couldn't conceal the fact. The size, the regulation haircut, the jacket and tie, the walk and posture were all giveaways. People saw Mills and moved along. Unless they wanted to pester him about the developments in the Christmas Killer case. Jake bit back a scowl when reminded of the sensationalist nickname.

Now Mills was ambling up to Jake, a goofy grin on

his face that was intended to obscure the seriousness of his words. 'If the shrink is right about him being here, I sure as hell can't see him.'

Mills was right. The only way they could have got anything useful out of the service was if they had had enough warning to set up a sting operation. If they had got a volunteer task force together to police the event, the odds were high that the killer would have been one of the volunteers. It had happened before. Jake figured they could maybe try something like that on the one-month 'anniversary' of the first kill, if they hadn't made an arrest by then.

He tried not to think about how many victims this guy would have racked up if they had to wait *that* long.

Asher was there, in a three-piece business suit. His bulk and his thick neck meant that he didn't look especially dignified. In fact, he looked more out of place than anyone. *If chief of police was an elected post, Asher would have struggled*, Jake thought.

Harper, on the other hand, was looking if not immaculate then pretty good in his dark suit. His tie was a discreet maroon, and his regulation pale shirt matched his complexion. Although Jake noticed that his hair was not perfectly groomed – some of it stuck out at an angle – his shave was close as the cut on an Augusta green. The combination of untamed hair yet effort with the razor gave him the right look for a grieving widower. It was sick, but Jake knew that if Harper performed well today and at the funeral, he was a shoo-in for mayor.

Jake scanned the crowd. Although it was thirty minutes to the start of the noon service, several hundred people were already there. Many had gone into the old church, which had been opened for the occasion. Some were lighting candles. Others were kneeling at the abandoned altar. He didn't know who he was looking for.

He was aware of a shadow looming to his left and turned to see the smiling face of Father Ken.

'I am glad to see you could make it, Detective,' he said.

'I wouldn't have missed it,' Jake lied. He could see Asher, beckoning him over to the PD podium at which he stood. Jake offered Father Ken a nod that was half an apology for stepping away and half an unspoken commitment that they would continue their pleasantries later on.

Jake approached Asher. 'Let's get started,' said Asher, aiming his mouth away from the array of microphones bearing the logos of local radio stations and television affiliates. The podium had been set up outside the large ornate wooden door of the old church. With so many community representatives and press in attendance, Asher had decided to hold an impromptu press conference. Jake hoped that the press would be more respectful standing outside a church, but then he remembered the bedlam at the construction site on the day they discovered Marcia Lamb's corpse and found himself not very hopeful at all.

'I want you two square behind me,' Asher said to Jake and Mills.

Jake winced. 'Sir, I think—'

'I don't care what you think,' Asher interrupted. 'You two are the lead investigators on this case, and you stand here so that the whole community can see you. This is as much about calming people as it is about appealing for fresh witnesses.'

Jake had to concede the colonel had a point.

'I'll be letting out some information,' Asher continued, 'but the eyeballs – I don't want any mention of them.'

Jake nodded.

'Any theory on why the third victim wasn't killed in her home?' Asher pressed as if the question had just occurred to him.

Jake barely paused to think; it was a question he had already considered. 'Candy didn't live alone. Too risky for him. A roommate is an unknown variable – not only a potential witness, were she to return unexpectedly, but someone else he would have to kill in order to preserve his own freedom. Such a scenario opens up the possibility of mistakes, which is not our guy's style. So he doesn't take the risk – he does it outside. One time. I'd expect him to go back to the established pattern next. Invading their space seems to be part of his signature.'

The colonel made a strange gesture with his head and shoulders – like he was trying to shrug, but the sheer awfulness of Jake's scenario had drained him of the energy to complete even that basic gesture.

'I am going to say we are following several strong leads and have identified a number of potential suspects. It's a lie, but it will buy us some more time.'

As Asher turned to the podium, Jake reached for his sleeve. An unprecedented gesture, one that Asher may not have experienced since at least three promotions ago, but Jake's instincts were tingling. He had an idea. 'One suspect, Colonel. We have one suspect. Let's put this prick under pressure,' he hissed. Asher nodded grimly. Message received.

Jake half-turned to let his eyes rove over the crowd gathering in the narrow shadow of the podium. Was his target among them? *Let's see how you react when you think we're on your tail.*

The press corps had swollen considerably over the past few days. Now all the major regional papers had their own people in Littleton. Some of the nationals too. The work for stringers was drying up. All the news channels had their own OB units in place, big trucks with logos and banks of satellite dishes and aerials. He had heard rumours that several foreign correspondents were in Littleton.

Under FBI classification rules the Christmas Killer was still a 'spree' rather than a 'serial' murderer. A 'cooling-off period' followed by another kill would muddy the categorizing a little, but Jake was beyond caring about labels. Spree, serial or mass – his target was a highly dangerous and evil individual. And he needed to be stopped.

Jake distracted himself by eyeing the throng of reporters. He found himself looking for one face in particular, a face he could not decide if he wanted to see or not. His former best friend, Adam Banks, a Chicago-based journalist, should be here somewhere. But Jake couldn't see him. Good – he didn't want to pick at that sore again. Banks was the one blemish on a perfect record.

Chuck Ford was here, of course. He was looking a little grubby beside the big hitters, but his face had the eager furtiveness of a rat scavenging for carrion. Clearly, his plan was to stay on top of this story at all costs.

By now the colonel was reading out his prepared statement, and Jake was only half-listening. He knew the drill – a few words about the victims, then an appeal for help. Asher would dwell on Marcia Lamb because of her child, and on Belinda Harper, whose grieving husband was at the service. He was going to skip over Candy for a variety of reasons.

Jake felt a twinge of guilt and rage when this thought blew through his mind, a brief flash of a need to get justice for Candy more than the other two women. A strange, barely articulated conviction that in death – especially the humiliating, inglorious kind suffered by Candy and Belinda and Marcia – there should be no hierarchy.

'We believe we know who the killer is,' Asher was saying, 'but knowing it and proving it are different things. We are appealing to the public to help us give this killer the needle, as he deserves. Someone knows something. Someone has seen something. You might not realize it now, but some small thing you saw on the night of any of these three killings might be the final piece of information we need to make our case. Please come forward, in complete confidence. We are all on the same side. We need to make our streets and our homes – our community – safe. As it should be.'

It was four minutes to twelve, and nearly time for the start of the service. There would be no time for questions.

Chuck Ford had thrust himself to the front of the pack. His arm was raised, his face a frozen mask of righteous anger that probably wasn't genuine. 'You've identified a suspect?'

Asher looked a little startled because of the way the question had been bellowed at him. He turned and looked at the clock on the steeple of the church. He had time to answer Ford's question. He looked at Jake, who tried to shake his head without shaking his head.

Asher turned back to Ford. 'We have an idea who we are looking for, yes,' he said. 'That is all I'm willing to say at this point.'

You should have given him nothing.

'Should the people of Littleton – the citizens of

Indiana – be feeling like prisoners in their own homes? It's Christmas, Colonel!'

To his credit, Asher maintained his cool. 'There is no need to panic. The usual precautions that people would observe should also apply in this case. Don't accept lifts from strangers, don't let them into your homes, don't give out personal details.'

It was a platitude, and it wasn't convincing. Jake wished that Asher would utilize the tried and tested 'No comment.'

'Are we safe?' demanded Ford. 'Yes or no?'

Asher hardened. 'I've already answered your question, Mr Ford. Any more questions?' He looked up, trying to make eye contact with literally any of the other reporters.

But Ford wasn't going to let go of the bone. 'He's killed three times; he's left three crime scenes. You have plenty to go on and you claim you have a suspect. Why isn't the Christmas Killer in custody yet, Colonel?'

Jake could see Asher's fists balling. 'We have a city-wide task force working the investigation. Leads are being followed, suspects tracked. Rest assured, the full resources of—'

'*Suspects?* So now there are more than one?'

'Er . . .' Suddenly Asher looked like a drowning animal. Jake could have killed Asher for saying too much.

'If you can't handle this, why has the FBI not been called in?' Ford went on.

Jake knew the answer: no police department,

however out of its depth, wanted to give up jurisdiction over a high-profile case and admit it was beyond them. Besides, there was no federal aspect to this particular case. It had not crossed state lines, and unless the governor specifically requested it, the FBI could be no more than consultants. But Jake knew there was no way to explain that to a pack of rabid journalists without giving them ample opportunity to paint Littleton PD as glory hunters putting the public at risk rather than calling in the big guns.

Asher gritted his teeth while the other reporters took notes and snapped photographs. Jake feared for the fellow's mood when the morning papers arrived, showing his harassed face beneath less-than-flattering headlines.

Ford was not finished. 'Why is the case not being handled by an experienced Littleton officer? I understand the lead detective has only been in the city a few weeks.'

Jake felt it like a knee in the guts. He stepped forward and took a spot next to Asher at the podium. He glared down at Ford, now only a foot or two away.

'We are doing the best that we can,' said Jake, keeping himself from snarling. 'We know this town; we know how to investigate a murder. We'll find this guy.'

'That's not very reassuring for the people of Littleton. Don't you think that it's time to call in the *experts*?' said Ford.

'We are the experts,' said Jake.

'You're an outsider,' said Ford. 'Maybe a few bodies here and there is acceptable back in Chicago. Maybe you let them build up before you do anything. But here in Littleton we value human life—'

A wave of something dark fell over Jake. He couldn't stop it. He took half a step forward, his shoulders squaring.

'Austin!' shouted Asher.

Jake managed to rein himself in.

Ford stepped back and then feigned a stumble. He threw his arms out and fell into the crowd of journalists.

'Don't hit me!' he shouted at Jake. The cameras flashed, and Jake felt rough hands hauling him back. Mills and Asher had rushed forward. The colonel's face was in his, screaming admonishments that Jake's raging brain could not decipher. The only thing he was aware of was the sly grin on Ford's face as other reporters helped him to his feet.

'What the fuck was that about?' Asher yelled, pushing Jake back towards the podium.

Uniforms swarmed the makeshift stage, blocking Jake from photographers desperate to get a shot of the lunatic cop. Jake didn't care. He was letting his body go limp, against the commands of his mind, which urged him to fight off Asher and Mills, then charge at Ford and give him what was coming to him. But the two cops held him tight even though they didn't need to. And this just made him hotter and angrier.

They took him around the side of the church, and more uniforms stepped in. Jake shoved Asher away from him. 'I'm all right.'

'You are not all right!' shouted Asher. 'Attacking reporters? What the hell's the matter with you?'

'I didn't touch that asshole. But I should have. I should have taken a good swing at him, knocked his fucking teeth down his throat.'

'Snap out of it,' said Asher, and he held Jake to the wall by his shoulder. 'I know you didn't touch him but it's not the point. You lost it. You went for him.'

'He goaded me. He made it personal.'

'I don't care,' said Asher.

Jake took some deep breaths. 'How did he know about me? Who told him I was from Chicago? Where does he get off, questioning my professionalism?'

'I think you proved his point on that one,' said Asher. He relaxed his hold and Jake slumped forward, panting.

'Austin, I hate journalists as much as you do.' Asher spoke more softly now. 'There's not an ounce of integrity among them. But we can't shout at them, and we can't make threatening gestures at them, especially when the cameras are pointed right at us.' Asher looked around as if to check no one was listening, then he lowered his voice even more. 'We took you on because we believed your story about what happened in Chicago. We took you on despite the charges.'

Jake narrowed his eyes. 'They were dropped.'

'Dropped or not, we took you on because we figured the affray was a one-time thing.'

'He—' Jake started.

Asher held up a hand to stop him. Apparently Asher wasn't interested in excuses. 'There are people who want me to bring in the FBI. And you just gave them the ammunition they need.'

'We can handle this as well as the FBI,' said Jake. It dawned on him how badly he'd just fucked up.

'We mightn't get the chance,' said Asher. 'First, you're going to apologize to Ford. Publicly.'

Jake said nothing.

'Then,' said Asher, 'I'm going to let the press know that you are taking anger management sessions with the department shrink.' Jake's head snapped up at that. 'That will not be a line, Detective. You'll start the sessions on Monday morning. Understood?'

Jake nodded. He was too angry to say anything. He'd lost control, and right now there was no way of knowing what damage it had done to the case. He had removed himself from his own subtle surveillance operation. If the killer was among the crowd, there was no way that Jake would know because he had been too busy measuring his dick against Chuck Ford's – letting that asshole sucker him into making a fool of himself.

Had Jake cost himself and his department what might have been their best chance at latching on to the killer?

42

Saturday, 4 p.m.

This was his quiet place, his sanctuary. Here he felt safe. He could let down his defences and be himself, who he truly was. There was no need to pretend in this room.

The television was on, a sitcom he was half-watching as he prepared for his work. An episode cynically centred on the season, but the gravest concern of the lead character – a hapless single father – was whether he would have time to travel from New York to Connecticut in order to buy his brat of a daughter the 'special' doll she had demanded.

Disgusting . . .

He was surrounded by the instruments of his trade. Most of them he would never need to utilize, but those who had come before him had used them. Some looked positively frightening, with straps, clamps and restraints.

The piece he was cleaning now had been invented in 1542 by an English witchfinder. That made it a bit unusual, as most of the instruments had been devised by the Spanish Inquisition. It was a big, cumbersome device, awkward to carry, but one man could just manage it. And it fitted into the back of his car.

The head crusher was ingenious. It was a frame about two by three feet, with a helmet in the middle. Under the helmet was a chin strap. He could move the helmet up and down by turning the screws. It could be slowly tightened until the skull began to deform under the pressure. It had built-in manacles to restrain the wrists, so that the victim had no escape from the fate they deserved, but he didn't use them; he bound their hands himself.

It was a squeeze to get the helmet over a modern head. The device was four centuries old, and people had been smaller back then. But once it was on, all he needed was a few turns of the screw.

But he needed to clean it after every use. Heads tended to bleed, and the blood dried on the mechanism, making it difficult to turn.

And there were the clumps of hair.

The news came on, so he put aside the crusher for a few minutes and brought up the sound. The first item was the three murders. He watched the flickering images of the police chief, Asher, making an appeal for witnesses to come forward. The colonel was staring directly into the camera and talking about having identified a suspect. That wasn't true. They were completely in the dark.

You would have told me if they were on to us.

Behind Asher were the two investigating detectives. One had a goofy look, while the other just looked uncomfortable. He peered more closely at the screen. He had seen this man before.

But where?

Then it was back to the anchor in the studio.

'That was Sally Hallbrook reporting from the press conference outside the Church of Christ the Redeemer in Littleton, Indiana, where the Christmas Killer has already claimed three victims.'

The Christmas Killer? Yet more tarnishing of the season.

The voice on the television continued: 'There were dramatic scenes after the press conference, when one of the detectives, Jake Austin, appeared to attack a reporter and knock him to the ground. Back to Sally Hallbrook in Littleton to tell us more.'

The screen switched to the end of the press conference. There was that detective again, who appeared to lunge suddenly towards one of the hacks. There was a snarl of anger on his face.

I do *know him . . . of course I do . . .*

He had seen that snarl, but it had been so many years ago. The face had changed, but he could see how the basic features were unaltered.

Who would have thought it?

He straightened the head crusher and used it to haul himself up from the floor.

And now I know who should be next . . .

43

Sunday, 18 December, 7.30 p.m.

The lights were subdued, and gentle violin music wafted softly over Jake and Leigh. They were in a small Italian restaurant, a bottle of red wine on the table between them, and subdued conversation all around them. A murderer was on the loose, and while the locals were trying to get on with their lives, it was clear that until the killer was caught, the general atmosphere in Littleton was going to be tense.

La Dolce Vita might or might not have been the best restaurant in town; Jake didn't know. All he knew was that they had gone there the first week they had arrived, and it had been good. He would have preferred a steak house and a twenty-ounce sirloin, but tonight was about spoiling Leigh.

His chicken cacciatore was tasty, and there was plenty of it. Leigh had opted for langoustines al pomodoro. It sounded good, until he realized that it was just a fancy name for small lobsters in tomato sauce.

'Fish in ketchup – I could have cooked you that at home,' he said.

'Yes, and left all the pots for me to clean up afterwards,' she replied.

He was able to forget that there was a killer at large, that he had almost punched another journalist and eaten humble pie, that he was getting up early on Monday to meet a therapist that he was trying to deny he was attracted to. He was able to focus on his gorgeous wife. And she *was* gorgeous tonight. The soft candlelight caught her golden hair, and her eyes sparkled. Being away from the baby for a while seemed to have lifted a decade from her face.

'You could pass for a college senior,' he said.

'You're not so bad yourself – in this light you could pass for forty,' she replied. Over dessert and her third glass of wine Leigh was loosening up. She'd even stopped calling home to check on the kids, who were being watched by Melissa, a niece of Mills. In fact, a smile had been on her face all day, ever since three generations of family had finally banded together to put up the Christmas tree. It had been fun – Jake's mom remembering past Christmases, his daughter forgetting to be sullen.

Things were feeling *normal* – just for a day.

'I didn't always love wine, you know,' Leigh said now. 'When I was five I took a sip from my mother's glass and spat it out on the table.'

Jake laughed. 'Five? You started early!'

'What were you like when you were five? I bet you were an angel,' she said with a wink.

He nodded in agreement. 'Perfect from birth.'

'Come on. Everyone has something to say about their childhood. You never talk about yours.'

That one came from left field, but Jake paused and gave it some consideration. 'We travelled a lot,' he said finally.

'I'd love to be able to talk to your mother about it,' Leigh said, her voice sounding sad. 'What was she like?'

Jake noticed. Leigh had asked, what *was* his mom like? No real emphasis on the past tense, but her meaning was clear. In their house now was the relic of the woman who had raised him. Leigh was asking what the *real* woman had been like, before the dementia. Unfortunately, it was a question Jake couldn't answer.

'It's weird, but I don't have that many clear memories of my childhood,' he said. 'I have some, but I don't know whether they're real or not.'

Leigh looked at him, her head cocked to one side. 'You must be able to remember something.'

He went on: 'You know the scar I have on my right hand?' He showed her a white mark near his index finger. 'I have no idea where it came from. For as long as I remember, it was just there. I can't even guess. How's that for weird?'

Leigh smiled. 'Most of us don't remember a lot before we were five,' she assured him.

'I don't remember a lot after five either,' Jake said. 'I don't know who my father is, or what he was like. Most of my real memories start around junior high. Before that it's just images and flashes. None of them have ever made sense.'

'You probably remember more than you think,' said Leigh. 'Maybe you could bring it up with the therapist.'

Jake wanted to tell her that he was not seeing a therapist; he was merely following department procedure after an incident. But he didn't want to talk about Gail. Something stirred in him when he thought about her.

Just then Leigh's phone rang and she rolled her eyes. 'No one ever calls me, and the one time they do . . .' Leigh reached into her purse and took it out. She looked at the number on the screen and her smile froze. 'It's home.'

Jake told himself that Melissa was probably asking where the baby formula was, but that didn't feel right. He leaned forward to listen in as she took the call, his heart rate rising.

Leigh went pale.

'We'll be right there,' she said, standing up.

44
Sunday, 9 p.m.

The fireworks were over when they got home, but the babysitter was still upset. Faith was standing almost rigid with catatonic fury. Baby Jakey was crying, and Jeanette was blissfully unaware, watching a repeat of *Desperate Housewives*, although most of the screen was now obscured by a collapsed Christmas tree.

The room was a teddy bear bloodbath. White balls of fluff were everywhere, and heads and limbs were scattered. It was carnage. Jake winced when he stepped on a pink bear ripped up the middle from crotch to neck. There was a severed head on the table, impaled on scissors. He knew the head. It belonged to a teddy bear that had been given to him by the guys in Chicago.

Leigh initially recoiled, then stepped forward and screamed at Faith, 'What have you done?'

Not knowing what else to do, Jake got out his wallet, pulled out a fifty and gave it to Melissa. It was twenty more than they had agreed, but he shoved it into her hand. She was sobbing slightly.

'I'm sorry, Mr Austin. I couldn't stop her,' she said.

'Don't worry. I'll take care of it.' And the babysitter scuttled out of the door.

Faith ran up the stairs, her hands covering her face. Leigh stood in the middle of the room, screaming up at her. Jeanette was turning up the volume on the television until the noise felt like it was crawling into Jake's skull. He could feel the headache and the ulcer beginning again. This was nuts. Right and wrong could be discussed later. He needed to bring order to his house.

He took the remote from his mom and killed the sound, just leaving the flickering images, which he unveiled by standing the Christmas tree back up. Then he took Leigh gently by the shoulders and guided her to the sofa.

'I'll bring Faith back down. We need to talk this through, but you need to get a grip on yourself first. OK, honey?'

Faith had locked herself in her room, but a sharp rap on the door brought her out. Her face was red and there were tears running down her cheeks. Jake felt a stab of sympathy for his daughter and placed an arm around her shoulder. Then he remembered all the toys, now torn rags littering the living room.

'You're in trouble,' he said in a level voice.

His daughter followed him back to the living room. Leigh had Jakey in her arms, and he had stopped crying. She was already tidying the mess while she cradled the baby. The practicality of his wife often took Jake by surprise.

Faith stood at the bottom of the stairs, looking at the ground.

Leigh glared at her. 'What's all this about, young lady?'

'I don't know,' muttered Faith.

'Something must have triggered this,' said Jake. Then he softened his tone. 'Something had to upset you – make you mad.'

'I don't know. Jakey was screaming and he wouldn't stop. Grandma was being as stupid as usual. I was trying to play with a doll, and it broke. And then I . . . just got angry.'

At that moment Jake's mother stood and came over. She had a beautiful, peaceful smile on her face. She put a hand on Faith's shoulder.

Faith brushed her hand away brusquely. She glared at her parents. 'See?!'

'You've destroyed all of Baby Jakey's things. Why?' Leigh asked again.

'I don't know!' wailed Faith.

This was going nowhere, and there would soon be tears all round again. Jake intervened. 'Go up to your room, and we'll discuss your punishment in the morning,' he said.

Faith turned and ran up the stairs.

Jake helped with the tidying, and within a few minutes the room looked normal again. They found one teddy that was undamaged, and Leigh settled Jakey in his cot with it. Then she sat beside Jake.

'What will we do?'

'We can get new ones. He's so young, he doesn't even know what he's missing.'

'That's not what I meant,' said Leigh. Jake knew. He knew they had to talk about what had happened.

'I hate to keep saying it,' said Leigh, 'but the strain of your mother changing every day . . . on top of the move and the new baby . . . it's all getting to her. It's getting to all of us. I've been trying to warn you.'

'We need to stamp this behaviour out right now,' said Jake. The curse of being a cop was that you knew too much. He had seen this before: destructive behaviour in childhood leading to something worse. It worried him on a professional level. And he knew from experience a cop's professional eye should never be turned on his family.

Nothing good could come of that.

'We have to punish Faith severely over this,' he said. 'Let her know how seriously she has stepped out of line. We'll ground her for a month. We won't let her friends over, and we'll take her phone. And she has to replace the bears out of her allowance.'

'That's a bit severe,' said Leigh, seeming genuinely surprised at what he proposed. 'She's only twelve.'

'Doesn't mean she's not old enough to know better.'

What he didn't say was his biggest fear. That the psychological quirks of his family, the strange way of looking at the world, had not skipped a generation, as he had hoped.

Had it taken hold of his baby girl too?

Leigh stroked his arm. 'She's twelve, Jake. She's experiencing changes.'

'People move house all the time and they don't—'

'No – *changes*.' She looked him in the eye. 'This could be hormonal. Every girl gets edgy as her body prepares for her first period.'

Jake blushed. Women's issues were not something he felt comfortable with. And the thought of his precious daughter growing up brought its own concerns.

'Don't worry. I'll talk to her in the morning,' said Leigh. 'And I'll work out a suitable punishment. One that makes her think, not one that'll build up more resentment to fuel whatever this is.'

Secretly Jake felt delighted that the responsibility was being lifted from his shoulders. Just then Jeanette turned from the television and looked at him.

'You were always like that as a child,' she chirped. 'Always throwing things around and breaking them. Terrible temper you had.' Then she turned back to the screen.

Jake turned all his attention to his mom. 'Oh yeah, Mom? Like when?'

But his mom was gone again. She kept her eyes on the silent episode of *Desperate Housewives*, ignoring Jake as if he hadn't spoken at all.

45

Monday, 19 December, 7 a.m.

When Jake arrived for his shift, there was one car in the station's parking lot. As he walked towards the door, Gail got out and joined him on the steps.

'I hope it's not too early,' she said. 'The chief said you'd be too busy to squeeze this in during the day.'

'It's fine,' Jake said.

Jake showed her to the small conference room. He left her there while he ducked into the detective bureau to make a couple of coffees, which he brought back.

'You didn't bring your couch?' he joked.

She smiled politely, but it was clear that today was not about fun. This was business. Jake sat on the plastic chair she had set out for him.

'Have you had counselling before?' she asked, blowing on her coffee.

'Whoa there!' said Jake, smiling. 'This isn't counselling. We chew the fat; you sign the paperwork, and the colonel gets off my back.'

Gail looked at him for a moment before she spoke. 'That's not how it works,' she said. 'You pushed a journalist and threatened to punch him.'

'I didn't push . . .' he started, but he knew there was no point arguing. Whatever he had or hadn't done physically, there was no getting around his temper. He realized he sounded like a child, protesting his innocence. 'I have no problem with journalists,' he went on.

She picked up a file. 'I've been doing my research. This isn't the first time.'

'I didn't push Ford yesterday.' He kept his voice even, but his blood pressure was rising.

'But the other time? Adam Banks?'

'That was . . . a very different situation.'

She looked at him. 'Tell me about it.'

'Me and him had a difference of opinion . . .' He shifted in his seat. 'I am not a violent person.'

'You hit a man a few months ago and got yourself suspended. And then you wanted to hit a man yesterday,' she said.

Jake didn't answer. He knew how it looked.

'Detective, I believe in my profession,' Gail told him. 'And I'm not going to let you get out of this simply because you want me to. I can't sign off on the paperwork until you start talking honestly. So we could be meeting here every day for the foreseeable future. Understand?'

The thought flashed through Jake's mind that spending an hour with this woman might not be such an ordeal. Then his mind flashed to an image of his wife's exasperated face after their daughter's teddy bear massacre. A wave of self-loathing tumbled through his chest, as powerful as any leak from his ulcer.

Gail gave him time to take a breath, then she continued. 'You're not comfortable with direct questions so let's start with small talk. You're new to Littleton?'

'Moved here from Chicago a few months ago, just before Jakey was born.' He could see where this was going.

'And why did you leave Chicago?'

Why? There were so many reasons.

'We wanted a quieter pace of life, somewhere nice to bring up the kids.'

'You could have moved to the suburbs,' she said.

He couldn't dance around it. She had his file.

'There were personal factors as well.'

'You mean the fight with the journalist?'

He let the silence hang for a few minutes, but finally he nodded. 'That was one reason.'

'Tell me about it.'

'Banks was a buddy of mine. We were at school together, then I went to Chicago and joined the PD. When he moved to Chicago we would meet up most weeks for a few beers.' Jake paused and picked at his fingernails.

'And . . .'

'One night I was heavy into a case, and it was getting to me. I met him that night, and I had one too many.'

'Did you get into a fight?' Gail asked.

'No.' Jake rubbed the back of his head. 'Umm . . . we

had a solid witness to a major gangland hit, a guy who could put two of the big players away permanently.' He stopped to clear his throat. 'But it was a tough case to make; the witness had to be carefully managed, and kept safe. I told Adam about it, friend to friend.'

Jake stopped and looked out of the window of the office. After a long moment of silence he looked back at Gail. She nodded for him to continue.

'Turns out "friend" doesn't appear in journalists' dictionaries. Two days after I told him, the story of the witness was on the front page of the fucking *Chicago Tribune*, morning edition.' Again he paused.

'Yes?' encouraged Gail.

'And our witness did not live to see the evening edition,' said Jake. He could see the man's face in his mind: young, tough, no-bullshit kind of guy. Jake had told him that there were risks involved in being a witness, but he still wanted to testify. Said something about 'good people not standing by . . .'

'Wow,' said Gail. 'That must have been rough.'

'It was. He was just married—'

'I meant on you.'

Jake paused. He had never thought about it like that. It was his fault the guy had died. He deserved no pity. 'I nearly got fired. The case fell apart. The two gang bosses walked. Had an ulcer ever since.'

'And that's it?'

He drained his coffee. 'Refill?'

'And is that it?' she asked again.

He shrugged. 'More or less. I got back on the job, but it was always hanging over me. So I came here. The timing was right – the baby . . . And my mother was beginning to show signs of a mental decline. She's living with us now.'

'You're changing the subject.' Gail just looked at him, silently waiting, the file in her hand like a gun she could raise and discharge at any time.

Jake caved in first. 'I went to Banks's house. I was furious. A witness was dead. He said he was sorry it had gone south, but he had done nothing wrong. I was shouting at him; he wasn't backing down. And I shoved him. That was all. It sent him halfway down the hallway. He took a bit of a tumble. Didn't know my own strength, I guess.'

'I've seen the medical report.'

Jake caught the tone. A simple shove would not inflict the injuries that she had read about.

'Well, Adam . . .' Jake wondered how to put it. Then he remembered who he was talking to. 'Adam took a swing at me. He missed. By this time my instincts and training were kicking in. It became an actual fight.' Jake sighed. 'He came off worse.'

Gail held up the report. 'Broken nose and two teeth missing.'

He nodded. 'There were charges but he had them dropped. That's what got me off the hook.'

'Any idea why he didn't press charges?'

'He knew he had it coming?' said Jake with a shrug.

'Or perhaps he valued your friendship?' suggested Gail.

'Then he shouldn't have sold me out,' said Jake swiftly, but the thought troubled him. He had never asked himself why Adam had walked away from the assault charges.

'And now?' said Gail after another pause. 'How is your life?'

'Everything is going swimmingly.' He didn't mention the trouble with Faith over the weekend.

'*Swimmingly?*' Gail said and smiled. 'You've had a move, a new addition to your family; you're looking after your mother, and it's going *swimmingly*?' she went on. 'Must be the first family since the Waltons where that's happened.'

Jake smiled and relaxed a little. This was safer ground.

'It's a fucking nightmare!' he said with a grin. 'My mom isn't capable of looking after herself. So when the vacancy came up here in Littleton I applied, got the job and moved my mother in with us. Leigh is finding it tough. Faith is finding it tough. And the baby's picking up on it. It's . . . stressful to say the least.'

'How do you handle stress?'

'Very well.'

'Hmm, I saw that yesterday.'

He laughed. 'You got me there.'

'Can you remember,' she began – they were on to standard psychotherapy now – 'if you have always been so short-tempered? Were you like that as a child?'

'I don't know,' he replied, trying not to sound glib or evasive.

She did not look like she was going to accept this. 'Come on.'

'I don't really remember much. Truthfully. There was always just my mother. She was a nurse, and we moved around quite a bit when I was young. I don't really remember my father. I must have been very young when he left us.'

'No contact since?'

Jake paused. He couldn't remember. It was not a thing he had ever spoken to his mom about. There were no pictures of his father, and he didn't even have a name. What the man had done for a job was a mystery. Where he had gone was another one.

'Does your mother ever talk about him?' Gail pushed. She reached out and touched him gently on the back of the hand. He wasn't sure if she was supposed to do that.

'I've asked her about him once or twice, but she never said much,' he said, feeling himself frown as he fought to focus. 'I vaguely remember a man when I was small. I don't know if he was my father, but I don't think I liked him. He frightened me. Other than that, nothing. Just vague memories. I'm not sure if they're memories or just fantasies I put together based on things my mother said.'

'That's not unusual,' said Gail. 'Lots of our memories are a mix of reality and fiction.' She sat back in her chair, staring right at him. 'You don't look convinced.'

Jake shook his head. 'It's not that I disagree,' he said. 'I just . . . feel like I don't really know who I am, where I came from.'

'Who you are is made up of so many different things. Your past is only one part of that. And you're a different person in different circumstances. You're one person at work, another person at home. You're another person when you're alone with your wife.'

Gail's voice almost tailed off at the last word. Her cheeks reddened a little. 'Do you and your wife get along well?' she asked.

How to answer that? Each day would need a different response. So he just shrugged.

Gail stood up. 'I think that's enough for today.' Jake felt a pang of regret that their meeting was over. He wanted to spend more time with her. He wanted it so much that he knew he absolutely shouldn't.

46

Monday, 10 a.m.

Two hours later the call came. He had been dreading it all morning, and when 9 a.m. passed, then nine thirty, he began to think he might catch a break and the call might not come.

There was plenty to keep him busy, to keep his mind off it, including a couple of false leads phoned in by well-meaning citizens who had let their paranoia get the better of them. It was the church service and the appeal for witnesses that drew out the whack jobs. There were plenty of people now, all willing to testify that they had seen a tall man or a short man, a black man or a white man, either before or after each of the murders. All fantasy: there wasn't a common thread running through them. But each call had to be logged and followed up. To miss one might be to overlook the vital clue that would crack open the case.

But with each false lead, Jake could feel his ulcer burning.

Then, at about two minutes to ten, the phone rang.

'Detective Austin,' he said as he picked up.

'This is Judy at the switch. There's a report of another murder. Can you take the call?'

The caller was a construction worker in a panic. 'Er, yeah. I found a body. It's horrible. I just went in to clear the place up, and I found it.'

'Are you OK, sir?' asked Jake. 'Where are you?'

'The warehouse over on Poughanni Road – the one we're going to knock down today. There's a body on the floor.'

It stood on its own on some waste ground. The interstate was edging close to it, and it was one of a number of buildings scheduled for demolition this week. By Christmas Eve parts of Littleton were scheduled to look like they were victims of a blitzkrieg.

Jake stopped at the wooden door and drew his focus inward, trying to keep himself centred. After a moment he walked through the door into the chilliness of the disused building.

The warehouse was vast and empty.

Mills tapped him on the shoulder and pointed: the far wall. Jake nodded. He could see it, a bundle of clothing that had to be the body. He set off across the cold concrete floor, and even from some distance away he could see that it had suffered the same death as the other three. Dark patches on the face where eyes should have been looked back at him.

The body seemed bigger than the others, though not

by much. And the clothes were wrong. Jake stared for another minute before the truth dawned.

'Shit!' he muttered under his breath.

The victim was not a woman.

'Ditto,' said Mills. 'This changes everything.'

Their theory was now untenable. They were back to square one. Again.

47

Monday, 10.25 a.m.

Jake scanned the ground, looking for anything the killer might have left behind. But it was useless, as he had known it would be. This was a man who took pride in his work. It mattered to him. He would not casually discard a cigarette butt or drop a candy wrapper.

You're taunting us, Jake thought. *Taunting us with just how good you are. You know that this is what we expect of you. You're taking delight in living up to expectations now, at the same time as confounding them. Showing us you're in complete control.*

Slowly he approached. His steps rang out in the silence of the building. It was incredibly cold in the cavernous space, and his breath condensed before him. His eyes darted left and right. He was looking for anything: a wet spot that would indicate where someone had stood and waited, or a dark patch that could be blood.

There were a few cans and bottles against one of the walls. The warehouse had obviously become a hangout for winos or kids' beer parties. Each one of the cans and bottles would have to be wrung through the mill of forensics. *Ronnie will love that.*

Now that Jake was nearing the body, what he was looking for were signs of a struggle. Something knocked over or out of place. But with the furniture and fittings long gone, there was nothing left as a record of the last twelve hours.

Finally he was there. He stepped towards the body and bent, gently laying a hand on an outstretched arm. It was as cold as a cut of beef. He pressed the muscle and it felt firm. Rigor was well established, advanced. The corpse had been here all night.

Jake stepped back again and just looked. The body was of a mature man probably approaching forty. White, well fed but not overweight. He had dark hair and looked a bit scruffy, but he certainly hadn't been living rough. Most murder victims come from the lower strata of society; not this guy. He was well dressed, but in a casual way. Unlike the other victims, this one had been laid out rather than dumped. But there was no element of staging to it. Some killers put their victims in elaborate poses as part of their signature. But this body seemed to have been laid out with a certain dignity, as if the killer had no more interest in it but was observing the decencies. The body was on its back, but his face was turned to the side.

Only the eyeballs were out. That was the first thing Jake had spotted, but now he looked properly. The head was the same as the other three – dark blotches of blood in the eye sockets, and bloody gelatinous strands of optic nerve leading to the lifeless eyes.

The facial features were distorted but strangely familiar. The distortion was caused by the destruction of the cheekbones and the crushing of the face. Jake could see the gaps in the teeth, and that the lower jaw had flopped down.

But, even so, Jake knew the man. His mind was able to reverse-engineer the face, imagining it with the jaw set correctly, the dental gaps filled in, the cheekbones restored and the livid white replaced with a healthy glow.

The dead man was Chuck Ford.

48

Monday, noon

Jake and Mills were still at the scene, but they were no longer alone. The warehouse was swarming with cops, lab techs and hangers-on. Outside the media were camped, and every time an investigator came or went he was harassed by a chorus of questions and demands.

'Four is the magic number,' said Mills. 'He's officially a serial killer now.'

'That's going to make it difficult to keep the Feds out,' said Jake. He was restless; he had gone outside more than once, but he kept coming back in. What was he missing? There had to be some clue he had overlooked. 'Did we ever get that hunk of skin from Makowski's shed tested?' Jake asked. But whatever the answer was, he knew that Makowski hadn't done this. Not a chance.

Mills nodded. 'It belonged to Makowski.'

Jake noticed that everyone in the warehouse was gawping at him under their eyebrows – even if trying to look like they weren't. Jake knew why. He had, after all, publicly assaulted the victim. He knew what was crossing their minds. If it had involved someone else, it might have crossed his.

Jake turned as the noise from the journalists gathered outside rose. Colonel Asher had arrived, and he bustled through the ring of journalists like a man on a mission, not saying anything but striking a determined pose that would hopefully make the afternoon papers. Then he was through, barging his way across the floor towards the corpse.

Jake stepped in front of him. 'We need to toss Ford's house. Mills has—'

Asher glared at him. 'What are you doing here?'

'I'm lead investigator.'

'You have history with Ford.'

'Are you saying I'm a suspect?' Jake had stepped forward, deliberately entering Asher's personal space. The chief was forced to take a step back.

'Don't be stupid, Detective!' Asher told him. 'You know how the press are going to play this one. You went for one of their own, and they're going to tear you apart. You'll be convicted as soon as their ink is dry.'

'Who gives a fuck what they print?' Jake said.

Jake could see Asher hadn't been prepared for this response. He expected to be the one doing the shouting. Now Jake was putting him on the back foot. It was deliberate. Jake was in no mood for a dressing-down.

Asher stared back at Jake. 'Mills is in charge now. He's leading, you're his secondary.'

'And he has the experience for something like

this?' asked Jake before he could stop himself. Immediately he turned and gave Mills a 'No offence' look, to which Mills responded with an affable 'None taken' headshake.

Asher glanced over his shoulder at the journalists in the distance. 'I have to give them something, even if it's bullshit. You will still be running the case the way you have been. But, officially, Mills goes down on the books as lead detective. Ego aside, Austin, you know it has to be this way.'

Jake held the colonel's gaze for a long moment but said nothing. He turned to look at Mills, who had a platitude ready: 'All that counts is that we get the fucker.'

Jake relaxed. *Focus on the job in hand. We'll sort out the politics later.*

49

Monday, 12.15 p.m.

Chuck Ford lived on Beachwood, which intersected Oakland Downes. That made him a near neighbour of the Harpers. Jake dismissed the thought almost immediately. He was trying to make connections where there were none. Marcia Lamb and Candy wouldn't fit into this neighbourhood. He was clutching at straws when he should have been analysing the facts.

Beachwood was not as upmarket as Oakland Downes, but it was a close thing. The houses were a bit smaller, the yards not so expansive. But the cars in the driveways were as new and as luxurious. It was a kind of Oakland Downes Lite.

It wasn't all residential; some of the buildings had been converted to commercial properties. Jake spotted one large old residence hosting a plastic surgery clinic, while another housed a firm of lawyers.

Mills pulled to the kerb about halfway down the street. The building they had stopped at was an old red-brick two-storey structure, quite large, with spaces for six cars marked in white paint at the end of the drive.

Two cars were there now. They had been there a while, judging by the layers of snow that had collected.

'Swanky,' said Jake.

'It's not all his – it's been converted to luxury apartments,' Mills replied. 'They went for way more than a cop's salary stretches to.'

'Were you interested?'

Mills shook his head. 'Beyond my budget. And it would have stretched Ford too.'

Both men got out of the car, and Jake surveyed the scene. He walked down the driveway. It was screened by trees and ornate hedging, so whoever approached would have been able to do so unobserved, especially at night.

I don't think that mattered to you. You have no fear of being seen. Why is that?

Jake had reached the door now. He had seen no signs of disturbance. The yard was beautifully maintained, with symmetrical flower beds, now just greenery. But none of the plants looked damaged. There had been no struggle here.

You got in again. How do you keep doing that?

Jake looked at the list of names on the front door. Six bells. Six parking slots. None of the bells had Ford's name on it. He rang one at random. Nothing. So he tried the next. The fourth one got a sleepy female voice over the intercom.

'Leave it on the stoop,' she said.

'We're police officers. We're looking for Charles Ford's apartment?'

'Chuck?' she sounded a lot more awake now. 'He's number 4. Is he in trouble?'

'Thanks, ma'am. Can you open the door?'

There was a buzz, and Jake pushed the door open. Both cops stepped in. There were three doors off the main corridor: two to the right and one to the left.

There was a stairwell on the left, and Jake went up to the first floor. It was the same as the floor below. Apartment 4 was on the left. Jake stopped at the top of the stairs and looked. Nothing seemed out of place. The corridor was clean and well lit.

Mills was beside him now.

'He got this far the way we did, and he probably just rang the bell and was let in,' said Mills. 'Somehow he seems to inspire trust in his victims.'

'You're learning,' said Jake. 'But it's never that easy. I'd say he broke in and surprised Ford.'

Mills stepped forward and said, 'Give me a minute before you go in. You know how sites become contaminated as soon as we arrive in force. I'm going to lift whatever's on the bell.'

Quickly he removed a small vial of powder from his pocket and put some on his hand. He blew it gently on to the bell, then took out a roll of tape, taking off an inch. He laid it gently over the bell, then pulled. He then stuck the tape to a small laminated card and put it in a clear evidence bag.

'We'd never be that lucky,' said Jake.

Mills reached into another pocket and took out a small wallet, removing some tools.

'I got the door,' he said.

As soon as the door opened, the coppery smell of freshly spilt blood wafted out into the hallway.

50

Monday, 12.30 p.m.

Jake assumed there'd be signs of a struggle within a few feet of the door. Ford was a mature man. He'd been round the block and would not be physically intimidated. He would put up a fight for his life.

The apartment was blessedly free of Christmas paraphernalia – not unusual in the home of a middle-aged bachelor – but it was still awash in colour. Whites and lurid lashes of reds and yellows. Even the paintings on the walls followed the palette. They were brash moderns, cheap reproductions of Kandinsky splurges. One of the paintings was on the floor. It had a hole in its centre, as if someone had stepped through it. A bedside table was knocked over, a pile of mail and takeaway menus on the floor. A chair was lying in the kitchen area of the large open-plan room. The linoleum under the chair was sticky with congealed blood.

You got in somehow. You sneaked up on him, and you hit him. But he was a big man, a lot stronger than the women you killed. You've had it easy up to now. But you fought as well. And you subdued him. You improvised a weapon.

Jake looked around. What would make a good

weapon? The picture? No, far too light. Then he saw it – a marble statuette of Rodin's *The Thinker.*

You grabbed the statue – that's when the table fell over. He was coming at you after your first blow failed to knock him down. He turned and came at you. You pushed him back – that's what knocked the painting off the wall. Then you hit him, and he fell right there.

You must have been out of breath. You must have been terrified, but there was no commotion in the building. No one heard. You were able to do your work.

Now Jake knew what to look for. He went over to the stereo – the volume knob was set quite high. Not so high that another resident would phone the police and complain, but high enough to drown out any sounds of a struggle inside the apartment. The stereo was off. He used his fingernail to press the *On* button, then *Eject.* Bruce Springsteen. That would do it.

'We need to get forensics to dust the stereo.'

'Check,' said Mills from the door.

When he woke up, you had him secured to the kitchen chair.

Jake went over to the chair and bent. There was plenty of blood and two teeth. There was fabric on the chair, probably from the restraints the killer had used. They were building a case, but they still needed a suspect.

Ford had to know you, otherwise you would not have got past the door.

Trouble was, Chuck Ford knew a lot of people.

51

Monday, 1 p.m.

Within an hour of the initial report, the white van of the forensics team had arrived. Dr Ronnie Zatkin came herself.

'I need everyone out so my team can do their job,' she said. Like a no-nonsense schoolteacher she steered the uniformed cops from the apartment. Then the forensic photographer began his work, snapping picture after picture.

'After he's done, we'll begin dusting for prints,' she told Jake. 'Then we can send in the team to collect blood and other samples. But it will be well into evening before you guys can have the room.'

'Can you tell me anything now, Doctor?' he asked.

'We've had a quick look at the body. Too early to confirm it, but the cause of death is likely the same mysterious instrument,' she said. 'Now, can you leave the room and let us do our job?'

'No problem,' he said, walking past her to one of the doors off the main living room. It was a small study, lined with books. There were plenty of notebooks and scraps of paper, and an open laptop on a desk.

'You can't go in there,' shouted Ronnie. 'We won't get to that room until tomorrow. You can go in then.'

'I need to go through Ford's computer now. He knew things about the case before we released them. We need to know what he knew, and we need to see if what he was working on made him a target of the killer.'

Ronnie sighed. 'At least pull these on,' she said, handing him a pair of latex gloves. 'And give my team ten minutes with the keyboard before you begin.'

'Deal.'

'And don't let anyone know I let you in.'

Ford's chair was a bit high for Jake, but he wouldn't be here too long. Disregarding Ronnie's request, he was about to hit the power key but noticed it was already on. *Thank God.* So he just moved the mouse a bit, and the screen lit up. *Chuck was working when you arrived. Did you knock, and did he just let you in?*

Jake quickly scanned the article Ford was working on. Mills read over his shoulder. There was nothing new in it – speculation about possible links between the three women, and an unnamed psychologist musing about whether the Christmas Killer might have killed before Marcia Lamb. The same thought had passed through Jake's head.

He closed the article, and went to the file directory. Ford was a hoarder. Every word he had written for the last few years was still on the hard drive. There were thousands of articles. And the names on the files didn't give much clue as to what was in them. This could take months and, even then, might not show up anything.

Jake glanced at the door to see if Ronnie was looking in. When he was sure that she wasn't he quickly typed 'Christmas Killer' into the *Search* box. About fifteen articles came up. He scanned them and concluded that Ford had no Deep Throat within the Littleton PD. His information just came from dogged working of the usual sources. And listening in to the police radio.

'Try the victims,' suggested Mills.

Jake typed 'Marcia Lamb' in the box. She didn't appear until a week previously, when the killer began his killing spree. Next he tried 'Candy Jones', who appeared in an article two years back after being hauled before the courts on a hooking rap. She got a week of county time and a fine of $200.

But 'Belinda Harper' turned up in dozens of articles. Jake quickly ran through them. The first few seemed to relate to a charity dinner, a fund-raiser or a library or school committee so he dismissed the rest.

'She was squeaky clean,' he said.

Next he typed in the chief suspects. 'Guy Makowski' produced a handful of hits, mostly related to union activities at the steel mill. There was also a court case where he'd claimed compensation after an accident. Nothing else, and nothing to ring any alarm bells.

Then Jake typed in 'Sonny Malone'.

'This should be interesting,' said Mills as the list of articles lit up the screen. There were plenty of references to Malone, all relating to court proceedings, but none in the past few years; Malone had been off the streets in jail.

'A big nothing,' said Jake. 'Might as well leave it to the techs.'

'Try "Mitch Harper" before you quit,' suggested Mills.

'Why not?'

He typed in the name then hit the *Return* key. Mills sucked in his breath; they had struck the mother lode. The search box read, *Your search has shown 728 files.* That was far too many to wade through right now, with a forensics unit waiting to go through the whole apartment.

Jake was about to switch off the computer when one of the 728 files listed caught his eye. What stood out was that it was a folder rather than a document. Dated four years ago, it was simply labelled 'Harper File'.

A whole folder on Mitch Harper. Was Ford following his campaign trail?

Jake opened the folder. It contained eight documents. One was named 'Deposition of Witness A, Call Girl'. Another was 'Deposition of Doctor Shawcross'. Others were tagged 'Statement' or 'Account Of'. Obviously Ford had been collecting statements for a major article, and he had stored the information together. The final article was the one Jake decided to read first. Its title: 'Harper Scandal'.

52

SEX SCANDAL OF GOVERNOR-IN-WAITING

by Charles Ford

Littleton councilman and Democratic high-flyer Mitch Harper is tonight battening down the hatches as his career flounders amidst allegations of a year-long relationship with a local prostitute.

The married politician, who had harbored ambitions for the state governorship, has been left reeling by the accusation that he slept with the high-class escort, as well as engaging in violent and deviant sexual practices.

The escort went public after being hospitalized by the popular young attorney. He allegedly assaulted her during a heated sex session at a hotel in the capital. Police were called during the incident.

This reporter has spoken to the woman in question, Leanne Schultz, who alleges that she began her affair with Councilman Harper last October, when he hired her and another escort and took them to an Indianapolis hotel. Councilman Harper was in the capital for a Democratic Party fund-raiser. His wife, Belinda Harper, was not with him on that occasion.

'He seemed nice,' said Ms Schultz. 'We began to see each other regularly, at first when he was on business in Indianapolis. But soon he was sending a car to pick me up for nights and weekends away. I traveled to Washington with him just after Christmas.'

It is believed that Belinda Harper was completely unaware of her husband's meetings with Ms Schultz. She has given no comment, but a close friend told this reporter that Mrs Harper is 'shocked and heartbroken.'

According to Ms Schultz, it was not long before Councilman Harper began to display a darker side to his character. As the affair progressed, the councilman's demands became more extreme. He experimented in bondage and sadomasochistic practices. Ms Schultz began to fear for her safety.

'He liked to give it rough. The sex became more and more brutal; I felt as if I was being raped. I tried to break it off, but he threatened that he would tip off the police about me if I ever stopped seeing him.'

Things came to a head on a night two weeks ago, when Councilman Harper was in Plainfield for a conference, where he was to deliver the keynote address. Ms Schultz went to his room after the event.

'It began as normal, but I soon knew this was going to be one of the brutal sessions,' she said. 'He had a belt, and he wanted to whip me. I said no. I tried to leave the hotel room, but he stopped me. I began to scream, and he became physically aggressive.'

Ms Schultz suffered a broken nose and bruised ribs in the assault. Other guests at the hotel heard the disturbance and phoned the police, who took Ms Schultz to Plainfield Private Hospital. She was released after treatment, but decided not to press charges. However, she is understood to be considering bringing a civil action against Councilman Harper, who refused a request for comment.

Councilman Harper was first elected to the city council in Littleton six years ago, and was returned with an increased majority two years ago. He has been spoken of as a candidate for higher office, but this latest scandal appears to have curtailed that ambition.

A senior source within the Democratic Party said, 'Mitch is a great guy, but if you can't keep it in your trousers, maybe politics isn't the game for you. It will take him a long time to come back from this.'

53

Monday, 2.20 p.m.

Jake sat back from the computer. He looked up at Mills, who seemed as stunned as Jake felt. This was something new. He had known none of this about Harper. Surely someone could have filled him in?

'Do you know much about Harper?' he asked Mills.

'Mitch? I've met him plenty of times,' he replied. 'I knew he was a bit of a horn dog, but I didn't know *this* about him.'

Just then Dr Zatkin looked in.

'I'll have to move you guys. You've had plenty of time,' she said. 'You better not be touching that keyboard!'

'No, ma'am,' said Jake. 'Ronnie, can you come in for a moment? Do you know Mitch Harper?'

She looked puzzled. 'As much as anyone else does. Why do you ask?'

'Can you tell me about him?'

She shrugged. 'Trained as an attorney, qualified top of his class. He came home, set up a practice, married well and moved into politics. He got on to the city council at his first try, the youngest member in twenty years. We thought he was a high-flyer.'

'Thought?' asked Jake.

'His career stalled a few years ago,' she explained.

'Oh yeah,' said Mills. 'I remember that.'

'People said he'd go for governor,' Ronnie said, 'and who knew what after that? He had that presidential air about him. But it all seemed to slow down for him about . . . four years ago.'

Jake looked at Mills. They knew why.

'There was a scandal, wasn't there?' he said.

Ronnie looked puzzled. 'I don't think so. His career just seemed to go quiet for a while. He seems to be back on track now, though. They say he'll be your next mayor.' She came into the study and shooed them out. 'Why'd you ask?'

'It's something we need to look into,' Jake told her. 'We'll get out of your hair now.'

She turned to walk out of the room and Jake used the moment to close the screen of the laptop and pop out the power lead. He picked up the slim computer and draped his coat over his arm to conceal it. He followed Mills out of the building.

In the car they began putting the pieces together. An up-and-comer like Harper was at the time would have had the connections to make an assault charge disappear. Hospitals – especially private clinics – could be persuaded to turn a blind eye to a hooker's broken nose. The whole thing could have gone away; but Chuck

Ford had found out about it. Maybe the woman had gone to him.

Jake opened the laptop, balancing it on the dashboard.

Mills saw what he had and his eyes widened. 'You did not just take that!'

'Keep your eyes on the road,' Jake told him. 'Park up round the corner.'

He picked a file at random as Mills pulled over. The file included the date of publication and the paper the article had appeared in. Then he went back to the 'Harper Scandal' file. There was no dateline and no publication. The article had not been published, which meant Ford had had a change of heart. Why? Had Harper got to him? Threatened him or bribed him? Most likely bribed, based on the look of the apartment. Ford was doing better than a simple hack journalist had any right to. Had he sold out?

If he did, he was a despicable prick, thought Jake.

'We need to locate Leanne Schultz. I wonder if she's still in Indianapolis?' he said to Mills.

'Not any more,' said Mills, holding up his phone to show a web page. 'She was killed in a hit-and-run about three years ago.'

'Of course she was.' Jake tried not to smile, tried not to let himself believe that things might now be falling into place.

Harper had got rid of the prostitute. Got rid of his wife. He had got rid of a journalist who knew where the skeletons were hidden. And he was offing others unconnected with him to make it look like a crazed serial killer was on the loose.

It might fit. But Marcia Lamb and Candy Jones were still a problem. Why them specifically? Harper was milking Marcia Lamb for all she was worth, politically. Was he really ruthless enough to kill a pretty young woman for a sound bite on single mothers and early-release programmes? Yes, he was. If he was ruthless enough to do what he had done to his wife, he was ruthless enough to kill Marcia Lamb. Candy – another prostitute – he had probably just enjoyed. And those killings provided great cover for the two killings he had really wanted to do.

'I wonder, did he sleep with Candy too?' Jake muttered.

You're worse than a serial killer. You have no conscience. To you, this is just work . . .

54

Monday, 3 p.m.

Zatkin had broken his balls over the laptop theft, but Jake convinced her they were both likely to face disciplinary action if it came out that he'd removed evidence from the crime scene. Anyway, he'd returned it to the house after copying all he need on to a memory stick.

Now Jake had new prey in his sights.

The plan was simple. They did not want this to look like an interrogation of a suspect, but at the same time they wanted Harper to be in no doubt that he was in the machine. The wheels were grinding. This was an initial interview; they wouldn't let him know what was really up until they were sure they could nail him.

At City Hall Harper vacillated. He came down to meet Jake and Mills in the lobby and shook their hands. But once he had them in his office, he pulled his mouth tight with apparent regret. 'Guys, I've told you everything I can about Belinda. I'd love to help more, but I have a meeting at three thirty that I'm prepping for, and I'm swamped with funeral arrangements. Can one of you drop by the house later? Say, after seven?'

'I'm afraid not, sir,' said Jake gently. 'Your wife's killer has struck for a fourth time. Everything needs to be followed up urgently. You understand.'

There was a pause. Jake watched Harper's eyes carefully.

'OK,' said the councilman. 'I guess I can spare ten minutes.'

Jake put on his best apologetically sympathetic face. 'We're going to need a bit longer than that, sir – we can't leave any stone unturned now. Public safety. We have a car waiting. We can bring you across to the station house, then return you here in time for your meeting.'

Harper sighed and ran his fingers through his hair. Then, with a single nod, he set about gathering his coat and briefcase.

'We appreciate it, sir,' said Jake, maintaining his sympathetic face as he quickly scanned the room. For what potential clue, he had no real idea. He was just working on a cop's instinct.

Harper's office wasn't as grand as Jake had expected it to be. The room had been recently refurbished, painted white; the table was cheap and the chairs didn't look comfortable. A picture of his wife was on his desk, but the walls were bare. Harper clearly didn't plan on making this office any kind of home. He had his eye on another, more prestigious, space.

The mayor's office.

'We are so sorry to be pushing you at a time like this,' Jake continued. Harper had his coat on by now, and was fixing the cops with a gaze that was neither challenging nor submissive. Jake tried not to let his own eyes show that wheels were turning in his head, but he was thinking hard. Was Harper showing the signs of pathological dispassion necessary to commit the crimes the cops were investigating?

Jake made sure his face was all business and courtesy as he went on: 'We let it go the past few days because your grief was so fresh, but we hope that you can face talking about your wife now. We really need to explore every aspect. Belinda was the second victim. With this sort of profile, the killers often move on to random victims – as appears to have happened in Littleton – but there is often a link, however tenuous, to the first few. We hope some small random detail might provide the clue to find the man we're looking for.'

'I understand,' said Harper. Jake could see he was holding up better than might be expected. Today he was impeccably groomed. He looked like he had stepped off the cover of *GQ*. The waft of aftershave was almost effeminate. His eyes were clear. The traces of red were gone.

'It's not easy to talk about her yet,' he went on. 'Or even to think of a life without her. She was my rock.'

Jake thought that Belinda was more like Harper's rocket right now. He was up twelve points since her death. Whatever the problems in their marriage, she had been a shot of political Red Bull to his campaign. But he dismissed the thought as uncharitable. Harper irritated him, yes, and he was suddenly looking like a viable suspect – but Jake knew he had to keep an open mind as best he could. Because, whatever the councilman might think, this whole sad business was about more than Mitch Harper – there were three other victims with grieving families who deserved justice and closure.

'Can't we do this in one of the conference rooms here?' Harper asked as they walked out of the door. 'I haven't been home since it happened. This place feels more like home to me after what that bastard did.' As they walked past the front desk in the lobby, Jake caught the receptionist looking up at Harper with big puppy eyes. Harper's grief and stoicism was playing very well to the gallery.

'The station would be better for us,' Jake said firmly.

A flicker of suspicion crossed Harper's face, and he became blunt. 'Why?' he asked.

'All our files are there. We can cross-check things immediately instead of putting them on the long finger and risk missing some important detail.' He played his trump. 'This is our job. We know how to do it best.'

There was no arguing that one, especially with the receptionist listening. Harper conceded by motioning for the detectives to continue leading the way.

Outside City Hall about a dozen journalists were waiting in the cold. There had been a few already there when they'd arrived, and Jake figured they'd put the word out. The colonel was not going to be happy – *discretion*, he had urged.

One of the reporters stepped forward. 'Detective, can you fill us in on the current leads? Is Councilman Harper now a suspect?'

Chief and only suspect, Jake thought, but this had to be handled right. Ford might be gone, but his breed lived on. This was a herd that needed culling.

He knew he should have said, 'No comment,' but he gave one, as a way to let Harper think they were on his side. He also wanted to see if Harper might say something to land himself in the shit. 'Councilman Harper has just lost his wife. He is helping us put together her final moments, to try and put her killer behind bars, where he belongs.'

Harper smiled weakly and addressed the reporters, who were so influential as to what the rest of the voting public thought: 'I suppose I have to get used to this now.'

Jake eyed the councilman closely as he got in the car. He looked like he was already used to it. And he also looked like he didn't exactly hate it.

55

Monday, 3.45 p.m.

'Interview with Councilman Mitch Harper. Time: fifteen forty-five. Present: Councilman Harper, Detectives Austin and Mills of the Littleton Police Department,' said Jake. They were seated in a triangle, the two detectives facing the suspect.

'Hold on a minute,' interrupted Harper. 'Why is this being recorded?'

Jake wrestled the grimace away from his face. Harper had got suspicious before they had properly begun. Either he was a paranoid innocent man, or a very cautious guilty one. Either way, their interview had just become much more tricky.

With an effort, Jake smiled. 'You are a person of interest because you are strongly linked to the case, but you are not a suspect.' Jake left out the last word of that sentence – 'officially'.

Harper relaxed and nodded.

'We need to try and form a clear picture of what type of person Belinda was, and what she did with her life,' Jake continued. 'Then we can see if any of that intersects with our investigation.'

'OK,' Harper said.

'You knew her from high school?'

'No – yes. I knew her, but she was a few years behind me. Seniors didn't mix with freshmen. But she was stunning, the head cheerleader when I was in senior year, so I knew her a bit. When I came back to town after college we met a few times, in bars and things. And we clicked. Eventually.' He smiled ruefully. 'I had to chase her. And I wasn't the only one.'

Jake smiled back at him. 'I never met her. What sort of woman was she?'

'She could be a charmer. She had a way of wrapping men around her little finger. Back then guys were swarming around her like bees on a flower.'

'And in later years?'

'No, she didn't encourage that. You won't find any obsessed admirers in the closet,' said Harper. 'Her work took up most of her time and energy.'

'I understood she didn't work,' said Jake.

'Her *charity* work,' Harper clarified. 'She was on a lot of different committees – mainly educational, working with young single mothers and such.' Jake felt his brow knit as he wondered if Marcia Lamb had been aided by such a committee. Could there be a connection between victim number one and victim number two?

'She was the chair of the Carnegie Library Committee,' Harper continued. 'Belinda gave a lot to the community. And of course she worked for me. A politician's wife can be a full-time job.'

Jake put his thoughts of connection to one side, making a mental note to pick them up again as soon as this interview was over. 'Did you enjoy working with her?'

Harper paused to consider the question. 'I don't suppose I really worked *with* her. She was like part of the back-room team. She worked to support me, rather than working with me. But yes, I did enjoy it. She was a remarkable woman.'

Jake was frustrated – the dead were always mythologized. He needed an insight into the real person. 'Working with someone, and living with them, you'd get to know them fairly well. Did you ever see any signs of – I don't know – a temper?'

Harper looked surprised. 'No.'

Jake looked at him. He let Harper be the one to break the silence. Let Harper acknowledge that *he* was the one made uncomfortable.

'I suppose we all have our moments,' he said. 'Why do you ask?'

'Routine. I'm just wondering if she might have had a fight with someone, something that could have triggered the attack. A possible revenge motive? Do you think that's possible?'

'No,' said Harper, a little too fast. 'Bella didn't have a temper.'

Now Harper was using his pet name for her – that was a good sign. Jake smiled, inviting a confidence. 'Come on – you were married all those years. Never a blow-out? She never lost it? Threw a vase?'

Harper laughed. 'You're married, I see. Yeah, there was the occasional fight. The usual stuff – silly things. I was out too late; I came home smelling of alcohol . . .'

And other women's perfume? Jake wondered.

'She had a thing about my cigars, so I quit,' Harper was saying. Then he added, 'For her.'

Jake needed to rein him in ever so slightly. Harper feeling the need to impress upon the cops how much he did for his wife was not good – it showed that, at the very least, the councilman was feeling prickles of anxiety. He might not be convinced that he was in the frame – not just yet – but he was definitely conscious of the possibility . . . and he wanted to avoid it.

Jake couldn't let this happen. Not before they were convinced, one way or the other. He had to keep it light – give a little to get a little. It was his turn now.

'My wife is a lovely woman,' he said. 'I'd take a bullet for her. But she can nag like the best of them . . .' Jake affected a chuckle. 'Last week I came home from a late shift. I had stopped at a bar for a few beers. She threw a plate at me. Worst thing was, my dinner was on that plate!'

Harper laughed again. 'I never had a plate *thrown* at me. But I got served the occasional plate of cold shoulder.'

Both men smiled. Jake's smile was sympathetic, the friendly cop. Harper's smile didn't reach his eyes.

Jake tried again. 'She's Italian,' he lied, feeling like a boxer peppering a well-drilled opponent with quick jabs, hoping to lure his guarding gloves down from his chin, exposing it to a knockout punch. 'She goes over the top sometimes. I took her out for dinner one night. Got a call from work and made the mistake of answering it. She walked out, drove home and left me stranded.'

'Bella once cut holes in the seat of my suit pants,' said Harper. 'It was fifteen years ago. I was just starting out, and I had only two suits. And she destroyed one. I didn't even realize until I was with some very prominent people. Thank God I wasn't going commando, you know what I mean?'

Jake put on a sympathetic grimace. Then he offered a laugh like it was a great story. It kind of was. 'You must have really pissed her off to get that kind of reaction.'

But he had pushed too fast. The shutters came down. 'Like I said, we all have our moments. But Belinda is – was – great, and we could not have been happier.'

Back to 'Belinda'.

'I'm beginning to get a picture of her,' Jake said, accordingly retreating to generalities – the boxer going back to the jab after missing an ambitious uppercut. 'She was a strong woman.'

Harper nodded.

Jake jabbed again. 'She could be a bit of a wildcat when she was upset. A lot of level-headed women can become a bit vindictive when they are upset.'

Harper said, 'My dad always told me women are crazy by nature. What can you do?'

The jabs were not getting through. Harper's guard was too solid. What bothered Jake was that Harper was able to deflect and parry Jake's questions. He didn't know he was a suspect but he wasn't taking the chance. Jake had interviewed dozens of grieving widowers and widows, mothers and brothers, and one thing they all had in common was that they got upset when they remembered their lost loved one. Harper was holding it together well – too well. He was too conscious of what he was saying, too aware of how his words might be interpreted – and this almost seemed as important to him as helping the police find his wife's murderer.

Is it your political training, or am I looking at the face of a killer?

Time to find out.

'It sounds as if Belinda could be quite volatile,' said Jake, changing the angle of the jab and looking for Harper to give up simple parrying. He wanted him to try a little bobbing and weaving – maybe then he would step into the path of a haymaker. 'Was this something she kept behind closed doors, or did it ever break out in public?'

Out of the corner of his eye he could see Mills shifting in his seat. He was already paying attention, but now he was even more alert and focused. Mills got it: Jake was subtly asking if Mitch and Belinda ever fought in public. Jake couldn't ask this directly: he had no grounds for holding Harper and, once the word 'lawyer' was mentioned, the interview would be over.

Answer the real *question*, Jake mentally urged Harper. *Did you guys fight a lot? Did she reserve her hostility for you, or did she spread it around?*

'We heard she had a minor altercation with a man named Guy Makowski a few weeks ago, and that in retaliation he kicked her car.'

Harper's eyes went blank, but not before they flared to signal that something had clicked in his head. But whatever thought he had had, he was not going to share with the detectives. The shutters were down again, this time for good. Jake knew he was about to be sandbagged.

'If there's anything you feel you'd like to say, I'm listening,' he pressed. 'Any little detail could be crucial.' *And it will be bad for you if you conceal anything.* 'This guy has killed twice more since he took Belinda from you,' he added, wondering if he used the word 'constituents' he might get more play from the councilman. 'And he'll kill again, unless we catch him. Do you want that on your conscience?'

Harper just stared at him. There was defiance in his look. Then he slowly shook his head. 'I have nothing more to say, Officer.'

'Detective,' Jake reminded him.

'Apologies, Detective.'

There was a long silence shattered by the sound of Mills clearing his throat. 'Who wants coffee?' he said, clearly trying to lighten the tension. Barely waiting for a response from either man, Mills stood up from the table and left the room.

Left Jake and Harper alone together. Jake could feel his fist, under the table, beginning to clench. The councilman was holding something back. But what? Why wasn't he telling them everything when his wife's killer was still on the loose?

'So, are we done here?' said Harper. 'I think I've given you enough of my time.'

And then he smiled. It was the smile of a man who knew he could not be touched. Jake felt the burn spreading through his belly – this time it wasn't just the ulcer.

'We're done when I say we're done,' he said. It came out stronger than he had intended.

'Really? I was under the impression I was helping you with your inquiries,' said Harper.

'Four people have been killed. You need to be straight with us.'

'And I have been.' Harper leaned forward. 'And now you need to do your job.'

'Look—' said Jake.

But the councilman cut him off. 'No, *you* fucking look!' He pointed his finger in Jake's face and it took everything Jake had not to snap the finger in two. 'If you're threatening me, Detective, I want to tell you something—'

Mills came back into the room, mobile phone pressed to his ear. 'You're needed outside, Detective,' he said to Jake. 'Can we stop the interview for a few minutes?'

'Fine by me,' muttered Harper.

Jake got up and stormed out of the room, slamming the door on the way out.

56

Monday, 4.15 p.m.

'Jesus, Austin,' said Mills as they stood outside the interview room. 'There was no phone call; I just had to get you out of there. You were—'

'I know there was no fucking call,' said Jake, his voice coming out in a snarl. He turned away from Mills and walked down the corridor to the detectives' office.

He walked straight to the back of the open-plan room. There was a door leading to a tiny canteen, and he went in. It was empty. He slammed the door behind him. Harper, with his smugness, was getting on his nerves. Jake needed to get himself under control if he was going to get anywhere in the interview. He held his head in his hands and tried to breathe through his mounting anger. But it wasn't working. His pulse was racing, and his head felt light.

He had been working flat out all day. He hadn't eaten. Maybe that was why his head was swimming, unable to properly focus. There was a vending machine in the canteen. He reached into his pocket and took out four quarters. He bought himself a Snickers bar that he didn't really feel like. The machine gave the familiar dull *whirr* noise, and he saw the metal spiral begin to move with agonizing slowness. It pushed his Snickers bar out, and it dropped off the display. But the reassuring *thunk* of the bar falling into the tray didn't follow. He looked down. It had got stuck.

He put his hands on the machine and shook it, trying to dislodge the bar. Nothing happened. He pressed the coin return button, but the machine did not refund him his four quarters.

'Fuck you,' he said.

He grabbed the machine and shook it as hard as he could, hearing it scrape against the floor as he dislodged it from the spot where it had stood for a decade or more. He kept on shaking, but still nothing happened. He slid his hands up the edges, thinking that more leverage might do the trick.

'Shit!' he gasped, as his palm ran over a jagged edge of metal. 'Fucker!'

His fist was moving before he could stop it. He punched the machine – once, then again. The glass front shattered beneath his knuckles.

As the glass rained down on his shoes, Jake took a deep breath. He felt the warm wetness on his hand. He looked down. His hand had multiple gashes on the palm and back and knuckles. Already droplets were peppering the floor at his feet.

There was no first-aid box in the canteen but there was a roll of blue paper towels. He ripped off a few sheets and wound them around his bleeding hand. The paper reddened immediately. Jake took a tea towel that was lying by the coffee machine and wound it tightly around the tissue. Makeshift work – a cop's speciality.

He stormed out of the canteen, through the detective bureau, through the open-plan office that housed the uniforms, traffic guys, drugs and vice – ignoring the startled looks they gave him – heading towards the reception, where he knew there was a first-aid box.

He was almost there when a shadow flickered at the edge of his vision. He looked up.

Not now. Not fucking *now.*

It was Johnny Cooper. He had somehow got past the reception desk. If anything, he was looking worse than a few days ago. He was emaciated and swayed slightly as he walked. Except that 'walked' was too generous a term. Johnny was flat-out stumbling. Jake could smell the stale beer breath, which was competing with the urine stench in a race to get far away from Johnny as quickly as possible.

'I'm sorry, I had to do it,' he was saying. 'You *know*. You understand. Journalists, they're the lowest of the low. I had to go to his house and kill him. He's been writing bad things, evil things, unholy things—'

Jake had had enough. Hand or no hand, this would be dealt with immediately. He gripped Johnny's shoulder, feeling the bony ridge under the cheap fabric of the man's coat. Jake turned Cooper and propelled him to the front desk and the public area.

'Officer Meredith, arrest this man for Murder One.

Throw him in the holding cell and keep him on ice until I'm ready for him,' he said.

The young uniform, a look of confusion on his face, stepped up and took Cooper by the elbow, leading him away. Cooper looked a little disconcerted. Jake wondered if he might actually protest his innocence, now that his twisted confession fantasy seemed to be getting a result.

That would be the cherry on the faecal sundae Jake was trying to keep contained in his burning belly.

He glared around. There were nearly a dozen guys in his sight, and at the front desk he could see Sara, a phone to her ear.

'Listen up, you jerk-offs,' he shouted. 'How the fuck did that lunatic just walk right past all of you?' He glared at them. A number of people looked back, clearly uncomfortable. 'No answer?'

'It's just Johnny,' one of the guys said. 'Sara was tied up, so he came into the office. Big deal.'

'And what if it hadn't been "Just Johnny"? Huh? What if someone had come in with a knife or a gun? A fucking al-Qaeda man could have come in with a bomb strapped to his fucking chest, shouted fucking "Allah-hu Akbar!" and blown us all to shit, and you wouldn't have known anything about it until your heads were flying out of here.'

He could see the stunned looks on their faces, and he knew he had gone too far, but he couldn't stop himself.

Then one of the traffic guys stood up, a grizzled veteran near the end of his twenty. 'Detective,' he said, the word sounding like it tasted bad in his mouth, 'you need to get a grip. You're out of line.'

Jake let the statement hang in the air for a moment. Of course that was how they were going to react – Jake was not local, and had transferred in from a major city. Though it was never said, least of all by him, the implication of such a career path was that Jake had been demoted, that Littleton was a league – maybe two – below somewhere like Chicago. So Jake's advice, his assessments, were always going to be taken as condescending, and his compliments patronizing – even if they weren't.

He had to ignore the fact that he did think the Littleton guys weren't doing things the right way. He could bring any procedural complaint up later – after he'd caught this killer. For now he needed these people on his side, so he had to play nice. But he couldn't.

'There's a fucking killer still out there!' he yelled.

The Littleton cops simply turned away and went about their business – whatever they were doing before Johnny Cooper's show-stopping arrival. Jake considered following up, then realized there was no point. They weren't going to listen to him. He had had his claws, however shallowly, into Mitch Harper, and his grip had been loosened by Johnny. Like an Olympic hurdler whose stride is disrupted, he was going to clip the next hurdle.

He just hoped that clipping it would not take him right out of the race.

He turned and marched into the interview room where Johnny waited.

Johnny looked up as Jake entered the interview room. His eyes were big, and his face was pale. Jake could see he had been crying.

'Please help me,' Johnny said. 'I need to be stopped. I don't know why I did it. I saw him on the television, and the voices told me I had to do him too. I said no, but they made me. I'm so sorry . . .'

Jake could feel the band of pressure around his forehead squeeze a notch tighter with every word Johnny uttered. His teeth were grinding. He had heard enough. Leaning forward until he was right in Johnny's face, Jake said, 'Stop wasting my time. You didn't kill Ford. You didn't kill anyone, and you never will.'

Johnny recoiled as far away from Jake as he could. His lip trembled.

'You know why you won't kill anyone, Johnny?' Jake sneered, putting extra emphasis on his next word: '*Ever?* Because, in your own sad, pathetic way you're sicker than the guys who actually do have the *balls* to go out and take a human life. Because you *want* to be a killer.' He made sure he hit the word 'want' as hard as he could. 'You think about it. Dream about it. Probably jerk off over it sometimes, when you can get it up. Which I bet is extremely rare these days. But you just don't have the *guts* to actually do it.'

Johnny looked at him, eyes blinking rapidly.

'I . . . I . . . I killed plenty,' he said.

'You didn't kill anyone.'

Jake reached up and roughly wiped his brow. As he did so the towel came loose from his hand, and he felt some of the blood smear across his face. Some drops flicked off and landed on Johnny.

Johnny flinched and rubbed at the drop on his shirt. 'But I'm—'

'I'll tell you what you are!' yelled Jake. 'You're a bum who desperately wants to be noticed,' he said. 'You're a pathetic little man who everyone ignores. If you can't be a nice guy, you'll be a bad guy. Anything to get some attention. Am I right, Johnny?'

His blood was boiling. He didn't care. He grabbed Johnny by the shoulders, blood from his hand streaming over the bum's clothes, and shoved him from the holding cell.

'You don't have the guts to be a killer,' Jake snarled as he led Cooper back through to reception. 'It's not in you. You're a nothing, a nobody.' Jake pushed him again and Johnny stumbled. 'I don't ever want to see you in my station. Not for anything.'

He propelled Johnny out of the front door and turned. As he walked back in, he could hear Johnny muttering behind him, 'I'm sorry. I'm so sorry.'

Sara was glaring at him. 'Detective, your hand—'

Jake didn't stop. He stormed to the room where Harper was waiting for him.

57

Monday, 4.50 p.m.

'Interview resumed with Mitchell Harper,' Jake said, his words almost drowned out by the interview room door slamming behind him.

'I thought we were finished here,' said Harper, a flicker of nervousness seeming to pass over his eyes.

'We haven't even gotten started,' Jake said. 'I asked you if you had anything to volunteer. You had your chance. Now let's get down to basics. I know your marriage wasn't perfect. I know Belinda knew about your affairs.'

Harper went pale.

'Yes, your "meetings" with a local working girl are not exactly a secret,' said Jake. 'Although I wouldn't have thought a guy like you would have to pay for it.'

'I don't know what you're talking about.' Harper avoided Jake's gaze; he seemed to be scanning the walls for a hidden door through which he could escape.

'I'm talking about Leanne Schultz,' Jake said. 'Ring a bell? The hooker you were seeing for a year.'

Harper's mouth fell open.

'She said you liked it rough. "Brutal" was actually the word she used.'

'I . . . It wasn't like that.' Harper looked shocked.

'No? What was it like?'

'It was . . . a mistake.'

'Probably not your first, and definitely not your last.' Jake wiped his face with his bandage. He could taste the blood from the cut in his mouth.

'Shouldn't you get that hand looked at?' said Harper, feigning concern.

Jake ignored him. 'How many of Littleton's hookers do you see?'

Harper ran a hand through his hair, his eyes widening and narrowing as he internally debated whether he should tell the truth or go the usual politician's route. Then he closed his eyes and shook his head. He'd made a decision. 'I strayed once. It cost me dear. But Belinda forgave me. She was a patient, forgiving wi—'

There it was. A contradiction. Jake leaned forward, ignoring the twinge of pain in his hand when he placed it on the table. 'You told me she was volatile.'

'Belinda . . . was a complicated woman.'

'What kind of "complicated"?'

Harper opened his mouth to speak, but nothing came out. He was floundering.

'Was she aggressive, Councilman?' Jake pressed, talking quickly. A barrage of jabs now. He was going to get through that guard to land the haymaker. He could feel it. 'I've been told she was a very *passionate* lady – you've described her that way yourself. Is it possible that her emotions could get the better of her on bad days? Maybe she struck back at you with a retaliation fuck?'

Harper's lips were moving, on autopilot, knowing that a response was needed, but still no sound came out.

Jake decided to change his angle of attack – whipped hooks around the ears to bewilder and disorientate his opponent. 'Where were you the night Leanne Schultz was killed in the hit-and-run?'

Harper looked stunned. His face was ashen, and his fingers, gripping the chair, were white. Then suddenly his face collapsed. He put his head in his hands as his body shook with sobs. After a moment he looked back up at Jake, wiping his eyes and nose with the backs of his hands. He got himself under control. 'Leanne was just sex. Nothing more. And she was right: it was rough. I lived out my fantasy. I thought there was no harm in it. We all have our . . . dark sides, right? Our secret wants?'

'Do we?' Jake asked, a savagely sarcastic tone in his voice.

'She pushed me. She said she was going to the press, and I lost my head. I hit her. I regretted it straight away. I took her to the hospital.'

'You didn't take her to the hospital. The cops took her to the hospital.'

'How do you *know* all this?' he whispered, looking at Jake with a mixture of fear and amazement.

Jake sat back in his chair. 'I've read Chuck Ford's files.'

'It was a low point,' Harper said.

Jake noticed that Harper did not register any surprise that the now-dead reporter had the information. 'How did you straighten that out?' he asked.

Harper shrugged. Beaten. 'I lied to the police. I perjured myself – and back then I had some influence. It just went away.'

'And Leanne Schultz?'

'She was cool about it once I paid her off.'

'And Belinda?'

'She called in a divorce lawyer. I almost lost everything. I *did* lose my place in the party – if it wasn't for that whole affair, do you think I'd be running for mayor of this hick town? I'd be state governor by now.'

'So how did you make Ford go away?' he asked. 'Threaten him?'

'Fifty grand.'

Jake let the silence linger. Let it stretch. He held Harper's eyes unflinchingly, knowing that the silence was the worst part for the councilman. In silence his mind would have less protection against the guilt. In silence he would feel the sting of that guilt more acutely. He would talk simply to drown out his own thoughts, hoping that would deflect the guilt. And if he kept talking, there was a chance that he would say something he should not.

'I did a lot of bad things,' said Harper. 'I betrayed Belinda. But I wouldn't lay a hand on her. You don't think I would kill her and Ford over that? She had forgiven me. And Ford was happy with his pay-off.'

'Convenient that I'll never be able to question *them* about that,' said Jake.

Harper recoiled as if he had been struck. 'Belinda did forgive me. We worked through it all.'

Jake could not resist the urge to lean forward. Put Harper under more pressure, he might crack. Jake could feel that the councilman's breaking point was close. A barrage of one-twos, and he might have Harper down on the canvas.

'I don't buy it. Here's what I think. Belinda didn't forgive you. She *never* forgave you. She stayed with you because there was something in it for her. She took a gamble on you all those years ago, banking on you becoming a man of influence – and you did. But you screwed around on her, and – no matter how ambitious she was – she just could not accept that. She could not forget it, could not simply let it slide. And you knew this, didn't you? You knew, as soon as you achieved your political goals, as soon as you became mayor, Belinda would have your balls in her hand for the rest of your life together. So you made sure that life together wasn't too long.'

'No,' Harper muttered. 'I didn—'

'And that fuck, Ford,' Jake continued, getting into a rhythm. 'That bastard was hanging over you like the blade of a guillotine. An easier decision – no dithering required. But then, once you've gone as far as butchering your wife, killing a hack journalist who already took fifty grand from you must be comparatively easy, right?'

'No!' shouted Harper. 'What are you saying? I didn't kill them. I couldn't. I loved Bella. She loved me. She made my life hell for a while. She punished me, and I deserved it. We were good.'

Time to switch up again. Another body shot to drag the guard away from the face. 'What was the sex like, with the prostitute?' Jake asked.

Harper didn't answer.

Jake pushed some more. 'Rough stuff, right? You like to hurt women. You like to cause them pain. You need to dominate, right? A powerful man in a powerful position, and in your home – your own home – your wife was ruling the roost, telling *you* how things were. You couldn't handle that – but you couldn't take it out on Belinda because she had the trump cards. One word from her to the press, your career is over. So you seek out nameless whores. Whores nobody cares about, and nobody defends. Dominance without reprisals – just the way you like it, right? The way things never were with your wife. The wife you ended up—'

'No!' screamed Harper. He seemed years older than when they had picked him up.

The door of the interview room crashed open. Mills burst in, his face red and grim.

'Detective Austin! Outside.'

58

Monday, 5.10 p.m.

Jake followed Mills out of the interview room and back to the detective bureau. 'Don't you dare ever walk in on one of my interviews. I was about to get a confession, and you screwed it up.'

'Look at yourself,' said Mills. 'You look like a fucking mad man!'

'I'm going back in.'

He tried to shove past Mills, but Mills held him off. It took everything Jake had to not act out the flashes that played through his mind – flashes of him hip-tossing Mills to the floor and pinning him there with a knee pressed between his shoulder blades. He let Mills push him until he was facing a small mirror on the wall.

'Look at yourself!' Mills said again.

Jake saw. His hair was wild. The blood from the cut on his hand had soaked through the towel and there were dark stains on his cuffs. Specks of blood and rivers of sweat made his white shirt see-through in places. Streaks of blood were on his cheeks and around his lips from where he had unconsciously rubbed his face during the interrogation.

'Shit,' said Jake, and he looked at his hands.

'Yeah,' said Mills.

Jake closed his eyes, his mind filling with a rushing sound like the drone of an aeroplane mid-flight. He had *chosen* to punch the vending machine; no one had made him. He had *chosen* to lose the plot against Harper, going after him like a psycho; no one had made him do that either.

He was losing it, and he had no one to blame but himself.

'How much damage did I do?'

Mills shrugged. 'You did a tough interview. But it's a quadruple homicide. You'll probably get away with it. Another five minutes, and he'd have walked on a dozen different technicalities.'

Jake looked at Mills, whose face was creased with concern. Mills was the precinct joker. Seeing him look so serious, Jake realized how close he had come to a line he had vowed never to cross again.

'Go home, Austin,' said Mills. 'I'll finish up with the councilman. You hang with the family and unwind a bit. Unless there's another murder overnight, I don't want to see you back here until after lunch tomorrow.'

59

Monday, 7.45 p.m.

Jake wanted to go home by way of a bar, but he knew one beer would probably lead to five. He was also still relatively new in town, which meant that he was thin on drinking buddies whose conversation could drown out the dialogue his head was having with itself. So he drove straight home. He stopped in his driveway and sat in the car for about ten minutes, trying to let the tension and anger drain from him. The day had been a rough one; he didn't want to bring it home with him.

He had a feeling his family would have had a rough day of their own.

When he got inside, Leigh gasped at his bandaged hand.

'It's fine,' he told her, 'just a little gash.'

She removed the tea towel and grimaced. 'It's more than a little gash,' she said. 'You need stitches.' She looked him in the eye and stroked back his hair. 'I'll clean it up for you.'

She reached up to one of the high cupboards and took out a small canvas first-aid satchel. She removed some gauze and cut it into neat squares. Next she cut some strips of adhesive plaster. But just then there was a loud wailing from upstairs. They looked at each other, barely breathing. Jake knew they were thinking the same thing. *Sometimes he goes back to sleep* . . .

But no. The wailing built to a crescendo.

Jake sighed. Leigh shook her head. 'You are not picking up Jakey with this bloodied hand – you'll traumatize him!' She gave him a weary smile before going upstairs.

After he'd bandaged himself up as best he could, Jake sat in the living room and watched television for a while, trying to unwind. But the news was all about the Christmas Killer, Littleton's first serial.

Four victims, but Jake tried to put it in perspective. By serial killer standards, the Christmas Killer was small fry.

Has he killed before? Have I just failed to spot a pattern? Tomorrow morning he would go through all the old files on homicides, see if anything emerged. Then he remembered: he was at home tomorrow morning. He'd phone the idea in, let Mills handle it.

His mind drifted to Orville Lynn Majors, Indiana's only other serial killer. Majors had been a nurse at a hospital in Clinton, and during his two years there the death rate more than quadrupled. When he was dismissed in 1995, the death rate returned to normal. Majors was convicted of six killings but was suspected of more than 120.

'Dad!'

It was Faith, and she was shaking him. 'Dad, Mom

has been calling you for like five minutes. Dinner's ready.'

Jake snapped awake with a start, mingled and mangled images of Majors and Mitch Harper fading from his mind. This was bad: he was with his family, and he was obsessing on serial killers. He really needed to get a grip on himself. Following his daughter back to the airy kitchen, where his family were already seated, he saw his mother at the head of the table. Faith settled into the seat beside her, and Jakey's high chair was next. On the other side of the table was his space, while Leigh was on her feet, draining spaghetti.

'I see you've decided to join us,' she joked.

'Sorry, I . . .' Jake thought about explaining but decided not to. It wasn't exactly suitable dinnertime talk.

There was silence for a while as everyone tucked into the food. Jake looked around at his family and it felt like he wasn't really part of it. Like he was hovering above them. There was a bite of heat to the bolognese sauce, as Leigh always added a few chillies. Normally he loved her cooking, but today even the chillies didn't taste good. It was like all of his senses had been turned off.

Jeanette broke the silence with a verse of 'White Christmas'. 'Bruce loved that song,' she announced to no one in particular at the end.

'Mum, can I be excused?' asked Faith.

'We're a family,' said Leigh steadily; 'we eat together.'

Faith looked daggers at her but said nothing.

Jeanette chose this moment to launch into 'Silent Night'. Faith turned from her in disgust. In the process she knocked over a glass, and milk spilt on the table.

'Faith, be more careful,' said Leigh.

'I *am* being careful!' yelled Faith. This set off Baby Jakey.

'Now look what you've done,' Leigh said with a tut.

Jake heard all the discordant harmonies in the cacophony, but he didn't react. No irritation that another family dinner had descended into the kind of domestic chaos that he knew so well. No exasperation that his beloved daughter was developing a world-class talent for finding reasons to rage at anyone in the room. He realized he was feeling nothing. He told himself that after the day he'd had – the flare-up at the station, the near-miss with Harper – he was just drained.

After dinner he sat with Leigh for a while on the porch. It was freezing but quiet. Both of them wore overcoats, their breath coiling around their heads with every exhale. Without the noise, Jake felt a little better.

'What punishment did you decide on for Faith?' he asked.

'She's going to buy Jakey some new toys from her allowance,' said Leigh.

'And that's it?'

'That's it. Her actions have consequences, and she'll live with those consequences. But we're not going to punish her beyond that.'

‘And what if I disagree?’

Leigh laughed and lightly punched his upper arm. ‘You need to be a fully functioning member of this family to get a vote. Trust me; I know what I’m doing.’

Jake tried to return her laugh, but he couldn’t. He had to admit his domestic life functioned despite his lack of engagement with some aspects of it. And that was because Leigh picked up his slack. Then he thought about it a bit more. She was coping with a new baby, a move to a new state and her crazy mother-in-law.

‘I suppose it’s out of the question for you to get an hour free tomorrow morning?’ she asked.

‘For you? Anything.’

‘I’m not joking, Jake. I need to take Faith out to get her some new winter clothes.’

‘I have the morning off.’

Leigh stared at him for a long moment, clearly trying to figure out if he was joking. When she realized he wasn’t, her face lit up. ‘Perfect. I’ll take Faith into Indianapolis and we’ll spend the morning doing some Christmas shopping. It’ll be good for us to get some quality girl-time. And you can watch Jakey.’

I’d rather catch a killer, he thought. But he kept that to himself. Instead, he echoed her: ‘Perfect.’

60

Tuesday, 20 December, 8.15 a.m.

Faith had sulked the night before when she had heard she was to go shopping with her mother, but when the morning came, she was up early and clearly excited. The moody teen had been shaken off like a wet raincoat, leaving the sweet little girl Jake had known for the first eleven years of her life. At breakfast she chatted inanely and tickled Jakey under his chin. Jake had been about to stop her, but he saw that the baby was delighted to be getting attention from his older sister. In fact, Jake thought this was the first time he'd seen Jakey laugh properly. It was like music.

At nine Leigh and Faith left, and Jake was on his own – apart from his mother and his baby son. *This should be easy*, he thought.

Jake was in the middle of reading the paper's football coverage when the baby began to cry. He put down the paper, picked up Jakey and ran through his mental checklist, hoping that basic childcare had not changed much since he had done it with Faith. First he burped him, then he rubbed his back. He bounced him on his knee and even tried to sing. But then he got the smell.

Obvious – why hadn't he thought of it? Some detective he was. It was not at all pleasant, but Jake had been to four crime scenes in the past week, so changing a nappy was nothing. The baby immediately settled and was soon sleeping gently in his Moses basket. Jake carried him into the lounge. His mother was sitting there when he walked in.

'How are you feeling this morning, Mom?' he asked in a breezy tone.

She muttered a wordless reply and didn't look up. So he let it go. He could kill an hour with the newspaper.

But when he turned back to the football something about the report jarred. He looked at the date on the paper. It was two days old. He threw it away – but calmly, so as not to set off Jakey. The television was tuned to CNN. That and Fox News were the only news channels his cable subscription included. He saw his own image appear on the screen – thankfully, it was not the incident with Ford.

His mother muttered, 'Be more careful.'

The next item was the Springfield asylum story. By now Jake could almost recite the news word-for-word, but his mother turned the volume up.

On screen a team in white boiler suits was combing the grounds of the asylum, and all construction had come to a halt. Nothing new had been found, and the forensics weren't back yet on the two skeletons they'd unearthed. Both seemed to be young children, a girl of around seven and a boy a bit older. In the absence of facts, the reporters had to speculate.

'A number of people have come forward to tell their stories,' the reporter at the scene told the anchor. His face was arranged in a typical Isn't-this-horrible? grimace, but his eyes could not contain his professional glee at such a discovery. 'All the stories are depressingly similar. Witness after witness has told me about being abused by a Fred Lumley, who was the warden of the asylum. Mr Lumley is now the subject of an FBI manhunt.'

The camera cut to one of the witnesses.

'He took away my childhood,' cried the woman. 'He raped me repeatedly, from the age of eight until I was eleven.'

The reporter nodded sympathetically, then asked, 'Did anyone know?'

'I'm sure others knew, but no one did anything to stop him.'

'Why do you think that is?'

'Everyone was afraid of him,' said the woman with a weak shrug.

'And what effect did the abuse have on you? On your life?' the reporter asked.

The woman sniffed before answering the reporter's loaded questions. 'I tried to commit suicide twice. I became an alcoholic, and I've never been able to hold on to a job. That man didn't just take my childhood; he stole my whole life.'

Another witness, a man this time, told of being raped on his ninth birthday, and about taking an overdose when he was fourteen.

The report cut back to the anchor's live feed. 'The FBI is now coordinating a nationwide manhunt for the warden, Fred Lumley. He has been missing for thirty years or more, and they assume he will have changed his name and his identity. Authorities now believe Lumley disappeared because he knew that the abuse of the children in his care was about to be uncovered. He is also the chief suspect in the murder of the two children whose remains were discovered last week. FBI experts have created an image of what Lumley might look like now.'

Jeanette seemed almost in a trance as she stared at the screen. Jake found that he couldn't tear his gaze away either.

The screen filled with two black and white pictures: Lumley how he used to be and how the Feds' computer predicted he would look today. There was something familiar about the face, but that was the danger with reconstructions. They used common elements of all faces. Jake looked hard, with a relaxed mind, for about thirty seconds – long enough to be satisfied he did not know Lumley, then sat back. His mind was turning.

Maybe he's moved to Littleton and started killing again, he thought. *The way things are going, it's not that far-fetched.*

Baby Jakey woke with a whimper. That's how it started. Jake was over straight away, rocking the Moses basket gently. That only seemed to make it worse. It wasn't long before Jake found himself in the middle of a storm of noise, as the baby opened his throat and let out a full-blooded howl. The volume took Jake by surprise. He realized with a start that this was the first time he had been in charge of his son. Leigh was always there to take him when the crying started.

He picked Jakey out of the little basket and cradled him in his arms. But the baby arched his back and nearly fell to the floor. So Jake hugged him tight to his chest, hoping the sound of his own heart would somehow calm him. But either his heart was on strike, or it was muffled by his shirt and jacket, because Jakey still struggled. His face was turning red, and his eyes were watery. The sound of his screaming was tearing through Jake's head.

The band of pressure was back.

Jake went through everything. He offered the baby a bottle, but Jakey turned his head and refused it. He checked, but the nappy didn't seem to need changing. He rubbed Jakey's back, burped him gently, bounced him, rocked him. He even sang to him. Nothing worked. The baby screamed louder.

He looked to his mother. Jeanette had turned up the volume on the television.

Thanks, Mom. That's what was missing.

Jake pulled the remote out of her hand and killed the sound. 'I need your help here,' he said.

'Yes, dear,' she said gently. 'Is there a problem?'

Jake just stood there, with his screaming son in his arms, and looked at her. She wasn't being sarcastic. 'Jakey's crying.'

'He's a baby. That's what they do. But if you really must have him quiet, maybe Leigh can help?'

Jakey screamed louder. Jake wondered if, intuitively, he had picked up on the mention of his mother's name.

'She's in the city with Faith,' said Jake, almost shouting to be heard over his son's cries. 'What should I do?'

His mother looked at him for a moment, then smiled. 'Perhaps he's hungry?' she suggested.

'I've tried.'

'His nappy might . . . ?'

'I've tried everything! What did you use to do when I was a baby?'

She looked at him blankly.

'Never mind!' *I thought this stuff was supposed to be instinctive to mothers?*

The pounding in his head was back. It was going to be a long morning.

61

Tuesday, 2 p.m.

Jake had been relieved to hand Jakey over to Leigh once his wife was back from her girlie morning with Faith. As soon as his son started to quieten down, it felt like Jake's skull opened. In a good way. He felt some of his perspective returning. He had needed the break from the case, even if it was a mad domestic farce. Something else to occupy his mind would sharpen his focus on his work once he got back to it. He left the house ready, determined. He was going to nail Harper.

As soon as he reached the station, he realized that he had not asked Leigh or Faith about their morning, how it had been. Was Faith her old self? Had the break done Leigh any good? He might catch hell for that when he got home, and he would deserve it. But he told himself the case was about to break. He could feel it. And once Harper was booked, Jake would make it up to his family. He made this a vow as he entered the detective bureau.

Mills spotted him. He had a big grin on his face as he stood up from his desk. 'Me and the boys have chipped in to buy you a little something,' he said, bending down to pick up a cushion. 'It's for the next time you use the vending machine.'

There was a guffaw from the men behind Mills.

Jake allowed Mills a moment to enjoy his joke and even offered an indulgent smile. But the truth was, he wasn't in the mood. He was here to put Harper away.

Mills stopped smiling and put down the cushion. 'I cut Harper loose shortly after you went home. Boy, was he pissed off . . . once he'd stopped crying.'

Pissed off? Surely Harper should have been little more than simply relieved to be getting out of there.

Getting away with murder.

Either Harper was a murderous bastard who was also completely in control of his emotions and absolutely aware of how to manipulate the people around him, or . . .

Jake chased the thought away. The 'or' was too awful for him to contemplate.

'I think you've just made yourself a very powerful enemy, Austin. He'll be our next mayor, and he'll be in a position to make things very uncomfortable for you.'

'Not if he's on death row,' said Jake with more conviction than he actually felt.

They heard a yell from across the hall as Asher called. Jake walked into the colonel's office. Asher was behind the desk, his tie undone.

'I heard you gave Harper a tough grilling last night,' he began. 'You think he's our guy?'

Jake eased himself into the chair opposite Asher. He considered his answer. 'He's looking good for it.'

Asher looked down at his desk, considering his response. 'We pursue Harper, we do it under the radar. Understood? I can't risk blowback on the department if he becomes mayor. Our pockets are empty enough.'

'Yes, sir,' said Jake. 'Is there anything else?'

'There's been another find.'

'Fuck! Where did—'

'Not a new body,' said Asher, holding up his hands. 'Just a bone.'

'A bone?'

'It's a human bone.'

Who gives a shit?

'I've asked the uniforms to preserve the scene, and I want you to drive out and look at it.'

'Look, sir,' Jake said, taking a deep breath to try and hold himself back. 'I need to spend all my time on the serial. I'm not—'

'It's on another part of the interstate construction site,' said Asher, 'about half a mile from where Marcia Lamb was dumped.'

Now Jake was interested. 'Is it fresh?'

'They say it's old,' said Asher.

He sighed. 'Then send someone else.'

Asher looked at him. 'Last I remember, I was still the boss here. I want you to go look at it, not someone else. You're the guy with the eye. From what we know already, the bone is old, but it was placed on the site only a few days ago. That makes it fresh. Someone went to the trouble of digging it up and bringing it to the same construction site where we have a killer dumping fresh bodies. You know as well as I do, we have to look into any possible connections here.'

As he left Asher's office, Jake caught a glimpse of a slim woman walking into the station, and his heart squeezed in his chest. Had he missed an appointment with Gail Greene this morning? No, he wasn't due to see her again until Thursday. Two sessions a week over two weeks, anger management taken care of. So had Mills brought her in for something case-related?

He turned and put on a big smile, walking confidently up to her. As he drew near he could see she was upset. He turned his smile into a frown.

'Gail?'

Her face was white, and when she looked at him it tightened immediately. She was not in tears, but Jake got the feeling from her expression that she was probably the kind of person who had long since trained herself out of crying.

'You asshole,' she spat.

Jake tried not to look surprised or hurt. 'Excuse me?'

'I've just been with Johnny, and he's in a bad way. You did a real number on him, Detective.' She had adopted a mock-congratulatory tone.

He sighed, buying himself a few seconds – the better to curb his reaction to Gail's sarcasm. 'Dr Greene, we're in the middle of a murder investigation—'

'Johnny is a sick man. What you did yesterday was cruel. You've set him back years, and you've jeopardized any chance I had of helping him.' Her top lip curled, her face showing a disgust that took Jake aback. 'I hope you're proud of yourself.'

'He was obstructing our investigation.'

'He's fragile, and needs respect and understanding.'

'He was putting people's lives at risk. Without his interference, who knows what we could have done with the saved time? Candy Jones and Chuck Ford might still be alive now.'

He knew that he was overplaying the significance of Johnny's obstruction. Knew also that there was a certain sly malice in his accusation. What he did not know was who he was trying to kid.

'Asshole,' she repeated and turned to the door. Jake felt about four feet tall. And he also felt angry with himself. He had barely managed a word in his defence, and what he had said was a none-too-subtle suggestion that Johnny Cooper – sick, near-helpless Johnny Cooper – was in some way culpable for the crimes of the evil man who was still out there, probably planning his next attack.

The guy was still out there, though. And that was all that really mattered. This thought fuelled his next question. As Gail reached the door, he called out, 'I suppose that means my Thursday appointment is off?'

Gail did not stop; she just pushed through the door without looking back.

As Jake turned back towards the detective bureau Mills was standing there, again with the big grin. 'Trouble with the girlfriend? Don't worry, the make-up is always more fun than the fight.'

'Fuck you,' said Jake, brushing past.

It was time to nail a killer and get his life back.

62

Tuesday, 2 p.m.

Austin, you weren't meant to be a part of this story. You're a complication now. You will have to be dealt with.

He felt good as he looked at the four photographs pinned to his wall. He felt invincible – and invisible. The cops were running in circles, like puppies chasing their tails. Regardless of what they told the newspapers, they were nowhere near tracking him down.

Everything was following his plan. The only problem he could see was Austin. The detective had nothing, but his eyes were always open and alert, the eyes of a man who never stopped thinking. His eyes were the window into a mind that raced down every alley of thought, sometimes doubling back, looking for a clue or an idea to latch on to. Such men could be dangerous.

I know what you're doing. You're trying to imagine being me. You're trying to trace my thoughts and see through my eyes. And if you are who I think you are, you just might be very good at that. I'll have to be even more careful . . .

He stood and poured himself a small shot of Scotch. It was one of his few indulgences; always single malts, always from Islay. He savoured the smoky peatiness of the whisky. He let the warmth flow through his chest, chasing away the bitter chill of uncertainty now that this complication had entered the picture.

No matter. I'm the master, and I have my plan – a new plan. You don't know it yet, Jake, but I have you in check. And if you make even one wrong move, it will be checkmate. Game over.

He took a deep breath and drained the whisky.

I hope it doesn't come to that.

I always liked you as a child.

63

Tuesday, 3.30 p.m.

Mills drove while Jake sat silently.

They stopped at a part of the construction site that looked a lot more developed than where Marcia Lamb and Belinda Harper had been dumped. The blacktop had been smoothed and rolled, and workers were busy painting the road markings. Or at least they should have been. All work was suspended. The foreman was fuming.

'We should have just thrown the fucking bag in a dumpster and kept working,' Jake heard him say as they arrived.

'I could see why that would have been tempting,' he said, 'but there are laws against that.'

The man turned to face him. 'When can I get my men back to work?'

'Maybe today, maybe next week,' Jake told him. 'This is now a crime scene.'

Mills added, 'We'll do our job and be out of here as quickly as we can, sir.' Jake wondered when his partner had managed to learn such diplomacy.

The worker who had found the bone was lingering

just behind the foreman, clearly eager to tell his tale and lead them to the spot where he had made his discovery. But even cops not as adept as Jake and Mills would have needed no tour guide. The spot was obviously just up ahead, where a group of workers had formed a loose, lazy ring. A uniformed cop was with them, sipping from a paper cup of coffee.

Jake was furious. 'Patrolman, you were ordered to secure the scene. Why haven't you done it?'

The officer looked up, surprised. 'Nobody's touched it.'

'But you have all these people standing around, trampling on potential evidence.'

The man had the decency to look sheepish.

'Clear it now.' It felt good to assert his authority. The way his day was going, he had to take some control back. The officer began to herd the workers back towards the site office.

Now he was on his own. Mills was hanging back, giving him the space to work. What he was looking at was a hell of a lot better than what he had been seeing for the past few days. For a start there was no blood, no scattered teeth and no dangling eyeballs; just a tattered white plastic bag, with a rock on it to weigh it down. That was all.

He scanned the area.

The worker who had found the bag was hovering nearby.

'Did you put the rock on it?' Jake asked him.

'No,' the guy said. 'It was there when I spotted the bag. As soon as I saw the bone, I called you guys.' He leaned in. 'Is it human?'

Jake turned back to the bag. Interesting. The rock had been put there to ensure the bag didn't get mistaken for garbage. Whoever had dumped it *wanted* the bone to be found.

But why?

As he approached, he saw nothing of interest. The fresh tarmac was clear. He bent down and used a pen to open the bag, then looked inside. There was a bone there all right, and it was human, as far as he could tell. It looked like a femur. It was about fourteen inches long. Jake was no anatomist, but he thought that made it the bone of an adult but not a tall one. *Maybe a woman?* The surface of the bone was rough and discoloured, and there was not a trace of flesh attached. The colonel was right: it wasn't recent. On the surface of things, this bone had nothing to do with his case.

And yet it had been dumped on the interstate. And that sort of fitted with the previous crimes. All the bodies apart from Candy's had been dumped on sites associated with the new road.

Jake allowed himself to assume this old bone *was* related – just for a moment.

It might make the killer a man of a certain age, depending on how old the femur turns out to be. But no . . . Why had he kept this bone, for all those years, only to produce it now? It doesn't fit.

It couldn't fit.

Jake ran through the other potential explanations. It could be – and most likely was – a copycat with his own anti-interstate agenda. The construction companies were leaking money on all the delays. That was a result for the protesters.

It could be kids playing a prank. That possibility couldn't be discounted, however extreme and unlikely it sounded to his mind's ear. If he had the resources, he'd send uniforms to the graveyards to see if anything was disturbed.

He straightened up and walked the site, but nothing struck him as out of place. He came back to the bone and took out his mobile. Time to ring the lab.

'Ronnie? Austin here. I'm sending you in a bone.'

'Great, thanks. I'm twiddling my thumbs around here,' she said.

Jake ignored the playful sarcasm. 'We found it in a plastic bag on the new interstate. It looks like a femur.'

'Sounds like you don't need my help at all, Detective.'

'Very funny. Get back to me as soon as you can.'

He took one last look around the construction site. If it wasn't for Candy Jones, he'd still like Makowski for this. But Makowski had been in custody the night Candy was killed.

Of course, Candy could have been killed by a copy-cat.

Jake had four victims who could fit into a kind of neat box – two with definite links to Harper, one who was a prostitute, which Jake knew Harper used, and one who could very likely be described as a dress rehearsal for the main performance.

Jake told himself not to see connections where there might not be any. There was only one indisputable link between the four murders.

The new interstate.

Jake didn't know what, but there had to be something about the road – its construction or location, or some other kind of significance he was not yet seeing – that bound these murders together.

But what?

He looked up at Mills. 'I need a drink.'

64

Wednesday, 21 December, 9 a.m.

Jake was barely inside the detective bureau when Sara came to find him. She was pale.

'Detective Austin,' she whispered, 'it's Johnny . . .'

Would this guy ever learn? Would Sara? Just because there wasn't a fresh kill overnight didn't mean Jake could waste his morning on this lunatic. He had taken the dressing-down from Gail, and part of him knew she had been right to give it. But he was damned if he was going to provide a babysitting service for every sicko in Littleton.

'Deal with it yourself, Sara,' he said, making to move past her. 'I need to—'

'Please, Jake.'

There was something in her voice and a look in her eyes. No mischievous twinkle suggesting this was another prank. This was different. Jake got up and followed her to the front desk, thinking that maybe Johnny's constant appearances at the station had worn Sara down.

He was also thinking that, if Johnny tried to lay claim

to the femur, he might just beat the crazy bastard over the head with it.

At the front desk Johnny stood with his hands thrust into the pockets of a purple bathrobe which, even from ten feet away, radiated a stench of cheap cigarettes, piss and BO. His shoulders were hunched, and the skin around his eyes formed two deep pools of black. He looked like he hadn't slept last night – and maybe not the night before either. But he wasn't twitching today. He was standing still, glaring. There was something in his eyes that gave Jake a momentary prickle of unease. There was a focus there – a kind of clarity in Johnny's hostility.

But now was not the time for his bullshit.

'I thought I told you I didn't want to see you here any more,' he said. But he kept his voice even. He wasn't going to overdo it like he had on Monday.

'I did it.'

'I'm sure you did. Whatever it is, it can wait until your next therapy session. I understand you're getting treatment from Gail Greene. She's very good.'

Jake came from behind the desk and approached Johnny. Now was the time to escort him out and put an end to this mess. He reminded himself to do it gently – he did not want to give Gail Greene another reason to come back to the station and call him an asshole.

But Johnny took a step back. 'I did it,' he shouted. 'You challenged me, and I did it.' He took a hand out of his bathrobe pocket and held it up. The hand was red with blood. 'See?' he shouted triumphantly. He began to pull his other hand out of the other pocket.

Jake reacted instinctively, pulling his gun from his shoulder holster and bringing it up in a two-handed shooter's pose, aiming right at Johnny.

'Take your hand out very slowly and raise both hands over your head,' he bellowed.

The shout brought out a number of cops, uniformed and plain clothes. They saw Jake with his gun drawn and reacted instantly. Within seconds, five men had guns trained on Johnny Cooper.

'I did it this time! I *do* have the guts.' He said it calmly, and he wasn't moving. Nutcase or not, he had enough sense not to draw a shower of lead on himself.

'On your knees, Johnny – now!' shouted Jake.

Slowly Johnny lowered himself until he was kneeling. Both his hands were covered in fresh blood. As he knelt, his robe swung open. He was naked underneath except for a vest, which was also red with blood. Not his own – there was far too much for him to be walking and talking . . .

Then his face seemed to cave in, and his body shrank.

'My God! What have I done? I'm sorry. I'm so sorry. I only did it because he told me to. It's what *he* wanted.'

Johnny was pointing two blood-coated fingers at Jake.

65

Wednesday, 9.30 a.m.

Johnny was in a holding cell, cuffed. He had gone quietly, saying nothing more beyond a few muttered apologies and reiterations that he had been 'challenged' to take a life. He was on the chair, but curled up like a sitting fetus, and he was rocking gently, crying softly to himself. Back and forth. Back and forth.

'We need to check out his place,' said Mills. 'See if there's anything there that ties him to the others.'

'He's not the serial,' said Jake. 'There's just no way. His statements contradicted—'

'No shit,' said Mills. 'But he *has* committed a murder – from the looks of it, a messy one. The press is gonna be all over it, finding links. We have to follow it up, even if it's just to rule it out.'

Jake nodded.

'Two cars have already gone out,' Mills continued. 'They're holding one for us. Are you OK?'

Was he? It was too early to say.

Ten minutes later they were on skid row. Johnny Cooper lived in a three-storey apartment block in one of the roughest areas of town. It was the kind of place that should have eaten a man like Johnny alive but it probably did more to feed the beast of his dementia.

They pulled up behind the two black and whites. Three of the cops had gone inside, but one had stayed out with the cars. Mills locked the doors, something Jake hadn't seen him do before. It was that kind of neighbourhood.

They walked into the apartment block. There was no intercom system. The door pushed open, the lock broken. The cops were on the first floor. Jake and Mills walked up the unlit stairwell, which stank of urine and worse.

The landing looked like a refuse tip. There were cans and bottles everywhere, with plastic bags, old cereal boxes and dirty nappies too. More worryingly the ground was littered with needles, some broken and rusty, some newer. Jake also spotted a few used condoms.

'Classy place,' said Mills.

The door was closed.

'You're up,' said Jake.

'No need. I took these when we searched him.' Mills waved a bunch of keys in the air. 'You wouldn't remember; you were pretty out of it back at the station.'

Was I?

Jake felt slightly numb as he watched Mills put the key in and turn it.

As soon as the door cracked open, new smells wafted out to mingle with those of the fetid corridor – stale onions, burned toast, vomit and a filthy carpet – but the unmistakable smell of a dead body lorded over them all.

'He really did it this time,' muttered Mills.

Jake tried to meet his partner's gaze and found that he couldn't.

He walked into the tiny apartment. Two doors led off the dual living and bedroom. They were both ajar. One opened into a tiny kitchen, the other into a toilet. Jake deliberately slowed his breathing and tried to get into the moment.

Tried to get into the fucked-up head of Johnny Cooper.

He started with the crummy sofa. Shreds of tobacco on one of the cushions.

You were sitting here. Rolling a smoke. The one thing you had, your confessions, had been taken away from you. You felt vulnerable and alone. You didn't like it. You sat there, thinking and thinking, getting angrier and angrier.

Jake let his eyes roam over the room. What happened next? A chronically messy bum living in squalor – it was hard to spot what was out of place in such a man's living room. But Jake saw it – an unlit hand-rolled cigarette on top of the ancient television.

There was a knock at the door. So you got up to answer it. You don't get many visitors and, this time, you were feeling like you needed someone. Someone to talk to. So you got up – quickly. You put the smoke on the TV.

But who's at the door? Who would knock on your *door? What does Johnny the Snitch have that anyone else would want?*

Not money. Or maybe it was *money. A useless smoke-hound, a mooch, always with his hand out even to other people who everyone knows have nothing.*

Was that who made the mistake of knocking on your door? Someone worse off than yourself. Someone who, if anything, would be missed even less. Someone asking to borrow a few dollars, just for a couple of days – he swore he'd pay you back just as soon as he had it.

You were angry. Mad as hell. You didn't have the cash, but you told him you did.

You invited him inside.

Jake looked back at the cluttered living room. Not there – it was a small space, but to a man about to commit his first murder it would look too open. His victim, whoever he was, would have space to move, furniture to hide behind – any number of inanimate objects to use as a makeshift weapon.

The living room just wasn't practical – and, besides, Jake knew that, had the murder taken place in the living room, the place would be awash with red, as Johnny had been when he turned up at the station.

He also knew that the toilet was far too small for Johnny's purposes.

That left the kitchen. Jake hadn't seen it yet, but he knew instinctively the body would be there, coated in whatever blood had not spattered Johnny.

He was a man – can't imagine too many women would come here. And any who would, would almost certainly come with a friend. He was a man, a man who was jumpy, just like you.

Maybe strung out. He'd have to be, to not be able to look you in the eye and see that there was something different there tonight, something wrong.

You didn't do it straight away. You decided *straight away, but it took you a few minutes to wind yourself up for it. So you asked him to stay in the living room for a moment while you got the money. He probably thought you were afraid he was here to scope out your place, find where your stash was hidden. So he played along, stayed in the living room. And you went into . . .*

Jake followed his instincts – and his nose – and walked towards the small room on the left. The kitchen. The smell grew stronger. He stopped at the doorway, letting his mind continue churning.

Of course it was the kitchen. That's where the knives are. And you wanted to show me that you had 'the guts'. So it had to be a knife – it had to be messy, bloody. *You ducked into the kitchen for a moment, and he sat down on the filthy couch, thinking nothing of it.*

You breathed in and breathed out, gathering yourself. Then you made your decision. 'Here it is,' you called out. You knew he'd come to you, unsuspecting – all he's thinking about is the cash. He doesn't think it's weird that you suddenly suggest he comes into the kitchen.

As he bunched his hand into his jacket sleeve and reached for the kitchen door, Jake's breath caught in his throat. But was he simply apprehensive at seeing yet one more dead body in Littleton, or was he imagining this scenario just a little *too* clearly?

The kitchen door opened outwards. In Jake's

experience this was often the case in poorly designed shitty houses like these. It gave him the sensation that he was pulling up a curtain on the scene within.

Mills groaned and turned away. Jake felt like doing the same, but he didn't let himself – this was his doing. A weak bulb cast its lazy light over a tiled kitchen floor that may once have been white but was now a grisly medley of piss-yellow and blood-crimson. The yellow was a sign of Johnny Cooper's neglect, his years of living in squalor.

The crimson was his single moment of utter frenzy.

Jake crouched in the doorway, staring at the body of Johnny's victim. He lay face down on the tiles, his face – black, weathered and with flecks of grey in his unkempt beard – for ever set in a mask of pain and shock. From the ragged dogshit-stained boots all the way up to the torn tracksuit bottoms and faded black denim jacket, Jake knew that his initial assessment had been correct. A smoke-hound – someone so deep in the gutter that they would come to Johnny Cooper for a handout.

'That sick sonofabitch,' said Mills, peering over Jake to get a closer look at the corpse. 'Did he jack off?'

Jake followed Mills's finger. A splashing of grey-white stain was on the collar of the denim jacket. Standing up, he leaned as far as he dared into the kitchen. It was definitely semen on the victim's jacket. Jake turned and looked at Mills, who – for the first time since he had known the man – wore a look of absolute outrage.

'Did he jack off on the vic?' Mills asked again.

Jake shook his head. 'Gail Greene indicated that Johnny may have presented with symptoms of necrophiliac tendencies—'

'Don't fucking dress it up, Austin,' said Mills, his voice hiding none of his exasperation.

'No,' said Jake. 'He was wearing a robe, remember? Probably it came open, loose, during the attack. The euphoria of the moment, as he stood over the body, probably got the better of him.'

Jake didn't need to say any more than that. Mills puffed out his cheeks and turned away. Jake stood beside him in the filthy living room. The place where Johnny Cooper had spent his last moments of freedom, stewing over insults Jake had thrown at him in the station.

Jake imagined Johnny sitting with his bloody hands – the ones he would later point at Jake – held in his lap, rocking back and forth on the couch, thinking to himself that he'd done it. He'd really done it.

Now the serial confessor had something to which he really could confess.

Jake suddenly felt sick.

66

Wednesday, 11 a.m.

The station was unnaturally quiet when Jake and Mills returned. Everyone knew Johnny; they all regarded him as a harmless nut, and many of them had given him a bill from their wallets. Now he had killed, and it was like the family dog had turned on them and needed to be put down.

Jake spotted Gail Greene's car as she pulled up. But this time his heart didn't skip a beat. He didn't want to face her because to face her was to face the fact that it had been his taunting that had pushed Cooper to this. Jake had the same blood on his hands as Johnny did.

He walked the short distance to the detective bureau. A few of the guys were around. Mills had gone ahead and was at his desk, going over witness statements. Jake walked up to his partner. 'Mills, I want to talk to Johnny.'

'No way,' said a cold voice behind him. Normally the husky tone would have caused a slight tremble in his knees, but not now. He turned and looked at Gail Greene.

'I'm sorry,' he said softly.

'Not good enough. Johnny was a sick man. You changed that. You turned him into a killer.'

Jake took her by the elbow and pulled her into the canteen. He winced when he saw the damaged vending machine.

'I need to talk to him,' he whispered through gritted teeth, 'to find out—'

She pulled her elbow from his grasp. 'If he blames you? I think you'll find everybody blames you.'

'Gail—'

'Don't you dare try to play dumb, Jake. You know what you did, and you're smart enough to know that you did it because you just *have* to be the smartest guy in the room. You're the alpha male, the dominant one. And now there's a killer out there who's fooling you at every turn. You can't get a handle on him so you take it out on other people. You don't need a professional to tell you this, because you already know it. The unfortunate part with guys like you: it's always *in retrospect*. After the damage has been done.'

Jake let his eyes drop to the ground. He wanted to respond, but what could he say?

She wasn't finished. 'This isn't the first time you've lost control. Didn't you learn anything from what happened with your friend in Chicago?'

'Ex-friend,' said Jake.

'It's always someone else's fault,' she snapped. 'Now a man is dead, and Johnny's life is ruined. Whose fault is it now?'

Jake knew the answer to that.

'I hope you're happy with yourself.' She strode past

him to the door but did not leave right away. Instead, she turned back and said, 'I've recommended to Colonel Asher that you are not to communicate with Johnny. It's the least you can do for him now.'

Jake felt a pang of irritation as he watched her leave. He really didn't have time for this. Johnny Cooper was no longer a priority. And Johnny had made that decision himself.

His phone buzzed. Glancing down, he saw it was Leigh. More problems.

'What's up?' he asked wearily.

Leigh's voice was strained and clipped. Not angry or worried. Just tired, resigned. 'Your mother has gone for another one of her walks.'

There it was – the burning deep down in his stomach. He half-expected to look down and see smoke wafting from a hole in his flesh.

'What happened?'

'I don't know. She was sitting quietly watching the news. I went upstairs to give Jakey a bath, and when I came back down she was gone.'

'How long ago?'

'Within the last twenty minutes.'

Jake rubbed his eyes. He'd have to take an early lunch.

He walked out of the canteen back into the detective bureau. Gail was standing at the desk, talking to Mills. He barely glanced at them.

'Jake . . .' she said.

He kept walking.

67

Wednesday, 11.30 a.m.

Jake drove around the house in ever-expanding circles. It shouldn't be difficult; his mom was on foot and hadn't been missing long. Roughly twenty minutes by the time he had left the station, plus the six more minutes Jake had been driving. That meant she had had less than thirty minutes of walking time. She was elderly; that meant about a mile radius, maximum. But how many city blocks did that cover?

Traffic was light, but the highway construction was creating problems everywhere. There were diversions throughout the city, and Jake found himself driving down smaller roads that he was less familiar with. He needed GPS.

Suburbia, with plenty of leafy lanes and avenues, and lots of nice houses, most of which should have been decked out in garish Christmas decorations. But most of them had been taken down – hardly anyone seemed in the mood right now. And if the PD didn't break this one swiftly, Jake could imagine the next few Christmases being tainted by association.

If his mom had stuck to the roads, he might find her.

But if she went into driveways or a park, he could cruise for the whole day with no luck.

To top it all, he wasn't quite sure where he was. The streets of Littleton all looked the same to him: the same green hedges, turned brown now by winter; the same well-tended yards; the same mom-and-pop stores on the corners. The only real landmark was the steeple of the Church of Christ the Redeemer. He was in the heart of the construction zone now, with signs everywhere saying LOCAL ACCESS ONLY and DANGER – CONSTRUCTION. Dust hung in the air and settled on all the surfaces, and most of the vehicles were diggers. The church, slated for demolition, stood out by its height. At least it gave him a point of orientation. That was something.

Jake looked at the church. Two lanes led to it, and there was an area of open space in front. It was secluded, the perfect spot for an old woman to lose herself in.

And there was one! Jake felt an instant shot of relief diluted with confusion – could that briskly walking woman really be his mother? If it was, she was moving faster than Jake had seen her shift in years. She was walking as if she had a destination in mind.

Jake turned the car and headed down the street. As he drew near, he recognized her coat, and then he pulled level and could see her face. He stopped the car and got out.

'Hi, Mom.'

'Oh, hi, Jake,' she said with an automatic smile.

She recognizes me today – that's something.

'Mom,' he said, rushing round the car to hold her by the shoulders. 'What are you doing out?'

'I'm just looking for someone to talk to,' she went on, trying to sidestep him.

'You can talk to me,' he said, blocking her path again.

She looked at him for a moment, then looked away. 'I'm just looking for someone to talk to,' she repeated.

It was sad. She was making sense and seemed perfectly lucid. But she didn't know who she needed to speak to and couldn't tell him why. It was like her brain was still engaged but was travelling down a track that never quite intersected with anyone else's. But seeing her focused like this, fixated on an idea, however bizarre, was better than seeing her thoughts scattering to the winds.

'So talk to *me*,' he offered again.

'No, dear. I need to talk to someone.' She set off again and Jake walked beside her.

'I know a psychiatrist,' he suggested.

'No!' she shouted, grabbing his arm. 'No doctors! I want you to promise me, Jake. Don't bring in the doctors.'

Jake didn't know how to respond. Not only was she moving with more urgency and ease than he had seen in a long time, she had rather a strong grip on his arm too. Her long nails were sharp – even through Jake's sleeve. It was a grip he remembered from childhood: strong, dominant but flexible. He was suddenly struck with a memory from his childhood: *trying to escape her is useless; she has me too tight.*

He shook the thought away, and his eyes fell on a familiar figure walking up the street towards them. It was Father Ken, the priest from the condemned church.

'Detective Austin, hello.' The old man was smiling and had his hand extended. It was encased in a thick winter glove, making the handshake awkward. 'Is everything OK?'

Jake felt embarrassed. 'My mother had just gone for a bit of a ramble, but I'll be taking her home now.'

'A pleasure to meet you,' said the priest, turning to Jake's mom. 'Your son is doing a fine job policing our community. I hope you're proud of him.'

Jake's mother looked at the priest, her face re-forming into the old familiar blankness.

Father Ken looked from Jake's mother to Jake. 'I'm just returning from my morning walk. Why don't you both stop in for a cup of coffee? I'm just around the corner.'

Although he wanted to get back to the investigation, Jake thought he could spare a few minutes. If his mother was so set against doctors and psychiatrists, perhaps she might talk to a priest?

Just then Jake's pager buzzed. Irritably he took a quick look. It was the office. He killed the sound, then turned to Father Ken. The priest was smiling.

'Anything urgent?'

'It can wait.'

'Don't you be worrying,' said the priest. 'Go do what you have to do. I'll look after your mother and drive her home in half an hour or so. Let her relax and enjoy a cup of coffee, and you can be on your way.'

Jake hesitated. 'Are you sure?'

The priest smiled. 'I have nothing else to fill my day. It's not a problem.'

Jake felt relieved. Ten minutes, he'd be back on the case. He could do without the hassle and drama of returning to the house and having to deal with Leigh and Jakey on top of his mother.

'Thanks, Padre.'

He could hear his mother talking behind him as he turned away: 'Father, I think I'm ready to unburden myself now.'

As he walked briskly to his car, Jake wondered what, exactly, his mother needed to unburden herself of.

68

Wednesday, noon

This is too good. Simply perfect. A kind of divine destiny. Austin and his mama both dropped into my lap. Your guiding light led them to me. You really do work in surprising ways.

He did his best to look sympathetic as Jeanette Austin began to open her wicked, sinful heart to him.

'I feel my mind is slipping, Father. There are days when I don't remember things that everyone thinks I *should* remember.'

He smiled and nodded.

'Sometimes I wonder if this is my punishment.'

'Do you feel you need to be punished?' he asked her.

'Yes,' she said. 'For all my sinning.'

'I know,' he muttered. Of course he knew.

'There's no need to upset yourself by going through it all again. I understand,' he said.

He understood, but at the same time his hand, under the table, gripped the cosh tightly. For a moment he considered killing her right away, but that would have created problems. Her son – a detective, no less – would wonder why he hadn't driven her home, and within a very short time Father Ken's work would come crashing down on him, unfinished.

'Jake has forgotten everything,' she went on. 'He's completely blanked it out, as if it never happened.'

His hand relaxed on the cosh. *Maybe not today* . . . If Austin had really forgotten everything, then that meant his guard was down about it. He was vulnerable to a sucker punch from the past. That was good, very good.

You have taken away his memory, and now my pieces are in place. It shows the righteousness of my work. Soon it will be checkmate.

'And did you have any other children?' he asked her, even though he knew the answer.

'Never,' she said with a wistful smile. He noted that she answered without hesitation, as she would have answered any question he asked. She seemed to be in his thrall still, even after so many years. If he asked her to take up a knife and plunge it into her own chest, he believed she would do it without question.

'Jake has a daughter,' she went on. 'In some ways she reminds me of Jake when he was a boy. It frightens me. Maybe you could talk to her?'

It's an intriguing idea – to put my head in the lion's mouth.

His decision was definite. He would not kill her today. That would be rash. He had been smart up to now, and he was not prepared to let that desert him. Besides, he hadn't helped Jeanette and her son escape their troubles all those years ago only to kill them now. That would be cruel.

And I am not a cruel man.

It would make no sense to undo the good deed I did back then, unless I have to. I'll let her go. But the Lord has delivered Jake Austin to me. That is no accident. I know what it means . . . I see it all now. The beautiful design of his master plan for us.

The three of us . . . connected by that place.

Father Ken stood up calmly, feigning a stiffness in his hips that wasn't there.

Raising his arm he made the sign of the cross over Jeanette, muttering a blessing. Then he smiled.

'Jeanette, let me take you home.'

She followed him out of the house and to his car like a woman in a trance.

69

Thursday, 22 December, 8 a.m.

The protesters were roughly the same bunch as last week, the Monday that everything had started turning to shit. Why did they need so many cops to control this chicken-shit demo? Even the brass were out – Asher was at the head of the gaggle of cops, lips pursed tight, shoulders square and arms gesturing nonsensical directions and instructions. He was posing for the few cameras.

'There's the prick,' shouted a familiar face. Jake didn't need to look to know it was Guy Makowski. He had seen him at the forefront of the protesters, shouting the loudest. Jake had hung back specifically to avoid a confrontation. So much for that.

Makowski was apparently trying to get at Jake. He was a strong guy, and if his emotions were running as high as he was pretending, he probably could have broken free of the guys holding him back at any time. But that was not his intention. He was using the old schoolboy ploy, issuing a challenge he knew he wouldn't have to make good on. Asking for a fight he was too much of a coward to actually have – his friends were his cover.

Jake walked away to stand beside Father Ken in the shadow of a withered oak tree. The priest nodded and smiled weakly at Jake. They had exchanged a few words the previous evening when he had dropped Jake's mom home. She hadn't seemed much better, despite chatting with the priest.

'You OK, Father?' Jake asked.

The priest nodded. 'I'm going to see if I can talk sense into them. We both know the work isn't going to stop.' A multi-billion-dollar development was not going to be derailed by a handful of well-meaning protesters or violent nutcases. The priest strode towards the protesters, who were chanting their slogans.

'Save our church.'

'Re-con-struc-tion, not de-struc-tion.'

The crowd fell silent as Father Ken reached them.

'It's the Lord's will,' the priest said. 'Christ said the kingdom of heaven is *within*. And he was right. Our church is anywhere we gather in love and fellowship. Our church is not a building.'

'My church is a building!' yelled a woman. Dressed severely, she appeared to be in her fifties.

'Margaret, I know how attached you are to this place. But the diocese has already provided a modern church with modern facilities.'

'And what about our families?' shouted another woman.

Jake sighed, knowing that the debate had taken its usual turn. The graveyard was what it really came down to, not the church building. No matter how carefully it was done, people felt their loved ones' remains were being desecrated.

'That's why I'm here,' said Father Ken patiently. 'To ensure that the remains are treated with proper respect. They will be properly reinterred. You have my promise. This is the Lord's will. He wants it so, and we must acquiesce.'

Just then there was a rumble as the first digger moved into the small graveyard, and a wail went up from the crowd.

This was a waste of Jake's time. But in a sense it was also a release. He had no leads to follow, but he couldn't obsess on it, because he wasn't behind his desk looking at empty files.

I have to get back to it, look at everything with fresh eyes, he thought. *I've been missing something from the beginning, and I'm still missing it now.*

He walked over to Asher, whose face showed a mixture of apprehension and annoyance. He may have been a bit of a blowhard, but he knew cops, and he clearly saw on Jake's face what was coming.

'You want to keep the FBI out of your jurisdiction, sir?' said Jake. 'The best way of doing that is to keep your best people on the hunt.'

Asher's cheek twitched as if he was biting back an insult. In the end he just turned down the volume a little. 'After your last few days, you really think you qualify as one of the best?'

Jake hated to admit it, but he had no answer to that. 'Colonel, we have to keep pressing. It won't be long before the Feds start looking at Littleton and wondering if they should send some agents over. But they'll be doing it based on *our* casework. They'll have a dream of a head start to make a collar that isn't rightfully theirs.'

Asher was having none of it. 'If the casework is so good, and the Feds' job will be so easy, why haven't you caught this fucker already, Austin? Or is that how things were done in "Chi-town"? You let them kill and kill and kill, just to . . . What? Make it interesting?'

Jake wondered if the disdain in Asher's face was aimed at him or the city of Chicago. Maybe it was aimed at all cities in America – the cities that wouldn't employ him, the cities where he could never make it. Did Asher try and fail to get a city cop job somewhere? Did it eat at him now?

'No, Austin,' Asher went on. 'You will shut up and do as you are told. And you'll do as you're told somewhere that isn't where I am.'

Jake shrugged, biting the inside of his cheek to keep the smile off his face as a moment of clarity hit him. 'Fine.' He started walking back to his car.

He didn't need to turn back to know that Asher was glaring at him as he left, absolutely seething. But after cutting Jake down to size Asher could hardly call after him and ask him where he was going and what he thought he was doing.

As he reached his car, Jake caught the eye of Father

Ken, who was back under the oak tree. In the foreground a digger was clawing slowly at the earth. Elsewhere, protesters spread numbly away from the church grounds, defeated. Even Guy Makowski was nowhere to be seen.

Jake gave Father Ken an upward nod as he opened the door and got into the car. As he pulled away, he saw the priest giving him a gentle half-smile.

Jake almost admired him. He was taking the demise of his church rather well.

70

Thursday, 10 a.m.

Back at the station all was quiet. Jake put a call through to the lab. Ronnie picked up.

'I need more on that murder weapon report,' he began.

'And a hello to you too. I'm typing it up now. I'll email it when it's done.'

'Want to tell me now?'

'It's a medieval device called a head crusher. It gradually pulverizes the skull.'

'Jesus . . .' whispered Jake.

'It was used during the Inquisition and also by English witchfinders. It was perfect for extracting confessions because you could put on the pressure, then ease it and prolong the torture over several hours.'

The instant he heard the description, Jake knew they had it.

'First the jaw cracks . . .'

You wince at the noise of the jaw cracking.

'Then the lower teeth grind into the ones above . . .'

There's no more talking after that.

'The intracranial pressure causes the eyeballs to pop out of the skull . . .'

You pretend not to, but you like that part.

'Some of the devices had pockets to collect the eyeballs, but—'

'He doesn't harvest the eyeballs,' Jake interrupted her.

Jake googled 'head crusher' as he listened and studied the images that came up. They all showed a wooden or metal frame with a helmet and a large turnscrew above it. They looked infernal.

Ronnie continued: 'Eventually the pressure builds to the point where the skull itself cracks and the brain contents are squeezed out.'

You watch that part. You watch and make sure your work is done.

'Death occurs only at that stage. In the early stages, once the skull has been secured, the torturer would often beat on the helmet with a pipe, and the pain would vibrate through the . . .' Ronnie took a second to search for the word '. . . uh, *subject's* whole body. Some people were released after torture, but they were never the same again.'

Jake nodded even though Ronnie couldn't see him. Which was a good thing, in a way, because she wasn't there to see what he could feel was a blank, unemotional look on his face. She had described almost unimaginable human suffering, and by the end of it her analytical tones were weighed down with a kind of basic human horror, at once empathetic to those who suffered the torture and astonished that members of her own species could devise such methods of pain-infliction. One look at Jake's face, and she would have questions. Questions that he could not answer.

Starting with *How can you listen to such a tale and not be affected?* Weird thing was, he could never empathize with victims as well as he could with a killer. It wasn't that he didn't care, it was just that he couldn't feel them so clearly. He was closer to the killer.

Jake found himself suddenly very glad that Gail Greene wasn't listening in.

He tried to affect a tone that mirrored Ronnie's as he asked, 'What sort of a mind would invent a head crusher?'

'I hate to think,' she said.

Jake was silent for a moment, then said, 'It fits the MO. And he could carry one in a car. The profile we built up has the killer owning his own car. But where would you get a head crusher these days? Should I run checks for recent burglaries at museums?'

'Believe it or not,' said Ronnie, 'people buy and sell that kind of stuff all the time – there's quite a market for it. I did some searching online. They appear to be quite a thing on the S & M scene, but the ones they use wouldn't have the power to do the damage we're seeing on the victims. I suspect our guy is using an old one bought through a specialist antique dealer. Either that, or he made it himself to the, uh, traditional specifications.'

'Well, that's something,' Jake said. 'We'll start phoning round these dealers and see if anyone sold one to someone in the area.'

Jake's other phone began to ring.

'I got to go, Ronnie,' he told her. 'Thanks for this.'

He hung up and took the other call.

'Detective Austin?' said the voice on the other end. 'This is Special Agent Colin Reader, FBI. Do you have a minute?'

Fuck! The Feds were going to step in and claim jurisdiction.

'What's it about, Agent Reader?' He decided to play it friendly and informal but respectful. Equal to equal. Showing deference at this stage would be a mistake.

'You have our leg.'

'Excuse me?'

The agent chuckled a little, then went on: 'I'm working the Springfield asylum thing, and we've found a third body. And this one is missing his femur. We heard you guys found a femur yesterday near the Christmas Killer dump site.'

'We found a bone – it's with the lab now,' said Jake.

'Ours was old and an adult.'

'Yeah,' said Jake. 'Call Dr Zatkin in the forensics lab in Indianapolis. Tell her I said to give you everything.'

'Thanks, bud. I owe you one.' But the agent didn't hang up. 'Think there's any connection between our cases?'

Jake paused. It may have been an out-of-the-blue

call, and Reader didn't *sound* like an asshole, but that didn't mean there wasn't a possibility that the guy was working a scam, digging for scraps of info on their case. 'I doubt it,' said Jake, aiming for a tone that was neither too friendly or too stand-offish. 'Your guy is probably long dead.'

'Yeah . . . But still. One heck of a coincidence.'

Jake was wondering how a bone from a town miles away had ended up in Littleton – and been dumped deliberately so near their crime scenes. Now he knew where the bone came from, he had to rule out pranksters and highway protesters. Though he wouldn't admit it to the FBI, this latest development troubled him.

Just as Jake ended the call with Reader, Mills burst into the detective bureau. He was actually running, a panicked look on his face.

'Adult skeleton found,' he said to Jake, grabbing some stuff from his drawer.

'I know,' said Jake. 'I've just been talking to the Springfield team—'

'Not in Springfield,' said Mills. 'At Christ the Redeemer.'

What the fuck? Jake got up and ran out after Mills.

71

Thursday, 2 p.m.

At the church Jake ran up to the first uniform he saw. 'What happened?' he said.

The uniformed cop – young but not a rookie – was all business even though his eyes suggested he was a little freaked out. 'They lifted out a coffin, and there was a skeleton underneath it. One that wasn't on the foreman's list. So he called us over. Foreman thinks it's probably just some unrecorded burial from a hundred years back. But I don't like to speculate.'

Jake nodded at him, appreciating his demeanour and attitude. He followed the cop through to the graveyard. It was quieter than this morning, with the machines silenced. Workers stood around idly, a sight Jake was getting used to seeing.

The foreman ambled over. 'Detective,' he said. 'We were using the crane to take out the coffin when someone noticed something underneath. We realized—'

Jake held up his hand to the foreman. 'Thanks, the officer already filled me in.' He went closer to the hole in the ground. 'We'll need to take a statement, sir.'

'Er . . . is it suspicious?' he asked.

'We have to treat it that way until the lab tells us otherwise,' said Jake.

'OK.' The foreman shuffled a little bit. 'So what do I do? Do I send the guys home? We're really behind schedule as it is.'

'Tell you what, you move to the other side of the graveyard and get to work over there. We'll seal this grave and do our thing. You weren't going to finish the job today anyway.'

'No, that's true, conceded the foreman. 'With all the formalities and paperwork and everything . . .' He eyed the protesters in the distance. 'I can live with that.'

As the foreman went off to get work restarted in another spot, Jake took a moment to look at the grave. It was a narrow one, a single rather than a family plot. A small earthmover was at the head of the excavation. There was a mound of mud on one side. Perched on the other side of the hole was the old wooden coffin, its brass handles heavily corroded.

'The unaccounted-for skeleton is still in the hole,' said the cop.

Jake walked over and looked down. The skeleton was lying in the earth about six foot below him. In the deep shadows it was impossible to make out anything. He turned to the cop.

'Flashlight?'

The guy unclipped a penlight from his belt and handed it to Jake. He shone it into the grave, but its weak light didn't help much. Jake didn't want to wait so he bent down, placed a hand on the edge of the grave and lowered himself into the hole.

'You can't do that,' said the cop.

It was a long drop, and Jake felt it in his knees when he hit the dirt. He threw out his arm to steady himself.

'Hey!' said the cop.

Jake ignored him.

He bent and shone the flashlight on the skeleton, which seemed to be complete. The flesh was long gone, but some hair still clung to the skull, and the clothing was tattered but recognizable. Judging from what he could see of the clothes, the person had died in the late 1970s or early 80s. And he was male.

This was no ancient burial site. Someone had been hidden under the coffin. Which meant it was a murder. This was something they were going to have to look into.

He quickly searched the clothes. The scene was so old there was no fear of disturbing forensics. They weren't going to be lifting any prints after years in the ground. He found nothing in the pockets.

He was taking out his phone to call Asher when something caught his eye. The skull was uneven, depressed at one temple. Had the guy been deformed? Maybe someone with severe mental and learning difficulties?

Then he looked closer, shining the penlight at the cranium.

The jaw was fractured.

No.

Several of the teeth were missing.

No way . . .

There were cracks radiating from the top of the skull.

It's . . . It's you . . . You did this.

Just then the big machines went silent.

He could hear the foreman shouting, 'Detective! Detective Austin!'

He tried to scramble out of the grave, but he couldn't. It was too deep.

The cop from earlier appeared over the side of the grave. He reached down to help Jake up. 'Detective, you need to see this!'

'They've found another one,' said Mills, appearing from another area of the graveyard, panting and red-faced. Jake ran towards him, wiping the mud from his hands on to his coat as he went.

They got to where the foreman was standing just next to the cab of an earthmover. He didn't say anything but his face was pale and his eyes were wide.

The second grave looked much like the first. Jake peered down. He could see remains. He looked up at Mills. He could see the same thought was rushing through Mills's head. *Two graves excavated. Two bodies found.*

Jake looked around the small cemetery and counted the gravestones. 'Shit, Mills, we could be looking at up to two dozen unsolved homicides,' he said.

He shone the flashlight into the grave and focused on the skull. It was difficult to tell, but it seemed to have the same deformity he had noticed in the first one.

'Both skulls have the jaws broken and teeth missing,' he said to Mills.

'What . . . ?' said Mills.

Jake left Mills's unfinished question unanswered. Right now there was no answer to give. They were either on the trail of two mass murderers from two separate eras . . . or a stone-cold professional with literally decades of experience in killing and getting away with it.

72

Thursday, 6 p.m.

It's all out now, just like you wanted it to be. This is your will and your work.

The news on the television – and on the radio in the kitchen – was wonderful, now that he had adapted to the new plan.

Father Ken was relaxed, happy that it was working out the way the Lord wanted it. He was pottering around, tidying his house, and as he worked he remembered. It was good to reminisce. So many years had passed since it had begun, but he remembered them all in clear detail. He remembered them with such clarity he sometimes wondered whether they were real memories or if his head was simply full of elaborate fantasies. At times it was difficult to decide, especially as the years went on.

They'll have found Georgia now, I expect. She was the first soul I saved.

He remembered it like it was yesterday. Georgia was a troubled woman who couldn't stop herself from sinning. Always sins of the flesh. She was a fornicator, and often with married men or young men who knew no better. But *she* should have. She led them astray then came to Father Ken for forgiveness.

The worst, most wretched kind of Christian. The kind that viewed religion as a safety net – a safety net that was somehow magically reinforced at Christmas, as if the season was a source of year-round credit, excusing sins committed the rest of the year. A safety net into which they could always let themselves fall, safe in the knowledge that they would bounce back, up and away from retribution and punishment. They were calling Father Ken the Christmas Killer – if only they knew he was trying to preserve its purity.

He would never forget it. Georgia had come to confession and told him that she thought she was pregnant. What was she to do? He was horrified. He wanted to climb into her side of the confessional and choke some sense into her. But he followed the rites of the Church and absolved her of her sins. When he came out of the box a few minutes later, she was the only one left in the building. She was kneeling by the votive candles, labouring over her penance, a dozen pious rhymes cleansing a soul so black.

That was the first time he had heard the Lord's voice. Father Ken did as he was instructed. Why would he argue? He had walked up behind Georgia, a couplet from *Hamlet* – it was always *Hamlet* – running through his head: 'Now might I do it pat, now he is praying. And now I'll do't. And so he goes to heaven.'

He had placed his hands around her throat and

squeezed. She had struggled, but he was strong back then. A younger man, powerful. Soon he felt her resistance begin to wane. He kept crushing until her kicking became little more than spasms, then they died out and he felt her body go limp. But he kept squeezing, squeezing until his fingers grew tired and fell from her neck.

Then he stood back, expecting to feel horror. Shame and horror, regret and remorse. But that was not God's plan. Instead Father Ken twitched with elation. The excitement of the epiphany that told him, this – *this* – was the only way to save his flock from sinning. He must help God to do his work. He would become a fisher of souls.

But first he would have to dispose of the body.

You put the thought into my head.

His mind cleared quickly. There was to be a funeral the following morning, and the grave had already been dug. So he simply took Georgia outside and laid her in the empty hole, covering her with just a few inches of soil. It was a bit of work, but the next morning the funeral took place; the coffin was lowered in, and the gravedigger arrived and filled in the grave.

No one was any the wiser. It was not the Lord's plan for anyone to know of Father Ken's work.

It took him a while to refine his technique. He had to be alone with those he was rescuing, but his collar made that part easy. Then he had to incapacitate them. If he hit them too hard they couldn't wake up to confess. If he didn't hit hard enough, they didn't go down. A soft cosh proved the ideal solution.

He needed them to come round after that initial blow so they could hear the charges against them and admit their sins. They needed to beg the Lord for forgiveness. They needed to be on their knees before God, like all true penitents. To make it easy for them, he bound their hands in prayer. He knelt and prayed with them.

Then he gave the final turn of the screw and they danced screaming to their maker.

Everything he did was backed by sound theology, which was how he knew the voice in his head was not leading him astray. He had read about the Tribunal of the Holy Office of the Inquisition, and the great work it had done in Spain and France, weeding out heretics. The Inquisition had been sent into decline by the rise of Protestantism, but that did not make its efforts any less righteous. The inquisitors had done great work with the head crusher five hundred years ago. Father Ken would continue their grand, noble tradition.

In all my years not one has resisted confessing. Then they die, blessed and with their sins expunged.

Your beautiful and merciful will must see them swiftly through purgatory to the gates of paradise. Why else would you charge me with this mission?

He had been carrying out his crusade for decades now, his righteous strikes occurring every few years whenever he came across a soul that was set for damnation. And where better to hide the bodies than in a graveyard? The saved sinners deserved the consecrated earth. But fourteen months ago it had begun to unravel. The bishop had told him that the Church of Christ the Redeemer was to be knocked down, to make way for a new interstate. Father Ken had smiled and nodded, and made the right sounds about the Church being 'for progress', but he knew what this progress meant. His work – his half a lifetime of crusading – was about to be unveiled. And people would not understand. How could they, being such godless souls? They would only understand once they were *saved*, once they could see – from a celestial plane – the canvas on which the Lord was painting, with Father Ken as one of his brushes. They would drag him before their court, and force him to explain his actions to a judge who claimed to be speaking on behalf of the Almighty, but Father Ken knew better.

Then, after weeks of panic at the prospect of the earthen curtain being raised to reveal his work, Father Ken had another moment of pure, blissful clarity.

You wanted to let the world know. You wanted me to have my day of recognition.

The Lord's plan was simple: kill more frequently and dump the bodies in public. And Father Ken, his good servant, had done as he was bidden.

Marcia Lamb I liked, but she was an unmarried mother, and that was setting a bad example for her daughter – the poor girl had already been conceived and born out of sin. I could not let her continue to live among it.

Belinda Harper was a simple choice once she told me in the confessional about her adulterous affair. She said it was to punish her husband over his own indiscretions, but only God can decide who is to be punished.

The Jezebel Candy was an easy choice too.

I do wish I had not enjoyed killing Chuck Ford quite as much as I did. But he was a bearer of false witness for greedy profit. It was fitting that I laid down his life for you.

And, Lord, they all repented before they died. Their souls were cleansed, and I watched them ascend to heaven. It was glorious.

Praised be thy holy name.

How it would all end was a question that had crossed Father Ken's mind more than once, but he had trusted in the Lord. And the Lord had delivered.

You gave me the means of deliverance by sending me Jake Austin. That was an unexpected twist, but it told me I was on the right path. A path that, I can see now, is turning back on itself. A path that will end where it began.

You don't want me to end my crusade. You want me to save some more souls.

He looked up and stretched out his hands in praise.

'Thou art with me; thy rod and thy staff, they comfort me.'

But there was no harm in taking out an insurance policy . . .

73

Friday, 23 December, 11.30 a.m.

Caffeine and adrenaline were keeping them going. Jake and Mills had already spent three hours poring over old files and reports. Missing people from three decades ago were being cross-checked with the seventeen skeletons that had been recovered from the graveyard the day before. And there were constant intrusions from the press, local and regional – and some of the regional guys were having their stories picked up by Associated Press. Pretty soon more eyes than ever were going to be squinting at Littleton, Indiana.

Most of the remains were relatively old, but one skeleton still had much of the flesh attached and was in a summer dress similar to one Jake had seen Leigh wear only two years previously. It gave him hope that there would be a missing persons file in the database that could give him a break in this thing. But the database was stubbornly throwing up nothing at all, and Jake was getting frustrated. That's why he had volunteered for the coffee run.

As he walked up the steps to the station carrying two

coffees and a box of Danish, he felt a little lighter, a little less tense. His eyes had stopped aching, and he was thinking he might have a shot at looking at things again. He might see something he had missed before. Or, failing that, his time out of the station might have coincided with a miracle. Maybe Mills had found among the bones a hastily written note from a victim, identifying his or her murderer.

Had any cop *ever* been that lucky?

But when Jake used his toe to open the station door, he almost turned and left. Gail Greene was waiting for him in the lobby.

Not today. It's bad enough without you.

He took a deep breath and walked up to her.

'I'm sorry,' he began, but she was saying the same thing.

They looked at each other and shared a smile.

'I was a bit harsh on you the other day,' she said.

'I deserved it. I stepped way over a line, and Johnny paid for it.'

'You can't be held responsible for another man's actions,' she said.

Jake didn't know what to say next. His tongue had gone dry.

'Coffee?' he said.

'That's sweet of you. Want to go for a walk?'

Five minutes later they were sitting on a public bench overlooking City Hall, the box of Danish between them. The weather was sharp but dry. Jake was just in his jacket and could feel the cold. Gail was dressed for the weather in a big coat and gloves.

'I'm sorry I couldn't take you somewhere nicer, but a cop's salary doesn't go far,' he joked.

They sat in silence for a few minutes, then Gail turned to Jake and asked, 'Do you have any contacts among the team investigating the Chase Asylum thing?'

He looked surprised. Was this her excuse to come to the station? She could have asked him this over the phone.

'Why?' he asked.

'I've been following up a couple of leads on Johnny's medical history. Turns out, among other places, that he was actually a resident of the Chase Asylum for several months. He was sent there because he had been disruptive in his foster home.'

'Whoa.' Jake took a sip of his coffee, which had quickly got cold. It was weird the way cases and circumstances sometimes converged. But he knew that he would drive himself insane looking for hidden meanings, so he did his best to keep his mind clear.

'I don't know if it's relevant or not,' she said, 'but I think the people working that case might want to talk to Johnny. He was an in-patient around the time Fred Lumley went missing.'

'I do know one guy working Springfield,' said Jake. 'Colin Reader. I can put you in touch.'

'Thanks. And it might help Johnny to unburden. He

might have seen things, or suffered things, while he was there. In talking with him I get the strong feeling that the key to his behaviour is in his past. Something is eating away at him, and it might be what happened at the Chase Asylum.'

Jake thought it more than likely. Enough people had already come forward to say that Lumley had abused them. Why not one more?

'I'm going to see him right now,' said Gail. 'Do you want to come along?'

Jake's instinct was to say no. He didn't want to upset Johnny by reminding him of what he had done. Or maybe it was his own guilt stopping him.

'Don't worry,' said Gail, clearly registering the look on his face. 'If there was any chance of setting Johnny back, I wouldn't have suggested it.'

Jake shrugged. He had nothing on except a quadruple homicide and seventeen bodies from previous decades. And yet at that moment the guilt he felt about Johnny was exerting just as strong a pull. A strange fascination to see the damage he'd caused.

'OK.'

Also, he wanted to spend more time with Gail.

74

Friday, 12.30 p.m.

Johnny Cooper was being held in the secure wing of the psychiatric unit adjacent to Littleton General Hospital. The corridor was bright and airy; Johnny's room was more spacious and comfortable than the dingy apartment he had occupied up until two days ago. When Jake and Gail looked through his door Johnny was sitting in an armchair, staring up at a television playing reruns of an old sitcom. He had a smile on his face, a smile Jake knew was nothing to do with what was on the screen.

'They've medicated him up to cloud nine,' he whispered to Gail.

'What did you expect? He's been through a lot.'

Jake and Gail went in. Gail sat on the bed. Jake sat on a hard chair on the other side of the room. Johnny kept his eyes on the screen.

'Hey, Johnny,' Gail said. 'How're you doing?'

He continued to stare.

'Anything you need?'

Nothing. Jake stood and switched off the television. That might help.

Finally Johnny looked at Gail. 'Hi, Doc,' he said. Then he looked at Jake.

'This is Detective Austin,' Gail said. 'Do you remember him?'

Jake shrank back into his seat. Suddenly it felt wrong to be in this room. But Johnny turned back to Gail and didn't say anything, it was as if he didn't recognize Jake.

Gail leaned forward and touched his arm. 'Johnny, I wanted to ask you a few things. Is that OK?'

Johnny said nothing. He just looked down at her hand and nodded.

'Did you grow up in Indiana?' Gail asked.

Johnny looked up for a moment, then nodded again,

'You were fostered?'

'Fostered in a lot of places. "Like the last dog in the shelter, couldn't find a permanent home." What does that mean? Someone once said that to me, but I could never figure out what she meant.' He smiled.

Gail didn't smile back. 'You got in trouble quite a bit.'

'I did?' He frowned. 'I don't remember. That might be why they put me in the old asylum.'

Jake exchanged a quick glance with Gail.

Johnny's little smile came back. 'They'd changed the name to Springfield Hospital,' he said, his voice a low drone now. 'But it never stuck. We all knew what it really was.'

'How old were you then?'

'Seven? Twelve?'

Jake felt frustrated. This could take for ever. Years of psychiatric problems and strong doses of whatever chemical cocktail he'd been given had left Johnny's brain screwed.

But Gail persisted. 'Was anyone ever mean to you in the asylum?'

'The chef.'

Jake saw Gail grip Johnny's arm a little tighter as she asked, 'Did he hurt you? The other kids?'

Johnny nodded vigorously. 'Yeah, he hurt us. Hurt us with his food. It was the worst, Doc. We got fish on Fridays. No one liked fish, but he just kept on giving it to us.'

Jake felt a prickle of futile fury in his throat. Fury that a guy like Johnny, not evil by nature, had to live – or rather exist – stranded between madness and lucidity. Jake wanted to fix him, but there was no fixing this.

Johnny wasn't finished. 'But there was one nice nurse. I liked her. A big woman. She had the same name as you.' He pointed at Jake. 'Nurse Austin. Nice black woman. She was always smiling, singing to herself. She gave me hugs.'

Jake nodded as the poor crazy bastard rambled on. Then Johnny fell silent for a moment, during which Gail aimed a curious look at Jake. He offered a shrug in response.

'How's Benny?' Johnny asked suddenly. 'I hope he'll be all right.'

Gail looked confused.

'The man he . . .' said Jake. 'Johnny's *neighbour*,' he told Gail, hoping she'd get what he was implying.

Gail was as gentle. 'Johnny, Benny is dead.'

'Dead?' said Johnny. 'He won't be too happy about that. But maybe it'll stop him touching me for a buck. The man's always touching me for money. Do I look rich?' He stared back at the blank television screen. 'Dead, you say? Really? Wow . . .'

Johnny looked quite pleased for a moment.

Because now he has something to be genuinely sorry about.

Gail stood. 'Bye, Johnny. It was good to see you.'

Jake turned the TV back on then followed Gail from the room.

'Goodbye, Doc,' said Johnny, his eyes never leaving the television. 'Keep safe, Bruce.'

75

Friday, 2 p.m.

Gail was driving Jake back to the station when it started to snow. Littleton may have been drained of all Christmas spirit, but the sky didn't give a shit.

Gail was explaining Aquinas syndrome.

'Like Johnny, the sufferers usually have some sort of paranoid schizophrenia or a delusional disorder,' she said. 'They also have deviant sexual desires. Paedophilia and necrophilia are common. That's why Johnny ejaculated after killing Benny.'

Jake didn't tell her that he had pretty much figured that out already. He and Gail had only just got back on good terms, and he was going to need her help to anticipate the killer's next move.

'There's one thing you should understand,' Gail continued. 'What you did triggered Johnny to act his delusions out. But at that point, given the multitude of problems he has, *anything* could have triggered it. The pressures were building. If it wasn't you, it would have been someone else. So don't beat yourself up over it. It wasn't your fault.'

'Thanks,' was all Jake could say to that. He appreciated

her attempt to make him feel better, but the truth was, it *had* been his fault. And he would carry that with him, like his ulcer, for a long time to come.

Gail pulled into the police station parking lot and they sat in silence for a few minutes. 'You don't want to go back inside,' she said.

'Is it that obvious?'

Gail smiled.

'This one is beating me,' he told her.

'Ha! The Jake Austins of this world don't get beaten.'

'I used to believe that,' he said. 'But if the bodies in the graveyard are linked to the murderer of Marcia, Belinda, Candy and Chuck, then this guy's a professional who's been doing this a very long time. If these skeletons are connected to our . . . fresher vics, then we're hunting the worst kind of serial killer – someone cold, someone smart enough to change his MO when he knew the churchyard was going to be dug up. A man not motivated by any kind of frenzy, but maybe a twisted intellectual conviction that what he is doing is somehow right and just.'

Gail said nothing but just listened.

'Of course, the potential length of time these killings are spread over suggests a man of a certain age,' Jake went on. 'And men of a certain age become less physically capable. That's nature. The body breaks down. Could an older guy *really* have overpowered two streetwise women like Candy and Marcia? Marcia had a daughter that she wanted to get home to, a daughter she *loved*. She would have fought tooth and nail to stay alive. And Chuck Ford would not have been easy either.'

'A blow to the back of the head with a heavy object can cut anyone down to size,' Gail offered.

'Maybe you're right,' he said. 'But what if . . . what if our guy is a copycat. That would mean he knew about the original murders, murders the police apparently never suspected. But *how*? Is he the son of the original killer, maybe? An "apprentice" of some kind?'

His brain searing with questions that made it hurt, Jake leaned back against the headrest. Each new question left him more confused.

'He can't get away with it for ever,' said Gail, clearly trying to be encouraging.

'He can,' Jake replied. 'If it is just one man, he *has* been getting away with it for ever. Seventeen missing people, and nobody's alarm bells went *ding*. Not one . . . The case is so cold now I haven't a hope.'

'But if it's just one man, you could—'

'It's a road map of dead ends. I can't link the victims. I can't see a motive. I'm pretty much screwed unless I get very, very lucky.'

Gail fell silent. Something about her expression. She was making a decision.

'What?' Jake asked, turning to look at her.

Gail nodded once, coming to a decision. 'I have to tell you something. Maybe I should have said it before, but it's hard to break professional trust. Belinda Harper was one of my private patients.'

That got Jake's attention.

'She was coming to me because she was depressed. She said she was having an affair with a man in retaliation for the affairs Mitch was having. I tried to tell her that it was a negative, destructive way to deal with the situation, but she wouldn't stop seeing him.'

'Wow,' said Jake.

But where does Chuck Ford fit in?

'Do you know who she was having the affair with?' he asked.

'She would never tell me,' said Gail.

'I have to find this guy. He might be unconnected, but I have to track him down. Something he knows, something he's not even *aware* he knows, might . . .'

He tailed off when he noticed that Gail was looking at him with concern.

'You're burning the candle at both ends,' she said in answer to his look. 'You need to step back and let others help you out.'

That would never happen. 'It's all on me and Mills. Me, really. Mills seems to be able to brush it off at the end of the day.'

'The stress is damaging you. I can see it,' said Gail.

'I'm fine,' he insisted, the words appearing to wake up his ulcer, which trickled a bit more acid, as if to say, *Fuck you, Jake. That's not your call.*

'Really?' Gail turned to stare straight at him. 'Who's looking out for you?' Her hand had moved, taking hold of his. She was looking into his eyes. Her scent was coiling around his head and neck like a noose.

Who is *looking out for me?*

Jake turned his hand until he was holding hers. He started to lean forward to kiss her. She leaned in too. But Jake felt a pang of guilt stronger than any acid burn. With his free hand he fumbled for the passenger-side door.

'I'm sorry,' he muttered. 'I'm really sorry.'

He got the door open and dragged himself out of the car. He marched across the parking lot, then up the steps and into the station.

He didn't look back.

76

Saturday, 24 December, 5.49 a.m.

The man behind him was getting closer. He could feel the menacing presence but he couldn't make out the face. He never could. But as the man touched him, he turned and screamed, and then he was slashing the man with a knife, his skinny twelve-year-old arms barely strong enough to break the flesh. But after a couple more tries, he finally had the knife inside the man's belly. And there was blood, blood everywhere . . .

Then Jake woke up.

It was always the same dream. Not every night, but at frequent regular intervals. And he could never see the face.

Jake hadn't slept well. Guilt and desire wrestled in his head, and neither had won. But they both kept sleep away. He felt like an asshole for coming so close to kissing Gail. He felt like even more of an asshole when he acknowledged that there was a part of him that regretted *not* kissing her.

The clock on the bedside table showed five forty-nine, but he couldn't take any more of this. He needed to get away. He knew he couldn't face Leigh for a family breakfast. He worried that his face might give something away.

Trying not to make any noise, he began to dress. Leigh stirred, and he froze.

'What's up?' she asked groggily.

'I have to go to the station. The paperwork is piling up.'

'My hero.' She turned in the bed, drew the covers over herself again, and was soon breathing deeply.

As Jake left the house he felt a deep sense of disappointment in himself. He hated how Leigh trusted him so much. He wasn't sure he could live up to her trust.

The station was almost empty; the night shift ran on a skeleton crew. There was one guy on the desk, and two cars patrolling. There were four cops sitting around drinking coffee. Jake poured himself a cup, but he didn't want to talk. He didn't feel like company right now.

Carrying his drink, he went to his desk and powered up the computer. Sitting down, he took a sip of the coffee. Strong. Far stronger than the stuff the day shift brewed. But he guessed the night guys needed a bit of a booster sometimes.

He had one fresh email with an attachment. He clicked on the message. It was from Colin Reader, the FBI guy. The message opened, and Jake read it quickly.

Detective Austin,

Thanks for the heads-up on the bone. Dr Zatkin was very helpful. But how did it get over to you guys? I need to know. If you find out, keep me in the loop.

We had one of our artists do up a facial reconstruction on the skeleton. It's quite good, about 70% accurate, he says. Would you mind having a look over it, maybe post it around the station? We're hoping it might jog a memory.

Thanks,
Colin

Jake clicked on the attachment and it began to download, line by line, from the top.

It was a drawing. Now he could see the eyes. They were cold eyes, a nondescript grey colour. But there was nothing you could do about that; the eyes on a reconstruction always looked dead.

With every new line that appeared Jake felt more and more nauseous. About ten seconds later, the image was complete and Jake's mouth filled with saliva.

Apart from the eye colour, he could have been looking at a mirror.

What the hell?

It was a joke. It had to be.

Mills must have sent it to wind him up. But Mills wasn't smart enough to send a message from a convincing fake FBI email address. He wasn't that technologically knowledgeable. Jake checked the address in the sender's box. It was an official FBI address, no doubt about it. Maybe Mills had managed to put Reader up to playing a prank? But that couldn't have been right – he'd only spoken with Reader a couple of times but the Fed hadn't struck Jake as the type to waste his time with jokes.

The image was genuine.

Jake felt a moment of panic. *There has to be an explanation.* But he couldn't think of one. Unless he was losing his mind.

He passed the morning unable to resist taking repeated looks at the picture. Each time he brought up the window he hoped that the face would be different, that it would have somehow changed itself. But it had not.

Around ten thirty Mills stopped by Jake's desk. 'Howdy, partner,' he said.

With a start Jake minimized the image on the screen.

'You all right, buddy?' asked Mills.

'Yeah, I'm fine. I just have things on my mind. The case is getting to me, I think.'

'I know. Night guys said you've been in for hours. Take a break. Go home and relax. Wrap some gifts or something. Don't leave it *all* to the missus – that's a sure way to get yourself some couch time. Know what I'm saying?'

Jake smiled at Mills.

'I'll do that.'

But an hour later, when Mills left the station, Jake was still staring at the screen. His mind was a riot of thoughts tumbling over each other, but he kept coming back to one question: *Why does a long-dead man in Littleton, Indiana have my face?*

77

Saturday, 6 p.m.

Jake passed the day in a daze, barely aware of the people passing in and out of the station, vaguely aware of a twitch that he had developed.

The detective bureau remained blissfully quiet. On most Saturdays the bureau operated with a skeleton crew just like the night guys, the detectives taking turns on a four-weekly rotation. But today it was even quieter than usual as folks clocked off to go home and be with their families. Jake shook his head clear of images of subdued Christmas dinners under the cloud of threat and violence that had settled over Littleton.

You really have killed Christmas, Jake thought. Then he cursed himself for being flippant.

It was dark outside when the night shift clocked on. Around the station the uniformed cops readied themselves to go out on patrol. There was always a little more activity in the darker hours on Saturdays – bar fights and such, drawing out the squad cars. When the first siren wailed, Jake came to his senses. Like snapping out of a dream. He really needed to get a grip. But how?

Talk it out, that was what they said. He picked up the phone and dialled Gail's number.

When the phone on the other end of the line started ringing, he asked himself, *Why Gail? Why not Leigh?* He told himself it was because she was a counsellor. But she didn't pick up, so it was a moot point. Thinking of Gail brought back yesterday's conversation in the car. Something she had said about Johnny's Aquinas syndrome was playing on his mind, but he couldn't quite put his finger on it. He replayed the conversation in his head.

Then he went on the Internet and googled the condition. Very little came up and nothing to resolve whatever it was that was bothering him. So he googled 'head crusher' again. This time he didn't just look at the images; he read the articles. Religious zealots would put heretics in the device, and squeeze their heads until they confessed their sins. Often they continued with the pressure until the victim died. Just as often the penitent – or what was left of them – was released from the device and put on trial. The inevitable result was death at the stake. All done in the name of God.

That triggered something.

Jake turned from the screen and picked up a copy of the medical report from Ronnie. It was long and detailed, and he had skimmed over parts of it. But some parts stuck out. He ran his eyes down the pages.

Yes, he was right. All the victims had had their hands

bound together from the elbow to the wrist. There was ante-mortem bruising consistent with restraints on all the victims. He held up his own arms and pushed them together, elbow to elbow and wrist to wrist. The only practical way of doing it was with the palms facing each other.

Their hands were bound in prayer.

Now he was on track. The killings had a ritualistic aspect, suggesting a religious motivation. He went through the victims in his head again. Marcia Lamb was a single mother raising a bastard child. Belinda Harper was an adulterous wife. Candy Jones was a prostitute. Chuck Ford was a ruthless journalist, opportunistic and without morals, a man who profited from the exploitation of misery.

They weren't evil people. But perhaps in the eyes of a religious nut . . . ?

Jake thought about the people he knew in Littleton, the ones who claimed deep faith. Certainly a number of people who had turned up at the demonstrations didn't want the old church torn down . . .

But what about . . . ?

No. It was crazy, what he was thinking now. No way could it be true.

And yet he couldn't shake the feeling – a tingle of conviction that was almost always right.

Jake went through the evidence bit by bit.

He would have had access to the graves at Christ the Redeemer; and those skulls had suffered the same damage as the Christmas Killer had inflicted on his victims. If all the murders were committed by the same man, that meant the perpetrator would have to be well into middle age or perhaps a bit older. And old-fashioned in his views too.

Jake grabbed his coat and left the station.

78

Saturday, 8.40 p.m.

Jake was running now. Why hadn't he seen it? As he climbed into his car he had his mobile out and was scrolling through his contacts, looking for Mills's number.

Father Ken Laurie. Unbelievable.

Jake let his mind flood with images of Father Ken's face, trying to see in retrospect what he may not have seen when he was with him. Any hint as to the evil beneath the smiling kind-old-boy features that he made good use of. But as he focused on Father Ken's face a strange flickering vision invaded his mind. His finger hesitated over the *Call* button.

The image in his mind was not a memory of one of their meetings. The Father Ken Jake was imagining was younger. His hair was thicker and darker, his skin didn't have any wrinkles. And Jake's mind's eye was looking *up* at him.

Like the view of a child.

A strange sense of familiarity made Jake shudder, even though he could feel sweat running down his body. Behind the young Father Ken scenery seemed to come into focus, filling out the vision. A dull grey autumn sky, clouds hanging low over . . . what? He couldn't see. He was outdoors, in some kind of garden, but what? And where? And why was none of this confusing him?

Jake shook himself and lightly slapped his own cheeks three times. Gail was right – he had been working too hard, obsessing. And he had not slept well last night, because the dream had returned, and . . .

The dream.

Jake got that same shiver of familiarity. He could feel his chest tightening, his mind working like an engine, asking so many questions he couldn't decipher a single one. Things were making sense but without making any sense at all.

He put the phone back in his pocket and started the car. He could call Mills in a while. He needed to understand first.

Driving through the quiet streets he tried to prepare himself for the confrontation. He had no idea what he would say to Father Ken. *Do I know you? Did you kill those people?* His ulcer was leaking like a foundering oil tanker, and he had to fight the urge to pull over and vomit by the roadside. He kept driving. The church steeple was like a guiding beacon, and soon he found himself on the right leafy streets. He turned down one, and there it was – the priest's house.

I can't believe I left my mother alone with you.

There was nothing parked outside, but Jake didn't

give it a thought. He drew his car to a stop. Then he did something he hadn't done since he'd arrived at Littleton – he checked his service weapon to make sure it had a full clip. Satisfied, he got out of the car and walked up to the priest's door. He knocked. No answer.

The lights were out.

He could be out killing someone right now.

Jake ignored the calm voice in his head saying something about a search warrant and questioning how he would ever explain his actions to Internal Affairs, if it came to it. He took a step back and kicked the door. It was old and a little rickety. It came right off.

He raised his gun as he walked in. Nothing. Through the first door. He quickly scanned the living room. It was empty. He went through to the kitchen. That was empty too. That left upstairs. He took the stairs at a run, two at a time. It wasn't how he had been taught to do it, but then the police academy had never run a class on raiding the home of a man you've been having nightmares about from years before you met him.

At the top he could see three doors, two of which were open. He tried the first door. It led to a bedroom. Nothing. The second door led to an office. The final door was closed. He opened it and stepped into a small bathroom. All empty. No sign of the priest.

The tightness in his chest eased a little bit. Father Ken was out. Jake would call it in shortly, but first he'd have a quick look through the house in the hope that it would throw up some kind of explanation.

He needed to understand.

The bedroom was small. It was a simple room, nothing out of the ordinary. A crucifix hung on the wall above a queen-size double bed, with blankets rather than a quilt. On the bedside locker were a clock, a pair of reading glasses and a stack of books – a mix of popular history and thrillers.

The office contained a computer that looked about ten years old, a printer, even a fax machine, and piles of books. Most of the books seemed to be Bible studies or medieval history, with the occasional weighty theological tome. There was a very comfortable chair, the stuffing bulging in places, that Jake assumed the priest used himself. There was a second chair, more modern – a bland mass-produced thing. Probably for visitors, Jake reasoned.

He went back downstairs to the living room. It was also perfectly ordinary, giving no hint of the monster who dwelt there. A twenty-year-old Hitachi TV sat in the corner, with a doily and a dried flower arrangement on top. The furniture consisted of a simple but comfortable three-piece suite and a coffee table. On the coffee table was a chess set, with a game laid out. Jake looked at it; black was about three moves from checkmate.

Jake started to doubt his own theory.

The final room he searched was the kitchen. Again it was the very ordinariness that struck him. Neither obsessively clean nor disgustingly filthy. On the counter there was a box of cornflakes and a dirty bowl. A jar of Nescafé instant coffee was open, with a spoon sticking out. The table was simple and had just two chairs. The guy lived alone; he wouldn't need any more settings than that.

I'm wrong. This isn't the house of a killer. I'm overwrought. I've made a horrible mistake.

Jake knew what he had to do: phone it in and square the broken door with Asher. He could probably wriggle out of it, say that he had come to talk to Father Ken about something else and got the impression there were burglars in the house. He had overreacted enough around the station, Jake thought Asher might just buy it. Maybe he could give Father Ken a few bucks for a new door and that would be that.

He was getting ready to switch off the lights and leave when something caught his eye. A yellow Post-it note on the fridge door. He went over and as he drew closer his legs went weak, and his heart grew cold.

The Post-it had a mobile number and three words.

'Jake. Call me.'

79

Saturday, 9.15 p.m.

Jake fumbled with his phone and keyed the numbers in with shaking fingers. He forced himself to focus and tried again. The phone rang.

'Jake,' said a voice he recognized as Father Ken's. 'Thank you for calling. Are you still at my house?'

'Yes.' Jake felt like a child – scared and weak. *Looking up at him, a man of authority.* He scanned the room, trying to focus on the here and now, not on the returning vision of a young Father Ken. The vision that was becoming clearer.

'I'm sorry I can't be there.' The priest's voice was calm. Soothing. 'But I had to leave in a hurry. I'm sure you understand.'

'Yes,' Jake said again. He wanted to say more, but nothing would come.

'You sound shaken, Jake. Why don't you help yourself to a drop? The bottle's by the sink.'

Jake looked and saw a bottle of Scotch.

'I . . . I . . . I need to speak to you, Father,' he said.

'Yes. You have questions. I'll do my very best to answer them for you.'

Jake sat down. Normally he planned an interrogation, but there was no time for that now, and he had a feeling that all of his usual strategies would be useless against Father Ken.

'You killed them, didn't you?' he simply asked.

'You'll have to be more specific, Jake. Who did I kill?'

'The skeletons we found under the coffins in the graveyard.'

'Yes, I killed them.'

He'd found him. 'How many?'

'Mine is a select flock. You have to be a sinner to join. And you have to confess fully and sincerely to leave.'

It was all about the confessions. Jake blinked against the montage in his mind – the faces of Marcia Lamb and Candy in the awful archaic torture device, screaming for mercy and absolution, still clinging to the hope that the madman who was doing this would let them go, if they just confessed.

'They all confessed, Jake,' said Father Ken, his voice as level. 'In the end. And they all went to meet their maker with their sins absolved.'

The calmness of the priest's voice did something to puncture the numbness in Jake. So what if he was a man of the cloth? Jake had heard this type of tone on other killers. He was a psychopath, deranged. No better than any other murderer. And when he reminded himself of this, Jake felt a surge of strength in his body – a surge of strength that felt vaguely like the cockiness he would present to his mother as a teenager when he looked to challenge her authority.

'What's murder, if not a sin, Father?' he asked. 'You have a different rulebook than the rest of us, huh?'

'It was his work. I am just his servant.'

Jake was getting frustrated. 'Will you kill again?'

'If the Lord wills it.'

Jake needed to establish himself as the dominant one in the conversation, the one with the status. Ask the questions, get the answers. But he couldn't.

'Something on your mind, Detective? You always did have a habit of going off into your own little world when things didn't go your way.'

Jake was helpless to stop the child-like voice slipping past his lips. 'Father, do you know me?'

'Yes. I knew your mother too.'

'How?' asked Jake. 'I . . . I don't understand how it's possible. We'd never been to Littleton until I transferred here.'

The priest made a noise that was halfway between a sigh and a laugh. 'My oh my, you really don't remember anything, do you?'

Jake shook his head, forgetting that the priest couldn't see him.

'We're old friends . . . aren't we, Jeanette?'

Jake sprang up from the chair, feeling his heart somewhere near his throat. 'Where's my mother?'

'Here with me.'

Jake's head started to spin. He paced up and down

the small kitchen, but there was no air in his lungs to speak.

'She's safe . . . for now. But be warned: no cops, no APB, no telling your partner. Let's keep this . . . in the family.'

'Where are—'

The line went dead before Jake could finish his question.

80

Saturday, 10.10 p.m.

Jake hit the brakes hard and was thrown forward against the steering wheel as he brought the car to a stop outside his house. He had driven straight home. There was only one thing he could cling on to: maybe Father Ken was bluffing.

But something about the way that the old priest had said 'in the family' sent a cold chill through Jake's gut that doused even the fire of the ulcer.

He scrambled out of the car without even killing the engine. He shoved the door closed. Long strides ate up the path, and he threw open his front door.

In the living room Leigh was half-asleep on the sofa, in a white bathrobe. She jumped up as he charged inside. For a moment she was wide-eyed, obviously fearing they were being robbed. But her face softened when she saw who it was.

'Jake, hi.' Her soft expression quickly became concerned again. 'Are you all right?'

He grabbed her by the elbows. 'My mother – where is she?'

'Didn't you get my messages? I assumed you were out looking for her. She's gone walk—'

'Shit.' He ran from the room into the hall, checking the coat stand. Her coat was still there. He ran up the stairs. Across the corridor the baby began to howl. Jake pushed open his mom's door and checked her room. Hat and scarf were on the dresser. Her purse was missing. Quickly he threw open drawers, tossing the contents on the floor. No purse anywhere. Why had she taken it? Was she expecting to be picked up?

You bastard. You told her you would come for her. You set it all up.

Leigh had followed him up the stairs.

'It's OK, Jake. She's done this before. You'll find her.'

He didn't answer; he kept tearing the room apart. The purse became more important with every second that passed. If she had taken it, that meant she had gone voluntarily, and the question was, why? If she hadn't taken it, she had been abducted, and the question was, how?

'Where the fuck is it?' he muttered.

'Jake, you're scaring me,' said Leigh, her voice trembling. 'You're not going to find her in the drawers. You need to get back out in the car and take a ride around town, like before. She'll be OK.'

'She'll be dead,' he muttered. He turned to Leigh. 'Pack. Now.' He snapped it out like an order, and he could see the shocked look on her face. But there was no time.

'Do it,' he repeated.

'Jake, I'm not going to leave the house on Christmas Eve.'

'Stop arguing and do what I tell you! For once, Leigh, just do—'

She cowered. 'Jake,' she pleaded, 'talk to me!'

'Grab what you can; I'll get the kids.'

He ran from the room into their own bedroom, picked up the screaming baby and shoved him into Leigh's arms.

'I'll pack his clothes. We'll buy nappies on the way.'

Leigh put Jakey back down in his cot and stood in front of Jake. She hit him hard in the chest. 'On the way *where*?'

By now Faith had woken up, and stood in the doorway, staring at her parents. Her eyes were sleepy at first, but her anxiety cleared the fog away.

'Faith, you have five minutes to get some stuff together,' Jake told her.

'What have I done now?' she whined.

'Just *do it*.'

The shortness of his tone brought a wet gasp from his daughter. She lingered in the doorway as stunned as if he had slapped her.

He turned to Leigh. He bent forward and whispered, so that Faith wouldn't hear, 'The killer's got my mother.'

Leigh looked at him, her eyes narrowing for a fraction

of a second before she saw that he was neither joking nor crazy. Her face went white. He had seen this look before, several times after Faith was born. When things got too much for her, Leigh got angry. Destructive. And Jake could not afford that right now. He had to keep Leigh busy, focused. He threw a bag on the bed. 'Please, baby, start packing.'

Leigh, in a daze, began to fill the bag. He watched her for a moment, but she was moving too slowly and throwing the wrong things into the bag.

'Forget it,' he said, pulling the bag away from her. 'Buy whatever you need. Get dressed. I'll get Faith. You're leaving right now.'

Ten minutes later Leigh was in the driver's seat of her car, with Faith beside her. Jake's little girl was pale and wide-eyed, her voice shaking as she asked, over and over again, 'But where are we going? *Why* are we going?' Her voice was drowned out by the screams of Jakey, strapped into his car seat in the back.

Jake barely heard either of them. He opened his wallet and took out all the cash he had.

'Drive out of town,' he told Leigh, 'as far as you can go, and get a motel for the night. Don't tell me where. In the morning I'll call you. The cash should get you through until then. This will all be over in the morning.'

Jake saw Faith looking from parent to parent, her eyes getting wider and wider, and her breathing a series of strangled whimpers. He did his best to look confident. 'I'm just playing safe, that's all. Probably overreacting . . . Silly dad!'

Leigh nodded, trying to mirror his bravery for Faith. 'I'll call—'

'No phones. Keep it switched off, and only turn it on once an hour, for two minutes at most.'

He bent and took her face in his hands, kissing her deeply.

'I love you,' she told him.

'I love you too.'

He watched the car screech off, not moving until they were out of sight. He was just walking back inside when his mobile phone buzzed. Jake answered, knowing whose voice he would hear.

'I have a job for you.'

Jake did his best to sound in command. 'I'm listening.'

'You know the Chase Asylum?'

What did the Chase Asylum have to do with anything? The throbbing in Jake's head was beating like a drum now as his mind opened to a whole new world of horror. Was Father Ken connected to the dead children as well?

Just how high was this madman's body count?

'Yes,' Jake said.

'There's something in the asylum that the builders and the FBI haven't found yet,' said Father Ken. 'It's your job to get it for me. Tonight.'

'Did you kill those children?' Jake asked.

'Take a flashlight. Call this number as soon as you arrive. And remember, no police.'

'Can I speak to my—'

But the line had gone dead.

81

Sunday, 25 December, 1 a.m.

It took Jake until well past midnight to reach Springfield and another fifteen minutes to find the Chase Asylum on the outskirts of the town. He killed the headlights on the car and cruised the last quarter-mile, pulling silently to the kerb a hundred yards short of the gate of the asylum.

The streets were silent and still, as they no doubt had been every previous Christmas Day. But this year it was different. And only Jake knew *how* different.

He got out and walked a bit closer, sticking to the shadows. After twenty minutes' observation he was happy the site was deserted. The FBI's excavation team obviously got Christmas off. That was the difference with a cold case; a few more days wouldn't make a difference. There was most likely a security guard around somewhere, watching the scene – for double time, probably – but Jake couldn't see him.

Getting into the grounds of the Chase Asylum was easy. Much of the surrounding wall was already down, replaced with wire fencing. Jake walked along the wall until he found a gap where the fencing was loose and clambered through. He looked across fifty yards of overgrown lawn towards the dark hulk of the building. He stayed low and watched. He saw nothing, and heard nothing. The only thing he felt was the sharp sting of the night air nipping his cheeks, the gentle patter of snow as it fell upon his shoulders.

He made his way towards the building. The night sky was clouded, providing great cover. When the moon broke through Jake dropped to the ground. The moon stayed out for more than five minutes, and he lay still, watching. He was glad he did as he doubted he would have spotted the flashlight in one of the upstairs windows otherwise. Whoever held it was moving. Jake followed its progress along the line of windows, and then it disappeared. A few minutes later the flashlight appeared in a downstairs window. It was the guard doing his round.

The moon concealed again, Jake resumed his approach, reaching the wall of the building. He took his time. He slowly circled the building in a clockwise direction, looking for doors or open windows. The obvious entry point was the front door, but there was a low light just inside it where Jake assumed the guard had his work station. He risked a quick look through a nearby window. He could see a desk and some monitors showing the gardens. None of the cameras seemed to cover the asylum interior. There was a radio on the watchman's table cackling out an old rock and roll track Jake thought he recognized.

Jake squatted behind a bush and waited. He knew enough guys in security – mostly retired cops – to know how they worked their shifts. The likelihood was, this guy would do a round, and then he'd sit at his desk for thirty minutes before doing his next one. From where Jake squatted he had a clear view of the table where the radio was playing. Six minutes later, he saw the bobbing flashlight coming down a corridor. The security guard sat down at his table, took out a Thermos and poured himself a coffee.

Jake inched along the wall to the corner of the asylum. He had about thirty minutes.

He ran round the side of the building, hugging the walls to avoid the cameras, until he was as far from the main entrance as he could get. He found a window that wasn't secured from the inside, and slowly pried it open. There was a creak, but he hoped he was far enough away that the security guard's radio would drown the small noise.

Once inside, Jake took out his torch and risked a quick scan of his immediate surroundings. It looked like a classroom. There were finger paintings and posters on the wall still. Too much work for the demolition team to bother removing them, so they would all be swept away with the rubble. He walked to the wall and took a quick look at the paintings. Some were ordinary scenes you'd see in any classroom – kids outside perfect detached houses, with trees in the yard – but a high proportion were quite disturbing: images of vicious dogs, monsters, children running from a shadowy figure. All of them seemed to be rendered in shades of angry reds and blacks. The products of damaged young minds.

He stepped into the corridor, checking up and down before he walked on. With its military-style grey and cream walls and high ceiling, this corridor looked eerily familiar to him.

Why?

He took out his mobile and texted the priest's number.

I'm in. Where to?

Moments later the phone lit up.

The day ward. Know it?

Somehow, Jake *did* know it. He stopped thinking and moved automatically, turning right at the classroom door. He ignored the first intersection but at the next went left. He was using a muscle memory he never knew he had. Everything felt familiar except for the fact that the lights were off. Jake found he could picture these halls in harsh electric light.

This new hallway was wider than the last and led to a double door at the end. Jake walked to the double door. He pushed it open and stepped into the day ward.

He felt sick. It was empty now, just empty spaces where the beds had once been. But it was exactly how Jake had pictured it. Something drew him to the wall along the left, halfway along. He looked at the wall, covered with graffiti.

There it was: *BRUCE WUZ HERE*.

His legs went weak and he stopped breathing. 'Bruce' again. And now he knew . . .

How did he know?

When did I come here? he asked himself over and over again.

He reached out and ran his fingers over the rough letters, then he leaned against the wall and tried to bring his mind under control. He called the priest.

Father Ken answered first ring. 'I'm here,' Jake whispered.

'Good. Go down to the nurses' station. It's—'

'I know where it is.'

'Of course you do . . .' He heard a smile in Father Ken's voice.

Jake walked to the far end of the room, where a built-in desk had not yet been removed. From what he had seen of the hospital so far, that seemed to be the pattern: a lot of the removable stuff had been taken, while the fittings were going down with the building. It was probably cheaper that way.

'Look up at the ceiling.'

Jake looked up and saw the ceiling – low, only about three feet above his head – was covered with dirty white plastic tiles.

'Start at the corner near the door and count four tiles along the long wall, then three in. That tile is loose.'

Keeping the phone to his ear, Jake climbed on to the desk and reached up with his free hand. He found the tile and pushed. A choking cloud of dust fell on him, and he struggled not to sneeze.

'Good,' said the priest. 'You should find it there.'

Jake reached his hand up into the space and felt around. His fingers met a few wires, cobwebs, dead flies and lots of dust. Then he felt something hard. It was small and moved when he touched it. He reached further in and removed the object. He turned on the torch to illuminate his find.

It was a long kitchen knife, solid steel. Some of the rivets on the handle had rusted with age, and the blade could have done with a good clean. But otherwise it was perfect. He looked closely at the wooden handle. There were dark stains that flaked off when he rubbed them. Blood. Was this one of the knives Father Ken had used in his killing spree?

No. Father Ken wasn't the type to use a knife.

Then why would he want it? It was well hidden and would probably have been buried under tons of rubble once the building came down.

'I've found the knife,' he said. 'I presume that's what you want?'

'Yes. You've done well.'

'Do you want me to get rid of it?'

'Oh no,' said the priest. 'I want you to keep it safe, just like I'm keeping your mother.'

Then the line went dead.

Jake stared dumbly at the phone for several seconds before shoving it into his trouser pocket. He wished he could see the priest's plan in the same way he could see everything else, but where Father Ken was concerned he could make out nothing. Nothing at all.

And Jake was getting a strong sense of certainty that this place, this building, had something to do with that mental block.

82

Sunday, 2.30 a.m.

As Jake crossed the day ward to the door, he knew he was in serious trouble. Father Ken had everything – not just Jake's mother, but secrets about Jake himself. Secrets that kept Jake bound up in whatever sick wild goose chase he was involved in. Briefly he considered calling it all in. But just as quickly he realized he could not do that. He was on his own now. In legal terms his actions tonight amounted to obstruction of justice. If he explained, he might escape a custodial sentence. But his career was over.

Jake told himself to worry about that once he had his mother back.

He had to move quickly, get out of the window while the guard was still sitting at his station, and get the hell clear of the grounds. But he didn't do that. He felt an urge to stay and let the ghosts find him.

There was one ghost in particular that he wanted to meet. The ghost of the long-dead man who shared his face. So instead of turning back down the hall he'd come along, he turned right and continued deeper into the building, looking for the stairwell that led to the basement. He took a left, checked round the corner for the guard, then ran down the corridor. He passed large wards on either side. At the end of the hallway he took a right then a left. The basement door gaped open in front of him. He hadn't made a single wrong turn on the way.

He hesitated at the top but he knew he had to go down. Maybe here he would find the answers that would chase away this maddening familiarity.

He began to climb down into the darkness, his torch showing the way in front of him, but it was a penlight and lit little of his surroundings. There were a few rooms down there, but Jake was drawn towards one in particular. It was an office, and the door was closed. It was the first closed door he'd come across. Gently he pushed the handle, but it was locked.

He put his shoulder to the door and gave a speculative push. It creaked. There was some give there. The wooden frame was rotten from damp. Even though he was all the way down in the basement, he didn't want to risk the noise of a kick. So he shoved as hard as he could, easing the pressure at the final moment when the door gave.

His penlight revealed row upon row of metal filing cabinets. He pulled on one drawer, and the tray of files slid out easily. He pulled out a file at random and flicked through. It was a medical report on one of the patients. He scanned the tags – they were alphabetical. This should be easy.

Tonight he would get his answer.

He went to the first cabinet. He guessed third drawer down, and he was right. He found the AS, AT, AU and AW files. AU – he ran his finger over the dusty tags until he found AUSTIN. His heart began to pound in his chest. He could hear it.

There were three files with the name Austin.

AUSTIN, Catherine.

AUSTIN, Gerald.

He held his breath. Surely the next file would bear the name Jake . . . But it didn't.

AUSTIN, Jeanette.

Slowly, almost reluctantly, he pulled out the file and opened it. On reading the first page, the relief flooded through him.

His mother had been a nurse! It made perfect sense. In spite of himself, Jake smiled, almost laughing with relief. That had to be why he recognized the place, even if his memories had taken on an infuriatingly spooky form: his mom had worked here. Of course his mother's old workplace was familiar to him. He wasn't losing his mind. He had never been a patient. He was going to be all right.

At some point he would have to ask his mother why she had never mentioned that they had lived around here before, especially when Jake had announced he was transferring to Littleton. But he would ask her that question, and many more, after he had saved her from Father Ken.

Jake tucked the file under his arm and pointed the

penlight towards the door. He walked out of the office feeling lighter and more sure of himself than he had in days. He was going to fix everything – catch the killer, save his mother, explain to Asher what he'd done. This was going to work out. He could feel it.

As he walked through the basement towards the stairwell, the torch beam caught a sign on one of the doors. He looked. WARDEN.

This was once Fred Lumley's office.

The door was unlocked, and he pushed it open. All the furniture was gone, but like upstairs no one had bothered to remove the pictures from the walls. There was a large oil painting on one wall opposite where Jake assumed the desk used to be. He shone the light on the painting and almost dropped it. What he'd seen hit him like a physical blow.

He steadied himself, holding the penlight like a gun as he walked towards the painting. The picture showed a man standing in an office, shelves of books behind him. One hand rested on the back of a chair, and he stared out of the canvas. He was dressed in formal trousers and a collared shirt with no tie.

Jake was looking at a painting of himself.

He reeled as a storm of images assaulted his mind: images of spraying, spurting blood just like his nightmares.

Jake screwed his eyes shut, an instinctive reaction – but that just brought the mental images into sharper focus.

I'm fucking losing it!

He forced himself to look at the other pictures on the walls. A few photographs remained. Most of them were in black and white, and faded. One showed happy people in groups on a lawn, another showed what looked like a graduation.

He was drawn to one of the pictures: a black and white framed photo of two men at what looked like an event in the asylum grounds. One was the man who looked like Jake, the other was a much younger Father Ken. The caption beneath read, 'Warden Fred Lumley, with Father Kenneth Laurie'.

Father Ken was smiling.

So you were *here.*

Suddenly Jake heard a creak, and a loud voice called, 'Who's down there?'

He killed the torch and waited. The silence was probably only a matter of seconds, but to Jake it felt like an hour.

The security guard was more conscientious than Jake had thought, and soon he heard the sound of footsteps descending the stairs.

Jake silently slipped the photo from the wall and shoved it into his mom's personnel file. He waited until the guard had got all the way down to the basement. He kept a close eye on where he knew the doorway to be and the hall beyond. Right on cue a swell of pale light illuminated the hall, sweeping in a crazy arc.

And then a second one joined it – two guards.

The torch beams bounced off the walls of the office. One of them caught an old mirror and bounced back, and for a moment Jake saw two men in dark suits, lights held in left hands, guns in their right. This wasn't the guard doing his rounds; they were FBI. It seemed they had not abandoned the asylum for Christmas after all. Jake had miscalled this one badly.

He kept low, waiting for his chance. The lights swept the room. At the point where both torches were pointed away from him Jake sprang, rushing between the agents and hitting them both with his shoulders as he passed. It hurt, but he knew one of the agents had been put on the ground. The other was still on his feet, but had dropped something – hopefully his gun. Jake bounded up the stairs, trusting his instinctive knowledge of the asylum to guide him. He wasn't going to risk turning on his own torch.

He got through the door at the top, and could hear the first of the FBI men already on the stairs. Down the corridor he ran at full speed. There was nothing to trip him – he remembered that from earlier. Down past the day ward, turn, then into the classroom.

The window was still open. He was out and running across the grass towards the perimeter fence. But he could hear the two agents emerging from the building. He was through the gap in the fence now and running the hundred yards towards his car. From the shouts of the FBI guys, he put them at thirty yards or so behind. As he ran Jake fumbled in his pocket for his keys. He was at the car, and the key hit the lock first go. He was in; the engine turned and caught. Jake hit the gas, and he was off, keeping his face low so that the two agents – who he could see running towards where his car had been – couldn't make him out.

He was safe. If he didn't lose his way on the minor roads, he was home free.

But the Feds had his licence-plate number.

83

Sunday, 6 a.m.

Father Ken was not answering his mobile. Jake had tried four times already, and the lack of a response was driving him crazy. He was still wearing yesterday's clothes, and he carried the dust and grime of the asylum with him. He knew he looked like shit: the reaction of the colleagues, those who had drawn the holiday short straw, when he got to the station told him so. They avoided him. No one approached his desk. It was like there was a sign hovering over him warning them away.

Time was ticking; it would not be long before the FBI traced his numberplate and came looking.

He took out the photograph he had taken from Lumley's wall the night before. It was dirty and he could barely make out the details. The two figures in the foreground – Lumley and Father Ken – were clear, but the others were obscure. Jake took out a tissue and rubbed the glass.

It seemed to be some sort of a presentation day or craft fair. Behind and around the two smiling men was a group of people, both children and adults. Some were holding artwork; others were smiling awkwardly; a few seemed uninterested, looking the wrong way. The style of the clothing, as well as the long hair and moustaches of the men, dated the photo to the era of Jake's childhood.

Some of the people in the photograph were clearly staff. One was a nurse, a heavyset black woman with a large Afro. She looked young, about twenty. Her face felt oddly familiar to Jake – a friend of his mom's? – but, try as he might, he couldn't remember who she was.

Jake opened his desk drawer and removed a magnifying glass. He looked at the woman carefully but still could not make the connection. Then he spotted she was wearing a name tag. He couldn't make out what it said. He removed the back of the frame and took out the photo. He placed it under his desk lamp. Now it was slightly clearer. He looked through the magnifying glass and adjusted it until the badge was as clear as he could make it. Now he could just about make out the name.

JEANETTE AUSTIN.

He sat back in surprise. *What? Why is she wearing my mother's name tag?*

Jake stood up. He needed to clear his head, to think. He was suddenly very aware of the fact that he hadn't eaten in he didn't know how long. He hadn't even had a coffee since getting to the station. A jolt of caffeine might get him thinking clearly.

He went into the small canteen off the detective bureau, but no one had made coffee that morning. Christmas. So he walked into the main recreation room of the station. It was about twice the size of his sitting room at home, with comfortable chairs scattered around and two coffee tables. There was a counter with a coffee machine, a cupboard full of mugs and plates, and a small fridge. The room also had a television on a stand. It was showing a replay of a preview of the annual Christmas Day football game. A cleaner whose name Jake didn't know was relaxing with a magazine.

Jake took the remote from the table and switched to CNN.

'Hey, I was watching that!' said the cleaner.

Jake raised the volume. The cleaner went back to her magazine, muttering something about cops being 'full of themselves'.

The TV news rotated through an entire cycle while he watched, and then returned to the second story of the day: the Chase Asylum killings.

'In an overnight twist, the manhunt for Fred Lumley has turned into a homicide investigation,' the anchor said.

'FBI experts have done a facial reconstruction of an adult skeleton found at the Chase Asylum, and have confirmed that the adult male is former warden Fred Lumley, who disappeared more than thirty years ago. Until this find, Lumley was wanted for questioning in connection with the deaths of at least two children at the institution, which closed down three years ago and is now due for demolition as part of wide-ranging plans to regenerate the towns surrounding Indianapolis.'

The screen switched from the anchor to the FBI reconstruction. Jake winced as the picture filled the screen. It was the photofit that the FBI man had emailed over yesterday, the one that looked just like him.

'Hey, Detective,' laughed the cleaner, looking up from her magazine. 'Do you have a twin we don't know about?'

Jake didn't answer. He just took his coffee and returned to his desk. There was something he needed to be sure of. His mother's file was in the drawer beneath the photograph. He took it out and began to read it. But everything was wrong. His mother was never five feet nine tall. She never weighed one ninety-five.

And she was never black.

Maybe there were two Jeanette Austins, or maybe the files had been tampered with. Maybe it was an honest mistake. Jake had no idea.

If Jeanette Austin wasn't his mother, then who was? *And who the hell am* I?

84

Sunday, 9.15 a.m.

He'd had a pleasant night.

His sense of a destiny being fulfilled, of a circle reaching completion, was getting stronger and stronger. The good Lord had decided it was time for him to reveal himself to the world. And that plan, which scared Father Ken at first, now filled him with joy.

How perfect that he would be saving souls on the anniversary of Christ's birth. His only regret was, he couldn't save them all. But he could manage one more. Of course he could. He would kill the old woman to save her. But first he would have to get the instrument of her sin.

That is why I need the knife.

85

Sunday, 10.45 a.m.

The drive to the morgue was a lot quicker than the last time. Traffic was light on Christmas Day everywhere in America.

There was no receptionist working, so Jake let himself in and walked to Ronnie Zatkin's office. She wasn't there. Jake found her down in the morgue, surrounded by a couple of twenty-somethings examining the seventeen skeletons.

She looked up as he walked in. 'Hi, Detective. Merry Christmas.'

'Thanks. Can I get a minute?'

Dr Zatkin nodded and led the way towards her office.

'I had to call in help,' she explained to Jake, pointing at her dutiful deputies as they walked past. 'These guys are final-year students from the Indiana University School of Medicine. There's no way my staff could cope with seventeen cold case autopsies on top of their normal workload. The only way we can get them done is by calling in the cavalry. Luckily, these kids are all desperate for experience. Looks good on résumés, you know?'

They got to the door of her office and she was about to open it when Jake stopped her. 'Do you have another lab we could go to?' he asked.

She nodded again and led him into a small room off the morgue and closed the door behind them. 'What's up?' she asked.

He placed a plastic bag on the stainless-steel work surface, then removed the old kitchen knife he had recovered from the Chase Asylum.

'I need to know: are those dark stains on the handle human blood?'

Doctor Zatkin put on plastic gloves, picked up the knife and examined it under a bright light.

'Looks like it. I can see some residue where the blade sinks into the handle. I could take a scraping from there and test that.' She started towards a microscope in the corner of the room.

'Before you begin, Ronnie,' said Jake, 'this has to be between you and me. No one else can know.'

She looked at him and shook her head slowly. 'That's not the way we're supposed to do things.'

'And I'll bet working on Christmas Day is not the way you're supposed to do things either. But you're here, aren't you?'

She looked at him for a long moment. 'You're in a bind,' she said, her voice halfway between question and statement.

Jake thought about agreeing, maybe even telling her everything, but . . .

'It's best I don't tell you,' he said.

He could see she was reluctant but intrigued, and finally she nodded. She opened a drawer and took out a small vial of luminol. Dimming the light, she sprayed the knife handle. After a second or two it began to glow slightly – a very faint blue. It lasted about thirty seconds, then faded away.

'It's blood,' she said.

'What type?'

'Hold on – the test doesn't even tell us if it's human or animal blood. I need to collect a sample.'

Briskly she reached for a spatula and scraped it along the edge of the knife where it met the wooden handle. She dropped the black specks that came off into a small test tube. Then she added a clear liquid from one of the bottles on the shelf above the workstation. Within minutes, there was half an inch of pink liquid at the bottom of the test tube.

She took out a pipette and filled it, depositing some drops on a small card.

'I'll know blood type in the next two minutes,' she explained.

'What about DNA?'

'You don't want to wait – that will take hours. Unless you had something you wanted me to compare the DNA with?'

Jake didn't reply.

They watched as the blood samples on the test card reacted with the enzymes.

'How's the case going? Any fresh leads?' Ronnie asked.

Jake mumbled a non-answer, and Ronnie gave up on the small talk. Both of them just watched: some of the patches of pink remained uniform while others began to form clumps of darker material.

After a short while, Doctor Zatkin said, 'The blood is AB negative. I don't know if that's what you were expecting, but that's all I can tell you for now. I'll run the DNA test, and if you have anything to compare it with, drop it in.'

Jake, on autopilot, nodded his thanks.

AB negative – that's the same blood type as me.

'How common is AB negative?' he asked.

'It's the rarest blood type of them all. Forensics love it: it's the best blood type for eliminating suspects. Maybe one in a hundred and sixty people has it.' Her smile dropped and her eyes widened. 'Don't tell me it's from the Christmas Killer?'

'No, it's not.'

Ronnie shrugged and didn't push it.

It went against one of the earliest lessons a detective receives when he is first trained – do not make assumptions. Do not jump to conclusions based on one piece of evidence.

But, this time, Jake couldn't help it. The odds were short enough that he was beginning to see it clearly.

It's Fred Lumley's blood.

Fred Lumley was my father.

86

Sunday, 11.30 a.m.

Jake left the morgue and drove back towards Littleton. The DNA results would tell him for sure, but he didn't need them to confirm what he already knew.

He was clear of Indianapolis and driving through rolling countryside when his mobile buzzed. He glanced at the number, thinking it might be Father Ken – actually hoping it was. Instead, he saw the PD's switchboard number.

He pulled over and answered.

'Austin, where the fuck are you?' The voice at the other end was Colonel Asher's. He was pissed off – likely because he had been called in on Christmas Day.

'On my way back in, boss. I was at the morgue.'

'I don't give a fuck where you were. What were you doing out at the Chase Asylum last night?'

As the words hit him Jake felt the blood drain from his body. That's why Asher had gone in. They knew already. He had hoped for a few hours more.

Jake leaned and rested his forehead on the wheel. It was over. He couldn't go back to the station now.

'Austin, do you have an explanation?'

Jake took his head off the wheel. Outside, traffic thundered by, but he didn't really hear it. 'I wasn't at the Chase Asylum,' he said. It was a shitty lie and wouldn't buy him time.

'Don't fuck me around. Two FBI agents saw the ghost of Fred Lumley in the asylum last night. He knocked them over and ran, but they got his licence number and tracked him down. Do you know who the ghost was?'

Jake didn't answer. What could he, realistically, say to that? One look at any image of Lumley, and Jake's mistaken-identity defence would be shredded. But he didn't need to answer because, from the way he ploughed on, Asher wasn't really looking for one. He had clearly had it with Jake days ago, and getting dragged in on Christmas Day had not done anything to improve his opinion. 'They want to know what you were doing there,' he said, 'and why you were contaminating evidence. I have Special Agent Colin Reader in my office right now. He wants a word.'

'No, sir,' said Jake.

'Detective, you'd better—' snapped Asher.

'I have to follow up something. I'll be in later.'

'Austin, get back here now, or I'll put an APB on you. Every cop in the state will have your picture, they'll have—'

Jake ended the call and tossed the phone on to the passenger seat. He fired the engine and pulled on to the road without any idea of where he was going. Things were closing in on him fast. It wasn't just his career on the line; it was his mother, his family and his whole identity.

Where the fuck is Father Ken?

If Jake could track down the priest, he could save his mother. That was the only thing that mattered right now.

He took his eyes off the road to pick up his mobile again. He hit *Redial* to try the priest. He could hear the phone ringing. It seemed to go on and on.

Finally, Father Ken answered. 'What can I do for you, Detective?'

Give me back my mother. And my life – all of it.

But Jake didn't say that. This was a negotiation, and the secret of successful negotiation was to keep calm.

He made a show of taking a deep breath. 'Forgive me, Father, for I have sinned . . .'

'Too late.'

Jake tried again. 'I want you to help me,' he said. 'I have questions . . . about me.'

There was a hiss on the line, and the signal came and went, but Jake managed to hear Father Ken say, 'Fire away.'

'OK, we'll start at the beginning. Did you kill Fred Lumley?' Jake asked.

The sound of laughter tinkled through the bad connection.

'Is that a yes or a no?'

'Jake, I do the Lord's work. But I am not the only one who does.'

'What about my mother?' Jake asked. 'Is she still safe?'

'Your mother?' Father Ken was feigning confusion. 'Do you mean Jeanette?'

'Who else would I mean?'

'Jeanette . . . Austin?'

'Yes. Jeanette Austin, the woman you kidnapped, you . . .' Jake bit back the insult. The negotiation had been taken right out of his control. 'My mother . . .'

'That's funny,' the priest said and laughed again.

What was Father Ken up to, making him talk in circles? One last sick power play? A show of ultimate dominance – that he could toy with the younger man because he had all the cards?

'Thing is,' Father Ken continued, 'I don't see much Jamaican ancestry in your features, Detective.' Father Ken laughed at his own joke, his mirth echoing down the line to Jake.

Echoing . . .

Jake took the phone away from his face so Father Ken wouldn't hear the thrill of hope in his voice. He knew exactly where the priest was.

When he spoke again, it was in the same little-boy voice he had not been able to control the night before – only this time it was a con. He was feeding Father Ken's hunger for power. 'I don't understand . . .'

'But you will, Jake,' said Father Ken. 'You will.'

The priest ended the call. Jake could imagine him smirking, laughing to himself, thinking that he was safe – that Jake was completely at his mercy, that there was no way he would ever be found. But there had been something about the call, the connection, that had been poking the nerve synapses in his brain all through the priest's taunting. There had been an echo on the line, and not only the electronic echo of a faulty connection. It was a physical echo. The priest was in a big enclosed space. But the connection had been poor too – like he was underground . . .

Father Ken had not gone on the run at all. He was hiding beneath his beloved church.

'The Lord has many instruments, Father,' Jake muttered. 'And one of them is coming to get you.'

87

Sunday, 11.45 a.m.

Jake had to act fast. By now Asher would have put out the APB he'd threatened. Every cop in the city would be on the lookout for his car.

He was ten minutes from Christ the Redeemer. He floored it and let the siren blare. To hell with drawing attention to himself – he was far beyond worrying about that. He followed the spire of the church and was close within seven minutes.

A drive past was too risky, so he pulled up short and put his mobile on silent. He rummaged in the glove compartment, taking out his Beretta 92 semi-auto. There were eight rounds in the clip, and one chambered. Nine shots – more than he would need. He slipped the gun into his shoulder holster, then took out a torch. The knife he had recovered from the Chase Asylum was in a plastic bag on the passenger seat. Without really knowing why, Jake took the knife out of the bag and slipped it into his jacket pocket.

He got out of the car and walked up to the church, not even bothering to duck his head against the driving snow. He barely felt it now.

The scene was becoming depressingly familiar. The little cemetery was blocked off with a temporary hoarding set up by the construction crew, overlaid with black and yellow police tape he himself had helped put up. Jake didn't expect there to be security cameras, but he wasn't taking chances. When he got to the church grounds he crossed the grass verge rather than walking on the gravel. He reached the main door. It was closed. It was huge and made of oak, about twelve feet high, but there was an inset door on one side. Jake tried it and it gave. He pushed it open, fingers wrapped tightly around the edge in case he had to brace it against a whine.

Then Jake stepped into the darkness.

The church was little more than a vast cavern, with nothing at all inside. All the pews had been removed and sold through junk shops and antique outlets down in Indianapolis. There were blank patches on the walls where the Stations of the Cross had been taken down. The only things left in place were the ornate stained-glass windows, dappling the interior in an eerie orange, green and blue gloom. At the far end Jake could see the altar, a plain limestone plinth with a cross embossed on the front and a marble top. The altar was as empty as the church, and the tabernacle door was open behind it, like God himself had deserted Christ the Redeemer.

Sticking to the walls, Jake slowly made his way around the church. It was eerily peaceful. He could hear the rustle of wind through the bare winter branches outside, and in the distance the rumble of holiday traffic. Inside, all was silent, but as he neared the altar he became aware of another sound, faint at first. It was a moan or a chant, seeming to rise up out of the depths of the darkness. The moan rose and rose in volume, seeming to coil and spiral in the air, before crashing down into a long drawn-out single note that cannoned off the walls of the church.

The moan faded and died, but Jake was moving now, moving fast towards the sound. He crossed to the altar. There were two doors, one on either side of the tabernacle. He tried the one on the left. It opened into the sacristy, the little room where the priest dressed for Mass. Empty. He tried the other door and was immediately hit by a musty smell crawling out of the open doorway. Squinting into the darkness, Jake could see stone steps spiralling down.

Now the sound was unmistakable. That was his mother's voice, chanting and moaning. He could make out words: she was praying, or begging, for forgiveness. He recognized the formula from his childhood: the ritual of confession.

'Forgive me, Father, for I have sinned . . .'

'That's right – beg the Lord for forgiveness, sinner.' The voice of Father Ken rose in a crescendo.

Jake saw the next five seconds play out in his head, clearly – triumphantly. He would take the stairs two at a time, charging down into the basement below. He would take the butt of his gun to Father Ken's head.

Not the skull, because he was an old man who probably couldn't survive such a blow, and Jake wanted him to spend whatever time he had left rotting in jail. He would whip him across the jaw. At least it would stop him talking.

Let's see how you like losing your *teeth, Padre.*

But Jake did not follow his own script. He couldn't – his cop's training overrode his emotions. This was an unknown environment, and he didn't know the layout; he had not observed the target or the victim so he had no idea how the players were arranged. Any action would be slowed by the half-second Jake would need to get orientated once he was in there. And he knew from experience it was hard to be adaptable when your heart was in your mouth.

So he took the steps slowly, making sure to place his whole foot on each step, heel and toes touching the stone simultaneously to reduce the noise of creaking shoe leather or gently cracking metatarsal bones. He stopped before the final turn, the feeble light from the basement just catching the tops of his shoes. He listened.

His mother was still pleading for forgiveness. Her voice was low and weak, tired.

'Please, Christ, forgive me my sins,' she rasped. Her words were coming in short bursts that seemed forced from her throat. 'Mother of mercy, forgive me.'

'Real penitence only comes when you admit your sins,' said Father Ken. 'Admit your sins, and his divine grace will set you free, my child.'

His mother's voice was shrill, shrieking, and felt like a dagger in Jake's ears. 'I admit my sins! I admit them.'

Jake was itching to storm into the crypt and open fire. But he couldn't. He had to hold back and make sure he had a clean run at the priest. He also knew that Father Ken – for all his years – had to be considered a dangerous man. Jake did not want to think about how this thing would play out if he charged in and missed.

'I haven't heard you say it yet.' Father Ken was bellowing now. 'Your greatest, most grave and foul sin. Confess to what you did . . . Confess to the murder of Fred Lumley.'

A wave of shock flowed through Jake at that. His gun arm momentarily lowered. His mother wouldn't have killed anyone, not in a million years. She *couldn't* have killed Fred Lumley.

'I can't. I didn't kill Fred. I should have, but I didn't.' His mother was pleading now.

Jake knew she hadn't killed him in the same way he knew that it was Fred Lumley's blood on the blade.

'Liar!' Father Ken yelled. 'Confess your gravest sin!'

There was a scream, this one piercing.

Jake could listen no longer. He turned the corner and took in the scene at a glance. They were in a basement about sixty feet long, with an arched stone roof. The stone floor was bare. Against one wall lay three tombs. Against the other wall were lumber, ladders and old paint pots. It was half storeroom, half catacomb. His mother was kneeling in the centre of the floor about twenty feet in front of Jake. Her head was trapped in the murderous head crusher.

Her hands were raised in prayer, but Jake could see that they weren't bound together with rope or leather or anything else. She was praying voluntarily.

Jeanette's face was ashen and was beginning to distort near the jaw line. Father Ken was standing above and behind her, his hands on the screw. He was in his white alb with a purple stole around his neck. Jake had a flash of a memory from his childhood: purple was the colour of penance.

Father Ken seemed ready for another turn of the screw.

'Stop!' shouted Jake, drawing his gun and aiming at the head of the priest.

Father Ken looked up and nodded as he saw Jake. 'The confessional is normally private,' he said, 'but I think, under the circumstances, we can allow you to stay and listen to the sin and then the absolution.'

'Step away from her,' Jake ordered.

Father Ken had a determined look. 'Well now, I think we have a problem,' he said. He leaned forward deliberately, grasping the handle of the screw.

Jake cocked the pistol and squinted down the barrel, lining up the shot he didn't want to take unless he had to. 'I'm giving you one chance, you sonofabitch. You really do not want to fuck with me today.'

The evil priest kept his eyes on Jake's mom. 'If you shoot me, Detective, you might kill me. But it won't save Jeanette, because the force of my body falling will turn this screw. I might die, but I will still win. If you want to save your mother, you will drop the gun and kick it across the floor to me.'

Jake held his gun hand steady, then slowly brought his other hand up, settling his aim. He had a clear shot, even in the darkness, across the basement. He could take the priest out. But even as he thought it, he had to ask himself how tight was the screw already turned? How much more could his mother's fragile skull take?

'Be a sensible boy, and drop it,' coaxed the priest.

'Do as he says,' said his mother. Her voice became a scream as Father Ken turned the screw. Only a little, but it was enough . . . 'Please, Bruce!'

His mother's mistake drew Jake's eyes briefly to her. She did not have her hands bound; why wasn't she doing something to free herself? Why was she accepting this? It was like the priest had some kind of power over her. She had knelt willingly before his infernal machine and now was silently praying. He could see her lips moving with the words.

Jake turned his gaze back to Father Ken, who was glaring at him with a look that seemed to be half-warning him to obey his command and half-desperate for him to justify using the crusher. Slowly Jake lowered his arm and, bending low, put the gun on the floor. He kept his eyes on the priest the whole time.

Jake straightened. His body tingled with annoyance at himself – he had not followed a basic rule of training for hostage situations. *Dismantle your weapon. Neutralize your opponent's advantage as best you can.*

'Kick the gun over here,' said the priest.

Jake did as he was told, all his senses on alert, his muscles poised for one lunge. If the priest bent to pick up the loaded gun, he would have to take his hand off the screw . . . and if his hand was off the screw . . .

'Relax, Jake,' said Father Ken with a smile. He didn't move for the gun. Jake tried not to let his disappointment, his rising panic, show. 'There are things you need to hear. Isn't that right, Melanie?'

'Yes,' whispered Jake's mother.

'Speak up. I don't think he heard you,' said the priest.

'Yes,' she said.

'Melanie?' whispered Jake.

Father Ken's lips curled in a grim arrogant smile. 'And you seemed like such a close family . . .' He loomed over Jake's mother. 'The floor is yours . . . Melanie.'

Jake's mother turned her eyes as far as they would go, so that she could look at Jake. 'My name is Melanie. Melanie Sands. I was a patient at the Chase Asylum.'

'Very good,' said the priest encouragingly. 'Go on.'

There was a haunted expression on Jake's mom's face, an expression that was caused by more than the pressure on her skull.

'I knew about Fred Lumley,' she whispered. 'We all knew. He was abusing the children. And we did nothing about it. Forgive me, Father.' Her voice was low. Jake strained to hear.

'There's more,' urged the priest. 'There's more sin to be confessed, Melanie.'

'Some of the children disappeared. And we knew he had killed them. But we were too scared of him to do anything about it.' Tears were streaming down her cheeks now, and her voice was strangled – as though she was forcing the confession physically out of her mouth.

'He killed them?' asked Jake, hearing the pain in his own voice echo back at him, as though the walls of the crypt were rejecting him, rejecting his pain. As well they should – his biological father was a child abuser and a murderer.

'Oh yes, he killed them, all right,' said Father Ken. 'Daddy was an evil man, Jake.'

Jake was stunned. He'd got the answer to a question he'd been asking his whole life, and was now wishing he hadn't.

'I will never forgive myself . . . for not doing anything . . .' said Jeanette. She looked hard at Jake. 'I tried to stop him. I tried to help you. But I couldn't. I wasn't strong enough.'

Jake's words were hoarse, barely audible. 'What are you talking about, Mom?'

'I couldn't keep him away from you,' she said, face crumpling and her voice collapsing to a wail. 'He said you were his son and he could do what he wanted . . .'

Jake felt his stomach lurch like he had gone over the top of a roller coaster. His mind pulsed with vague flashes of memory, and he tried to push them aside.

'I'm sorry, Bruce,' said his mother. 'Forgive me.'

'Mom . . .' Jake said, but he couldn't finish the sentence. The words were choking him. The memories were flooding back now, memories of a young boy and a man who scared him. Jake had thought the shadowy spectre in his dreams was a figment of his imagination, the product of a naturally skewed and twisted mind. The kind of mind that made him a unique and effective cop. But now he knew – his mind was twisted because he had *inherited* that trait.

And there was something else he knew, another explanation for why he had turned out the way he had. Why he had the ability to anticipate criminal behaviour, second-guess the moves of psychopaths.

How else could he have turned out after having grown up inside Chase Asylum?

88

Sunday, 12.45 p.m.

'I'm so sorry, dear, that I did nothing to stop it,' said his mother.

'But you did stop it,' said Father Ken in triumph. 'Confess to the warden's murder, and I will absolve you of your sins before you meet your creator.'

'I can't!' Jake's mom cried. 'I saw him beat Bruce, and I was paralysed and did nothing. I only wish I had had the courage to take his life, Father. I swear to you, I'm telling the truth on this. I was a patient, but I had privileges. I did some work in the office, and they gave me some spending money. I went down into the basement to give some documents to Mr Lumley. I heard a noise in the office, and I walked in . . .'

Yes. Jake could remember it all now. He could finish his mother's story for her.

I was looking down at the floor, trying to squeeze my mind out of my body and into a gap there under my feet. It would help me block out the pain of what my father was doing to me.

My head was filled with rage, and also with shame. How could he hurt me so much?

And then she walked in. She saw me in a position of complete humiliation. I wanted the gap between my feet to open up and let me drop away. I imagined it happening. But it didn't. It never did.

I was never so lucky.

I was crying and in extreme pain. He had promised I would get used to it in time, but I never did. Through my pain, though, I now felt joy – hope. Melanie had caught him, and that had to mean that he would stop. Or at least lay off me for a while, and go after someone else. Melanie had bought me some time, even if it was only a little. I loved her so much at the moment. She seemed like the bravest, most heroic person in the world.

But then Dad twisted around and shouted at her. He was in a rage because she had just barged in. She hadn't knocked. He called her names, names I didn't know the meaning of, but I knew they were bad words. I could tell because they made Melanie cry. And I hated my father even more.

He said he would make her life a living hell. He said no one would take the word of a lunatic like her over that of a respected . . .

'. . . medical man like him.' Jake's mom was telling the story while the scene played through Jake's mind. 'I tried to back out, but he followed me and pulled me back into his office. He held me against the table and pushed my legs apart . . .'

Jake's mom let that last statement hang in the air, the way Jake had seen abused women do in countless interviews. Nothing else needed to be said.

Father Ken, however, did not feel that way. 'He raped you,' he said. 'And that's when you killed him. Confess, and it will be over.'

I can see Dad's body there on the floor, and all the blood. All the sticky blood, and it's everywhere. It's on my shirt and my shoes, and splattered on my face. On Melanie's face too, and her clothes. There was so much blood. Who would have believed one man had so much of it inside him?

Melanie was standing over the body with blood on her hands and was leafing through the phone book. She was picking up the office phone. I guessed she was scared. Then she was talking to someone, and I could hear what she was saying, but not what he was saying.

'Father, he's dead. You have to come. I don't know what to do.'

Then she turned to me and told me that it would all work out because the priest was a good man, and he would know what to do for the best.

And finally Jake knew where he had met Father Ken Laurie before, had the explanation for why he could visualize the younger face on him. Father Ken had come when Melanie had called him. He was the kindly man who had come in and said that everything would be fine. It would all work out for the best because God had a plan that was bigger than them all.

'You were there that day,' Jake said to Father Ken.

'We all were,' he replied.

Now Jake could remember it clearly.

Father Ken had rushed down the stairs to the basement. He had surveyed the carnage and run to Melanie, who was sitting near the desk.

'Is he dead?' she asked.

The priest nodded.

'He was a bad man,' she went on. 'He was evil. You have to help me. What will I do? I have to get the boy out of here.'

'For the sake of the boy, I'll help you, Melanie,' said Father Ken. 'He deserved to die because of his sins.'

Father Ken had put the body in a thick canvas sack he got from the maintenance room. And then he had found cleaning fluids and a bucket of water and instructed Melanie to get down on her knees and begin scrubbing.

When the room was clean, he took the knife and put it in a small bag.

'You need to get far away from here,' he said to Melanie. He looked around the office and saw some papers on the desk. They were the employment papers of one of the nurses on the staff: Jeanette Austin.

'Melanie Sands must disappear for ever. Take the boy with you. Pretend he is your son and you are a nurse called Jeanette Austin. God knows you've spent enough time here to know how to act like one. This deed has set you free.'

'Thank you, Father,' she said.

'Go now, while it's quiet. I'll handle the body,' said Father Ken.

He bundled them out of the building and pushed them gently in the direction of the gate.

'Go as far away as you can,' he said. 'Bruce, this nice lady will look after you and take care of you now.'

He had taken Melanie aside and whispered something in her ear, but Bruce had listened in, and he had heard what Father Ken said.

'Melanie, I tell you that this is your penance. Raise that

boy well, so that you may atone for the sins you have committed today.'

Bruce knew then that he wouldn't be living at the asylum any more.

It was the first time in his life that he had ever felt safe.

89

Sunday, 1 p.m.

Father Ken's hand was still steady on the screw handle.

'I have never stopped being grateful, Father. I raised Bruce like my own,' said Jake's mom, her words coming in pained gasps, short and sharp.

'It wasn't your right to kill Lumley,' said Father Ken. 'You are not the instrument of the Lord. You are still a murderess who would one day have to atone for your sins. You must confess before I send you to paradise.'

'But, Father, I didn't kill him.'

And then the final memories came flooding back to Jake. All the pictures, the vague imaginings, the bad dreams, were beginning to make perfect sense.

He was holding her against the table, and he was pushing between her legs. He had pulled her skirt up, had pulled his own trousers down. I knew what he was doing. I'd seen him do it to other girls and boys.

He had also done it to me.

Melanie was a nice lady. She had taken me into the woods one day and shown me a kingfisher by the river. And she had tried to come to my rescue tonight. I had to do something . . .

There was a knife on the table. I picked it up. I only wanted him to stop. I hit him with the knife but it bounced off his back. He stopped what he was doing and turned around. He looked really angry and seemed to be taller and wider than ever before. He came at me. And I was frightened. I knew that look in his eyes. He came at me and grabbed for the knife, and I pushed it against him to stop him.

This time it went in.

My hand was wet with the blood.

And then I hit him, again and again. And each time the knife went in, and my hand got wetter and wetter. He looked surprised when the knife first went in, and he stopped for a moment. Then he tried to take the knife from me, but I kept hitting him. And then he was weaker. The blood was coming out of him the same way I had seen water come out of a burst pipe in the shower room one time. His hands were no longer as strong, and I was able to hit him harder.

He was on his knees, and then he fell on to his back. But I kept plunging the knife into him. I was enjoying it. He wouldn't hurt me for a long time. Maybe never again.

The knife was slippery with the blood, and I lost my grip. I cut myself, the blade giving me a scar that I could never explain . . .

Until now.

And then she was pulling at my shoulders. That's why I stopped. And because my arm was tired and felt very heavy.

He wasn't moving. He was just lying there, his leg twisted under him where he had fallen. His eyes were staring up at the ceiling. The evil look was gone. There was blood on his face and on his arms. I could see a big gash on his cheek.

I turned, and Melanie folded me into her arms.

And I remember that I was smiling.

90

Sunday, 1.01 p.m.

'Say it with me: O my God, I am heartily sorry for having offended thee, and I detest all my sins . . .' Father Ken was chanting.

Jeanette joined in: '. . . because I dread the loss of heaven and the pains of hell . . .'

They were both chanting it together: '. . . but most of all because they offend thee, my God . . .'

Father Ken had a triumphant look on his face, and he was staring straight at Jake. Jake could see the priest's shoulders tensing for the final turn of the screw at the end of the act of contrition.

Jake let everything drain out of him, all the misery he felt at his discovery and all the questions he wanted to ask his mother – or the woman he had *thought* was his mother. He had to let it all go, just for now, otherwise he would never get the chance to sit down and ask her those questions.

Jake suddenly threw himself at the priest. He covered the twenty feet in barely a second, driving a shoulder into his ribs and forcing him back from the crusher.

Jake had timed it perfectly. Father Ken fell back

without managing to apply any more pressure to his hideous device. Jake stumbled, falling on top of him.

Father Ken was twisting, trying to get out from under Jake. And he was strong. Jake struggled to maintain his grip as the evil priest writhed and wriggled. He remembered his high-school wrestling days and tried to spread his weight, pushing down hard on Father Ken. He could hear the priest's breath coming in wheezes, and knew he was struggling for air. Jake came up on his toes, forcing his shoulder down on the priest. At the same time his arms circled Father Ken's head, applying a holding lock. The priest bucked another time, but Jake was tightening his grip. He was in control now.

Then Father Ken got one hand free, and Jake could feel him reaching. Jake tightened his hold, but the priest wasn't trying to get away. Too late Jake understood. Father Ken managed to grab Jake's little finger. He yanked, and there was a crack as the finger broke. Jake yelled, helpless to stop his arms going limp and his grip relaxing. He felt Father Ken turning underneath him. Then the priest was struggling to his feet and running towards Jeanette.

Jake rolled to his feet and moved as fast as he had ever done in his life. He tackled Father Ken high, pushing him past Jeanette and running him face first into the wall. There was a satisfying *crack* as forehead hit stone, then the body of the priest went limp in his grasp. He let him fall to the floor. He stared at him for a few moments, watching the faint rise and fall of Father Ken's back as his lungs took in shallow breaths.

He was unconscious.

Jake turned his attention to the head crusher. A quick glance confirmed it was a standard thread, and he frantically spun the handle counter-clockwise. It was well oiled, though it still moved stiffly. A few turns, and he could see the helmet begin to move upwards. A few more turns, and Jake managed to pull his mom free.

His mom? Jeanette? Melanie? He didn't care. She was the woman who had saved him from his father. The woman who had raised him as her own son. He threw his arms around her, and she sank into his embrace.

91

Sunday, 1.04 p.m.

'I am so sorry,' she whispered with her lips. She couldn't move her jaw.

Jake rubbed her shoulders mechanically as they held each other. She was injured, he knew that. But how badly?

He pulled his head back to examine her as best he could in the darkness of the crypt. He could see a deep bruising stain on the top of her head, visible against her silver hair. He could feel the wetness. Scalp wounds bled like a bitch, but that didn't mean they were serious. He had freed her before her jaw had been completely broken, before her eyeballs bulged and burst out of her skull. But she was old; how quickly could she get over what had happened?

She might never recover.

The thought came like a punch, and he felt weak at the knees. He could not let her slide away from him again. He needed her to keep a grip on herself just a little longer.

'Mom, there are some questions I have to ask – some things about my past I have to know.'

She did not respond except to repeat her whisper: 'I'm so sorry . . .'

'Melanie!' He snapped her real name. He needed to break through the barrier. 'My real mother? What was her name? Why did she leave me with Lumley?'

Her lips moved, but no sound came out.

'Melanie, please . . . I need a name,' said Jake.

She didn't reply.

He persisted. Jake wondered if the doors were closed completely. Another name might jog her memory. 'Did you know someone named Johnny Cooper? Did *I* know him? Were we friends?'

But Jeanette just continued to mutter apologies to no one in particular.

Jake was sinking into despondency when he felt her arms tense around his shoulders. Too late he was aware of a change in the light, as if someone was moving in the shadows behind him. He tensed his shoulders to throw Jeanette out of harm's way, but then he felt a blow like the kick of a mule.

It hit him right between the shoulder blades, and he crumpled to the ground, face first.

Jake kicked out backwards, like a wild bull. It was a blind strike, but the feel of a shin bone beneath his heel was wonderful at that moment.

'Damn you,' gasped the priest as Jake heard him stumble back.

Jake took the opportunity to spin on to his back. Father Ken was standing about four feet away from him, a big slab of stone in his hands. It must have weighed twenty pounds. Jake said a silent prayer of thanks that the man wasn't twenty years younger. If he had been strong enough to aim it at Jake's head instead of his shoulders, the fight would have been over at the first blow.

As Father Ken raised the stone, Jake started scrambling away. He heard the grunt of effort from the old man as he heaved the stone.

It was like being stamped on by a crazed horse. Jake felt his left shoulder buckle, and from the pain shooting through him knew the joint had been wrenched from its socket. He was on his stomach now, his left arm mangled and somehow wrapped around his left leg. He felt Father Ken sit heavily on his back. He tried to move, but his arm was dead under him.

Then he felt the chain going around his neck . . .

The priest was strong. His gnarled hands were tightening the links, drawing the chain tighter and tighter around Jake's throat. Jake felt an intense pain as his Adam's apple yielded to the pressure of the chain, a sensation like crawling flame to the side of his neck as Father Ken's weapon constricted his jugular, cutting off the blood supply to his brain. He couldn't breathe, and he felt his energy draining with every heartbeat. Then a milky cloud descended over his eyes, and the pain went away. His head was twisted to one side, and his mind swam. He could hear nothing over the roar in his ears.

Then Jake felt the chain loosen. Felt the weight of the priest lift as he fell off Jake's back.

Jake rolled to his right, avoiding his damaged left arm. He struggled into a sitting position. It felt like he was swimming through syrup. His breath caught in his throat as he tried to draw in gulps of oxygen. His mom was attacking Father Ken, plunging what Jake could now see was a kitchen knife into his torso over and over again. It had to have fallen from his pocket during the scuffle.

Jake staggered to his feet, ignoring the agony in his shoulder as the blood and feeling flowed again through his body. He gazed at the surreal sight of his mother stabbing at the priest over and over again to the beat of the pounding in his head, which made what he was seeing seem distant.

'Forgive me, Father,' she was screaming. 'Forgive me, Father.'

And she kept driving the knife into the back of the priest, even as he crumpled to the ground.

'Mom – no!' shouted Jake, reaching out with his good arm.

Father Ken was crawling now, scrabbling desperately away. Jake's mom walked up to the grovelling priest and bent down, her left hand on his shoulder, steadying herself. She raised the knife over her head.

'Stop!' howled the priest into the darkness.

Then the knife fell.

92

Sunday, 1.10 p.m.

Jake stood in the open door of the church, trying to orientate himself. He had a blinding headache, made worse by the bitter cold, which seemed to slam against his skull. Blood vessels had burst in his eyeballs from the strangulation, and he knew it would be days before his vision settled properly. He thought his shoulder was dislocated, but the worst pain came from his finger. In the light he could see that it was badly swollen, and the top two portions were bent at an angle away from his palm.

He looked at the woman he had thought of as his mother. She was swaying slightly, and her hands and the front of her dress were covered in dark splurges of blood. There was livid purple bruising under her chin, and the top of her skull was still crimson.

She looked at him blankly.

'Mom?'

There was no response. Her eyes stared into the middle distance, unfocused. Every minute or so she mumbled, 'Forgive me, Father.' Jake wondered if she was addressing God or Father Ken. Maybe it was no one at all. Maybe she was trapped in a catatonic state, repeating the phrase because her mind was like a stuck record. She was in her own space now, and Jake knew she might not be coming back from there.

It could not be put off any longer. She needed an ambulance. Jake reached into his pocket and groaned in agony. He had to use his wounded right hand because his whole left arm was useless. He gritted his teeth as he dug out his phone, then clumsily opened his list of contacts. Asher or Mills?

He chickened out and went for Mills. As he was about to dial, he realized the decision had been taken out of his hands. He could hear the distant wail of a siren. A moment later he heard the howl of a speeding engine and within a minute a black and white had skidded to a stop outside the church, lights flashing. Mills jumped out of the driver's side, reaching for his gun as he ran towards the church. Another detective – a guy called Baynes, who usually worked the night shift – had got out from the passenger side and was matching him stride for stride. They had obviously been dragged out from their homes. More Christmases fucked . . .

Jake stepped out from the doorway into view.

Both detectives stopped and stared. Jake stared back.

Baynes looked at Jake's mother and radioed for an ambulance.

'Is she OK?' asked Mills.

Jake shook his head. 'She was going to be his next victim,' he said.

Mills covered his mouth with his hand.

After a moment Jake said, 'He's downstairs.'

Mills nodded.

'Alive?'

'No,' said Jake.

'Was it Father Ken?' asked Mills.

Jake looked stunned. 'How did you figure it out?' he asked.

'The bodies in the graveyard,' said Mills. 'The only people with access to the graves were the parish priest, the gravedigger and three local undertakers. We had already eliminated the undertakers and the gravedigger. He was the only one left.'

'Oh. And how did you get here so quickly?'

'Colonel Asher has an APB out on you. But the dispatcher is sweet on me, and when your car was spotted she tipped me off. I think it's better that *I* bring you in.'

Jake shrugged, wondering who, exactly, it was 'better' for.

93

Sunday, 1.30 p.m.

Ten minutes after Baynes made the call, the ambulance arrived. Jake's mom was laid gently on a stretcher and placed inside. She wasn't responding to anyone. One of the paramedics asked her some questions but shook his head when he got no answers.

As the ambulance pulled away from the deconsecrated church Jake was pretty sure his own hopes were leaving with it. He would never get the answers to his questions. He would never learn who he really was.

But there were more pressing matters. How much of what he knew could he even tell anybody?

He turned to Mills, who was not looking comfortable. Beside him Baynes stood staring at the ground, clearly unsure of how to play this, and thinking it best to leave it to the day-shift detective.

'You know I have to arrest you? You're my partner, but you've crossed a line here, man,' said Mills.

'I understand,' said Jake.

'Colonel Asher will be here in a minute, and he still wants to burn your ass over everything else you pulled these past two weeks.'

Jake didn't answer.

'Internal Affairs are going to be all over you like flies on shit. What the fuck got into you, Jake? Breaking into the old asylum?'

There was so much he couldn't tell Mills. So much he couldn't tell anybody. He could never reveal how he knew it was Father Ken. That would involve revealing he was Fred Lumley's son, and that was a can of worms best left unopened. Especially as Jake was the one who had killed him. Asher might speculate on the 'ghost of Lumley' roaming the asylum, but Jake wasn't going to help him on that one. And, if anyone did manage to turn up anything about Lumley's son, all they would find was a child named Bruce.

A car was pulling up now, and Jake watched as the colonel stepped out. His face was redder than usual, and he walked with his chest thrust forward. He glared at Jake for a long moment, then turned to Detective Baynes.

'I'm going inside to look at the scene.' He turned back to Mills. 'Take Austin down to the station and arrest him.'

Mills nodded. 'Sir.'

Jake felt like a man walking across shifting sands who suddenly finds he's sinking. *Will I get out of this?*

Could he make up a story to account for all the facts? He had stopped the Christmas Killer. There had to be some credit due for that, surely. He'd solved twenty-one murders in one day. Where was his pat on the back?

Yes, he'd withheld evidence, but he could justify that – a victim's life had been at stake. His own mother. She was beyond making a coherent statement and would never be charged with anything. All they really had Jake for was breaking into the asylum.

A plan formed in his head so fast Jake was acting on it before he knew what its ultimate conclusion would be. He turned to Mills.

'I want my phone call.'

Mills reached into his jacket pocket and handed Jake his mobile.

'I need some privacy.'

Mills looked reluctant to step away.

Jake looked at him. 'I'm not going to get very far with my gimpy shoulder, am I?'

Mills nodded, then moved away.

Jake called directory inquiries and asked to be redirected. After a long moment his target came on the line.

'Councilman Harper? It's Detective Jake Austin here.'

There was a long pause and a sigh before the voice at the other end replied, 'Merry Christmas, Detective. What can I do for you?'

The voice was cold. Jake could feel the dislike crackling down the line.

'It's more what we can do for each other. I'll start with the good news. We caught your wife's killer.'

There was another pause, then a slightly incredulous 'What?'

'In the past hour. He's dead. Case is closed.'

A silence on the other end, then another heavy sigh. 'That *is* good news.'

'The bad news is that I'm in a bit of a mess, and I need you to help me out of it.'

'And why should I help you?'

Jake detected a note of apprehension in the councilman's voice. He clearly did not like where this might be heading.

'Because if you can help me make my problem disappear, then I can help you sweep Leanne Schultz back under the carpet again. And this time she'll stay there. You have my word.'

The councilman took only a moment to reach a decision.

'Is Colonel Asher there?' he asked.

Jake handed the phone back to Mills.

'He wants to speak to the boss,' he said.

Mills took the phone and walked into the church.

Jake stood under a yew in the churchyard, looking down the leafy avenue. Soon Jake could call his family home from their hiding place. Things would calm down now that he no longer had a serial killer on his plate at work. In fact, he did not think he would have much on his plate at all for quite some time. Asher was likely to be furious at being outplayed like this, and would retaliate by keeping Jake sidelined even after he was medically cleared to get back to work – which, it being the holiday season, might not be for a few weeks.

So Jake would get to spend more time at home, which would make Leigh happy. And if Leigh was happy, Baby Jakey would be happy. And if Baby Jakey wasn't screaming the whole place down, maybe Faith would level out.

Things might be normal again . . . whatever that was.

He turned back to the church. He saw Mills emerging from the doorway, a look of bemusement on his face.

'Seems like Harper's got your back,' Mills said. 'What did you say to him?'

Jake couldn't meet his partner's eye. Not just yet.

In a short hour he had slain the devil, then shaken another devil by the hand. And he knew things would never be the same again.